Sarah

GW00597361

Skye Elizab

The beautiful African savanna is the backdrop to this satisfying story. Sarah hopes its wild charm will suit her restless and independent spirit. She also longs to forget something she can't forgive. She doesn't expect the turmoil of elephant culling, disturbing dreams, the culture of witchcraft and shamanism and an annoying but attractive fellow worker, Mark, to get to her as they do. Skye Elizabeth's well-crafted and accurate descriptions transported me right there so I could almost smell the citronella and hear the wild animal noises.

Paula Vince
2011 CALEB Winner
& International Book Award Winner
www.appleleafbooks.com
www.justoccurred.blogspot.com

Author Skye Elizabeth's obvious love and understanding of horses shines through this intriguing tale. Its setting in the South African savannah makes for an unusual twist. And with a rebellious young horse whisperer searching for genuine fulfillment in her life, she learns relationships with those around her can be far more challenging that those with her beloved animals. A must read for young adults who enjoy adventure/romance stories "off the beaten track".

R S Galieh
www.ritastellagalieh.com
http://inspirationalromance.blogspot.com

I love the way that Skye has used her love of God's creation and horses in particular to convey the message of the Gospel to her readers in an exciting way. The beauty of the exotic setting combined with adventure, suspense, and romance provide a stunning backdrop to the beauty of the message of God's love and guidance. The book not only provides entertainment but a clear Gospel message. Just like Sarah, Skye has allowed God to use her gifts to bring a message of hope to her readers.

Tracey Davies, New Hope Church, Crows Nest

This book is indeed a must read to everyone who has a gift or on the way of discovering their gifts. It is in this book that I discovered that wisdom can also be associated with beginners. A book full of wisdom, inspiration and life!

In *Sarah's Gift*, the author's premise of an Aussie horse whisperer on an African safari with a twist is quite original. Vivid descriptions of landscape, horse wrangling, and themes such as God's forgiveness and purpose are woven skillfully into the story. I could see, hear and smell Africa.

For a first time author, Skye has done a brilliant job with this book, being able to tie so many different aspects into one volume. Adventure, Romance, Christian principles, the Gospel, people coming into relationship with Jesus and the outworking of that in their lives. Add to that the conservation aspect of the story and the caring for an endangered species. She has the ability to make you feel as though you are actually there, right in the middle of the story... on horseback, meeting new people and seeing new places. Can't wait for the sequel!

Sarah's Gift is a fascinating book that's full of adventure, deep emotion and spiritual redemption. Skye has successfully captured the atmosphere of the African bush - she makes you feel like you are right there, experiencing everything with the characters in her book. You can almost taste the land. The book was gripping right to the end; it was filled with on-the-edge-of-your-seat tension, engaging and real characters, and deep feeling. She's also conveyed the timely, relevant message of preserving our country and its creatures.

Sarah's Gift

BOOK ONE
of the

Dare to Follow

TRILOGY

elite ShadeTree Publishing

Sarah's Gift

by Skye Elizabeth Wieland

Copyright @ 2012 ShadeTree Publishing, LLC

Print ISBN: 978-1-937331-18-4

e-Book ISBN: 978-1-937331-19-1

Series ISBN: 978-1-937331-20-7

Cover art by Christos Georghiou

The purpose of this book is to educate and enlighten. This book is sold with the understanding that the author and publisher are not engaged in rendering counseling, albeit it professional or lay, to the reader or anyone else. The author and publisher shall have neither liability nor responsibility to any person or entity with respect to any loss or damage caused, or alleged to have been caused, directly or indirectly, by the information contained in this book. The information in this book does not necessarily reflect the opinion of the publisher.

Visit our Web site at www.ShadeTreePublishing.com

*To every adventurous heart
who knew they were designed for a greater purpose.*

Blessings
Skye 2014

PROLOGUE

Australia 1975

Ten-year-old Sarah cowered in her bed, her large green eyes staring toward the doorway. Her dad had just walked in the front door; he was drunk again from a night out with his workmates. A heated argument had started between him and her mum downstairs.

Echoing up the stairwell, her father's shouting escalated with violent speed, and her mum's shrill voice mounted with nervous anger. Covering her ears, Sarah clenched her eyes shut as tears forced their way out.

Why does he keep doing this?

Something smashed, then more yelling. Silence. She heard her mum crying. Sarah opened her eyes gingerly and glanced across her room at her suitcase that was still open and half-packed in the corner. Quickly slipping out from her sheets, she kicked it under the bed, and then dashed back to the warm safety of her blankets. If Dad discovered it – she didn't want to even think about what he'd do.

He did this all the time. Last time things went too far, and mum had planned for them to leave. In fact, they were going early in the morning. Where they were going, Sarah didn't know. All she knew was that she wished with all her heart that they had left before now.

Her dad started yelling again, startling Sarah from her thoughts. Her mum cried out and then stopped. Her dad kept yelling when Sarah heard another loud crash as something fell. The sounds of her mum groaning made Sarah sit bolt upright, skewing her covers about her bedraggled thighs.

1

She paused.

Nothing.

In sudden panic, she flew out of bed and ran down the steps two at a time. Sarah had no idea what she'd do when she got downstairs. For now, she wasn't thinking straight because something was terribly wrong.

Sarah skidded to a stop as she rounded the corner into the kitchen. Her dad was hunched and breathing heavy over her mum's lifeless form. Sarah could just see around his legs that her mum's face was covered in fresh bruises, and blood seeped onto the kitchen floor. Still in a drunken rage and annoyed that she had given up, he spat at the limp form, looking at Sarah with cold eyes.

"Git back ta bed!" he snapped.

Sarah stood frozen to the spot, staring wide-eyed at her mum, perspiration pricking at the skin on the back of her neck. Her mum wasn't waking up. She clasped her hands to her mouth and shook her head, eyes brimming with tears.

"I said, GIT BACK TA BED!!!" roared her dad. His voice boomed around the inside of her head, causing her to rock back on her heels. Her hesitation was all he needed to push him over the edge. He closed the distance between them, yanking and twisting her wrist. A slight yelp escaped Sarah's lips, as her father pulled her ear to his mouth, "You saw nothing here," he growled, the smell of alcohol strong on his breath.

Sarah's face burned as she mustered her strength and ripped her arm from his grip. Like a bolt, she took off, bursting from the back door and running for her life. Tears streamed down her face.

"SARAH! GIT BACK 'ERE!"

Glancing over her shoulder, she saw his dark figure silhouetted in the doorway of the house. Gritting her teeth and turning back into the wind, Sarah sprinted hard, willing herself to fly.

After running for what felt like an eternity, she slowed and stepped up the curb onto someone's front lawn, her cheeks flushed. Bending over, holding a stitch in her side, Sarah stepped onto the patio.

While catching her ragged breath, she banged on the door, crying out for help. An elderly man and woman appeared, suspicious lines forming between their brows as they tightened their night robes about them. Sarah spluttered out her situation between gulps of air, and the man quickly stepped inside and dialed the police and ambulance.

Sarah allowed herself to be led inside. Her stiffened shoulders relaxed a little only once the door clicked closed behind her.

Seating their unexpected guest in the living room, the woman covered Sarah's shoulders with a warm blanket and went to prepare her a hot chocolate to drink. Sarah wasn't very thirsty, but snuggled nervously into the blanket, raising her brows to see what would come of the phone calls as the people moved about the house. Timid, Sarah sank into the couch, her spindly legs tucked up under her.

She tried to block out the sounds of her mum screaming that still echoed in her head. Fatigue was overcoming her, but doggedly, she willed her burning eyes to stay open, lest she see visions of her mum's lifeless form behind her eyelids. The woman moved back into the room and sat opposite her, watching her with a drawn expression. Sitting up slightly and raising her brows at the woman, Sarah frowned when the woman simply shook her head. She wasn't told anything. Beyond all other things, Sarah needed to get to the hospital, see if her mum was OK. Why were the police taking so long?

After what seemed like an eternity, a police officer arrived at the house and Sarah repeated her story, a sick feeling growing in her gut as she watched the officer taking notes. Several other policemen had been sent to investigate, and soon enough, the officer excused himself to take a call on the two-way.

Sarah's hands fumbled in her lap. *Mum? Why won't they hurry up and tell me what happened to my mum?*

Later that evening, Sarah sat in a patrol car, listening glumly as policemen radioed back and forth. The officer, who had interviewed Sarah, glanced back at her from the driver's seat as he received word about an arrest. Sarah blinked through her puffy, tired eyes, pulling loose strands from the blanket that was gifted to her by the couple. She asked again about her mum, but the policeman offered no information except to repeat that they had no word from the hospital yet.

He drove on in silence, keeping Sarah prisoner to her thoughts and fears. She looked out the window as a light misty rain began to flick onto the tinted glass, enhancing the colors from passing shop windows and streetlights. Tiredness washed over Sarah. She had no idea what time it was, and she didn't even care. She resolved not to let herself rest until she found out about her mum.

The patrol car swung into the hospital loading bay. Sarah tugged herself upright, fatigue falling from her shoulders with the discarded blanket. The officer opened the door and motioned for her to follow.

In the early hours of that morning, as Sarah sat next to the hospital bed, her mother slipped peacefully away; never to be attacked by her husband again. The nurses roused Sarah, who had been drifting in and out of restless sleep, and informed her that they had done all they could, but her injuries were too much. Feeling numb, Sarah later allowed a nurse to lead her to a spare bed, where she cried herself to sleep.

CHAPTER ONE

South Africa 1990

It was October; the beginning of the summer months when rains were anticipated by all, and the air was mingled with the stirrings of change. The wind swept through Sarah White's loose tendrils of black hair like cool fingers of scented freshness.

Sarah gasped with awe as she watched the dawn opening like a stage curtain, rising in symphony as the warm, orange glow began to kiss the tips of the ever-plentiful African mopane shrubs. A delicate pink-hued mist in the bushveldt below was weaving its way up through the boulders and shrubs surrounding Sarah as she sat atop the small rise. Parties of exotic birds began their morning chorus; scarlet-chested sunbirds seeking out the life-giving nectar from the various seasonal blossoms; grey flycatchers darting to and fro, hunting insects; and the occasional woodland kingfisher as it descended toward the waterholes at the base of the hill beyond.

Sarah sighed as she raised her delicate hand, and with long, slender fingers, she tucked another stray piece of her thick black hair behind her ear as the soft wind kept chasing the loose bits about. Far from annoyed, though, her green eyes scanned the horizon as she allowed her skin to soak in the warmth. This place was magical. Similar to the dawns of her homeland, Australia, just the colors here seemed richer and more vibrant. She could see why many called it God's own country. Another rogue piece of hair flew across her vision, and Sarah casually blew it from her olive face.

Perhaps it was just her personal perception because of the hardships of home that made the place appear better. This place

5

reminded her of a spot back in Outback Queensland at home, where she'd frequently sit astride her horse, gazing over a land filled with woody mulga bushes. Here the land was dotted with both the woody mopane trees with their thick heart-shaped leaves that the elephants would often keep in check, as well as its relative, the lower mopane scrub bush. Back in Australia, though, the only dangers were wild pigs, dogs, or territorial emus. Here it was a different story.

She was now twenty-five, and since her arrival in this new country on her twenty-second birthday, this quiet spot just outside the protection of the Brennan's property had fast become her favorite place. Much to the alarm of her co-workers, who forever warned her it was against the rules and dangerous, she would come here as often as she could and just drink up the beauty of creation at dawn. It was where she could think, where she could clear her head and try to sort out some of the clutter, or perhaps just forget for a while. At twenty-five, sometimes her mind was a fog during all the whirl and chaos of normal life.

Her horse, Honor, yawned and licked her lips, half shutting her eyes against the warm glare of the rising sun. Sarah leaned forward over the animal's neck and scratched behind her ears. The palomino mare turned her head into Sarah's hand, enjoying every stroke.

Sighing, Sarah closed her eyes and tried to savour the stillness and beauty of the morning before time began to close in on her. She'd moved here from Australia four years ago as a volunteer to work for Johnno Brennan at his safari trail-riding establishment. Her skills as a trainer and horse breaker combined with her bachelor's degree in equine management made her a catch that Johnno was reluctant to lose.

Despite her slight figure and less than average height, Sarah had proven to all that her strength as good as any and that she was irreplaceable. After finding her feet, she'd fallen in love with the place and had sorted out her working visa to stay on indefinitely.

At several points over the last few years, she even contemplated becoming a permanent citizen of the country. The majesty, the beauty, and the dangers of this land enthralled her to no end. In Africa, she felt more alive than she'd ever felt before. Despite constant nagging from her family and friends to return back home to Australia, and with the current political climate in South Africa, Sarah insisted on staying, justifying her decision with the fact that she was out of harm's way, most of the time. Occasional word of rallies and new bombings of the railway would make her doubt her decision, but it was something she was loathe to discuss with her adopted family back in Australia.

She glanced over her shoulder. She might soon wear out her welcome, though. If she got busted out here again this morning, there'd be hell to pay. She wondered how many more times she would get away with riding out before work into dangerous territory before she'd be asked to leave and go back to Australia. While not as dangerous as the Kruger, this place was still known lion country, too dangerous to venture out into alone without protection.

Brennan Safari Trails was situated snugly along the western side of Kruger National Park (or "the Kruger" as locals liked to call it) in the Eastern Transvaal region of South Africa.

North of Brennan was the Letaba Ranch Game Reserve, where Sarah now sat perched, which boasted a large variety of wild game. Use of Letaba Reserve to take horse rides was the norm, but Johnno Brennan had just established tentative ties with the government to take some rides into the Kruger for overnight treks.

These treks were something Johnno seemed to be pushing more and more lately. The main riders they catered to were from South Africa and the surrounding area, but recent times had attracted the attention of some overseas tourism agencies.

Life was always busy in this part of Africa, but in a laidback, relaxing kind of way. It was part and parcel of the tourism industry, which grew strong along the border towns of the Kruger.

Sarah often overheard her co-worker Mark arguing with Johnno about the safety risks that were being imposed on them by venturing out into the reserve, but their boss always pushed for his own way. She wondered how long the horse business here would last with more and more local horses getting taken down by lions, and disease starting to creep in and threaten their stock. She'd heard rumor that, soon enough, the Kruger would be open to safaris with game-viewing vehicles only.

In many ways, Sarah felt like she still didn't fit in to this lifestyle and culture. It was a constant struggle to pick up the various phrases of the people that often mingled English with their Afrikaans. Even harder to grasp was the Zulu and Sotho languages. People kept assuring her that, with time, she would pick it up, or at least enough to get by.

Sarah felt as if she were sitting back and watching herself through a window. Her life was happening, but she still didn't feel totally present. Things seemed too good to be true at times. Sure, the work was similar to what she had done back home with her adopted parents, but there she mustered cattle and trained horses. Here, it was so much more.

She was employed for her degree in stable management and was expected to run the herd with the limited funds that were available. She helped take the trail rides and took on some horse training and breaking, much to the disgust of her co-worker, who maintained that they needed to get in old, reliable stock and stop wasting time on training new stock.

This part of the day, though, with the glory of the mornings, was the only thing that seemed to give her a glimpse of what she'd hoped she would feel in her heart while trying to live her dream of creating hope, meaning and purpose in Africa. Reality was so much harder.

Then a twig snapped behind her, followed by a dull thudding, jolting Sarah from her thoughts. She turned and saw Brandi trotting up the track on her little black pony, looking flustered and out of breath.

She was wearing new jeans and the Brennan's uniform shirt. A khaki work-shirt, with the Brennan Safari Trails emblem embroidered on the front pocket. Girls often wore tight-fitting singlets underneath so that when the afternoons were hot, they could strip off a layer of clothing.

Summers were hot and humid out here, and you did what you

could to stay cool. Sarah noted that Brandi already had the top button of her shirt undone in the rising temperature, her hot pink singlet peeping out from underneath.

Sarah was no better in her attire, wearing her work jeans and white singlet. Her uniform shirt was still hanging over the rail back at the horse kraals.

"What are you doing out here?" Sarah chided her, noting how she too had ventured into Letaba alone on horseback.

Brandi ignored the biting comment and, catching her breath, addressed Sarah urgently. "Johnno says that you've got to get back now!"

Sarah grimaced, "I'm not late, am I?"

Brandi paused and looked her up and down with exasperation, "No, you're not late...yet! But he said that if you don't come and do your job now, you won't have one! What are you even doing out here? Are you crazy?"

"Are you?" Sarah shot back with a challenging expression, twisting her lips. Red frustration crept up Brandi's neck, and when she went to speak, Sarah cut her off. "It's not like I'm in the Kruger!" Sarah retorted.

Brandi shook her head in dismay. "Still, it's lion country."

Sarah grumbled, her eyes darting back and forth, scanning through the thick foliage. Swallowing hard, Sarah took up her reins and turned toward camp. Brandi trailed behind her, glancing around as if they were being stalked.

Sarah didn't want to lose this job. This was what she had always wanted to do. *So why aren't I happy?* she pondered.

They picked their way down the small rise before breaking into a canter. Sarah sped ahead, not wanting to spend any longer than necessary talking to Brandi.

Brandi Coetzee irritated her to no end. She was one of those happy people who was always chipper, even when you rationalized that she should be having a bad day. When everyone else was normal, there she was: chirpy and praying.

Brandi was known as the person on staff who was always praying about everything. She went to some church in town, and Christianity was something that she took more seriously than most people Sarah knew who called themselves Christians.

Mark van der Merwe, another of Sarah's co-worker's, liked to call Brandi the "God-Botherer." He felt that if there were a God, he'd be sick and tired of hearing from Brandi all the time.

Sarah knew that she was supposed to take the younger staff under her wing, but something in Brandi just grated her nerves. Sure, Johnno found a good catch when he employed Brandi. Her father owned the saddlery in town, and she had learned all kinds of leatherwork, including mending saddles and other gear. And, while she was the most junior staff member on the team, she was still a valuable asset.

As they trotted into the campsite, Brandi sidled up to Sarah. "You scared me half to death doing that! Is Mark right? That you do that all the time, even though you are told not to? It's lion country, Sarah! And what's more, elephant territory! My uncle nearly got trampled by one! I've seen a cow take out a bakkie that got too close to her calf! I know you have been at Brennan's longer than me, but you are not in Australia anymore."

Brandi stopped talking, and Sarah wondered if she was about to change tack. Sarah was right. "Are you alright?" Brandi queried, her voice still shaking.

"Are we done?" The cutting words issued from the Aussie's mouth wounded Brandi's quiet nature for the third time that morning, and Brandi cringed.

Sarah rolled her eyes and vaulted off Honor, leading her away. As she turned her back on Brandi, Sarah felt a strange jolt in her chest, like a slight pang of guilt that she had been so abrupt yet again. Disturbed by the weakness, she brushed her feelings aside.

Glancing back, Sarah noticed with dismay that Brandi was still watching her, the younger woman's brows creased as she led her own horse away. Their eyes met, and Brandi, shedding her disquiet like a discarded coat, kicked up her chin with a brave smile.

Sarah shrugged and shook her head. *Happy people.*

Turning her thoughts away from the blonde Afrikaans woman, she tied Honor in her stall, leaving her saddled up, grabbed her work-shirt and strode to the tack-up area.

Mark was already there, saddling up horses. His face was set with aggravation, causing a nerve to twitch in his distinct jaw line as he glanced her way. With a casual air, she finished buttoning up her shirt as she approached.

"Sarah!" Mark yelled.

She rocked to a stop in front of him, ready to receive the verbal assault. She wouldn't give him the satisfaction of shaking her. "I know! I know! Lions, tigers and bears, Oh my!" Sarah clasped her hands to her cheeks as she quoted *The Wizard of Oz.*

Glaring at her for a moment, he shook his head of thick light brown hair. Sarah lifted her chin in triumph. She knew what he was thinking: *Sarah is Sarah; stubborn and full of disregard for any of the warnings he gave.*

Mark wasn't winning anymore, and he knew it. Moving along and bending to straighten her chapette, Sarah heard him wind up to speak with her, and she peeped under her armpit at him.

"Get Pete, Mac and Zander ready. The people are already here, and they brought two extra."

Mark sounded agitated, and Sarah knew better than to ask questions. Biting her lip in worry, she straightened up and began to brush and tack up the last three horses that were tied and waiting.

The other nine horses were ready, as well as Mark's bay gelding, Sniper, who was just getting bridled. Mark snapped the bridle strap into place and stalked off, leaving Sarah wondering. Extra tourists on a ride meant another guide, namely Brandi.

This many people riding in lion country upped the risks to the point that Mark's nerves wouldn't cope. Why did Johnno keep doing this to them? Did he want to go out of business?

Groaning, Sarah finished up with the horses and went to check in with Johnno in the office and get her two-way radio and rifle. Why were they getting ready this early anyway? She thought it was supposed to be a late ride today.

Johnno wasn't in the office, but was out in the foyer where twelve riders were being welcomed and directed to fill out their waiver forms. Johnno looked up; his white bushy eyebrows rising as Sarah walked in. Ignoring her, he continued his conversation with the young gentleman before him.

Sarah quirked her mouth; Johnno wasn't too grumpy this morning; otherwise he would have excused himself and spoken to her immediately about riding out alone again. Maybe, like Mark, Johnno was so used to her defiance that he'd given up.

She walked past the foyer, taking stock of the tourists who would be riding, before making her way back into the offices to retrieve her gear.

"You going to have a go at me this morning?" challenged Sarah, breezing past Mark.

Mark grunted in reply before looking up at her. "Nice of you to be around this morning to help, by the way." Mark tossed a radio to her, with a sarcastic twist to his mouth.

She flinched, "I'm not late, in fact. I'm still early."

"And so were *they*." Mark jerked his head toward the foyer, signaling at the tourists.

"That's not our problem, Mark. Let them wait outside. Who let them in early anyway?"

Then, in an instant, Sarah remembered the day. She didn't have time to react as Mark cut across her thoughts, speaking as if to a child.

"The boss said that we had to get on the trail early today. The park's board notified us yesterday that they need to cull again. They said the team would be in to start at noon. Or didn't you get that message?"

Sarah bit her lip. She'd forgotten.

"Well?" Mark pressed, stopping to stare at her.

"I'm sorry...," dropping the radio onto the side bench, Sarah closed her eyes and kneaded her forehead, weary of the conversation. "I forgot!"

Mark stormed off into the next room. Eyes widening at his dark mood, Sarah followed him through to the rifle safe and waited as he unlatched the locks.

"Forgot? You of all people should have remembered. After all, it is your beloved elephants that are getting shot this afternoon."

"If we need to get in and out before the culling, why are we even going into the Kruger? Why not stay in Letaba?" She cocked her hands on her hips waiting for a reply.

Eyes smoldering, Mark closed the gap between them, growling low, through gritted teeth. "Because what Johnno wants, Johnno gets!"

Stepping backward, Sarah shook her head, not following.

Mark glanced over his shoulder toward the foyer where Johnno was meeting the guests. "Those people are paying extra to see those elephants. Since the fences were taken down last month, the D-10 herd has moved into the Kruger. It doesn't even matter where we go, the fence is down; the elephants come and go as they please. The riders, they want elephants, we show them elephants. Got it?"

"But it's dangerous—"

"I know it's bloody dangerous, but it's our job, OK!?"

"But Johnno—"

"I don't care about what he says! Johnno is a money-hungry idiot!"

Mark stopped, as if he'd said too much. Sarah arched an elegant brow as he moved and closed the door leading down to the foyer. Turning back to her with suspicion, he tilted his head with irony. "I thought you liked it dangerous!"

Heat rose into Sarah's features as she struggled not to retort at him. Mark shrugged and turned back to the gun safe. His temper cooling, he handed her a Winchester rifle and ammunition.

"What Johnno wants, Johnno gets, and today...he wants us to take the people to see D-10 before they're culled."

Ignoring his words, Sarah turned to her own thoughts. She hated his persistent sarcasm and bad moods, but then again, hers weren't much better this morning.

Sarah cocked her head to one side, cradling the weapon. "Aren't the elephants important to you too?" She queried, feeling her own emotions coming back under control.

Mark shrugged again as he loaded the shells into his utility belt. His indifference caused a fresh surge of anger to rise in her.

"Why do you even work here, anyway, if you don't feel

connected to the wildlife?" She spat the words with more venom than she intended.

Mark started to pull an angry expression but smirked instead and replied, "The attractive tourists."

Sarah stood rigid, her clenched fists causing the biceps on her delicate and bare upper arms to bulge in response. She noticed him watching her, and it filled her with even more angst toward the man.

He held her gaze for a moment before exhaling loudly, his shoulders relaxing. "What's going on, Sarah? Don't you like it here? If you want to go home, all you have to do is ask."

Narrowing his eyes, he continued to watch her. Sarah turned away from his gaze. She knew it was his job to look out for her, keep her welfare in his priorities, but the way he sometimes went about it infuriated her. He was trying, though, she owed him that much.

"It's not that, Mark." She turned back toward him as he handed her the ammunition she was required to also carry on her belt. Normally, they wouldn't load the firearms unless Mark felt it was necessary. "I'm stressed," she admitted, sighing.

Mark's lip twisted into another smirk, and she knew that he just realized that he'd won the battle by drawing her out. "I can tell."

He picked up her radio from the bench and tossed it back to her. Holding the rifle, she lurched out and juggled it before securing it in the crook of her free arm. Mark's eyes danced with sardonic humor.

"Maybe you should flirt with some attractive riders yourself...might take away some of the stress."

Sensing the brief moment of professional sympathy pass, Sarah's brow furrowed as she grabbed up her first aid kit from the bench. She noted that it felt rather light and, glaring at him for not restocking last week, put her other items down and started stuffing fresh items into the kit from the shelving above. She pointedly ignored Mark, giving him the silent treatment, which didn't seem to perturb him the slightest bit.

Mark laughed at her pouting and said, "Another point for me!"

14

He flicked his index finger over his tongue and touched it to the air, making a hissing sound as if he were sizzling hot.

Sarah screwed up her face, "You're still in my bad books for real though, leaving me to do all the work again. Meet you at the horses."

Not waiting for him to answer, she huffed away to the next room, applied her sunscreen, and took up the radio, first aid, and rifle in her arms. Checking that everything else was locked and stowed away, she made her way out to make sure that all the horses were ready for the ride, without another glance at her superior. Mark might have been trail boss, but he acted like such a child!

Brandi was already in the greeting area with Jet, her black pony. She grinned at Sarah, the excitement of the job still fresh in her young heart.

Brandi had only been with them a few months.
Sarah wondered why Brandi was so different, not holding the same stress levels as her or Mark before a ride of this kind.

Brandi knew the dangers; she was always sprouting them off at Sarah. She had the disregard of a naive tourist, despite sitting through all the safety briefs.

A surge of jealously was roused in Sarah to be blessed with the same lack of apparent fear and nerves.

Sarah's mouth tilted back, dismayed that only after a few years on this job, her heart had already waned with the monotony and stress of it. She thought this was her heart's desire, to be part of a trail-riding safari in South Africa. To be training, managing, and riding horses, and be surrounded by the beauty of Africa's finest.

Brennan Safari Trails was a good place to work. The boss was passable, though he regularly put money over safety, buying in unsuitable horses and expecting her to deal with them. The staff was bearable, and she was doing what she always wanted. But, something was still missing.

Sarah shook her thoughts away. It was time to work and she needed to be on her toes.

Laughter and chatter filled the air as Mark led the twelve

riders into the tack-up area. Sarah sat on a log, propping her elbow on her knee and resting her chin on her hand. She watched with boredom as Mark settled the tourists and began the tiresome safety brief that would precede the ride.

Sarah watched Mark closely as he spoke. His earlier mood swing from temper to mischief had been replaced yet again. His face now carried a serious and drawn appearance as he went through the spiel, his eyes scanning the overly large group.

There was a young girl in the mix, and Sarah judged her to be about ten years old. Too young! Mark noticed it too, because his eyes kept flicking to the girl; a clouded look of concern crossing his features.

No one else would have noticed Mark's expression but Sarah. She knew how to read him most of the time. He often signaled her with his eyes when he found a rider he thought might need extra guidance. This was one of those times.

When his eyes passed her way, she nodded her head inconspicuously and saw him respond. Sarah knew that even though they often couldn't stand each other, they worked well together and relied on each other to watch the other's back.

Sarah tore her thoughts away from the young girl and examined the rest of the group. Most of them were overseas tourists, a rarity. No wonder Johnno was giving them what they wanted. Sarah wondered if Johnno had charged extra. No matter, the staff wouldn't see any of it, even though they did all the work.

The fact that Johnno kept taking unnecessary risks by booking too many inexperienced people and demanding that Mark and Sarah deal with it, was getting beyond annoying. And all in the name of money. It was a miracle that they hadn't been closed down already.

With the safety talk over, Mark nodded, grim faced to Sarah as he exhaled. She knew he was also worried about how young the riders were.

Sarah stood up to help them mount the horses as they filed over to her, even as she glanced back at Mark.

Rubbing his hands together, Mark was accosted by a tall, red-haired woman with an English accent. She seemed to regard the tall, tanned, ruggedly handsome Afrikaans man with the girlishness of a teenager with a crush. His eyes flickered Sarah's way in a plea for assistance.

Ha! This was her chance for some payback!

Approaching Honor, Sarah rolled her eyes and smiled to herself; she was not going to rescue him. If he joked that he was attracted to the tourists then he could get himself out of this himself. One point for Sarah!

As the riders bustled into action, Sarah moved into Mark's view only. Catching his eye, she flicked her index finger over her own tongue and touched it to the air, grinning a toothy grin that he would understand as the hiss that accompanied the action. A slight nod of his head showed his acceptance of defeat.

Curious, the redhead looked over her shoulder toward Sarah. Ducking her face with amusement, Sarah walked away.

Time to focus! Sarah started to think about the trails they would take in order to find the wayward elephants. This was going to be a long and slow ride with so many people. Hoping they would spot some interesting game today or else it would be a complete loss, Sarah also wondered if they all knew how to canter if they needed to ride out of harm's way.

Setting her face, she launched herself toward the group, where she was faced with a middle-aged, balding man who was waiting to be helped onto his horse.

As they headed out, Sarah rode along the flank of the group, observing the riders as they all snaked their way along the dry bushveldt. They weaved in and around the prolific mopane shrubs, ever watchful for game to spot.

Sarah liked this time of year. Soon, the rains would bring back the life and color of the scrubby dry landscape. Ever enthusiastic, Brandi was behind the group, relaying some tale from her adventures on the trail. Mark was, as usual, leading the group and telling them the history of the area and what game they should expect to see. They were still working their way through the large Letaba Game reserve.

Soon, they would cross the border into the Kruger, where the veldt would flatten out even more and the mopane would be thicker and harder to navigate.

Sarah saw a young lady in the middle of the group struggling to work out how to hold her reins. Her father rode behind her in exasperation trying to help: "Amy, just...I can't see...just try to kick him on and he might stop doing it."

"Daaad! I *am* doing that, and he keeps throwing his head around," Amy replied.

Sarah struggled against the anger she felt toward Johnno and forced a warm smile as she sidled up to help the girl. "Hi there. Need a hand?"

"Um....hello," stuttered the girl, as she pulled on the reins to get the horse to stop throwing its head. She struggled to even answer.

Sarah cut in, "First...relax. That's it. Take a big breath and make yourself flop like jelly."

The girl wiggled her body, and Sarah replied with, "Good job! Now you're relaxed. So sit up a bit now but keep loose, though. Don't let yourself go stiff. Now, loosen your reins right up."

"But he'll run away with me," protested the girl.

"Trust me, he won't. That's it. Loosen them right up. Good! Now, take another deep breath."

The girl sighed and flopped around in the saddle.

Sarah chuckled. "Now, he's just going to follow the other horses. Don't pull on his head or he'll get upset, like he did before."

Amy giggled in delight at being able to relax into the ride.

"What do you say, Amy?" prompted her father.

"Thank you," responded the girl. "You're right! He is following the leader."

"Most of our horses here do that. They're good like that. Look!" Sarah pointed toward a small herd of zebra that they were nearing. Amy gasped.

Somewhat satisfied, Sarah's mouth tightened as she moved on to help another rider. This was Sarah's life. Aiding people with the simple aspects of riding on the trail was starting to become an onerous chore.

She was disgusted with Johnno for not following Mark's and

her advice on limiting rides to experienced riders. A rider as green as Amy was surely lion fodder if anything went wrong. At the very least they should test them, give them a short arena lesson. It annoyed Sarah that Johnno didn't believe in testing and teaching some basics in the arena first.

Some of the basics could be shown in minutes in an arena, and then fine-tuning could happen on the trail. But no, it wasn't like that. Johnno just expected Sarah to fix whatever was wrong on the ride.

If Sarah had her way, that would be the first thing to change. Alas, she could not hope for such fortune. It would forever be as it was now. If Johnno moved on, Mark would take over and at least things would change for the better, but she doubted he would keep her on staff.

Sarah sighed, this isn't what her dream was supposed to end up like.

They moved on for quite some time, stopping here and there to do some birding, as Mark spotted the more elusive species. Many a bird watcher had ventured to Africa hoping to see some these exotic native birds, but this crowd was not interested.

"When are we going to see some elephants?" the tall red-haired English woman asked after a while.

Mark didn't bother to turn around and just kept the group moving. "Hopefully soon. We're almost in the Kruger."

Sarah watched with idle interest as they stepped through the unmarked boundary, and the landscape started to become denser and more scrubby as they moved into the Kruger.

"Look! Over there!" someone in the group exclaimed.

Several people pointed out toward an acacia, where a couple of willowy giraffe were stretching into the leaves and chomping away at the trees, shaping the canopies into perfect umbrellas, while solid little oxpeckers jumped about their hides, cleaning away the insects in a beautiful display of mutualism.

Mark halted the horses so everyone could watch then settled back into the saddle, cocking a leg up on the pommel. Several cameras slipped out from hidden pockets and began to flash and click away toward the unconcerned, haughty animals.

Sarah gazed around the heavy foliage to their left, littered with thick mopane shrub and red bushwillow trees. Prime hiding area for feline hunters. Shuddering, she looked toward Mark, ready to move on.

In the next instant, a gunshot rang out, making several of the horses jump. The giraffes' heads snapped in the same direction, looking for the intrusion into their peaceful grazing. Swiveling their ears back and forth in agitation, the lanky beasts began to move off.

Mark spun his horse to look for Sarah. "Sarah!" he yelled.

Sarah trotted up next to him, anxious. "I thought you said that they were starting at noon? It's only eight a.m.!"

"I know, Sarah!" he snapped. "I'll start over that way with the group." He pointed toward a grassy slope.

"Can you go up that rise where there's a clearing and have a look?" He kept his voice low so that only Sarah could hear. "This will stuff up the ride if they start now. These people want to see D-10 alive, not blood and guts."

Sarah nodded, relieved for a break in the routine, but concerned about the cull. Throwing all caution to the wind, she cantered ahead as Mark radioed back to base.

Mark tried several times to contact Johnno while he was leading the group down the track. "Mark to base, Mark to base. Do you copy?" Nothing.

Mark cursed under his breath in Afrikaans and glanced over his shoulder at the group. Nobody looked worried about the gunshot, but everybody was talking and looking around with excitement.

"Do you think it's hunters?"

"I didn't think that was allowed?"

"Surely not in the Kruger."

"I wonder if someone got attacked!"

"Mum, I want to go home. I don't want my horse to go crazy...."

Mark knew that this part of the Kruger was off limits to hunting, but with the current unstable climate of the country, who knew what a gunshot could possibly mean.

Since Mandela had been released from jail at the beginning of the year, all chaos seemed to be breaking loose as apartheid was losing its hold over South Africa. Right-wing extremists were unhappy with change, as President Frederik de Klerk wrestled to bring peace to the nation. Mark felt a pang of insecurity and guilt about his heritage.

Where are you, Johnno? Mark thought to himself.

He held the two-way radio up to his lips again and pressed the relay button. "Mark to Sarah. Do you copy?"

"Sarah to Mark. I copy you. Over."

"Can you see anything? Over."

"Nothing. Not even plains game. The wildebeest, zebra—everything is gone. The veldt is empty. It's eerie. Over."

Mark furrowed his brows. He couldn't hear the sounds of any vehicles from another safari. Still, someone must be out here. Without thinking, he reached down, touching his hand to his rifle.

Should he go on with the group, take them back and refund their money, or go another way?

Taking them back wasn't an option. He was reluctant to keep looking for elephants now. Mark rubbed his chin, trying to make a decision, and then turned to the group, preparing to make some kind of announcement.

"Well, they must have got it." He chuckled, trying to disperse rumors of danger.

A murmur of nervous laughter rippled through the group.

"But to play it safe, we'll go the other way through Scrubby Trail, back toward Letaba. It's a good trail to spot birds, and occasionally we get some big game there too."

Low grumbles resonated through the group, but Mark didn't care. He didn't care if Johnno had promised elephants; their safety was in his hands, and that came first.

Mark set his face and turned to continue, putting his radio to his lips again. "Mark to Sarah. Do you copy?"

"Yes, Mark? Over."

"Are you coming? We'll go to Scrubby, just in case. Over."

"OK. I just want to check something out first, just over the crest. Over and out."

"No, Sarah, it's too dangerous! Just leave it! I need you back with the group now! Over."

Mark frowned again. "Sarah? Sarah?! Blast it!" Mark shook his head. *Why must she go off and do her own thing all the time? Doesn't she realize how dangerous it is, or that she is part of a team?*

Mark clipped his two-way back onto his belt and started off again, trying not to imagine Sarah as lion's bait. He would try Johnno again later, but for now, he had the group to look after.

CHAPTER
TWO

It was silent on the lowveldt ahead as Sarah's eyes scanned the grounds she was becoming all too familiar with. When she'd first come from Australia, she'd only known it as savannah; but soon enough, she'd been educated on the ways of the land and its people and their terminology.

The lowveldt, as she now called it, was the low grasslands. Here she would find the comfort of the familiar herds. Zebra, wildebeest, and the occasional impala that made up the bulk of the plains game. Herons and Saddle-billed storks would be graceful in picking their way through the silts in the waterways or waterholes, looking for food.

But where were all the herds now? The rains would soon be coming, and Sarah knew that this waterhole would be overflowing onto the lowveldt, covering the base of the grasslands in a cool mirror of water that would team with many more animals.

For now, though, everything was dry, except for a lone waterhole.

Shielding her eyes against the sun, Sarah scanned further on, where the lowveldt gave way to the bushveldt, and where the mopane scrubs were so dense that she couldn't see past them. Nothing.

It was strange. This place should have been covered in animals, but there were none, like they'd all been spooked away.

Sarah's horse, Honor, was on full alert. She was looking toward a bank of red bushwillow trees by the waterhole, unblinking. Something was amiss.

The regular background noise of chattering birds and other animals was gone, replaced by a void that screamed with silence.

A sudden wave of panic hit Sarah like the oncoming rush of a train, and she fought the urge to turn Honor around and gallop straight back to the group. It was inexplicable, as nothing in the scenery had changed.

Doubt clouded Sarah's senses; she shouldn't be here. Whatever it was, Honor felt it too.

The horse jumped with fright, and started to toss her head, snorting and pawing at the ground. Her head then set in one direction, ears pricked forward. She stood motionless, transfixed by some distant danger. Every muscle in the great palomino under Sarah was tense, ready for action.

Was there a lioness crouched in the gently swaying grasses? Sarah felt both the urge to race to safety and the curiosity to see what was down there. She trusted Honor's instinct for danger, though, and resisted the urge to race away in case a lion or other predator was present.

With deliberate action, Sarah coughed loudly to put off any would-be predators. Nothing. Having waited long enough, she turned to step the horse back down the winding track to rejoin the group.

Once she felt the safety of more open ground, she pushed Honor into an easy canter, slowing to a trot as she neared Scrubby Trail and listened for the group. She caught glimpses of horses up ahead, and as the breeze ebbed and flowed, she heard snippets of voices in the distance.

Walking Honor now, Sarah tried to gather her thoughts. *What WAS that back there? It felt evil...supernatural, almost spiritual!*

In her childhood, Sarah remembered her mother trying to tell her about the bible and how there is a spiritual realm that we can't see.

But her mother was long gone, stolen away from her. She didn't share the same bond with her adopted mum, and in her adulthood she focused on other pursuits and was not really interested if there was or wasn't truth in her mother's faith. After all, it hadn't saved her mum.

It didn't matter, because Sarah made her own reality. She reasoned that if she believed that there was no spirit realm then nothing was going to bother her from it.

But back in the lowveldt...there was a presence...something was there that was unseen. Had it not been for Honor reacting, Sarah could have dismissed it as her wild imagination. She didn't like the feelings it stirred in her, feelings of a distant and forgotten sinking in the pit of her stomach.

Fear? She'd felt fear since entering adulthood and found it something to be respected; it taught her how to respond to dangers, how to keep on her toes. But this was different. This was something heavy, penetrating, debilitating— something she hadn't felt since....

Sarah shuddered, but quickly shook it off. *It was probably just a lion! This is stupid! There was nothing there!*

But then, that type of thinking was part of the problem. *Trust your instincts,* she told herself, closing in on the group. She was wary of the stirrings in her spirit.

"Hello, find anything interesting?" Brandi inquired as Sarah walked up to the group. The cheery greeting was in morbid contrast to the feelings Sarah had just worked so hard to suppress.

Sarah shook her head, and still feeling perturbed and a little indignant, she ignored the girl's question and trotted right past her. She checked over the group as she approached Mark and felt a sudden pang of guilt for leaving them so long and ignoring Mark's request to return. This many people needed more than two trail guides, especially with gunshots around and in lion country.

But she mustn't cave in front of Mark. Sarah composed herself, trying to appear aloof. "Did you miss me?" she asked, tensing up as she approached Mark.

He wasn't amused. "Have you got a death wish, woman? I asked you to return, I didn't want you to be separated too long. I'm also responsible for your safety when we are on duty. You can't just go off on your fanciful adventures and forget about work. We're here to make a living, remember?"

Sarah's face burned as she scoffed, "Ha! I thought you almost cared about me just then."

She glanced behind at the riders who were watching them

with interest. From the look of their faces, their ears had pricked to a conversation that was not meant for them. Sarah clammed her mouth shut, clearing her throat.

Mark followed her gaze before locking his startling blue eyes on her, his brows lowered. Sarah was momentarily taken aback and tried to recover her cavalier demeanor.

"You'd better get back to it, Mr. Safari Guide, and we'll discuss it later," Sarah forced a smirk and pulled back to the rear of the group to tend to riders again, sighing with relief.

From where she sat, she could see Mark shake his head, refocus, and resume talking with the riders closest to him, pointing out another small herd of giraffe and telling the group some interesting facts, such as the length of a giraffe's tongue and how their front legs are longer than their necks.

As the morning wore on, Sarah's panic and discomfort from the empty veldt dissolved. She trained her thoughts on helping people learn to ride better, staying out of Mark's hair and avoiding Brandi's constant questioning. Perhaps she would look into the mystery of the missing wildlife later when no one could see her slip away, or more easy, write it off as a lion.

As the ride wore on, it was the cull that began to weigh heavier on her mind. By the time they returned to Brennan's, she was almost consumed by her thoughts about it.

That evening, Sarah was in the staff common room, pouring a coffee, when Mark entered. She'd been alone for a while, worrying about the cull. So many elephants, so much carnage, just because the numbers were too great. Other areas of Africa struggled with their dwindling elephant populations after they had been hunted to the brink, some even claiming them to be endangered, but South Africa had healthy numbers in the Letaba Reserve and in the Kruger...maybe too healthy.

Animal activists had tried to stop the culling in the past, arguing that the elephants were endangered in some countries and that they should be relocated. The Parks Board tried relocating them several times, but it ended up costing too much money to tranquilize them and to have the vehicles on hand to shift them. In the end, it was easier for the government to give the order, "Cull," under the Elephant Management Strategy that the Parks Board had put into place.

They culled the multiple family groups in several steps, staggering the amount of clean up and carnage that occurred with each event by focusing on one herd at a time. Each clan numbered between nine to eleven animals.

The ivory that came from the culls was put under lock and key in large government storehouses. Nevertheless, Sarah believed that the underground black market was still a big issue with ivory, and that almost anyone could be persuaded with money.

Sarah sighed, looking up at Mark as he approached. She grimaced, waiting for his inevitable report. She could always rely on Mark to keep her informed about the culls, whether she wanted to hear them or not. Mark was like that; he liked to find out the facts about everything and seemed to enjoy sharing them way too much.

"I just had a call from the Parks Board. The D-10 cull went off well. They're still doing clean up now; they need to get the meat sorted before the sun hits it in the morning," he informed.

Sarah gaped at him, before slamming her mouth shut and turning away in disgust. She could feel him watching her profile.

"They started at noon, as they had planned. They didn't have anyone out earlier than that, so the shot we heard must have just been from someone else, maybe a neighboring farmer chasing off a lion or something."

Sarah shook her head. "No, it was more than that. It didn't feel right." She breezed past him in agitation, heading out the door to the common area.

Mark shrugged, and not taking the hint to leave, followed Sarah out onto the great deck surrounding the common area and overlooking the valley paddocks. Piet, the other older trail guide was already there, enjoying the quiet evening air with his wife, Romy.

Being polite, Sarah and Mark both nodded in their direction, "Evening."

Piet nodded back. Sarah watched them as they observed the tension between her and Mark. Pressing her lips together, Sarah watched as the middle-aged man leaned into his wife to hear what she must have thought of the scene. Confirming her suspicion, they both looked toward Mark and Sarah, quickly excused themselves and left.

Was there no escaping Mark tonight?

Attempting to ignore her insistent shadow, Sarah leaned on the rail with her coffee, gazing into the darkness. She flicked her eyes sideways at Mark and saw him fidget as if he felt awkward. *What did he want?*

"Well," he cleared his throat, "they'll be back in a month's time to cull the D-12 herd."

Not bothering to look his way again, Sarah made a scoffing noise in her throat.

"They need to do it, Sarah," he implored, leaning in to try and catch her eye.

She finally turned to regard him, weary of the pointless conversation. "Don't try to make me feel better, Mark, you kinda screwed that up by telling me all the details anyway."

He stepped forward and went to speak, but she shut her eyes and shook her head in growing agitation, cutting him off. "Why do you seem to enjoy taunting me with all the gory details?"

Pressing his mouth closed and holding up his hands in defense, Mark turned and walked away.

He'd tried. He'd failed. Sometimes it just wasn't worth getting into it with her. Mark found Sarah strong-willed and stubborn. She was too passionate about something that she knew nothing about. He wasn't fussed on elephant culling either, but he saw the need. It would cost way too much money to simply transfer them to other regions. It was easier to cull before the growing numbers began to ruin everything, including the business.

It may have been four years since her arrival, but Sarah was still new to this land, and she just didn't understand the way things worked.

Brennan Safari Trails was open seven days a week, which called for a roster with staggered days off for the staff. Their busiest time was weekends and holidays.

Of the seven staff members who lived onsite in their own African-style rondavels, Mark, Sarah and Brandi often landed days off at the same time. A fact that didn't sit well with Sarah. She tried to negotiate with Johnno to mix it up a bit, but he was happy with the arrangement and not willing to budge.

Why couldn't Sarah get days off with people who wouldn't annoy her, like Piet and Romy, or even Solomon – their loyal Zulu stable-hand?

Brandi had just gotten back from Sunday morning service at Sunny Bank Christian Fellowship, in the nearby town of Phalaborwa, when she saw Sarah working with Honor in the round kraal. She went and put her bible and knapsack away in her rondavel, donned her hat and came back out to watch.

She often smiled when she thought of Sarah's response to the correct terminology for things in South Africa. Sarah called a kraal a "horse yard" and a round kraal a "round yard." Wasn't the place at the back of a house with lawn and flowers called a yard?

Sarah had Honor loose and was asking her to trot several circles around the round kraal before changing direction in one swift motion. Honor was then allowed several more circuits in the other direction before Sarah held up her whip way in front of where Honor was headed, asking her to stop. Honor stopped, licking her lips, and waited for the next command.

Sarah directed Honor with a signal, and the horse slowly backed up. Sarah pointed to the left and the great golden mare leapt into a jubilant canter, going around the inside of the round kraal. Sarah stood in the center, watching as Honor settled into the responsibility of another couple of smooth circuits around the kraal, her blonde mane breezing out behind her gracefully arched neck. The palomino truly was a beautiful animal.

Sarah tilted her head and looked at Honor's hindquarters with

29

exaggeration. Sensing the subtle cue, Honor ceased to canter and turned to look at Sarah. Crouching to the ground, Sarah beckoned with the tips of her fingers. Putting her head low and licking her lips again, Honor stepped over to where Sarah waited. Sarah rubbed her hand down the length of the horse's nose and spoke quiet words that only the two of them could hear.

Brandi stood watching the quiet exchange, breath caught in her throat. Sarah stood and looked up at her observer with little enthusiasm.

"THAT was amazing!" Brandi praised, clapping her hands.

Sarah caressed the equine head that appeared over her shoulder. "It's all about the relationship. You could have this with Jet, too. It just takes time." She clipped the lead rope back onto Honor's halter and unlatched the gate. Sarah looked sideways at Brandi as she followed them to the tack-up area.

"Really? How? I mean...it was like Honor could read your mind."

Sarah was amused at Brandi's naivety and turned to make sport of the girl. "It gets better too, you know? It can get so good that you can ride bridleless out in the open...even do dressage or show-jumping."

Brandi stopped in her tracks, mouth agape. "No! That's unfair! Don't make fun of me!"

Sarah shook her head and laughed. "It's OK, Brandi, you might understand some day."

With that, she dismissed Brandi and went on her way. She didn't want to spend her day teaching Brandi how to be natural around horses. She had other things to do. When Sarah worked with Honor, she felt at ease. It made all the troubles go away.

If she could slip away unnoticed, Sarah wanted to go back into the reserve today and check out that place in the veldt to see if there was anything else out there. Knowing that she'd be shot, or worse still, fired, if anyone found out where she was heading, she got out her saddle and hefted it onto the rail next to where Honor waited quietly. She wouldn't be able to get into the office for a rifle without attracting unwanted attention, or even worse, discipline, but she still wanted to risk venturing out.

Sarah's eyes bored into Brandi as the girl stood looking awkward in the distance. Finally, Brandi broke gaze, deciding to leave and do her own thing. *Good*, thought Sarah, turning away with satisfaction to saddle her horse.

She wouldn't be gone long, and figured she wouldn't even need her rifle.

Within minutes, the sound of Honor's hooves echoed off the buildings as Sarah cantered away to investigate the mystery out on the lowveldt.

Jet stood grazing in the bottom paddock as Brandi walked along the top pathway toward her rondavel. Brandi clucked her tongue to get Jet's attention. The black pony raised its head, glanced over at Brandi and then resumed grazing, turning his back to her.

Brandi sighed, "Oh, to have a relationship like Sarah and Honor...."

Brandi recalled seeing Sarah call to Honor in the paddock, and Honor would come galloping up to her like a long-lost friend. How did she do that? Sarah said it was a relationship.

Well, Jet was good for Brandi. She didn't have any trouble with him. She didn't want to be obsessed with horses and put horses before God.

She also had mixed feelings about how Sarah often treated her. Brandi could be offended and harbor an attitude or she could keep on offering friendship, even if Sarah often fobbed her off. Those were the choices.

Brandi sighed and stepped inside her rondavel, determined that it was time to pray for her workmates and ask for help dealing with their attitudes.

The rondavels were modernized but modest. A westernized version of the native African-style huts, they were sturdy, simplistic and rounded in shape, with a thatched roof and mud and stone walls. Each one of the Brennan's rondavels boasted a kitchenette, small bathroom and separate bedroom area.

Brandi closed the door behind her, flopped onto the old musty second-hand couch that had been in the rondavel forever and began to pray that Sarah kept herself out of trouble.

Sarah stooped and ran her fingers around the sooty, burnt circle in the grass. Strange. She was on edge. She shouldn't be here.

There were several small bones lying there, arranged within the circle in some kind of pattern. Could a shaman have been here? A nerve twitched in Sarah's neck as she gazed over her shoulder, gauging the distance between herself and Honor.

She had done the unthinkable. Intending to venture only to the boundary of Letaba—which was forbidden enough on its own—Sarah couldn't help but pass into the Kruger. She needed to see this spot again for herself.

The herds of plains animals were all back on the lowveldt, grazing, seemingly unconcerned with the presence of Sarah and her horse.

Sarah glanced back at Honor again, narrowing her eyes at the empty rifle sheath on her saddle. This had been a stupid idea! There was no evidence of the cull in these parts. The other elephant herds would have been elsewhere when the cull took place. They liked to browse the shrubs and strip away at the mopane trees, leaving the branches bare and carving trails of destruction through the undergrowth, trails that Brennan's often used for rides after clearing the debris.

Everything here looked serene and beautiful. Trying to control her nerves and regret, Sarah stood and stretched her back out, watching as something splashed in the waterhole, sending a flock of birds to flight in fear. Several delicate impala skittered away, and an aloof-looking kudu looked up and meandered in another direction as a decent-sized Nile crocodile hefted its great scaly bulk onto the bank to bake its hide in the sun.

Sarah started to feel the heat too. She'd lingered way too long in a forbidden place. It was time to be getting back.

Most of the animals on the lowveldt were starting to settle back and laze out the hot part of the day. Honor was looking comfortable tied under the shade of a nearby tree, head down, ears drooped to the sides and back hoof cocked. Every now and then, she would flick her tail to rid herself of a stray fly that had decided to irritate her.

"OK, girl, let's get out of here," Sarah mumbled.

The horse didn't respond.

"Honor!" she shouted.

The mare jolted her head from slumber and regarded Sarah. Sauntering over, Sarah untied her horse, glancing again at the empty rifle sheath.

Honor shook some flies from her face and began to chew on the bit, ready to go. Setting her stance, Sarah mounted up.

The two headed back at a steady pace, eager to return to the safety of the property as soon as possible. Despite what Sarah found, she wasn't spooked today. In fact, she felt rather good; as if she'd just cheated death as she and her horse raced home.

It was nice and hot, and she was going to go back to her rondavel to do what the plains animals were doing: laze around in the cool for the rest of the afternoon. She hoped that Brandi didn't tell anyone about her going riding, and even more so, she hoped that nobody checked the electric fencing that protected the property and noticed that it had been tampered with.

Turning the fence back on and mounting up, Sarah looked back over her shoulder down the trail. No sign of Piet, Solomon or any of the other riders. Sarah breathed a sigh of relief that the morning group of tourists hadn't intercepted her on her travels.

Mark stepped out from his rondavel at noon. He stood outside his door and blinked at the sunlight beating onto his tanned features.

Rubbing his eyes and yawning, Mark scanned the quiet courtyard that housed their rondavels like a cozy little community. He scoffed at the thought of the staff being "cozy," more like "tolerable."

He'd had a late night sitting at his kitchen table, looking up park statistics for work. He also kept a selection of display folders, where he stored his collected newspaper articles regarding the Kruger. Many of the articles consisted of the names of the poachers who had been arrested or shot in action by rangers. Of course, there would be the occasional positive article on the tourism efforts of Brennan's or other safari businesses along the Kruger.

Mark's life revolved around work, and he had little time for much else. He sometimes visited his family in Johannesburg and caught up with friends, but most of the time, his life was career driven.

He was a good trail boss and was always on the lookout to improve what he knew about the reserves and wildlife spotting. Despite what Sarah had said about him not caring for the wildlife, Mark did care, to a degree. He cared that they would have great wildlife to spot on safaris to keep the business booming. He hoped to one day own his own safari business, or even to take over management of Brennan's.

Mark raked his fingers through his thick, wavy brown hair that was getting bleached tips from the sun and rubbed his chin. Why did stubble always grow faster when he had late nights? Oh well, it was his day off. No ladies to impress here. No ladies that would care, anyway. They'd seen him like this hundreds of times and had given up on telling him he needed a haircut or a shave. He rather liked the rugged wild-man look; it gave him an edge that some women found alluring.

Mark scanned the area again, his dark blue eyes starting to focus better. Where was everyone? It was really quiet.

Squinting against the sun, he calculated that Piet's morning group of riders should be returning soon. He thought about the other trail boss with disdain, hoping that Piet had led the group properly, slowing down enough to show and explain all he could of the flora and fauna. They were only riding around Letaba this morning, so it shouldn't have been too difficult for the man. He'd check in with him later when he saw him return, or perhaps visit

Piet's wife, who was working on administrative tasks in the office.

Rumbling interrupted Mark's train of thought. Was that his stomach? He went back inside his rondavel; he knew how to fix that problem.

Sometime later, Mark looked out his window and saw Brandi heading over to the main staff building. She stepped up onto the deck and sat on the edge, letting her legs dangle under the rails. Brandi crunched into the apple she was holding and rested her chin on the railing, watching Jet in the paddock below.

Mark thought Brandi didn't look like herself, she was too...somber.

Happy, cheery Brandi was somber? Why? He HAD to hear this!

There was nothing better to do here today until Piet returned, so Mark set out to talk to Brandi. Brandi looked up as she heard Mark clomping up the steps onto the deck.

"Goeie dag. Hoe gaan dit?" Mark called out to her.

"Hello, Mark. Goed, en met jou?"

They greeted each other in Afrikaans, and Brandi's downcast voice confirming Mark's suspicions.

He shrugged and answered, "So so," and sat next to her, mirroring her and resting his chin on the rail. "You bothering God again?"

"Hmmph! Did you just wake up?" Brandi scowled, rolling her face to regard him.

Mark sniggered, knowing he'd gotten a bite from his comment.

"Ja. I had a late night again, reading and on the phone," said Mark. "I found out about some more bush camps in the Kruger that will let us do overnight rides. And Olifants' bush camp also wrote me, letting me know that they'll have horse stalls set up for us, so we can use that stop, too. I'm not too fussed on Olifants, though, it's too far into the Kruger."

"That's good about the other bush camps. I still want to do an overnight one day too," replied Brandi, her tone glum.

"You will, Brandi. We've got one lined up soon, I think. You'll get to meet Jacob, Martha and their cheetah, and...Martha's cooking!" He drooled just thinking of it.

"Maybe. Johnno may not let me go if it's a small group." Brandi sighed, swatting a fly from her face.

"Hmm...that's true. You'll get to go one day, though."

They sat in silence for a moment, watching the horses grazing in the paddock below.

"So, what else is wrong?" Mark questioned, now concerned.

"What do you mean?" Confusion crossed the young woman's face.

"I mean, you're not yourself. Did something upset you or what?" Mark stared out toward the paddock, feigning boredom as he worded the question.

Brandi hesitated before stammering, "It's Sarah."

That got his interest.

"Sarah?" Startled, Mark sat up, looking at her with inquiry.

Brandi locked eyes with him, mild curiosity crossing her features at his reaction.

Regret, for not masking his surprise, clouded Mark's judgment. What was Brandi thinking? Could she read his thoughts?

If he admitted it to himself, he'd had a thing for Sarah for over a year or more. No one else appeared to notice what was happening, and he was careful to conceal it. He was always giving Sarah grief about everything, and constantly got upset at her for her rash decisions, but deep down, after a while, it had become apparent to Mark that his feelings for her were growing.

The realization left him both confused and annoyed at first. Sarah was getting under his skin and had no idea about it. She was forever pushing him away, thinking he was an arrogant, sarcastic fool.

Mark knew that he would never in a million years have a chance with someone like Sarah. He would only look like a fool if he tried. Did he look like a fool now? How much had Brandi worked out? He needed to tread with more caution around the subject.

Brandi sighed beside him, bringing his thoughts back to the present.

"What has she done now?" Mark cloaked his thoughts with a

slight indifference, even a sliver of annoyance.

That's when Brandi changed tact, defending the girl. "Sarah didn't do anything, Mark. It's just that, well, I think I'm jealous of her...in more ways than one."

What was with Brandi? He hadn't seen that coming.

Mark ducked his head, trying to hide his amused face by clamming his hand over his mouth and pretending to rub at the stubble on his chin. He controlled the smug expression and nodded in thought, saying nothing.

Brandi looked away, and Mark thought she looked ashamed.

"Ahhh, the green-eyed monster, eh? What are you jealous of?" Mark regained his aloof demeanor.

Brandi retorted, "I don't want to be jealous, Mark."

"Jealousy is just an emotion." Mark raised an eyebrow, all pretenses slipping away. "We all experience emotions, it's what we do about them that counts."

Brandi pondered this thought. Mark was right; the bible says, "Be angry, but sin not."

Brandi reasoned that the emotion was normal as long as it didn't lead to sin. It didn't make her feel any better, though. She needed to deal with her thoughts privately, with God.

The urge to walk away and have some quiet time was strong, but Brandi felt awkward about just leaving Mark in the lurch, even if he was acting peculiar. She thought that talking it out might help, but she realized that she needed to talk it out with God rather than Mark.

"Sooo...? Is it her looks? Her clothes? Her horse?" Mark tilted his head, prying for answers. His curiosity had now been more than aroused.

Brandi relented, "I just would love to have the kind of relationship with my horse that Sarah has with Honor. I mean, it's like in those children's movies where there's a mental connection between the kid and the horse. They look like they can read each other's minds." Slightly changing the subject, "What do they teach them about horses in Australia anyway?"

Mark nodded, knowingly. "Come."

They got up and started strolling past the staff rondavels and down the dirt track toward the horse facilities.

"Brandi, there's something you've got to understand about Sarah. She's not just a good rider. When it comes to horses, she *is* like the people in the movies. She has the kind of relationship with them that—like you said—they can understand. Sarah's been working with horses in an intuitive way before she even knew natural horsemanship was a method of horse training. She's studying it further now, but she just always had a knack for it."

They walked past the horse kraals and into the stables, until they got to a display window on the wall. Behind the glass were photos of Sarah and Honor that Sarah had tacked up near Honor's stable. The photos included a shot of Sarah riding Honor bareback and bridleless over a jump, Sarah's hair streaming out behind her as she held her arms out like she was flying.

Brandi reached up to touch the glass in front of the photo, her eyes wide in acknowledgment. "I've never noticed this before? She really did that?" Brandi looked at Mark, her eyes confused.

Mark nodded. "She does that kind of thing a lot. She's a show-off!"

"I thought she was joking," Brandi admitted.

Mark chuckled, "That's understandable. I was a bit shocked at first myself. I thought, 'You crazy woman! You'll get yourself killed!'"

Brandi laughed at his change in expression, but her eyes were glued to the photos in wonder. "She said it was all about the relationship."

"Ja! She's right, Brandi."

"What do you know about Sarah?" Brandi pried, giving him that curious look again from the corner of her eye.

Mark considered lying, feeling as though he was being led somewhere, but then giving up and leaning against a post, he revealed what he knew.

"Let's see...she came over from Australia about four years ago. She has a cute accent...." It was meant to come out jokingly, but Mark's tone took on an embarrassed edge that was not missed by Brandi.

A self-conscious simper played across his face, and Brandi

pushed at his shoulder.

"Come on, seriously."

She hadn't caught on! Mark sobered up, relieved, and tried to lead her away from his lapse, "I don't think Sarah had a great childhood. I don't know too much, but I do know that Sarah had a hard upbringing. She wasn't exposed to horses until the last ten years or so. I heard that she lived for quite a few years on a big cattle place in Australia as a foster kid, and the family adopted her and she stayed and learned the trade. That's where she learned all she knows."

Quieting a bit, Mark continued on, "I don't know anything about what happened to her real family, but I do know that she is a very strong-willed and independent woman. I'd say those are traits she picked up to look after herself in the early years. Honor was the first horse she ever owned, and Honor was a rescue horse that someone had neglected back in Australia. Sarah focused all her time and energy into her relationship with Honor. That's why it's so important to her. Lots of time and effort. She's had Honor for a long time, even paid the fortune it cost to fly her over here."

Brandi looked at the photo of Sarah on Honor again, wonder in her eyes. "Do you have that kind of relationship with Sniper?"

Mark cocked his head to one side, struggling with what to say, "Ahh, sort of. I mean, Sniper is a good doer, he's obedient and light...but I would never trust him enough to let him have any opportunity to escape from me. Horses are unpredictable. You just can't let go of your full control."

He looked at the photo of Sarah flying over the jump with her arms extended. "I don't do what Sarah does with Honor. I don't know any horse that I would trust enough, except for maybe Honor."

Brandi nodded, "I know what you mean."

They started to walk out into the sunlight. It was getting hot.

Outside, Mark stopped and looked straight at Brandi, "The thing is, Brandi, why are you so upset about this? Jealous or not, it's no big deal. You just have to be willing to spend every blinking moment with your horse and you can have the same thing. I, for one, have other things to do with my time."

He looked at her again, curious. "So why the hang up on the jealously bit?"

Brandi shuffled with discomfort, and Mark got the impression it was a Christian thing. Maybe jealousy was against her religion or something.

She swallowed and started to speak, "Well..."

Just then, they heard the sound of trotting hooves coming up the path from the tack-up area. Brandi welcomed the interruption.

They stood silent, watching as Sarah jogged past them toward the stables, carrying Honor's light endurance saddle and gear to put away in the tack room. Then came Honor, no bridle, no halter, just trotting along behind Sarah like a dog.

The horse smelled freshly washed, wet fur and sweat filling Mark's nostrils with that pleasant, familiar smell that he had come to know and love about horses.

Brandi just looked at Mark and shook her head in amazement. Sarah and her horse disappeared into the stables, soon reappearing, walking side by side.

Mark cocked his hands onto his hips and grinned at Sarah as she passed. "Show off!"

Sarah looked smug and ignored him, turning to Honor. "Don't worry, baby, he's just jealous!"

Brandi looked at Mark.

"Hey!" Mark called after Sarah, who turned, with question in her eyes. "Did you enjoy checking the Brennan's boundary?" He folded his arms across his chest, a look of suspicion on his face.

"Hmm." Sarah answered, nodding her head in affirmation.

"I thought as much," Mark frowned with disapproval, reading between the lines.

Ducking away from further scrutiny, Sarah went down and unlatched the gate, leading into the bottom paddock, and gestured for Honor to pass her into the pasture. Honor walked in quietly and then, spotting Jet, let out a whinny and trotted down to meet him. Sarah's face tilted with appreciation as Honor found a patch of grass, circled, then dropped into a huge, luxurious roll.

Mark and Brandi stood watching from outside the stables,

feeling as though they were intruding on something intimate. There was an amazing relationship between Sarah and her horse. None could dispute it.

Mark wiped some dust from his eyes, trying to fight against the rising tension in his temples. "That's why Johnno hired her. She's good with the other horses, too. She doesn't get them quiet enough to do what she does with Honor—that would take more time—but she does get them safe for people to ride. She was taken on as our Stable Manager, flank rider and instructor, but unofficially, she is also our breaker and trainer."

Mark watched Sarah from behind as she leaned on the fence post, looking at Honor. She was a slender woman, shorter than average. He considered her long, wavy black hair. It was loose today and fell in turbulent waves down to the middle of her back. Her soft hair was going a tint of auburn from being kissed from the sun.

Her olive skin was tanned from a life outdoors, but it also spoke of a heritage Mark couldn't put his finger on. Perhaps Italian? He would never know. Sarah's thick Aussie accent proved the only heritage she would share, and beyond that, she was a closed book to everyone.

His gaze followed her as she left the post and went up the path toward her rondavel, her slender hips, clad in tight denim jeans, swaying ever so gently as she walked back up the path toward home.

Brandi stood by feeling a little awkward, before she slipped away to go back to her place.

CHAPTER THREE

Tuesday morning Johnno called Sarah into his office.

"Hello, Sarah," he spun his chair around to face her, forming his fingers into temples against one another. "I've got a couple of new horses arriving this morning. They are green-broken, but need to be worked and educated."

Sarah groaned, "Why do you keep doing this?"

"Doing what?"

"Buying unsuitable horses?" Dipping her head, she kneaded her temple with one hand, her other hand cocked on her hip.

Johnno looked her up and down and continued, unconcerned. "We're booked up for this week with tourists, but the groups are all small. The others can handle it without your help. I want you to spend this week working with these new horses. Ja? When you think they're ready, join some rides into the reserve with a group, *not* on your own. Understand?"

Sarah folded her arms across her chest.

"Understand?" Johnno repeated, his voice growing stern.

"No worries, boss," Sarah conceded, sighing. *This was just perfect! More rejects! Why couldn't they get experienced, older horses? It would make more sense.* "I'll help the others saddle up and then get the kraal ready for the new horses. What time are they coming?"

"You know horses, and horse people for that matter. Could be anytime this morning," chuckled Johnno.

Sarah looked dubious.

"Don't get me wrong, Sarah, they'll be good mounts for tourists. I bought them from a quarter-horse stud near Johannesburg this time. They are high quality...well, they'd better

43

be for what I've paid. They are supposed to be quiet already. Don't look so worried, I'm not lumping you with feral horses again! These were expensive! Nothing but the best!"

Sarah gave him a flat look, doubt clouding her features. "Expensive or not, they are still not suitable for this type of work, Johnno. We need older, reliable horses. Young horses are susceptible to disease. The older ones seem to carry an immunity. Why don't you let me buy them? I could get you some good strong boerperde that have been doing this type of work in this terrain already...*and* they don't get sick!"

Imploring, she waited for his excuses.

"Nonsense, girl! I've seen you work; you can turn your hand at anything equine. These new, young horses will be ready in no time under your care—I know it."

He picked up a pen and started sorting through paperwork, dismissively.

"What about disease?" Sarah relented, not willing the conversation to be over.

"Well, you can buy some new vaccines or something," he wove the problem away with his hand, not bothering to look up from his work.

"Or something," Sarah grumbled under her breath.

Johnno put down his pen and papers with a sigh and locked eyes with her again. "Just go and try them, Sarah. You will not be disappointed."

She could tell from his tone that it was useless to argue any further.

"Yes, sir." Sarah dropped her shoulders, losing the battle. She would still carry reservation until she'd seen them and worked with them. "Thanks, Johnno. I'll be at the yards. Let me know when they come. I'll grab a radio."

It would be pleasant enough working with young quarter horses that had just been broken. Expensive in Sarah's mind could mean nice bloodlines, too. That would make them lovely to work with, but they weren't experienced enough for working with game yet. Sarah felt Johnno was just taking advantage of her skills and good nature.

To this point, Johnno had kept buying cheap horses that were abused, spoiled or half dead. He was stingy with his money and had taken an instant liking to the idea of a girl from Australia who had the skills to train and break broken-down and abused horses.

The truth was, Sarah hated trying to fix abused horses. It always took longer and broke her heart at the same time. Nevertheless, Mark and Sarah's desperate pleas to get in appropriate horses fell onto deaf ears...until now. Buying in young stock, now that was a change in routine. Maybe Johnno had woken up to the fact that Sarah refused to fix any more abused horses. He just didn't get it. It hurt too much; it was too...personal.

Sarah wondered, though, where he got the money for good horses all of a sudden. Brennan's was bringing in steady business, but often didn't have extra money to get quality gear and horses. Sarah noted that Johnno had also refurbished his house and office recently. Perhaps he had another investment, Sarah reasoned.

No matter, at least these new horses weren't from an abusive past. But could she keep them alive long enough to work into the program?

Mark looked up as Sarah came over to where he, Brandi and Solomon were saddling up for the first group of riders. She narrowed her eyes at the trio, thinking that Johnno had just told her he only had small groups this week. Why were three staff on a ride, then?

Sarah's hair was pulled back tight into a neat braid, hanging down her back like a soft ebony rope, and she looked ready for a hard day's work.

"You find out anything about these new perde?" Mark inquired. He grinned, looking toward Solomon and Brandi.

"What, you don't trust me?" Sarah replied, feigned hurt. She knew she was good at her job. She had done a great job with the other horses, especially Topsie, Suzie, and Zander.

Zander had turned into a great horse; he was a good looker, too. Sarah knew that Mark liked to ride Zander when Sniper was out of action. With new horses in, Mark would have to rely on Piet, Brandi, Solomon and the others to carry Sarah's load.

"It's not that," Mark grunted as he hefted a saddle onto Zander. "It's just that..."

"You need my help." Sarah finished the sentence for him.

Mark looked at her with exasperation, and Sarah smirked.

"It's OK to admit it," she grinned.

She overheard Solomon talking to Brandi a few horses down: "We're not good enough," Solomon said.

"It's not that either, Solomon!" Sarah called out, knowing that the Zulu man wasn't too upset about it, but rather was trying to join in the jest.

Brandi popped her head up from cleaning out hooves and caught Sarah's eye, an inexplicable expression in her face. *What did it mean?*

Shrugging it off, Sarah approached Mark as he was doing up Zander's girth. Ignoring him completely, she went straight to speak with the horse.

She could feel Mark look up at her as she rubbed her hand down the chestnut's sleek face with affection. His blaze and stockings looked super white today since the herd had been washed and groomed thoroughly after yesterday's dusty ride. No wonder Mark liked this horse, Sarah speculated. He was a nice horse to ride, too...now that he had been broken in.

When Zander had first arrived at Brennan Safari Trails his tail and mane were matted and knotted so bad that it all had to be hogged and cut off. He was covered in dirt, tufts of his dull coat and mane missing, bloated full of worms, and way too thin. And that was nothing compared to his temperament. Sarah had spent months with him before he was ready for anyone to ride. After hours and hours of groundwork and round kraal work, Sarah could tell most of a horse's past from what the horse itself presented in its attitude when she worked it. Zander was reactive and bitter, and had a deep mistrust toward people. She worked with him with care each day as he started to build relationships and trust in the people at his new home. He took longer than all the other horses to become good, but now he was considered one of the best rehab horses at the center.

With his new-found confidence, Zander was strong and fast and was reserved for the more experienced riders. Sarah combed her fingers through his sleek mane while Mark finished getting the saddle ready.

"You going to help or just stand around patting the horse all day?" Mark cut in, as he brushed past her.

This jolted Sarah's memory back to his original question. "The new horses," Sarah pondered aloud as she picked up a dandy brush and moved over to an unsaddled white pony, Lazer. As she groomed him, the gelding didn't even wake as tufts of long white shedding fur collected in the dandy brush and flew about the area, "well, Johnno said that he splashed out this time and bought freshies. They are from a quarter-horse stud close to Johannesburg. He sounded like they hurt his hip pocket a bit, so they must be good breeding at least. He said there was two of them, and that they were green-broken. Also that they are supposed to be quiet doers already."

"Typical," Mark rolled his eyes, appearing to not be the least bit surprised, before going onto saddling the next horse in line. "Geldings?"

Sarah shrugged her shoulders, "I forgot to ask."

"Hopefully they are. We don't need any more mares around here. We need to get rid of the ones we have." His voice strained as he lifted another heavy saddle onto the mare in front of him. Startled, the mare stepped sideways, causing Mark to have to move with her to fix the skewed-up pad under the sideways saddle.

Sighing with exasperation, but knowing it was his fault the mare moved, Mark went on to condemn them, "They get too moody when they're in heat, and they're just unpredictable."

Sarah's green eyes flashed.

Righting the saddle and pad, Mark yanked up the girth, straightening to face her. "I'm willing to make concessions for

Honor, but only because you won't listen to me. You know my warnings."

"I know, I know. A lion can smell a horse on heat a mile off. That's why we rotate the stock and leave the mares in heat here." Sarah swapped her dandy brush for a soft body brush and finished grooming the white pony before her.

"Would be easier if the boss bought what we asked for, though." Mark grunted, hitching up the girth again to tighten it.

"That reminds me, that mare of yours is in heat again. We'll need to leave her behind till she gets over it," Mark narrowed his eyes toward the palomino mare in the spare kraal.

As if on cue, Honor lifted her tail, airing herself out like a harlot.

"I rest my case!" Mark scowled.

"Well then, you could call it 'good timing' that the newbies arrive today," Sarah walked past him, slapping his shoulder as he shook his head at her horse. She threw the brush into the box and selected a hoof pick.

Chuckling, Mark grabbed one too and ducked down to clean out hooves.

Sarah shook her head, smiling, and went to do likewise to the pony.

Lazer was a white gelding, aptly named, not for being lazer-fast, but rather for being "a lazer." He was the slowest, laziest pony in the herd. He was also the fattest, thought Sarah as she picked up his back hoof.

The pony groaned and put his weight against her. Working with him rather than against him, she completed the task in silence. All four hooves cleaned out, she straightened, stretching her aching back out as she looked around, surveying the area.

Some horses were tied, ready for the trail ride, the rest were in their holding kraals. It was also worming day, so all the horses were together for the essential, if not happy, occasion. Twenty-four horses in all, including the four staff horses. Sarah knew they wouldn't be able to support many more horses at Brennan's.

Brennan Safari Trails owned a few hundred acres that once was farmland. They had access to the reserves as long as the horses left minimum impact on the native habitat. If the impact of the horses got too great, Johnno could even lose his newly acquired license to use the Kruger. If rides kept getting as big as they did the other day, with fifteen horses out on the trail, their way of running the business would need to undergo major change.

Mark would argue to the authorities that the horses caused less damage on the environment than the elephants. The main groups stayed on the designated trails; trails that elephants had started with their constant foraging. At least they still would have access to the private reserve of Letaba.

Sarah hoped that these two new horses were going to be good. If money was no longer an issue, maybe Johnno would be open to selling the mares one at a time and replacing them with reliable geldings. If he did that, she might even consider retiring Honor to Brennan's on a permanent basis to reduce the risk of a lion attack.

"By the way, good morning, Sarah," chirped Brandi, as she walked back from the tack shed with another saddle tucked under her arm. Behind her, Solomon carried two saddles in his strong arms. Sarah hadn't even seen them leave for the shed.

"Hi, Brandi, Solomon," Sarah greeted politely.

"Morning!" Solomon called, cheerily.

A hot feeling of guilt rose in Sarah's chest again. *Why did she have to be so rude to people? Had she even said hello to any of them this morning?*

Sarah had heard that Brandi wasn't herself the other day, but from looking at her today, you'd never have guessed it. Brandi never stayed down for long. Sarah wondered whether the reason Brandi was always so happy was because she'd found peace in a so-called God. Brandi seemed fulfilled and satisfied in life following the same God Sarah's mother had followed. It was like she'd found what she was looking for...found what Sarah was looking for.

Sarah had never felt anything like that. She thought she had with horses, but something was still missing—some kind of unexplained emptiness.

Sarah finished up Lazer and started on Bunny. Brandi had just put Bunny's saddle on the railing next to her. She was another palomino mare, somewhat smaller than Honor; Brandi liked to call her Honor's little sister, Truth, but Sarah had refused to change her name. It sounded silly to Sarah. "No sillier than Bunny," Brandi had argued with a pout.

The static sounds of the radio crackled to life on Sarah's hip: "Sarah, this is Johnno. Do you copy?"

She unclipped the radio from her hip and answered it, "Sarah here. I copy. Are they here? Over."

"Ja. Visitors the north gate. Can you run and let them in? Over."

"Will do. Over and out."

Sarah clipped the radio back on her hip and nodded to Mark, who inclined his head in reply.

"See ya, guys!" She called and took off at a jog toward the large double gates on the north side of the grounds.

Sarah waved goodbye as the horse truck pulled out of Brennan's gates and back onto the road. The owners of the stud had come out to deliver their progeny.

Sarah was impressed by their professionalism. She turned and observed the two new gelding quarter horses in the round kraal. Mark would be happy—no mares. Both were impressive-looking three-year-olds. One was a perfect pitch-black, sleek and shiny. The other, a red bay horse, with a rich black mane, tail and legs. The black horse was named Zulo, and the bay was Shar. Sarah saw no reason to change the names they had been given as foals.

Johnno appeared behind her from out of the blue, jolting Sarah from her thoughts. Being an ex-military man, Johnno had also tried his hand at being a park ranger for a while with the park authorities. For some reason, he didn't like that job.

After he retired from that position, Johnno invested his money in various projects he thought would bring him fulfillment and money. When those investments didn't pay, he moved on.

Sarah often looked at Johnno's hollow life and saw herself in it, just without the money to explore other options. Brennan Safari Trails was Johnno's last investment and was also the project that Johnno had kept going with growing success the longest, over eight years. In the beginning, he used to ride the trails on his trusty black gelding, Bandit, but soon grew tired and overweight, and he found that it lacked the fulfillment he sought.

After his knee-replacement operation last year, it was rare that Johnno ventured outside, opting instead for air conditioning and paperwork. He relied on his loyal handpicked staff. Bandit was also retired and spent his days grazing the paddock off to the side of Johnno's house.

"He looks like Bandit, doesn't he?" Johnno gazed with pride at the black version of the two new horses.

"I picked them out of a horse catalogue," Johnno chuckled to himself, pleased that he'd made the decision to buy from a stud.

"They always look different in real life, though," Sarah replied.

"Yes! They look much better!" Johnno agreed.

Sarah thought she saw the spark return to Johnno's eye. This would be an answer to all their problems! For a few months now, Mark had worried that Johnno was losing interest in the business; he feared that Johnno would grow tired of the investment and sell out, leaving them either without a job or at the mercy of a new owner, who might re-staff.

"Yes, he does. They're both lovely, Johnno," Sarah agreed.

An idea sprung to her mind, and swallowing hard, she put forward her idea, "Would you like Zulo made ready for you to ride?" It was a risk, but if they could get their boss back in the saddle perhaps he wouldn't sell out on them.

"Erm...maybe," Johnno cleared his throat repeatedly. "Just see what you can do. Get them ready for tourists, at any rate. I'll let you know what I'm doing when I see how he turns out."

Sarah nodded, knowing this was a cop-out. "Well, I'd best get started," Sarah slapped her hands together and, nodding to Johnno, left to get her gear.

When she returned, Johnno had left, much to her relief.

Johnno always made Sarah nervous. She didn't know what he was thinking. Sometimes he'd be quite amicable, other times he had a terrible temper. She went in and haltered up Shar, leading him out and putting him in a holding kraal nearby.

Sarah started with the gorgeous black Zulo. She threw her ropes, gloves and whip into the center of the round kraal with a loud clump. Zulo startled and trotted away from the commotion.

Sarah crouched down to see what Zulo would do next. She needed to gauge his temperament and personality, by pure observation. He stood facing the rail, looking for escape and sniffing the wood, his stomach heaving air in and out with drama. He watched Sarah from the corner of his eye. Sarah clucked, and the black quarter horse turned his head to survey her. He looked wary in the new environment, weary of the new stranger; the whites of his eyes reflecting his thoughts. He blinked rapidly, checking her out, wondering what to do next.

After what seemed like a minute or so, he shuffled his legs to stand and face her squarely. Sarah looked away and, standing up with care, walked two steps away from him, not looking back, no matter how tempted. She could sense Zulo watching her.

She then heard him drop his head and snort at the sand in the kraal. Sneaking a peek under her armpit, Sarah saw him look up at her again and chomp on his tongue, processing what to do with the situation. She was careful to make it appear that she wasn't watching him. He sniffed the ground again and took a few steps forward. He then stopped and looked back toward the holding kraal where Shar was busy eating some hay that Sarah had thrown in.

Sarah turned to face him and walked toward his hindquarters. Zulo snapped his head up to look at her again. Sarah immediately turned away from him, standing still, waiting.

Zulo looked at Shar for support, then back at Sarah. A long moment passed, until Sarah heard what she was waiting for. Zulo licked his lips and walked up to her shoulder.

Sarah waited as the horse sniffed her shoulder, making no attempt to launch herself at him. When the time felt right, ever so slowly, she turned and stroked his nose once then walked away

52

again, choosing to ignore the horse.

Zulo sniffed the air, unsure what to do, before following at Sarah's shoulder, looking for her leadership. She had respected his dignity, and now he was willing to follow her.

Sarah felt a wall of fear crumble away from the magnificent beast. With the horse's new-found confidence in her, Sarah turned and gave him a good stroking down his face and neck. Introductions had been made.

CHAPTER
FOUR

Sarah played with Zulo and Shar in the round kraal and around the Brennan's property for a couple of days, both on the ground and in the saddle, before she felt ready to take them into the reserve. After all, they had never been in close proximity to African wildlife before. They would need to learn to accept it as non-threatening, the same way they had learned that Sarah was non-threatening. This would take lots of understanding and patience on Sarah's part.

Shar was the first horse Sarah took out. As Sarah rode toward the boundary fence, she saw that the morning safari ride had already returned, so she wouldn't be able to join them. Perturbed, but not dissuaded, she dismounted and flicked off the electric fencing, before leading the horse into Letaba Reserve.

She took him around all the usual trails at first, and then cut into some of the tracks that only Sarah used. She tried to take Shar closer to the wildlife than would be ever required on a trail ride with tourists. She'd been able to get hold of her rifle this time, and it sat snug in the sheath on her saddle, thumping lightly against Shar's flank as he trotted along the track.

Sarah began by introducing the bay horse to the numbers of pale-colored impala that darted about in small herds amongst the scrub, their pale ochre coats blending well into the mopane foliage. If something was going to catch a spooky horse by surprise, it would be these benign dainty creatures with their black-tipped ears and sharp, warped horns.

Shar took most of it in stride, not in the least frightened by what he saw or heard, even when faced up to a lone rhino that Sarah found on her travels. If anything, Sarah found Shar inquisitive and curious about his new surroundings. When he did become worried by something, Sarah would use approach and retreat to get him used to it before she took him closer. She would take him right to the point where he got a bit worried, then back off again. Then she would return to that point and push a little further. With each approach, the horse would become braver and be willing to get closer to examine the offending object.

He was a fast-learning animal, and Sarah was suitably impressed. She opened him up on a nice stretch of track and savored the rush of wind on her face and the smooth rocking-horse motion of his easy canter. Shar was not going to take long to be rideable for the tourists.

Delighted, Sarah turned to head back to attempt to sneak out on Zulo as well. She was saving the best for last. She needed to get in and out before she was busted in the reserve without a group again. She'd need to keep an eye out for Mark on that account. If a ride was coming out this afternoon, she could link in with them with ease, but for now, she was still going to sneak out with the horse if she could.

The black horse, Zulo was a little higher than Shar in both physical size and spirit. Zulo had superior gaits; his only downfall being his nervous disposition. *Just like an Arab horse!* Sarah thought drolly. However, his movement was what made him a great horse.

Earlier she had marveled over Shar's seemingly smooth gaits, but once she rode Zulo, she saw that he outshone the other by a long shot. He would stop on a dime by just leaning back. He would walk-on with the slightest rock forward. It was as if he could read your mind. Sarah also believed that, given time, he would be slow and hesitant with a beginner as well, sensing their ability. This subtleness made him a far better horse, but his flighty temperament was more likely to be more suitable for more experienced riders at this point in time. She doubted he would ever be right for Johnno in his present condition.

Sarah felt that Zulo was going to be wasted on safari trail riding; he would have made a better show horse in Western sports. Still, this was Johnno's choice, and Sarah had to make it work.

Zulo was a little more dubious about the proximity of wild animals, blinking as he squared up to a kudu, which looked just as wary; his majestic twisted horns quivering as his muscles tensed, ready for flight. Zulo had gained enough confidence from Sarah's training to happily leave Brennan's, but he was overly alert and jumpy.

Some impalas deeper into the foliage suddenly caught his attention. Stiffened, he was trying to make out the identity and shape of the tiny, strange black markings that moved about in the mopane, as the impalas eyed him at the same time. One of the impalas turned away, and suddenly Zulo recognized that the black markings were not individual creatures at all, but part of the ears, eyes and head of a bigger creature. He snorted with feigned dominance. A rush of birds took off out of a mopane scrub bush nearby, causing Zulo to shy, losing his bravado.

Sarah gasped as the shock took her off guard. Only just keeping her seat, she regained her balance and pulled him up, bending over his neck to reassure him. Turning the horse, she took him further back, to where he felt comfortable, away from the impalas.

Once there, Sarah relaxed a little more and allowed Zulo to survey his surroundings, waiting until he felt safe enough to graze so they could move on. Sarah didn't believe in pushing a horse through fear thresholds. She found that the horse would trust her more if she showed it that she respected its fear. She also found that they would grow more confident quicker and be less likely to be spooked when they trusted people not to corner them and put them in scary situations. This could not be more true of the great black horse, Zulo, and Sarah worked hard to maintain his dignity.

He may have taken much longer to get used to the reserve, but Sarah found it was a pleasure to work with him, and she savored every minute of it. They had only been out in the reserve for about twenty minutes when Sarah decided she would turn back. She didn't intend to push him as far as she had Shar. Turning toward Brennan's, however, she had a moment of doubt.

Just a little farther? She looked over her shoulder. She had taken Shar right near the boundary in the Kruger to get him to see that rhino. Zulo hadn't had any such encounter. Just birds, impalas, and that kudu.

Turning him back around, she trotted him along a windy dirt track that led toward the open boundary into the Kruger. She stopped at the boundary, a wary feeling in her gut. There was nothing here at the boundary to show Zulo; she'd need to go in.

Touching her hand to the comforting wood of her Winchester firearm, she thought about going back. No, she'd brought him this far, she didn't want to waste that. The air sounded still. Looking ahead, Sarah bit her lip as she pushed Zulo toward a slight rise. Surely a little peek wouldn't hurt, especially now that she had gone this far. She would already get in trouble if she was found this far out; might as well make it worth it.

Making up her mind, they surged up the short incline and stood a moment taking in the view of the bushveldt. The D-12 herd of elephants liked to frequent this area. Sarah squeezed Zulo to start further along the track into the Kruger when she noticed the same eerie silence that she felt the other day. Everything was still.

Sarah felt a cold sweat break out on the back of her neck, and the hair rose on her arms along with the goose bumps. She spun her head around, scanning carefully through the mopane. She couldn't make out anything. It was too still, though.

Instinctively, she gazed up into the red bushwillow above her, searching for danger. Leopards? No, nothing. Pulling her gaze away from the branches above, she worried that a lion might be in the undergrowth, and she turned the horse. He wouldn't respond, but was frozen to the spot as he was with the impalas earlier. *Was she too late?*

She pulled his head around, maybe a little too hard, and he stepped off balance. Sinking her boot into his flank, she got him to move several steps. Zulo then stopped dead in his tracks, causing Sarah to jerk forward. Catching her breath and balance again, she looked down at the horse, color draining from her face. He was now fixated on several spots. Lions? They had to get out of there with all calm, lest the lion give chase.

"Let's go now, Zulo!" Sarah spoke, loud and clear, slamming her heel into the horse's flank again. It would take some time for him to forgive her, but they needed to move it—now!

Her own fear started to set in again. Reaching down for the rifle sheath, Sarah pulled out her gun, holding it across her chest as she struggled to hold Zulo's reins. It was dangerous and awkward.

It was too soon for the horse to be out here, too dangerous. He couldn't handle it, and now she couldn't handle him. The realization that today might be the day that breaking the rules broke her set in with grave enormity as Sarah tried to control her horse. Eyes wide and breath starting to come in short, sharp gasps, Sarah felt the sweat trickle down the back of her shirt as she scanned the close-packed mopane scrub, feeling eyes all around them. She wet her lips with her tongue, tasting the salt from the sweat beading on her upper lip.

Zulo started to shake, his ears stiffened in one direction.

"What's wrong boy? You wanna go back? I wanna go back. Let's go back!" She booted him again, trying to turn his head to no avail. Even the bit grinding into his cheek didn't distract him from his fear, but instead seemed to escalate it.

Zulo stood staring ahead down the winding track, oblivious to Sarah's words and actions. Sarah swallowed hard and tried to will herself to be calm for the sake of Zulo. The great black horse started to jig-jog on the spot and shake again. Finally, some action; she could use his flight instinct to get out of this predicament. He tossed his head again and jig-jogged, and Sarah slammed her heel into his flanks as she directed his head toward Brennan's. Here we go, gallop time!

The horse didn't bolt in reaction, though. Zulo reared with anger, suddenly throwing Sarah from the saddle into the dirt. Dropping the rifle, she rolled and jumped to her feet, adrenaline pumping, and took hold of the rifle, before grabbing the horse's reins. *Need to get back in the saddle, get out of here!* The words pushed through her mind, as breathlessly as the oxygen she was trying to get back into her lungs.

She shortened the reins and, jumping on one foot next to the jittery horse, prepared to mount. Zulo skittered sideways, avoiding her plan. Face burning, Sarah trying frantically to control him again, all her natural instincts pointing toward flight rather than calmness. *You don't have to kill me for coming out here now, Mark, I've done it myself.*

Zulo stopped rigid. The hair on the back of Sarah's neck started to prick up again as she prepared to mount Zulo again. Eeriness filled the air like a thick, constrictive blanket. She stopped trying to mount and looked around. What spiritual power was so great that it would cause all life to go silent within its sphere?

She let the reins drop and held up her rifle, turning it toward the mopane as she released the safety catch. Then she saw him. An old Sotho tribesman emerged from the mopane scrubs at the side of the track, about five meters away, and came hobbling toward Sarah and Zulo. He wore the traditional leopard skin clothing and headpiece of an African shaman, or witch doctor.

In one of his hands was a fresh elephant tusk with bloodied flesh on the end of it; the other held up a rifle. Both looked out of place with the man's traditional attire. His face was set with grim determination as he approached Sarah, limping, with one bad leg. Zulo snorted and started to tremble again, tossing his great head.

Sarah hadn't ever had anything to do with the Sotho tribesmen from the neighboring communities, but this man was intimidating. A shaman was seen as a holy man in his tribe. They were known to practice all kinds of strange rituals to protect the village from witchcraft, bad spirits and sorcery. To a Christian like Brandi, what they practiced in itself was akin to witchcraft.

Was he now trying to protect them from something? Protect her? What was he doing out here alone, in the Kruger, with a bad leg? Was he injured? He could have been taken by a lion. Was he really alone?

Sarah looked with trepidation past the man in search of others, half expecting to be rained upon with an assegai spear for trespassing. She wasn't trespassing, though. So, what did he want?

Maybe he was lost and looking for someone else. Those eyes! Sarah shuddered, feeling that he wanted to speak to her as his eyes pierced into her.

She took a bewildered step backward as she locked eyes with him again. Raising the bloodied tusk and the rifle into the air, he shook them at her, yelling something aggressive in Sotho. Sarah didn't have a clue what he was saying, but he was frightening her. He was angry! But at what? Angry at someone for killing the elephant? Angry at her for being here? What? Sarah's mouth dried up.

There was a moment of silence; the man's eyes were piercing straight through her with livid anger. The air was so intense that Sarah felt she would choke. Those eyes, so full of hatred and anger at something she couldn't explain.

They eyed each other down a moment longer before Sarah broke out of her frozen trance and bolted into action. Her horse sidestepped, ready to go and she swung herself into the saddle. Sarah was ready for whatever Zulo dished out as she booted him in the flanks. The horse reared again, coming out of his own fearful stupor, and they took off at a gallop back toward Brennan's.

Fading into the distance, she could still hear the man standing on the track, shouting at her, long after she had departed. His voice continued to echo in her head, long after she ceased to hear him. It wasn't her fault that he'd found a poached elephant! It happened all the time! Why was he yelling at her? Hot tears sprang into her eyes, the wind in her face making them sting as she rode.

The ride back to Brennan's felt like it took an eternity, but she didn't slow down until she got through the electrified gates of the property. Closing the gates behind her, she remounted and cantered back toward the stables, skidding to a stop in front of the old holding kraals and vaulting off.

She slipped Zulo straight into a spare kraal that was rarely used and overloaded with grass, and latched the gate. She then sank down onto the dirt outside the kraal in a shaking heap, her trembling hands reaching up to cover her face in grief. Sarah had been riding the new horses all day, she was tired, but it was no excuse for her to lose the plot. She had to pull herself together.

She wiped the fresh tears that threatened to fall from her puffy eyes and tried to compose her still-rapid breathing. Fear clung to the air around her, threatening to suffocate her. The tack area was still and quiet, except for the extra horses that stood dozing in their kraals, waiting for their dose of worming paste.

Mark, Brandi and Solomon were still out riding with the group, which would have left after she had. It was Piet's day off. He and his wife would have gone to town.

Sarah felt alone and scared, forgotten memories from her past raising their ugly heads. She hadn't felt this alone and frightened for a long time, not since that night when she fled for her life from her own home, from her father. She had been successful in blocking those memories from her mind, and now all of a sudden, they threatened to overtake her. But why, after all these years? Why would they surface over some shaman yelling at her? Was she going mad?

She rationalized that at least she would have time to recompose herself before anyone saw her and started asking too many questions. Standing, she turned in a circle, taking in the horse area, checking that nobody had been watching her. Sniffling, she slipped back through the fence and untacked Zulo. She threw the saddle and other gear on the fence rail. Grabbing up the rifle, she dashed across the grounds and into her rondavel, locking the door behind her.

She still felt like there were eyes following her. Still felt that eerie chill, burning to her bones, despite the hot and sultry air. Sarah clicked on her air conditioning and peered through the curtains as she drew them closed, and then withdrew from the window. She knew that Johnno would be around somewhere, but now that she was inside the safety of her home, she didn't want to leave.

The last time Sarah had felt this shaken was *that* day. The day she had seen both her real parents for the last time. Sarah sank onto her couch, the memories flooding back that she had worked so hard to forget.

The temperature in the room had dropped, and Sarah went to turn off the air conditioner again. Fresh waves of grief hit as she gave herself permission to remember her mum. Once permission was given, she was unable to stop the clear images that now flooded her mind. Images of her mum's sweet smile, her soft melodic voice as she sang to her God.

Then came the darker images of that night. Sarah curled up on the couch, hugged her legs to her chest and wept.

Brandi was putting away the gear from the ride when she noticed that Sarah had left her tack on the fence of the old kraals. Approaching with caution, she noticed that Zulo, one of the new horses, was in there, munching on the overgrowth. That was odd. This kraal was never used anymore because it needed some repairs. The gate hung at a precarious angle, threatening to fall off if a horse leaned on it.

The other holding kraals were full of the regular horses, but it was unusual that Sarah didn't put Zulo away up at the round kraal with Shar. It was also unlike Sarah to treat her gear so roughly. Something was wrong.

It had been another hot day and dark summer storm clouds had gathered to the east, bringing with them the low rumbles and promises of a light show and a good, soaking rain. Mark was systematically working through the horses, worming them all, as Brandi and Solomon unsaddled them and put the gear away.

"Solomon, I'll be back in a minute. I need to ask Mark something," Brandi said, starting toward Mark with deep concern. The Zulu man nodded as he continued to stow saddles away in the tack shed.

Mark looked up, wiping his sweaty brow, as Brandi appeared.

"Mark, did you treat the new horse, too?" she inquired.

Mark frowned, "I did Shar over at the round kraal, but it looks like Sarah isn't finished with Zulo yet. I hope she comes in soon, it's going to get a bit hairy for riding." He gazed up at the thunderclouds, which were rolling closer, just as lightning flickered in the distance, followed by a low and long rumble still a bit far off.

"But Sarah *is* back!" answered Brandi, "She put Zulo in the old kraal over here." She waved her hand toward the old decrepit wooden kraal in the corner. "She left the gear on the fence too—in a hurry, by the looks of it. Want me to put it away for her?"

Mark stood on the fence railing to get a look at the old kraal, "Hmm, odd."

Brandi made her way over to it and straightened out the edge of Sarah's gathered saddle blanket.

Mark furrowed his brow with concern.

"OK," he nodded, and Brandi swept up the gear and walked off. He was relieved that Sarah was back from riding, having a gut feeling that she'd snuck into the reserve today. But leaving expensive gear on the rails with rain on the way? Something was definitely not right.

"She must have had a reason. Ja, put it away for her, that would be great, thanks. I'll worm him in a sec," he conceded grudgingly.

Mark soon reappeared at Zulo's kraal with some worming paste and slipped through the fence. The horse had given up eating and now stood stiff in the corner, quivering. He was sweated up, but cooling down way too fast in the rapidly dropping temperature preceding the oncoming storm. He didn't look in a good way at all.

"What's the deal here?" Mark glanced over as Solomon appeared at the kraal, looking concerned. "Sarah would never leave a horse like this." Mark shook his head and touched the quivering wet hide.

"I'll get a rug," Solomon offered and was quick to disappear back into the tack shed.

Solomon returned with a rug, which Mark threw over the horse. Mark then wormed and fed Zulo, helped the others finish packing away their gear, locked up and went to look for Sarah.

It was getting dark as he knocked on her door, and almost as if on cue, heavy drops of cool summer rain started to splat on the back of Mark's shoulders and neck as the thunder tremors grew closer. There were no lights on in Sarah's rondavel, and Mark started to doubt that she was even in there. He knocked harder and waited. It was quiet and dark.

Mark turned to leave when the porch light blinked on. The click of the door latch brought him to attention, and he blinked as Sarah opened the door and the interior light streamed out.

Sarah stood there looking vacant. She looked like she'd been asleep, but her eyes were also puffy and red from crying. She rubbed her face, self-consciously. Just as quickly as Mark thought he saw Sarah looking vulnerable, the walls came straight back up and Sarah took on the pose of being in control again.

Mark squinted against the now driving rain and shuffled awkwardly, trying to squeeze under the overhang of the thatch roof. "Erm...may I come in?"

Sarah moved aside for Mark to enter. He worded his next question with care as he stepped into the dry home. He was painfully aware of the puddle he was creating on her carpet.

"Did you know that you left your gear out?" Cursing himself for sounding so heartless, Mark looked at his feet as water dripped from his thick hair onto the floor.

She blinked at him, defense rising in her eyes.

"It's raining," he said, stammering. "Brandi got your gear in for you," he added.

The significance of his sentiment was lost on Sarah, and her lips tightened. She threw on her rain jacket, and before he knew it, she ushered him back out the door, joining him in the rain and shutting the door behind them.

"Come with me. We need to talk with Johnno right now!" she said. Mark thought he caught a panicky edge in her voice.

Mark hesitated; he was getting drenched again. She grabbed his arm and hauled him up the muddy path toward Johnno's house, their riding boots crunching in the soggy gravel and mud as they marched. Much to Mark's relief, the rain lightened to a soft drizzle.

"Whoa! Easy!" he looked helpless at his imprisoned arm as her nails dug into his flesh.

She glanced up at him, puzzled, before she realized what she was doing and softened her grip, "Sorry, you must think I've gone crazy."

"Gone?" He muttered with sarcasm under his breath.

She let him go. "There's something important we have to talk about...that's all."

"What's going on?" gasped Mark in exasperation, picking up on her frantic mood.

Sarah shook her head, sending water droplets flinging out from her dripping hair, "Wait till we get inside."

They rushed on as the rain grew heavy again, washing over the campsite in convulsing sheets. The lightning show grew more frequent and intense as they knocked on Johnno's door.

The proud owner of Brennan's opened his door, agitated by the interruption to his quiet evening. Putting on his professional tone, Mark reported that the horses were all settled, fed and wormed, but that something was wrong with Sarah. Johnno smirked at Mark's calm demeanor as he gave his report in the drenching rain.

"Get inside!" Johnno said, waving them in. His amusement over their predicament turning to a scowl of discontent as he noted the puddles now forming on his carpet, "Wait there!"

The pair of drowned rats stood as Johnno retrieved some towels, throwing one to each of them and laying one with ceremony on the carpet where they'd wet the floor. They both removed their shoes, and Sarah her jacket as they stepped into the house.

"Have you both eaten yet?" Johnno asked.

Mark and Sarah shook their heads "no" as Sarah dried her hair with the towel.

"Mark, go in my office and ring for take-away," Johnno mumbled, looking tired and old.

He watched Mark go into the other room and sighed, turning to Sarah, who was still drying her long hair. She looked very upset, like she'd been crying; however, the rain could have flustered her on the way over.

Johnno sometimes got tired of Sarah and her upstart ways. She'd be off on her mare too much, or some drama would be occurring about the culling. She always knew better than everyone else, including him, and she was out to save the world. He conceded that she was a brilliant stable manager and trainer, and for that, he would never let her go.

"Come and sit, Sarah." He poured her a glass of water as she settled gingerly into his soft leather lounge suite, "Now, what on earth is going on?"

Sarah shifted her weight in the chair and looked into the glass of water. Mark finished his call and clicked the phone down, his long legs covering the distance from the office to the lounge in several strides. He took a seat next to Johnno, opposite Sarah, and leaned forward.

"Yeah, what's going on Sarah?" Mark asked, echoing Johnno.

Sarah swallowed, "Interrogation time, huh?" She put her glass down on the side table and took a deep breath, "It's this elephant culling...I think."

Mark flopped back into the couch and groaned, "Is that all?!"

"Hey! Watch the couch!" Johnno growled at him. Mark sat forward, fully aware of the effect his drenched clothing was having on his boss's furniture.

"Can I go home and get changed, Sarah?" he whined.

Sarah sighed, shooting Mark a warning glance. He sat with reserve, ready to hear it.

"It's not just the culling is it?" continued Mark.

Johnno waved Mark to be quiet so he could ask the questions instead, "What happened today?"

Sarah gave Mark another filthy look, still indignant that he would so easily dismiss her as one of those over-emotional women who wept for ages over something minor. She focused her attention on Johnno instead; perhaps he would listen. "The elephant culling," Sarah continued, "We have to look into it and get them to do something else. I think the Sotho tribes to the north of Kruger are getting upset with it. You know, the Pedi and other northern Sotho."

Mark leaned forward. Johnno looked thoughtful.

"What makes you say that?" Johnno asked.

"I...I was confronted today. Some tribesman, he was dressed

like a shaman or something, came out of the bush and blocked my path. I think he may have come from Lebowa. He started shouting at me and shaking a fresh tusk and a rifle at me. I don't know what he was saying."

"Where was that? You're saying he was on Brennan's? Trespassing?" Mark narrowed his eyes at Sarah with suspicion.

"Well..." Sarah dropped her gaze guiltily.

"I knew it!" Mark slapped his knee, sending a sharp spray of water outward. Johnno's thick neck flushed red with fury as he wiped the water from his glass coffee table.

"Sarah! Are you suicidal? You know the rules about that!" Mark shouted.

"I had my rifle!" she implored.

Mark sat back in the couch, rolling his eyes with anger.

"Mark!" Johnno spat, annoyed at the wet seeping into his couch from Mark's wet jeans.

Reacting like a shot, Mark sat up to prevent his wet shirt from touching the back of the couch.

"*That's* where the missing firearm is!" Mark said, as he rose to retrieve another towel for the couch. He pulled one from the pile Johnno had sat on a side table and draped it over the back of the couch and took his position again.

Ignoring Mark, Johnno continued, "If you are going to continue breaking the rules, Sarah, I'm going to have no choice but to ground you here. No riding at all!" Johnno's oversized jowls bounced up and down with vigor as his temper rose, and Sarah could see the spider veins in his cheeks stand out against his already flushed skin.

She went to protest, but was cut off by Johnno again, "It's that or I'll have to let you go." Johnno cut, killing the conversation, "You know what that means! Back to Australia!"

Sarah slumped in her chair, despondent, "Yes sir," she answered.

Mark cleared his throat, returning to the original train of thought, "But those rural tribes up in Lebowa never cared before, did they?" Mark looked from Sarah to Johnno.

Sarah thought she saw genuine concern in Mark's eyes. Was

he being protective? The thought both disarmed and frightened her further.

Johnno sat back and rubbed his hand over his face. "Well, the farmers don't care because elephant populations getting too big can cause damage to their properties if they break out of the Kruger boundaries. The tribes, though, I don't know. I didn't think they would object because they run livestock, too. Elephants could ruin their living."

Sarah tilted her chin, "Well, they care about it now! He was angry at me! He thinks we have something to do with it. We need to do something before the next cull. That's only a month or so away!"

She started to get quite agitated, her voice working its way up frantically, "They should be directing it at the Parks Board, not us! It's not our fault! I don't even agree with it. Why did he attack me? Why did he do it?! Why did he do it to *her*?!"

Sarah's face burned with embarrassment and anger with herself for the unexpected and revealing outburst, and she stood, trying to hide her face. She walked into the next room, hand to her lips with frustration, leaving the men in confusion.

"*Her*? Did she just say '*her*?'" Johnno sat blinking at the outburst.

Mark stood up and followed Sarah. He found her looking out the window, the rain drizzling down the glass in silver rivulets, illuminated every now and then by lightning. Her quivering hand was still to her mouth and she was shaking her head, tears running freely.

He walked up behind her, reached his hand out to touch her shoulder, but then stopped. He wanted desperately to turn her around and hold her, but he had to resist. She would push him away. He would look like a fool. He was livid at the thought of someone threatening her, but he knew that her outburst went deeper, more personal. It regarded something else, perhaps something from her past. Would she let him into her world? He doubted it.

He was no longer angry at her disobedience, her lack of respect for authority. He'd followed her out here, intending to comfort her somehow, but now he didn't know how to go about it.

Mark swallowed hard, "Sarah? Is that all there is to it?"

She turned and looked at him through tear-stained eyes and shook her head.

Mark persisted, "Do you mean, 'no, there's no more to it' or 'no, you don't want to tell me?'"

Sarah's lips tightened. Mark noticed her discomfort and stepped back, away from her. He looked beyond her, out the window and sighed. He was just messing things up again. She'd never see that his intentions were honest, even honorable.

Mark's eyes fell on Sarah for a moment, and then he walked back into the offices to rejoin Johnno. He felt Sarah watch him leave the room.

Turning back to the window, Sarah's mind filled with a whirlwind of questions. Why did he follow her? Why was he pushing her for answers all of a sudden when he didn't have the slightest interest in stopping the culling? Or was it something else? Was Mark developing feelings for her?

Sarah paused and gazed again over her shoulder toward the door where Mark had just been. Shaking the cobwebs from her head, she hardened her heart. She wasn't going to let anyone get close enough to her to break her heart ever again. She had worked too hard all these years, putting up her walls and trying to forget her past. No guy was going tear them down, no matter how attractive he was.

Behind the fortress Sarah had built, she knew that her heart was still a vulnerable and scared thing. That it wouldn't handle being mistreated. It was because of her past that she had never allowed any man to get into a romantic relationship with her. She just didn't trust people, particularly men.

Several minutes passed, and Sarah noticed the sound of a car arrive and drop off the dinner. She wasn't hungry anymore.

Nobody was taking her seriously. Sarah's shoulders sagged as she noticed her immense fatigue, the throbbing in her hip that she'd fallen on. The thought of a long, hot shower and soft bed appealed to her more than anything. She walked back into the room where Johnno and Mark had already started tucking into the aromatic take-away.

"Come and have some dinner," beckoned Johnno.

"Let's talk about this," said Mark.

Sarah shook her head, "Sorry for my outburst before. I think I'll just go home to bed," and with that, she breezed past the men and shut the door behind her.

Mark looked at Johnno, cryptic. "There's more to this than that Sotho man," he rationalized, stuffing his mouth with more food. Johnno nodded, deep in thought.

"Still," Mark continued, "I don't like the fact that someone came at her like that."

Johnno nodded in agreement and grabbed another slice of garlic bread, "We might have to look into it some more."

SARAH'S GIFT

CHAPTER
FIVE

Sarah was out on the Kruger bushveldt with no horse. The mopane was closing in around her, making her feel hemmed in and choked. Danger lurked like a fatal scent behind every bush, shrub and tree. Sarah felt cold and alone; the dawn wind felt as though it was rushing through her, chilling her to the bone.

It must have been just before sunrise, as the ground was still saturated with dew and the horizon took on a purple haze under the deep sapphire sky. *I have to get home!* Sarah thought.

The ground unexpectedly shook with thunder as a huge bull elephant stepped out from the mopane scrub, flattening it to a pulp in front of her. He flapped his great ears with aggression, stepping forward, muscles tensed. Sarah also tensed, bending her knees, ready to flee. The elephant raised his trunk and trumpeted, causing Sarah to flinch as the sound rang shrilly in her ears.

People get killed all the time from elephants charging. The hairs on the back of her neck rose as she fought to control her rising emotion. What should she do?

The elephant stepped closer, and without reason, Sarah raised her hands toward him like she was training a wild horse. The elephant paused as he lowered his great head, backing into the bushes from which he had come.

The sun broke upon the horizon, sending brilliant crimson and puce color onto the landscape. Sarah shielded her eyes against the glare that shone through the leaves of a mopane as she recognized the shape of a man appear.

"Sarah..."

She tensed, facing him squarely, "What?"

73

"Sarah..."

"Who are you?" Sarah lifted her hands to block the sun, narrowing her eyes to try and see the man.

"You have a gift," the man said as he moved into view. Sarah saw that it was not just the sun behind him that shone, but rather the man himself who shone with a light like no other.

Sarah couldn't make out the features of his face from the light, "Gift?" she asked.

"You have a gift," the man repeated, solemnly.

"Who are you? What do you want with me?"

Sarah then saw herself, sitting astride Honor as if from a great height. Down below she could see herself riding along the edge of a great river, leading a huge procession of some kind. She couldn't make out what she was leading from all the haze, and she thought it might be a herd because it was kicking up so much dust.

"You have a gift," the words echoed in her head.

Sarah flicked open her eyes, disorientated. She was in her bed. It had been a dream. That was weird. She rubbed her eyes and looked at her digital clock on the bedside table; it was four a.m.

Sarah rolled out of bed and onto her feet and shuffled into the kitchenette, flicking on her kettle. Stretching as she stifled a yawn, Sarah wondered what today would bring. She hoped that Johnno would have some luck with talking to the authorities today. Her feelings were still raw, personal memories from her past felt like they had been raked to the surface, and it made her feel worn out.

Sarah stayed around the property that day. She rode Zulo and Shar around Brennan's, concentrating on educating the new horses rather than exposing them to African wildlife. It was good to be able to focus on her work, but Sarah still longed to be able to work the horses amongst the wildlife. She had promised Johnno no more gallivanting offsite alone, though, and she intended to keep that promise, not just to keep her word, but also because she was still emotionally fragile about the whole shaman ordeal. She was at her most vulnerable right now.

Brandi walked past the round kraal just as Sarah was working Shar at liberty. She was careful not to disturb Sarah after Mark had warned her that morning that Sarah needed her space to deal with stuff.

Sarah saw Brandi and was perturbed at her silence. "Brandi!" yelled Sarah, stopping Shar and jumping up on the rails of the round kraal.

Brandi came straight over.

"Has Mark been talking to you about me?" Sarah came straight to the point.

Brandi looked down.

"What did he say?" demanded Sarah, stepping off the rail and folding her arms across her chest.

"You've been avoiding me, and that's not normal for you," Sarah's eyes felt like they were piercing into Brandi.

The younger girl took a deep breath, thinking about the previous Sunday when she had felt jealous of Sarah. "He didn't say anything about last night. He just said to give you some space."

Sarah searched Brandi's eyes and decided she was telling the truth. She hopped down off the rails, but kept looking at Brandi through the bars, "So, this church you go to...do they know much about supernatural things, like shaman? And dreams?"

Brandi was surprised by the change in subject. She bit her lip in thought, "Um, yeah...Why?"

"Hmmph!" Sarah nodded in contemplation, "I don't know yet, just wondering."

"Well, OK. You are welcome to come with me one Sunday if you want," Brandi ventured.

Sarah shook her head, "I don't think I'll need that, but we'll see."

Brandi nodded; she was beginning to think that she needed to pray a lot more for Sarah. Why was she ever jealous of her? It looked like Sarah had more turmoil brewing under the surface than Brandi would care to experience again.

"Well, I'll see you later," Brandi waved and left Sarah standing in the round kraal in thought. Brandi needed to go and get horses ready for an afternoon trail.

Mark clicked the phone down on the receiver and shook his head at Sarah. She'd been pacing the room behind him, chewing her thumb nail as he called the park authorities again about the elephant situation. When Johnno had called earlier, they had passed his number onto other people, promising that they would be calling back with information that same day. Johnno had tried them several more times, with no luck, before he had to make a trip into town to pick up supplies.

Sarah had come in that afternoon along with Mark, got the updates, and pushed Mark into ringing them again, "They won't take it from me Mark, I'm a woman! They'll patronize me."

"Rubbish!" Mark spat. "You just want me to throw my weight around because I'm a trail boss."

"Well?" Sarah waved him toward the phone.

Mark shook his head and picked up the receiver. Sarah paced and listened as Mark got numbers, rang another person, got put on hold and was passed onto someone else before they finally got through to someone in charge. Mark had to hold up his hand by this stage to stop Sarah from grabbing the phone and abusing them.

From what Sarah heard of Mark's side of the conversation, it didn't sound good, and she got more and more restless. "Well? What did they say," Sarah stood over Mark's chair with her arms folded.

Mark braced himself for the verbal onslaught and spun his chair around, "They said 'No.' It can't be done."

"I know they said 'No.' I could tell. But why?" She looked at her shorn-down thumbnail with dismay.

"They said that with the costs of tranquilizers and the vehicles and professionals—the transportation and all that—makes the translocations just not worth it. They go through the process and only get out a few elephants, and it costs an absolute fortune." Mark sighed and looked imploringly at her, "Can't you see that it's just not worth it? I think we should tackle this by getting the Sotho tribes off our backs, show them that we are not responsible. Fixing the elephant issue to make them happy is not the solution!"

Sarah shook her head, shocked, "You agree with them? With the park authorities!"

"Sarah, I don't like culling any more than you do, so don't start on me again," Mark slammed his hands on the desk and stood up, his face a mixture of hurt and annoyance. He was tired, and he was over having Sarah take out her frustration on him, "I just can't see any other way. Can you?"

Sarah stood silent, picturing herself in the dream. Mark was satisfied, "See? You can't! I'm going home. See you tomorrow."

He got up and left the office.

Sarah's eyes snapped back into focus, "Mark!"

He stopped in the open doorway, his brows raised.

"What if there was another way?" she asked.

Mark could see her mind working. He came back in and closed the door, waiting.

"Could elephants be mustered? Like cattle?" Sarah pressed.

"Sarah..." Mark shook his head, his tone doubtful.

"I know you think I'm crazy. It's only to get them over the border."

"Only? You're talking about Mozambique! It's just a few hundred kilometers across hostile lion country." Mark was incredulous, "And *if* they could be herded, it would still take a lot of people, money and effort."

Sarah hung her head.

Mark relented, trying to be patient, wanting to calm Sarah so he could get home and leave on a good note, "It's a great idea, but it's only a dream, Sarah. I'm sorry."

With that, he left the building to go home for the evening, shaking his head.

77

The following few days went along as usual, and Mark started to wonder whether Sarah had come back to her usual self. She spent the rest of the week working the new horses, and even started to venture back onto the reserves again, joining either Mark or Piet and the other staff as they led a few trail rides. Mark was satisfied that Zulo and Shar would at least be ready for Sarah to join the rides and help out on flank again while she continued to work them and he gave Piet the thumbs-up to take her along.

Mark beamed to himself as he stepped out ahead of the group with the frisky Sniper, that Mark had to keep in check. Sniper kept mouthing the bit and pulling at the reins, trying to get permission to race ahead.

The morning was brisk and dewy. It was supposed to be coming into the wet summer months, but by the feel of this morning, winter was still clinging in the air. Once everything started to heat up, Mark knew that the proper wet season would start with the big storms. They would all be able to sit on the great deck of the main building of an evening and watch the magnificence of the storms as they rolled in over the lands. It would bring new life on the reserve, more game, more tourists and, most importantly, more business.

Mark turned around to check his group. They seemed content enough, looking ahead at the herd of wildebeests in the distance and speculating as to whether or not there were any big cats watching from the bushes. Behind the five tourists rode Brandi, chatting away to the young woman in front of her. Sarah rode off to their right. She seemed distant, but then Mark reasoned that she was concentrating on educating Shar.

The group of tourists they had today were all good riders, but were more interested in spotting predators. Mark had no intention of searching out big cats and had no qualms in telling them so. They could book another safari in the safety of a game-spotting vehicle if that's what they wanted to see.

So far, Mark had taken them through the reserve and into the Kruger, along Olifants River, and found some giraffes, hippos and various birds, including a Saddle-billed Stork and a Secretary Bird.

The Secretary Bird was one of their favorites. Mark had pointed out how this great bird of prey was unique in its technique of hunting. It would trample a snake with its long legs before eating it. The bird had just been standing in the swaying grasses of the lowveldt, watching them as they passed, the black quills on the back if its head sticking up in interest. The group had groaned and asked for lions, cheetahs or any of the "big five:" lions, leopards, buffalos, elephants or rhinos.

So, that was Sarah's current task: big-five spotting. Mark had told her on the quiet that they were to avoid cats. Sarah had rolled her eyes at him, "Duh!"

They moved along the lowveldt, following the track that would loop back toward Letaba and back to Brennan's. So far, there was no sign of buffalo, elephants or rhinos. They had settled into the ride, and Sarah was convinced that they could get along without her immediate attention. She was able to flank ride from a distance and enjoy both looking for game and training Shar, without having her thoughts interrupted with the constant stream of tiresome conversation.

Lost in her thoughts, Sarah almost missed the leopard that was sitting in the bow of a tree, off to her right. It was hard to spot leopards at the best of times during the day, as they came out at night. This one was lazing on the branch, its great heavy paws, which were stained with blood, dangling down either side of the branch. The left-overs from an impala lunch hung limp over the branch next to the cat. He looked full and sleepy as he concentrated on grooming himself. *Perfect!* Sarah thought.

She picked up her radio to inform Mark. The riders picked up on what had been spotted, and murmurs of approval moved through the group. Mark had no intention of sticking around a leopard, though, even one that had already eaten.

He prepped the group about distance and noise level, and the group began to pass the tree at a safe distance, careful to keep moving and keep their voices loud. The cat sat up and watched the horses with mild interest.

Mark was well experienced with African wildlife, and he kept the group safe, but Sarah still didn't like the way the cat was watching them. She and Shar sat beside Brandi, off to the side, as they moved along; breathing a sigh of relief once they passed. The leopard yawned and went back to licking his great paws.

Brandi slowed down to allow Sarah to sidle up closer to her, "You OK?"

Sarah hesitated, "We just passed a big cat, Brandi, of course I'm not OK. I was nervous!"

"Is that all? You've been acting strange for a few days."

"Just drop it, Brandi. I'm tired, that's all."

Brandi nodded. She wasn't so sure, but she knew better than to push the matter. Sarah had been acting weird since the incident with the shaman. Mark had said that Sarah was fiercely independent, and Brandi knew her to be fearless. This shaman thing, though...Brandi noted how deep it had rocked Sarah.

Shaman were known to have strong spiritual powers, powers that didn't come from her Christian God. Brandi looked at Sarah, who was trying so hard to be strong on the surface. Brandi could sense her inner turmoil churning over something and she silently started to pray for her. *Please, Lord, give her Your strength. Make Yourself known to Sarah in a strong and powerful way, so that she knows that the fight is not hers to fight. Please, Jesus, bring Sarah into a knowledge of You, and what you did for her. Forgive me for judging her all the time. Please protect her from physical and spiritual dangers.*

CHAPTER
SIX

It didn't take long for Sarah to break her promise to Johnno, and she was back in her favorite spot, up on the track at dawn with Honor. She sat on the large boulder overlooking the bushveldt while Honor grazed with content behind her. Sarah just stared into the distance. She was numb from everything at the moment.

What was wrong with her? Was she going soft? Why were all her past nightmares haunting her now? Was it a sure sign that she was losing her mind?

Maybe she should pack up, leave Africa and chase another dream. Or was there another reason? Did she need to deal with things, like her feelings about her past, and face them? Sarah got too caught up in work to really try and think things through and figure out how she felt and what she wanted.

Why was she so adamant about this elephant thing anyway? What was she trying to prove? So many questions and no real answers.

She'd been having that same dream again. The dream where she was faced with some wild animal, and she would subdue it. Then the man would appear. The man with the shining face, who kept telling Sarah that she had a gift. Each time Sarah had gotten more and more confused. Who was he? What was he talking about?

Sometimes the dreams would take a dramatic and terrifying turn, and the man appeared to be warning her. She would be holding onto something that looked like a brown package, and the animals would overpower her as she tried her hardest to hold onto it. Those animals were often wild dogs, or lions.

Sarah hugged her knees to her chest and exhaled long and loud, watching the soft wisps of cirrus clouds on the horizon flick up with a tinge of pink and yellow from the rising sun. At least she didn't have to race off to work today. Her day off had arrived sooner than she thought.

Her week of working the new horses had dragged on tediously, with every day haunting Sarah to find answers to the pain in her heart and questions in her head. She felt ripped off by this to a degree. She was so weighed down with her pain that she was missing the enjoyment of it all. Working the new horses should have been the highlight of her month.

Reins dropped over Sarah's shoulder as Honor drooped her head to sniff Sarah's black hair. Sarah reached back and scratched her on the nose playfully.

"You finished eating girl?" At least having a horse like Honor made things feel just that little bit better in Sarah's life. This was all Sarah ever did though, work and ride. She had no other life. She had no other friends in South Africa.

She often missed her friends back in Australia. Sarah was not a very social person. Back home, she had a small group of really close friends as well as her step-brothers and that was it, but those people meant the world to her. Where were they now that she'd run away to another country, though? Did they feel like she'd ditched them? Did they care?

Honor's hot breath rushed in puffs down the back of Sarah's neck as the horse nuzzled her. Sarah pushed her nose away gently, "What do you want? I haven't got any food." Sarah asked Honor to back away and she got up, rubbing her hands on her pants. It was time to get back and go out somewhere. Anywhere.

Brandi was mucking out the stalls as Sarah returned to Brennan's on Honor. Brandi waved to them as they trotted up the track. Sarah slowed to a walk and stopped next to Brandi. She wanted to take Brandi up on her many offers to go into the town of Phalaborwa with her friends from church, just to get out.

However, now that she was in front of Brandi, Sarah didn't know how to get the words out and ask without sounding pathetic and needy.

"Morning, Sarah," Brandi greeted her.

Sarah cleared her throat, "Morning...um..." Honor dipped her head all of a sudden, to scratch an itch on her leg, sending Sarah lurching forward and throwing her off what she wanted to say.

Brandi giggled at Sarah's bemused expression. Then Brandi thought of something, "Say, Sarah, did you have plans today?"

Sarah felt a rush of relief that she wouldn't have to ask. "No, I didn't."

"Well, you know how I always offer for you to come along to my coffee mornings? I just wanted to let you know that the offer still stands." Brandi bent to pick up her wheelbarrow, expecting as usual that Sarah would find a way to be busy.

"You're going out like that?" Sarah sniggered, looking Brandi's soiled clothing up and down.

"No!" laughed Brandi in horror, "I'll shower first!"

"That's a relief. I didn't know if I'd cope being in the car with that smell."

Brandi nodded absently, before realizing with a start that Sarah had just accepted to come along, "Really? You're coming? I mean...great!"

Sarah laughed with apprehension, wondering whether she'd made a big mistake, "OK," she conceded, "let me go get cleaned up, and you definitely go and get cleaned up, and I'll meet you at your place in ten minutes."

Brandi nodded with excitement and rushed to drop off her wheelbarrow. Sarah walked Honor toward the stables, thinking that she might take her own car and follow Brandi, just in case she wanted to make a get-away. She wanted to get out, maybe ask some questions, but she didn't want anyone pushing Jesus onto her.

She was pathetic. With no friends, she had little choice at this stage but to hang out with Brandi and her churchy crew. Sarah had never felt so low.

Phalaborwa was one of the few towns in South Africa that sat right on the boundary of the Kruger. Situated in the Mopani district, it was a thriving mining town with a small focus on the tourism industry. It was dotted with various commercial businesses throughout the town to cater to the miners and their families. Phalaborwa had its own unique flavor, and it was only twenty minutes away from Brennan's.

Sarah sat with resignation in the passenger seat of Brandi's Land Cruiser, after Brandi had convinced her that it was a waste of diesel to take two vehicles, and that they wouldn't be doing anything that Sarah wouldn't be interested in. Plus the fact that the two of them together could get more horse feed while they were out.

Feeling trapped, Sarah wanted to be there to help load feed, and to make sure that Johnno had ordered the right stuff anyway. So, in the end, Sarah agreed. So far, her escape plan wasn't working out.

The girls sat in silence for a good part of the drive, before Brandi fished, "So, how are you anyway? Really?"

Sarah noted the genuine interest in Brandi's tone and wondered. Brandi had been trying to offer the hand of friendship to Sarah since she arrived at Brennan's. Sarah had always been put off by the fact that Brandi was a Christian, and that she was always happy. Brandi never seemed to care that Sarah pushed her around and away all the time, and for this, Sarah often felt ashamed, which compounded the situation. Now, when she was at her lowest, Brandi didn't gloat, or say "I told you so," or even push God at her. She was just there, offering friendship as she always did.

Brandi squirmed in her seat as she kept driving, focusing on the road, and Sarah noticed for the first time how hard it was for Brandi to try and relate to her as well. Soon enough, Brandi picked up the idle chitchat again.

"I'm so glad you decided to come out. You'll like my friends.

We like to go to Portico's. Have you been there before?" Brandi asked.

Sarah shook her head.

"It's brilliant. It's a coffee lounge, a bookshop and an art gallery all rolled into one. The whole place just makes you feel so relaxed. And you are allowed to read the books while you stay there, for as long as you like, without being obligated to buy anything. It's very artsy."

Sarah was gracious, "Sounds good."

They settled into uncomfortable silence again. Brandi was ecstatic. She thought to herself that even if Sarah didn't take to her and her friends, even if she was impossible to make a conversation with, at least she'd gotten Sarah off the property and given her a morning out. She'd still bless Sarah in some way today. Brandi knew who she was serving, and that gave her more joy than the reward of Sarah's friendship.

Brandi's friends were already there when they pulled into the car-park of Portico's. Brandi hadn't been wrong about the place. Sarah looked around in wonder, admiring the polished decking and tropical atmosphere of the cafe as they stepped onto the boardwalk. Many of the customers where sitting in the luxurious outdoor section at large tables, covered over with generous-sized umbrellas.

The deck was also lined with rows of palm trees that added to the shady and tropical feel of the place. There were huge terracotta urns placed around the inside of the deck, unfurling exotic ferns with lush green fronds. The walls were decorated with cast-iron candelabras and other decals, as well as various original artworks from local artists. Sarah hadn't even seen the whole establishment yet, but she was impressed.

"So you come here all the time, you said?" Sarah gazed around with approval, "It looks expensive."

"Ja, we do, but no, they aren't. They are quite reasonable here...Oh look, there they are!" Brandi grabbed Sarah by the arm and led her through the entrance and through to a short, round coffee table in the corner of an outdoor garden area. The coffee table was surrounded by large fluffy couches. Portico's was a strange combination of indoor and outdoor areas that complimented each other with splendor.

Beside the couch was one of the many floor-to-ceiling bookshelves containing both new and old books and magazines. Sarah caught herself still gazing around as she and Brandi stood before Brandi's group of friends.

"Hi, Brandi!" They all greeted her in a mismatched chorus.

Sarah judged that they all looked to be similar in age to Brandi. Early twenties or late teens. Brandi was nineteen.

"Hi, guys. This is Sarah. Sarah, this is Sally, Trish, Eric, Max and Kim."

Each person greeted Sarah with a warm handshake. Brandi and Sarah sat, and Sally handed them some menus.

Sally leaned forward, "So, Sarah, are you the Sarah that works with Brandi at the trail-riding place?"

Sarah nodded, "Yep, that's me."

"Oh, you're the girl that Brandi tells us is amazing with horses. She said that you break and train them, or something like that?" Eric quizzed with interest, putting down his cappuccino.

Sarah's mouth stretched, shooting Brandi a serious glare down her nose. Brandi turned red. Sarah didn't like people talking about her, but part of her was flattered that Brandi thought so much of her.

"Well, I try," Sarah admitted, relaxing her tone enough to show Brandi she didn't hold a grudge.

Brandi cut in with renewed excitement, "She's the stable manager! Sarah has this brilliant horse, Honor. She jogs around the footpaths without a lead rope, and this horse will just follow her like a dog."

Somewhat amused, Sarah warmed at the thought of Honor, "Yeah, it's true." She laughed while the others looked on in amazement.

Sarah was older than most of the group, but they accepted her immediately. They enjoyed coffee and cakes together, chatting about their livelihoods and interests. All awkwardness melted away from Sarah; this is what she'd needed. Brandi's friends were genuine, friendly and didn't appear to be judging her in any way.

Trish was nineteen like Brandi, and they had known each other from school. She had short black hair and looked sophisticated. She also had a thick Afrikaans accent. She worked in town at a shoe shop. Sally, the first young woman to speak to Sarah, had long blonde hair in a neat plait down her back. She owned a couple of horses at her parent's property just outside town. Then came Eric. He was one of those urban-type guys who spent a lot of time listening to music. He was also part of the worship team at Brandi's church, playing the electric guitar.

Last of all came Max and Kim, who were the oldest in the group. Max, twenty-two, and Kim, twenty-one, were the only married couple in the group. They'd been married for over a year now. Max led a small bible study group at church and also a men's group, where Sarah supposed they would all get together and talk about male problems.

It appeared that most of Brandi's friends were very involved with their church. They all met regularly and had some part to play in the life of the church. Sarah reasoned that this was their life, so what else would they talk about?

At first, Sarah kept waiting for them to launch their attack on her and try and get her converted to Christianity or something strange like that, but it never happened. With everything going on in Sarah's life, though, she was almost disappointed that conversation didn't turn spiritual.

It was time to take matters into her own hands: "So, can I ask something here? I don't know if you know anything about dream interpretation, but I keep having this one dream, sometimes it varies, but it's basically the same. I tend to write off my dreams, but this one keeps coming back. It's stressing me out."

Brandi blinked, in shock at Sarah's question. So was that why she wanted to come along? She wanted answers, but she thought she might get them from Brandi's friends instead of from her? Brandi's pride was hurt. *Sorry, Lord, please forgive me! Why do I struggle so much with my fleshly emotions?* Brandi then went quiet.

Max looked thoughtful, "Well, ja, the Holy Spirit helps people to know the meaning of dreams, but God is not just a quick-fix dispensing machine. You can't just..."

Kim put her hand on Max's arm, cutting him off.

"Sarah, what's your dream?" Kim asked.

Sarah's brows knitted together, rather put off.

"Um..." she started to explain, awkwardness flooded back in.

"It's alright, Sarah, tell us only if you feel comfortable," Kim regarded her, a gentle look in her eyes.

Sarah picked up her glass of water and took a sip, grateful to be let off the hook.

"Brandi seems to hear from God a lot about dreams," Max offered, looking at Kim with apology.

Sarah looked over at Brandi, who remained quiet, and fought with the urge to ask to go home. She had come all this way and humiliated herself in front of strangers that she had nothing in common with, and still had no answers. She resolved not to allow anyone to rob her of the opportunity of discovering what this dream might mean. With desperate ferocity, she launched into explaining the various dreams to them all, despite her fears.

Everyone sat listening with wide eyes. Max sat back, thoughtful, after Sarah had finished. "It's full of meaning," He pondered.

"What else did the man say to you?" Brandi piped up all of a sudden.

"Nothing...just that I have a gift."

"What did he look like again?" Eric took a bite from a cookie.

"Like I said before, he wore all white clothes, and I couldn't see his face."

"Was it covered or something, like a hood?"

"No, there was light coming from his face, light so bright that it obscured his features."

Everyone sat back and looked at each other, knowing expressions in their eyes. Eric pressed, "What did his hands look like?"

Feeling the victim of an interrogation, Sarah felt out of the loop. Judging from the expressions of those around her, they seemed to all know something she didn't, and she stammered to answer their questions.

"What? His hands? I don't know. Why are you all looking at me like that?" She felt her blood starting to rise, like they were making sport of her.

Sally put a hand on Sarah's shoulder, "It's OK. We're just wondering something."

"Wondering what?" asked Sarah, her eyes darting around the faces at the table.

Max put up a hand to silence them all, "Sarah, do something for us. Next time you have this dream, ask the man who he is. And ask what he wants you to do."

"Do you agree, Brandi?" He looked at Brandi, snapping her from her own thoughts.

"Who? Me? Yeah, that's what she should do."

Sarah frowned, wondering why Brandi wasn't her usual chatty self. What was wrong with her?

On the way to the feed store, Sarah couldn't take it any longer. "What's going on?" she asked with exasperation, "What have I done wrong?"

Brandi kept her eyes on the road, not giving away any of her feelings, "With what?"

"With you."

Brandi glanced over at Sarah, her defensiveness rising at Sarah's tone, "With me?"

"Yes, with you! You were so quiet back there at the restaurant. And you've been quiet at work lately. I want to know what I've done wrong that's offended you so much," Sarah inquired.

Brandi snapped her focus back to the road, trying to regain control of her own rising emotions, "You haven't offended me, Sarah," she answered in a controlled voice.

"Brandi! You're lying. I thought that was, what do you call

it?...a sin in your church!" Sarah snapped.

Brandi shook her head, "I'm not offended. It's something else," she justified.

"What?" urged Sarah, her voice rising an octave.

Brandi tore her gaze from the road and looked at Sarah with curiosity, "Are you sure you really want to know?"

"Well, I wouldn't be asking..." Sarah retorted.

Sighing with resignation, Brandi confessed, "OK, here we go," she said, letting the words flow. "I have struggled with how you treat me. I know I'm younger than you, and you have more experience, and you are better with horses and stuff...but you don't have to yell at me all the time and push me around." There was a stunned silence before Brandi went on, "And I'm kinda hurt that you wanted to come out to find answers, answers that you thought my friends could give you, but I couldn't. I feel used."

Sarah went quiet and looked out the window. She'd just been doing it again. Snapping at Brandi, when Brandi hadn't done anything wrong. Sarah didn't know how to react. Brandi was right.

"I'm sorry...," said Sarah, deflated, "sorry that I took my problems out on you. It's not your fault, and it was wrong for me to turn on you. No wonder you have been quiet."

Brandi kept concentrating on her driving. "Let's roll up the windows and put on the air conditioner," Brandi stated as they turned onto the road leading close to the mines.

The feed store was on the industrial side of town near the Phalaborwa mines. The air conditioner came on just as the first clouds of dust from the mines and smelted copper began to billow past them from large trucks.

"For the record," began Brandi, "I forgave you a long time ago...and I forgive you again now...but it takes longer for my emotions to kick in."

That caught Sarah by surprise; she didn't expect such strange logic. She felt an odd rush of relief, guilt and confusion at the same time. She needed to stop picking on Brandi.

Something still wasn't right between them, though. Sarah ventured, "So, why the distance? Why are you so quiet? It's not like you."

Brandi laughed, despite herself. "You sound just like Mark!"

Sarah nodded, "Ahh, this isn't the first time you've been asked, is it?"

Brandi watched her, "No, you're right. Mark asked the same thing...erm, look, it's alright. I'm just dealing with stuff in my own life right now. It's nothing to worry about."

Sarah was satisfied with that answer. She could relate to it even. Looking across at the younger woman, she added, "I'll try and treat you better, Brandi. You don't deserve me being rude to you all the time."

"Dankie, Sarah...that means a lot."

They settled back into a more comfortable silence as they pulled into the produce center. Brandi wondered whether things were going to start mending themselves from here onward. She thanked God for the breakthrough and prayed that Sarah would soon get answers to the questions about her dreams.

CHAPTER
SEVEN

Sarah didn't have to wait too long before she was assailed by the dream again. This time it was very different, though, as if somehow whoever appeared in the dream knew of her plans to test him out.

There was no bushveldt scene, no animals that Sarah was supposed to be leading or calming. Nothing except brilliant white space. Sarah stood waiting. Nothing happened, no one appeared. She felt a wispy rustle about her legs, and looking down, saw that she was wearing a simple white dress. She felt the soft fabric billowing lightly against her legs. She had bare feet on the cool white floor.

"Where are you?" Sarah called out, certain she was being watched. Her voice echoed against unseen walls, making her nervous. "If you are here, come out," she called, her voice shaking.

Without warning, the man appeared. He looked just like every other time—white clothing, face veiled by brilliant light. This time she noticed a blue sash hanging diagonally down from the white robe. Sarah felt the intensity of his gaze and lowered her eyes.

The man said nothing to her, but kept looking deep into her soul. What Sarah thought was a vivid white dress now looked dirty and dull in comparison with the light from this one man.

Sarah felt a strange mingling of compassion, love and, at the same time, imminent judgment under his scrutiny. *Who was this man?* She felt a strange knowing, as if he knew the conversation that took place at the café in town, and worse, she felt like he knew her deepest thoughts and fears, knew about her past. Under the silent gaze of those keen eyes, Sarah felt immeasurable understanding, without even one word spoken. It was as though this man knew everything about her whole life, even more then she did...and that unnerved her.

Sarah gathered her thoughts and ventured, "Who are you?" She squinted and tried to see into his face, but the light was still so brilliant, and it made her eyes water.

"I am the way, the truth and the light. No one comes to the Father except through me."

Sarah blinked, "What? I don't understand."

The man stepped forward and held out a hand to her. Sarah stepped up to him and reached out to take his hand, but recoiled in horror when she saw the scarring of a large hole in his palm.

She tried again to look at his face and took a step backward in the sudden blast of realization, "Jesus?"

Before she waited for an answer, Sarah fell to her knees, weeping. She knew it was Him.

In a rush of emotion, she felt like her whole life was exposed. She felt ashamed of her life and how she had lived it. Ashamed of her past and who she was. All her inadequacies came flooding to the surface under the exposure of Jesus' brilliant light. Who was Sarah White to be before Jesus? She couldn't bear to look up at Him.

Suddenly the intensity of the light lessened, and quivering, Sarah ventured to look up. The light veiling Jesus' face had parted and Sarah could look upon His features. Sarah saw His eyes and His expression. He smiled at her with such love and understanding, as she had never felt before in her life. It *was* Jesus. He could see her whole life, what she'd done, what she'd been through...and He still loved her. Again, He held out His hand to take hers.

Sarah couldn't believe that He would still want her. She took His hand and allowed Him to lift her back to her feet.

"Sarah..."

She looked at Jesus, tears flowing down her face.

"...I died for you. You don't have to carry this anymore," He said.

Sarah looked down and saw that she was carrying the heavy

brown package from her previous dreams. She knew that inside it were all her hurts, her pain, her fears and, most importantly, her past.

Jesus gestured to take the package that was a burden from Sarah, but she held it tight against her chest. It was her life! A silent understanding passed between them, and she knew that if she gave the burden to Jesus, she would feel absolute freedom from its bondage. Clutching the heavy package to herself, though, Sarah was scared, reluctant to hand it over.

Jesus's face radiated, still full of love, "Come to me, you who are heavy burdened, and I will give you rest. Take my yoke upon you and learn from me, for I am gentle and humble in heart, and you will find rest for your soul. For my yoke is easy and my burden is light."

Sarah shifted the heavy burden, and then placed it on the ground at her bare feet. Still holding onto the top handle, she asked, "What is your yoke...um...burden?"

"That if you confess with your mouth, 'Jesus is Lord,' and believe in your heart that God raised Him from the dead, you will be saved."

Sarah blinked, "Is that all? It's that easy?"

Jesus gazed at her with love.

"What about the gift you were saying I have? What do you want me to do with it?" she asked.

Jesus turned and gestured, and by the sweep of his arm, a glorious vista of lowveldt lands were revealed. "You have a gift that I gave you before you were even born, but you have not yet received it in the full. Walk with me. Be still in me. Build a relationship with me, let me carry your burdens, and your gift will come into full bloom. Your gift is part of my burden for you."

"But, what is it, exactly?" Sarah hungered to know more.

"You will know when the season comes."

A sudden crack of thunder overhead woke Sarah from her dream with a start. The rain was heavy upon the roof of her rondavel. She slipped out of bed to go and shut the windows against another storm. Her bedroom curtains slapped against the wall in wet fury, and Sarah could feel the cool rain that was intruding into her room. She shivered as she shut the window, amazed at the contrast between the peace in that blissful, but confusing, dream and the fierceness of a raging summer storm outside.

There was so much that happened in the dream that Sarah couldn't wait to go tell Brandi. She raced to her kitchen table, grabbed her notebook and pen and settled back into her bed to write down everything she remembered from the dream.

The following morning, Sarah went to help Brandi with the early feed-up. Brandi looked up in surprise when she saw Sarah approaching, "Sarah? Aren't you riding Honor before work? What's happened?"

Sarah shook her head, grinning from ear to ear, "The dream, Brandi! I had the dream again! And I did it!"

"You asked the questions?" Brandi stopped what she was doing and waited with hopeful expectancy.

Sarah could barely contain herself, "I know this sounds so silly—I don't know why I feel so great—but I asked the questions like Max said, and it was Jesus! I know it with my whole heart! And he had the holes in his hands and everything! He offered me love that I've never felt before."

"What?!" Brandi studied her face, eyes going wide with excitement, "What happened?"

"He asked something of me. He wanted me to give him something I don't know that I'm prepared to give."

Sarah went forlorn and wondered whether she would ever have the kind of freedom that was offered to her. It seemed too good to be true.

The faltering moment was stolen away as Brandi picked up the excitement, "Sarah, this is great! Wait until I tell the others! We do need to talk about it some more. The words that Jesus spoke to you, some of them came straight out of scripture!"

"Really?" Sarah was amazed. She'd never read the bible before, and that was a huge confirmation to her that this whole thing was very real.

"Ja!" exclaimed Brandi, her blonde ponytail bouncing up and down emphatically as she nodded.

Sarah stared blankly into the distance with amazement, "Wow, it's real..."

Trying to push aside their excitement, they both jumped in and got the early feed-up routine done with record speed.
Brandi couldn't get over the change in Sarah toward her, which occurred overnight. She hoped that the seed would fall on good soil with Sarah, and that it wouldn't get choked down by the weeds or rocks of the world.

Brandi determined that she would get Sarah back together with her friends soon. When Sarah was ready to pray with them and give Jesus her heart, she would need lots of support around her. God had big plans for this one, and Brandi was sure that the enemy's attacks were going to soon follow.

Work went along as normal all day for Mark, but he felt ill at ease. By the time the last ride had checked out and they were packing up the gear, the tension was so thick it could be cut with a knife. He'd been worrying about Sarah for some time now, since she'd been shaken up by the Sotho shaman. He thought she was back to herself last week, but recent action had proven otherwise. She'd been spending all her spare time with Brandi and completely ignoring him. Mark knew how much Brandi irked Sarah, but since she had her mini breakdown, she was getting closer to Brandi. It just didn't make any sense. Even from early this morning, Sarah was almost mimicking Brandi's chirpiness. It was unnatural, and Mark found it off-putting.

He supposed that his last conversation with Sarah hadn't gone too well, but to not speak to him all weekend, that was rough. He straightened up when he saw Sarah striding his way toward the tack-up kraals, carrying a bundle of bridles over her shoulder.

"Brandi's going to fix some gear tonight in the workshop. I

think we need to come down too and get the leather all oiled. Does that work for you?" Sarah asked him, her tone terse.

"Ja, I suppose," Mark grunted as he hefted a saddle onto his large shoulders.

"If you've got other work to do Mark, don't let us stop you. I could ask Piet or Solomon."

"What's that supposed to mean?" Mark frowned as he folded the girth across the top of the saddle in his arms.

"Don't worry about it." Sarah collected more bridles from their hooks on the kraals, and adjusting the weight of the full load on her shoulder, strode off in agitation.

"Sarah, wait! What's up with you?"

She stopped and waited. When Mark said nothing, she turned around, "What?"

He lowered the saddle back onto the rail and gestured for her to come over.

"Why are you so..." He struggled to search for the words.

"So what?!" she snapped.

"So happy around other people but so angry at me? What on earth have I done?" The girth slipped off the top of the saddle that he'd adjusted onto the rail, but he just watched it as the buckle fell into the dirt.

Sarah cocked her head to one side, giving him a chance to speak. "Think about it," she said.

There was a long moment of uncomfortable silence, and Sarah started to struggle under the weight of the bridles, but refused to put them down.

"I'm sorry," Mark spoke up after a pause, his features softened with sincerity. It had been hard for him to say. "I'm sorry for last week...about the cull. I'm sorry I got angry at you about it...and I'm sorry I pushed aside your ideas."

Sarah waited testily, the weight of the bridles pinching her skin. He searched her face, trying to gauge if he'd hit the nail on the head. From the look of her face, he decided he hadn't. He must have done something else, but what?

Mark shook his head with confusion, "That's not it, is it?"

She looked him in the eye, confirming his thoughts.

"No? Look, Sarah, I want to know why you're still angry with me. You've been avoiding me for days!"

Sarah grew even more impatient to get away from this conversation, "It's not that, Mark. I know where you're coming from with the cull. I know you tried to help."

"Do you?" He couldn't bear to look at her anymore. He felt it in his gut that she despised him. Any attempt to get closer to her would only make her hate him more.

"I've got a lot of things going on right now in my life, and I can see that you are really focused with work, so I won't bother you with it." Sarah sighed.

"I'm not too focused on work, Sarah! I'm worried about you!" The muscles tensed up in his neck as he realized what he'd voiced.

She regarded him with a strange look in her eye.

"...In a work sense," he corrected.

"I need to know you are good for work. Are you thinking of going home? To Australia, I mean?" Mark asked, a muscle in his jaw twitching.

"No!"

"Then what's going on? Why have you been avoiding me?" He was pushing too hard, and he knew it.

"I've just been busy. I'm alright, really. I can get through this and still work. OK?" replied Sarah. "Is that all? This is heavy!"

She turned to leave, but Mark kept after her.

"I'll level with you, Sarah..."

"Mark, this is getting heavy!"

She started walking toward the tack shed regardless, but slipping through the fence, Mark trotted up beside her.

"You've been acting very strange. I don't know what's going on with you anymore. You're going out, spending heaps of time with a junior, who apparently you couldn't stand before. You're..." his strange pause caused her to stop and arch her eyebrow.

"What?"

"You're different!"

"How?" Sarah snapped, feeling hot color rising up into her face.

"I don't know...you just are," Mark grimaced.

Walk away, man, just walk away!

Despite his own counsel, he kept digging the hole deeper, "You're acting off the planet. I mean...no, I didn't mean that...I meant..."

Shut up, Mark! Just shut it!

He looked at her hurt expression, fumbling.

"Sarah, I'm sorry. Can I help you in any way to get through this?"

She tilted her head toward him, "You *could* have offered to help carry these, seeing as you felt like chasing after me...but it's too late now."

She jolted the heavy bridles on her shoulder, and he lurched forward to take them from her.

"Don't bother, Mark!" Sarah blinked back hot tears and pushed past him.

Mark stood there bewildered. Every time he tried to talk to Sarah of late, he spoke out of tune and upset her. He cussed himself. *How stupid he would have just looked, chasing after her so! Did he look desperate? Would he never learn? What was it going to take to rebuild the rickety bridge between them, even if just to relate as civil work colleagues?*

Mark returned to the kraal, swung the saddle again onto his shoulders and trudged off to the shed. As he entered, Sarah whisked out, free of her load, avoiding eye contact with him. Mark shook his head, he deserved everything he'd just copped.

Mark felt dubious as he entered the workshop area that evening after dinner.

"Hello?" he called out.

A soft yellow light emanated from the back room.

"In here, Mark," called Brandi from her leather sewing machine.

Mark ducked under the low door as he stooped down into the room.

"Sarah coming?" he inquired, a twang in his voice. He cleared his throat.

Brandi nodded toward the door, "You just missed her; she took some gear and oil back to her place to work on. What did you say to her? She was as mad as a cut snake."

Too weary to appreciate Brandi's use of one of Sarah's Aussie terms, Mark grabbed the stirrups off one of the saddles against the wall, sat on a stool, and slid off the irons from the leather. He fumbled on the bench for a rag and tub of oil, and then began to work on the leather in his hand.

Brandi eyed him patiently, "Well?"

"I didn't think that I did anything to her," he admitted. "I'm trying to say the right things to her, but everything I say is offensive. She's supersensitive, and quite frankly, I'm tired! Tired of trying and tired of talking about it, already."

Making no move to push the issue, Brandi pressed her foot on the machine peddle to stitch up the girth she was working on. The loud machine whirled.

After a while, she paused, turning her serious attention to Mark, "Don't take it personally."

Mark chuckled, despite himself, "I suppose you're used to it from her."

Brandi ignored the jab and continued working. There was an awkward silence between the two for a few more moments before Brandi blurted out what was on her mind, "You have feelings for her, don't you?"

Mark's eyes shot up from the tub of oil conditioner, alarm in his face. *So she had noticed.*

His reaction caused a light to dance in her eyes.

"Don't worry, I won't tell anybody," she said and went back to her work, avoiding his gaze.

Mark furrowed his brows in concern, "Is it that obvious?"

Brandi pondered this for a moment before answering, "Probably not to most...but remember, I work with you both almost every day."

The hint of a smile grew on his face. To Brandi, Mark suddenly looked like a young, confused boy, not a twenty-seven-year-old man. He looked as if he didn't know which card to play next. He had no direction. As far as Brandi knew, Mark hadn't been in many relationships with women before. His life always revolved around his work. He lived, played and breathed safaris.

They settled into silent work again for a time; the whirling of the leather machine keeping them company before Mark sighed with resolution, "I'm going to talk to her, to try and make it right again."

He went to get up, but Brandi stopped him.

"Give her time, Mark...trust me. She is going through some things. Big things. She needs space and time. You going over will only complicate things."

Mark leaned back and with realization looked at Brandi with renewed interest.

"That's what she said, too. What do you know that I don't know?" he fished, cocking his head to the side.

Brandi looked up and tried to calculate what to say, "Erm...well..."

"Well what?" pressed Mark. "I used to know more than you, and I shared with you what I knew. Now you seem to know something I don't. You owe me!" He smirked, satisfied that he had her beat.

Brandi stammered, "It's not up to me to tell this time, Mark. I'm sure she will tell you when she is good and ready."

"How do you know that? She won't talk to me at all right now."

Mark flicked the cloth he was using onto a bench in agitation and went to put the stirrup leathers back next to the saddle they came from. He returned with the saddle and cradled it over his lap, taking a fresh glob of oil onto the cloth. He began to rub it into the surface in a circular motion.

Brandi groaned. She hated being stuck in the middle like this, "Mark, what I know is confidential."

"And what I told you wasn't?!"

"The difference, Mark, is that I know from first-hand experience...not from what I researched and found out from outside sources," Brandi snapped, losing her calm demeanor.

"Ahhh, so you can get angry," teased Mark, pointing a knowing finger at her. "I'm onto you! Christians can and do experience the same things as the rest of us."

Brandi raised her brows at Mark, "Of course we do! We're humans, not aliens, Mark! Sheesh! You're hard work sometimes, you know that?"

Mark grinned, "I try."

Feeling annoyed at Mark, Brandi continued to defend herself, "Sarah trusts me not to betray what she told me. I wouldn't do that to her, or to you, or anybody. If you want to find out something, you need to ask her yourself. I never should have let you gossip about her to me in the first place. I didn't realize that you found that information out from someone other than Sarah. So yes, I am angry. I'm angry that you would do that to someone who you say you care about!"

All the playful zest melted away from Mark, and he looked down at the table next to him, "I guess I am pretty immature, huh?"

Brandi said nothing and went back to her work. It was time for Mark to grow up in a lot of areas.

They continued working on their individual tasks in silence for another hour before Mark packed up his stuff and stood wiping oil from his hands onto his jeans.

"You won't tell her how I feel, will you?" he asked, a slight quiver in his voice.

An impatient expression crossed Brandi's face, "What was the point of everything I've just been saying? You know I won't."

She got up and stretched. "Thanks for helping out tonight," she tilted her head, looking weary.

"No problem," his reply was flat as he walked out.

It was getting late, and they would have to get up early again for work. Mark couldn't stop thinking about what Brandi had said; she was right. He didn't have upfront ways of doing things at times. He found it hard to relate to people face to face. The revelation left Mark feeling down.

As he walked across to his rondavel, Mark noticed that the lights were off at Sarah's and that she would have gone to bed.

Even if he had still wanted to, he wouldn't be able to talk to her tonight.

CHAPTER
EIGHT

The next night, Brandi had arranged for Kim and Max to come to Brennan's and have dinner at Brandi's. Sarah was helping Brandi try to make extra room in her small rondavel for the extra dinner guests, bringing in extra chairs from her own place and trying to arrange them in the small space.

"Any more dreams, Sarah?" Brandi asked.

"None. But I have been reading the bible you lent me."

"I hope you can understand it with all the notes and highlighting I've scribbled in it," Brandi looked apologetic.

"Oh, no! Those are the best bits! I'm sorry if I shouldn't be reading them, some of them are personal notes," Sarah bit her lip, worried that she'd stepped out of line. In truth, she couldn't help but read those parts. It helped her to understand Brandi more, as well as the bible.

"Of course you can read them. I lent you the book; you can read whatever's in it."

Sarah's shoulders dropped with relief, "Well, I love those bits. Your notes help me to understand it all."

"Glad it helps," Brandi's eyes lit up as she smoothed a tablecloth over her rickety old table.

"Did Mark turn up last night?" Sarah questioned.

"Ja. He stayed and worked on the gear you left in there."

"I suppose he was cranky about it?"

"Hmm...not at the oiling work," Brandi admitted, "He wanted to come and talk to you, and I told him to let you be."

Sarah's sighed with appreciation, but her eyes lit up as she looked out Brandi's curtain toward Mark's rondavel.

"That would have gone down well," Sarah replied with

sarcasm. "Thanks, though, I did want that time to myself."

"Anytime." Brandi tossed her head back as she put a salad on the table and went back into her small kitchenette to gather some dishes and cutlery.

Sarah checked the meat in the oven, and then got out some dressings from the fridge when they heard a car and saw the headlights shine through the curtains. Max and Kim had arrived.

They greeted each other with warm hugs, and then got straight into the business of having dinner and talking over trivial things. Sarah enjoyed every bit of it, but was busting at the seams to talk about her dream. They all insisted, though, that they should work their way up to it, enjoying dinner first.

Being with Brandi's friends felt like being part of a great family, the kind that welcomed everyone into their lives. Whenever Sarah was around them all lately—Brandi included—she felt loved, accepted and wanted.

After dinner, they tidied up together and then settled into the lounge with coffee and the chocolate cake that Kim had baked.

"So," started Kim with excitement, "you had something to tell us. Did you have the dream again?"

Sarah's expression brightened, "I most certainly did!"

Launching into a full, detailed account of the dream, Sarah read it out loud from her notebook, "And then Brandi lent me one of her older bibles, and I have been reading the gospel of Matthew."

Max looked at Kim and Brandi with a sparkle in his eyes. He pulled out his own bible from under Kim's handbag on the front table.

"Wait. I'll get mine...I mean, Brandi's." Sarah ducked over her things by the front door and grabbed the precious book.

Once they had all resettled in the lounge with their bibles, Max began, "So, has Brandi showed you where those scriptures are in the bible? You know, the ones that were in your dream?"

Both the women nodded with delight. It was the first thing that Brandi showed Sarah, and then Sarah's appetite had been whet for more.

"So, do you understand who Jesus is?" Max pursued, as he

leaned forward on the couch.

Sarah nodded, "I am learning more about Him as I read the gospels, but I wouldn't have believed that He was real except for my dream having the exact words from the bible in it. I've never read the bible, so that should have been impossible. That proved to me that whoever He was, He is definitely alive and real, and He wants to offer me something. I just hope He can help me with all the horrible feelings I've been dealing with."

Kim's serene expression lightened, "Sarah, have you ever stopped to wonder if the reason you are having these horrible experiences and dissatisfaction with life is because Jesus is trying to lead you to Himself?"

The thought put Sarah's mind into a spin, "That would mean that He had it planned all along. Would He have even planned all the bad stuff to happen in my life so He could get me to go to Him?" Sarah pondered aloud in horror, "Why would He allow that to happen?"

"Sarah, God doesn't want bad stuff to happen to people, but sometimes when it does, He can make some good come out from it," Brandi put a hand on Sarah's shoulder.

"But if God is so powerful, why would He allow stuff to happen like that in the first place? Couldn't He just stop it from happening?" Sarah's mind reeled into a whirlwind of horrible possibilities that perhaps this Jesus wasn't as safe as she first expected. Perhaps His burden would be worse than what she had now.

"God doesn't want a world full of robots. He wants children that love Him. If a child was forced—or programmed like a robot—to love his parents verses choosing to give his love to his parents, which would mean more to the parents?" quizzed Max.

"If the child chose to love his parents freely," answered Sarah. She was beginning to understand. "God gave us free will because He wanted us to choose Him over the other things in this world," she said aloud.

"Yes! That's insightful, Sarah. You've been reading," cheered Kim.

"I told you I had," said Sarah, full of wonder.

"John one-twelve," quoted Max, "*Yet to all who received him, to those who believed in his name, he gave the right to become children of God.*"

Sarah went back to her original thought, "So, we have free will to choose God or the other things of this world. But if bad things happen, He can still use it to bring good?"

"Yes," confirmed Max, "Perhaps God has shown you how empty you feel and how overcome you are by your past to help you to come to Him for help...to choose Him. Also, the things we go through help us grow into maturity, just like a baby bird coming out of an egg. It needs the trial of trying to get out in order to gain the strength it needs to survive. If you help a bird from its shell, it will never survive in the wild."

"You don't know about my past," interrupted Sarah, clouding up with uncertainty, "So, how do you know it's bad?"

Max turned to her, a knowing look in his face, "We all have a past. Most of us have had something from our past that weighed us down, some more than others. It's what we do with it that counts. In your dream, you were carrying a heavy burden that you didn't want to give up. That indicates a troublesome past of some sort, right? We've all had that. Jesus isn't going to take away your identity or your life when He relieves you of that burden. He will set you free from being dragged down by it."

Sarah wasn't so sure.

Max moved on, "So you know about sin. Romans six-twenty-three says that '*the wages for sin is death.*' We are born with sin. Even little babies have it. It's not fair, I know, but that's what happened when Adam and Eve ate from the apple. They cursed all of mankind with death. It doesn't matter how much we try to be good, we fail...right?"

Sarah nodded. She knew she had anger management issues, and that she sometimes lied.

"It doesn't matter if you try to stop sinning and go to church every day. You cannot get rid of it on your own. You're stuck with it...and the penalty is death in the end."

"But we all die anyway...eventually," argued Sarah.

"Ahh, but if you believe in Jesus Christ, you only die in body.

Your spirit will be saved. If not, your spirit will also die, which the bible says is way worse than your body dying."

"So, I just believe and that's it?" Sarah asked.

"Almost. You need to believe in what Jesus did for you." Max flicked open his bible, "Go to Romans ten-nine-ten."

The group flicked to Romans.

"This is one of the scriptures that was in my dream," Sarah blurted, wondering what else she would see of it.

"Yes, *'That if you confess with your mouth, Jesus is Lord, and believe in your heart that God raised him from the dead, you WILL be saved.'* But there's more: *'For it is with your heart that you believe and are justified, and it is with your mouth that you confess and are saved.'*"

Sarah looked at Max and then at the others, wondering whether she'd missed something.

"Sarah!" Brandi reached over, "It's verbal! The verbal confession is what saves you. Recognizing and believing that Jesus died for you and that God raised him from the dead is important, but it's only half of it."

Sarah shook her head, confused, "I know the guy died and that God raised him from the dead, but why is that so important?"

Kim leaned forward and took Sarah's hands, "Sarah, the penalty for sin is death. We cannot possibly pay that penalty because we are marred with sin. The only person who could ever pay that debt for us is someone who was not born with sin. Jesus was born from God, not Adam. He knew no sin. He was without fault. God sent Jesus down here to die for us in our place. When Jesus died on that cross, He did it to pay your debt of sin, so that you wouldn't have to. He did that for everyone, but not everyone accepts that gift. God raised Him from the dead again so that He could go and prepare a place for us. In the way He was raised, so too will all the Christians be raised when He comes back."

Tears welled up in Sarah's eyes, "Why would He do that for someone He doesn't even know?"

Tears of joy also fell from the eyes of Brandi and Kim.

"Because He knew you before you were even born, Sarah! He

loves you so much!" Brandi whispered.

"I think...I mean...I *know*," sobbed Sarah. "I know that from the dream."

Max leaned close to the group of women, who were now all huddled together, "Do you want to confess Jesus as Lord, Sarah? He wants your love, too. He wants you to love Him and for you to want to follow His plan for your life. You'll never look back. He has a plan and destiny for you that is beyond your wildest dreams."

Sarah laughed and cried at the same time. Could it *really* be that easy? Could this Jesus fill the hole in her heart? Could He color her world and make everything the way it should have been when she followed her heart and came to Africa? Could He give her the peace that she'd been searching for? Could He take away the pain of her past?

"Yes!" Sarah shouted.

"Repeat this short prayer after me, Sarah. '*I acknowledge that I am a sinner. I ask for your forgiveness, Lord. I believe that Jesus Christ is the Son of God, and that He died on the cross for my sins. I believe that God raised Him from the dead and that through Him, I can have life everlasting. I choose you Jesus, as my Lord and Savior, and I choose to follow you. Amen.*'"

Sarah repeated the prayer after Max and then wiped the tears from her eyes. She felt so much love and joy from these people in this room that she thought her heart was going to burst. Jesus loved her! God loved her! The revelation in her heart made her feel like she was walking on air.

"That's not the end of it, though, Sarah," Max was gentle but serious. "Jesus needs to heal your heart. You've been hurt."

Kim slapped Max across the shoulders, "She's been through enough for one night, Max!"

He nodded and laughed, "You're right."

"Isn't it amazing how just confessing makes you feel different, Sarah?" Brandi laughed, giving Sarah a warm hug.

"I know. I feel great! I feel light. I'm desperate to know more! I want healing too."

"It'll come!" Brandi laughed and collected up all their coffee mugs. "Who wants another koppie koffie?"

Max raised his hand, looking to Kim to see if she was having one. Kim nodded and came into the kitchenette to help Brandi. Brandi soon returned with Kim in tow, both wearing mischievous grins.

"Sarah, we did a little something for you, too."

"You what?" Sarah looked confused.

Brandi brought out a parcel from behind her back.

"Oh?" Sarah blinked with delighted surprise. "How did you even know I was going to pray that prayer tonight? You didn't have to get me anything."

Brandi shrugged, handing Sarah the parcel. Sarah's eyes went wide with excitement as she opened her own new women's study bible.

"Thank you! Thank you so much!" Sarah got up and gave the two women a heartfelt hug.

"Although," laughed Sarah, "I will miss Brandi's notes."

Brandi laughed, too, "That's ok. You can borrow mine whenever you need to, but now you can add your own notes to your own bible."

It was then that a knock came on the door. Sarah went and opened it, wiping her eyes that looked puffy and red from crying with joy.

Mark stood there and was taken aback when he saw her.

"You've been crying?!" he exclaimed.

Sarah stood feeling numb, not knowing how to respond.

"What's going on here?" Mark pushed past Sarah and stepped into Brandi's rondavel.

"Brandi!" He called out with authority, ignoring Max, who stood to greet him.

Sarah grabbed his arm with embarrassment, pulling him back toward the door. Brandi and Kim came back out from the kitchenette, where they had returned to make coffee, looking bewildered.

"What's wrong, Mark?" Brandi exclaimed, a frown creasing her forehead at his abrupt behavior.

"What's wrong? Why is Sarah upset?" he asked heatedly.

"Mark! It's fine," Brandi insisted, "Come in, have a coffee."

Sarah turned him around and started pushing him out the door, "No, he doesn't want a coffee."

She nodded to the others inside as she left, closing the door behind her.

Max looked at Brandi with concern, "Who was that?"

"That's Mark. He works with us here. They haven't been talking; I think they have things to sort out."

Kim handed Max his coffee, "He seemed overprotective."

Max rubbed his chin and sat to have his coffee.

Sarah took Mark away from the rondavels so they couldn't be heard.

"Mark, that was so embarrassing! You don't just barge into people's houses like that and demand to know what's going on."

"I was intervening."

"Intervening in what?"

"You're spending way too much time with Brandi."

Sarah brows rose with incredulous shock.

"She's a Christian, Sarah! A God-botherer! I can deal with that...but how do I know she wasn't in there with her churchy friends, converting you to some Jesus-worshipping, weird religion? She's been cryptic when I ask about you. I saw the car of her church friends, and you weren't home. Are they brainwashing you?"

"Whoooaaahh! Back up, Mark!" She held up her hands, "This has got nothing to do with you. What goes on outside of work hours with people is their own business, not yours! I don't know where you get off thinking you can do that!"

Livid, Sarah turned away from him, shaking her head. This time, he'd gone way too far.

Mark stood watching her, his voice stiff, "So you don't deny it? They were? Oh God, Sarah! I'm sorry if you think I'm acting like your father again or something, but..." he stopped himself.

Sarah spun and growled at him, "Don't mention my

112

father...*ever!*" With that, she ran into the darkness toward the stables, tears burning her eyes.

Mark furrowed his brow, wondering about the nerve he just pinched in Sarah, and then felt guilty that once again; he'd stuffed things up.

He didn't want strange people trying to give Sarah a God-crutch for her wounded life. He wanted to protect her from getting hurt all over again, but he felt like it was all out of his control, like it was never his battle to pursue in the first place.

Mark toyed with the idea of just going home, but felt the need to justify himself. He wandered back to Brandi's, and tentative, he knocked on the door.

Brandi opened it and looked at him expectantly, "Where's Sarah?"

"Can I come in?" Mark asked.

Reluctant, Brandi opened the door to let him in. She waited for an explanation.

Mark came in and faced Kim and Max, "I'm really sorry for my behavior just then. It was unforgivable." The rehearsed-sounding apology made Mark feel like a small boy who had been ordered by his parents to apologize for stealing something from a shop. He sighed.

Kim nodded courteously as Max studied him.

"I'm Max," Max replied, sticking out his hand. "This is my wife, Kim. We're sorry if we startled you by being here." He rested his hand on Mark's shoulder to show he took no offense.

Disdainful, Mark shucked the strangers hand away, blinking. He was not expecting an apology back.

"Well, that's OK. I was curious, but when I saw Sarah had been crying, I got worried."

"Where is Sarah?" Brandi asked again, growing irritated with Mark.

"I...I upset her again. She went somewhere to vent. I wanted to go after her, but I thought I'd better apologize first...let her be for a while. See, I do listen to you." He looked at Brandi, his eyes darkening.

Brandi gave a slight nod of approval. She was glad he was

taking some of her advice, but worried about Sarah being vulnerable right now.

"Well, you did kind of just waltz in here like you owned the place, Mark," Brandi said, giving a half-hearted laugh. "Thanks for coming back, but what did you do this time?"

Mark stammered with embarrassment, "Don't worry. I need to sort it out, though."

He went to leave when Kim stopped him, "Perhaps *we* should talk to Sarah."

Gazing her way with caution, Mark relented for no reason he could explain, and allowed Kim to clarify, "Sarah had been crying because we were helping her to deal with stuff in her life. We were showing her how she could overcome what's happened to her in her past. We don't think she was finished yet, though, and it might have sparked up again."

"You're strangers and you know what's going on with her past?!" Mark started, his voice raising.

Brandi gave him a warning glance and a shake of her head not to go there again.

"Not fully," admitted Kim, "But we've started helping her through it. And she may be vulnerable right now."

"I know she is!" Mark snapped, with more force than he intended. "I said something about her father and she nearly bit my head off."

Brandi and Kim looked to Max with expectation. He was, after all, the most mature Christian among them. He would know what to do.

Mark had messed things up by stepping in when he had, but perhaps it would trigger Sarah to release her burdens sooner.

"We should find her," Max decided, and they all left the rondavel, following Mark.

CHAPTER NINE

Mark found Sarah where he expected—sitting in Honor's stable in the straw, hugging her knees to her face and crying. Honor stood nearby, head lowered down, her muzzle resting on Sarah's shoulder.

Honor swung her head up when she heard Mark and the others arrive and gave a soft nicker, hoping they might feed her some grain from the feed room next door.

Sarah glanced up through tear-stained eyes, "Who's there? If it's you, Mark, you can go away."

"Sarah?" Kim ventured as she eased herself past Mark.

There was a long pause before Sarah murmured, "You can come in, Kim. Honor won't hurt you."

The woman put her hand on the latch to the stable door, but hesitated. She liked horses, but she wasn't so sure whether she was brave enough to be trapped in a small space with one.

When Sarah saw Kim hesitate, she started to get up. Kim ushered for the others to leave before Sarah would see them. Mark hesitated, but went with the group. He was still concerned. He didn't know these people; Sarah barely knew them. What were they telling her? They were Brandi's churchy friends, after all.

Outside, under the starry night, Mark sauntered away from Brandi and Max and sat on a log under a tree. He wondered whether he'd ever be able to repair the damage he'd done to Sarah.

He began to ponder if she was worth the trouble, but as soon as the thought came to him, he dismissed it. She *was* worth it. She had always been worth it.

After a while, Brandi came and sat next to Mark, "It's going to be alright, you know. I've known Max and Kim for years. They're good people. They know what they are talking about."

Mark stared ahead, "Hoe weet jy?" The quiet question was uttered in their mother tongue.

"How do I know?" Brandi repeated, "I just do. I've known them long enough to know that they can be trusted."

Mark and Brandi both heard something and looked into the darkness to their right. Max was pacing under a tree, his clasped hands to his mouth.

"What's he doing?" asked Mark, watching the man with suspicion.

"Praying," Brandi stated matter-of-factly while bending down and picking up a twig. She turned it in her hands, and then broke off little pieces at a time.

Mark watched Max's silhouette with narrowed eyes, "You Christians are always bothering God. I thought that he would get sick and tired of you all by now. Shouldn't you save your prayers for emergencies, like when someone is dying? I know that I would get annoyed, feeling like I was getting nagged every minute of the day."

"You don't see Sarah being this upset as an emergency?" Brandi asked Mark, a serious tone in her voice. "God is not limited like us in what He can handle. He wants His children to ask more of Him. He wants us to need Him, to rely on Him. He doesn't get bothered by us at all."

Brandi sighed. Mark would always be cynical about God, and she felt like she was wasting her breath.

"Maybe," muttered Mark, as he continued watching Max through narrowed eyes.

Shaking, Sarah came out of the stall and latched the door, then sat on the bench where Kim was waiting.

"What's got you so upset? Is it Mark?" asked Kim.

Sarah shook her head, "Yes...no...I mean, Mark's Mark. He's annoying, but it wasn't him; it was what he said." She exhaled, weighing up how much to tell this woman she barely knew.

She'd just put her trust, her hope, her heart in Jesus' hands; that made Kim and her sisters in the Lord. What did she have to lose?

Sarah took a deep breath as she tucked a loose strand of hair behind her ear, "He mentioned that he wasn't trying to be like my father. It just...triggered something," she sobbed.

There! She'd said it out loud. In vain, Sarah attempted to stop the flow of tears that were cascading down her face.

"What happened, Sarah? With your father?" Kim took Sarah's hand in her own gentle hands again. Her serene personality calming Sarah's inner turmoil.

Sarah had never told anyone about what happened to her family, except for one other couple who meant the world to her, Jacob and Martha, who lived at the bush camp in Kruger. They were the only two people in the world who she had ever trusted with her deepest secrets. She was so grateful that they were in her life, even if she did only get to see them when they did overnight trails into the Kruger.

Tonight was different, though. The grief felt so fresh and real, and it threatened to engulf her if she didn't release it. Without any logical reason, Sarah began retelling her story to a woman whom she hardly knew, but felt that she trusted beyond reasoning. Sarah felt a strange calm and detachment from everything as she relayed in vivid detail the events that occurred that fateful night.

Kim listened, quiet and intent, asking questions every now and then to clarify points. The whole time she was praying for guidance from the Lord to show her what to say and how to approach the subject. In the end, it was enough to simply share the pain, as Kim's tears fell with deep empathy.

When Sarah had finished telling her story, Kim embraced her like she was a child, "No wonder it's such a burden to carry."

Holding her tight, Kim cried with Sarah, the horror of the story playing through her mind. Sarah let her tears run unhindered down her face. It felt good to let all her pent-up sorrow and emotion from her past just wash out of her like a flood. Sarah knew that this was the burden that Jesus wanted to take from her, and all at once Sarah was more than ready to hand it over.

"How do I give Jesus this burden?" sobbed Sarah.

Kim spoke with a quiet calm, "It's as simple as shutting your eyes and pretending that you are back in your dream. You do that now."

Sarah blinked back her tears and shut her eyes, sniffling.

"Now, imagine the scene where you met Jesus in your last dream, Ja? Now imagine yourself placing that burden at His feet and walking away from it."

Sarah imagined the scene, but even as she placed the burden at His feet over and over again, she didn't feel any better. She didn't feel like she had let it go.

"Does that feel better?" Kim inquired.

Sarah shook her head. Something was stopping her from letting go.

"It's not working. I can't do it."

In an instant, Kim realized what it was, "Sarah, there's a blockage."

"Oh...?"

"We can kick this tonight if you're ready. Now, I know this next part is going to be hard, but it's the only way that you can truly be free of that horrid burden. Are you ready to hear what it is?"

"I think so."

"Here we go...you must forgive your father."

"What?!" Sarah's eye's flicked open and her horrified whisper was barely audible.

She closed her eyes, shaking her head. What he did was unforgivable.

"That's impossible! No one could forgive that," Sarah murmured.

Kim nodded, her lips pulled back in a understanding half-smile, "I know this is not an easy thing to ask, but Jesus wants to take away that pain. You can only give Him permission to do so when you forgive your father. Jesus forgave every sin when He

118

died on the cross. If you don't forgive your father then your father holds the power over you still."

Sarah took a moment to process this, as fresh tears flooded down her face. She tried to visualize Jesus again. She tried to hand over the pain of what her father did, but what he was too much.

She shook her head, dropping her fists into her lap with force, "I can't! Not yet."

Kim rubbed Sarah's back with compassion, "It's alright, Sarah. Whenever you're ready."

Kim got up and went to find Max. Sarah sat for some time, just trying to get her head around everything that had happened to her that night.

Mark kneaded his fingers into his temples, exhaling deeply as he looked at his watch, "It's getting late Brandi. How long do you think they'll talk? We've got to work tomorrow."

Brandi looked over at Mark, her eyes deep wells of worry. "Mark, Sarah is going through more than we know at the moment. She needs our support. You can go home to bed if that's what you're worried about. Nobody will mind."

"How can I support her if she won't open up to me?" he growled, ignoring Brandi's offer to escape.

Brandi sighed and watched as Mark stood up and paced.

"Do you want some advice from a girl's point of view?"

Mark squirmed, "Depends...but I guess I'm going to get it anyway." Rolling his eyes, he folded his arms.

Undaunted, Brandi went on with boldness, "First of all, get out of her face, you're starting to learn that one. Give her room to work through things."

"What? Like you guys are doing?"

Dubious, he gestured toward Kim and Max under the trees in the distance.

"She asked for our help with this, Mark," Brandi defended.

Mark snorted. Sarah was independent. It wouldn't be like her to seek help for anything, especially from strangers. What were they feeding her mind?

"Secondly," continued Brandi, "you haven't been overly supportive of her in the things that are important to her."

"What? The cull? I tried! I rang around to try and fix it."

"It's your attitude, Mark! You called around because Sarah pushed you too. She isn't going to want to get to know you if you are against what she cares about and wants to fight for."

Brandi looked over at Max and Kim, who were talking and waiting for them.

Brandi nodded to Mark, indicating that she was going join the others. Mark shrugged, turning away from her and wandering over to the fence, where he leaned his arms over the railing. He gazed out into the darkness of the paddocks.

Kim filled Brandi in on how Sarah was and indicated that she and Max needed to head home. They promised to pray for the people at Brennan's, particularly Sarah, and asked Brandi to keep them up to date.

As they strolled back to the car, Max and Kim glanced over toward Mark, who was still stoic, gazing into the darkness. They looked at each other, putting on a brave face for Brandi.

"I'd like to catch up with Mark again sometime," admitted Max. He felt a quickening in his spirit, that some deeper destiny lay within Mark. He couldn't put his finger on it, but Max was experienced with listening to the Holy Spirit and trusted God to work it out in His good timing, even if it made no sense to him.

Mark listened to the car leave the property and heard the soft footsteps of Brandi returning to the stables to talk with Sarah.

Soon after, the two of them walked quietly past him. Mark followed at a distance, listening to them saying their goodnights as he got into the staff room. He heard the dull clinks of Sarah's front door closing first, then soon after, Brandi's. So just like that, they go to bed, he thought, feeling dejected.

The silence in the air fell around him like a thick blanket as

Mark gazed up at the bright blinking stars. Could the stars see what was happening?

It was so beautiful outside at this time of year; he wished that, had circumstances been different, he and Sarah might have.... He stopped his train of thought before he got carried away.

He shuddered. It was late. He needed his sleep for work tomorrow, but what Brandi had said about Sarah sat heavy in his stomach. She needed to deal with stuff, and he'd been at her about it, and worst of all, he'd been offended when she didn't reveal anything. How selfish had he been? And then, the culling business—it was her passion. She believed in something strong enough to fight for it, and all he could do was keep shooting her down and telling her what he thought.

He sighed, *No wonder I've left a bad taste in her mouth.*

He looked up at the shimmering blanket of stars again and groaned. Running his fingers through his hair, Mark turned and headed back to his rondavel.

CHAPTER
TEN

"What's going on?" Johnno demanded in a gruff voice. "Where's Sarah this morning?"

"She's not feeling well," Brandi treaded with care around the subject. "I went to check on her this morning, and she was still in bed. Johnno, can I talk to you?"

Mark frowned as Brandi took Johnno aside to talk in private. Would Brandi make it worse?

"What's happened now?" grumbled Johnno with impatience.

"She's still shaken up about the tribesman thing, and she is dealing with issues from her past. Things have surfaced that Sarah is finding hard to process. She was up late dealing with it all, and now she is exhausted. I think she feels sick, too." Brandi bit her lip as she saw Johnno's displeasure.

"I don't care what she is dealing with, Brandi. If she's going to have late nights, she can wear it the next morning! I fully support her trying to sort out her life, but with a counselor, on her own time; *not on mine!* She still has to take responsibility." Johnno spun on his heel and headed toward the semi-circle of rondavels.

"What if she took leave?" Brandi called after him. She then grimaced, looking toward Mark, who was staring at her with displeasure.

Johnno turned to glare at her, his eyes wide, face growing red. Then he turned brusquely, heading for Sarah's rondavel. Mark groaned, reefing up the girth on the horse in front of him, buckling it into place and trotting after Johnno. Brandi *had* made it worse.

"Johnno!" Mark shouted.

The older man turned as he strode toward the staff room.

"Let me handle it, Johnno," Mark had caught up to the man with ease.

Pausing, Johnno nodded once and growled, "Hmmph. Tell her to be ready to ride in five minutes."

He stalked off back to the offices, his pudgy hips swaying from side to side. Mark hadn't seen the boss move that fast in years.

Johnno had heard the commotion the night before, and he wasn't impressed. If young people chose to stay up late and carry on then they could deal with the consequences, or find another job. Truth be told, he was disappointed in Sarah. He'd taken her under his wing like a daughter, but this moping around just had to stop! He was tired and old, and he wasn't in the mood for excuses.

Johnno was grateful that Mark was taking control, and he decided that he would process this group of tourists through to the greeting kraal, and then retire for a nap.

Mark rapped on Sarah's door, relieved that Johnno had relinquished the task to him, but unsure of how to deal with the situation. He knew that Johnno would have come down hard on her this morning, and something within him wanted to protect her from the brunt of it.

After a while, Sarah opened the door slowly, blinking at Mark through tired eyes. She screwed up her face, taking a breath to accuse him of harassing her again, when he held his hand up urgently.

"Sarah, I know you've been through a lot, but Johnno is really upset. You had better get organized and come to work. He's going to be back soon, and he seemed more angry than usual this morning."

A silent understanding passed between them, and Sarah nodded, ducking back into her rondavel to get ready.

Mark breathed a sigh of relief as he stepped away from Sarah's place, returning to the horse kraal to meet the customers. At last, they seemed to be on the same page, like they had been in the past.

Mark didn't want Sarah to lose her job. He couldn't read Johnno anymore, and he was afraid that Sarah would tip Johnno over the edge.

Sarah arrived shortly after, her bedraggled hair bunged into a hair tie. She lifted her chin toward Mark, Brandi and the other staff members who were there helping the riders mount the horses.

Mark nodded toward the stall where Brandi had put Honor. Honor's gear had been thrown over the rail. Sarah didn't mind; she was grateful. She knew that she would still be running behind as the others were almost ready to head out.

"Don't wait, I'll catch up," Sarah said as she sped up to brush and throw her saddle over Honor. She didn't want to be in the area when Johnno returned.

Moments later, Sarah was in the saddle, tightening her girth as Honor began to walk after the departed group. As soon as she was adjusted, boots back into the stirrups, Sarah lifted the reins, shifted her weight and urged Honor into an easy canter to close the distance between them and the group. Sarah glanced back over her shoulder, relieved that she had missed Johnno's wrath.

Catching up to the group as they got to the Brennan's electric gate, Sarah slowed to a walk next to Brandi for a moment and surveyed the group. Another mix of foreign tourists on safari.

Sarah walked Honor down the line and greeted the group. Much to her delight, a large consort consisted of Aussies.

"Can you get the gate, please, Sarah?" Mark hollered back over his shoulder as he saw her approaching.

Sarah vaulted from Honor's back and opened the gate, waiting with her horse as the group passed through. Closing it and resetting the power, she remounted and caught up again.

A Japanese couple had also joined this group, but they kept to themselves as the bulk of Australians all knew each other. The Aussies had travelled to Africa as part of a mission team from a church back in Australia.

Sarah was intrigued. Two of them relayed their story to her of how their team came over to help build an orphanage for the countless displaced tribal children who were without some of the basic necessities. As part of a thank-you gift, the church who had hosted them in Phalaborwa, and gifted them a horseback safari.

Sarah asked which church had hosted them.

"Sunny Bank Christian Fellowship," answered the bright young woman.

Sarah looked back over her shoulder toward Brandi, who was two horses behind, listening to the conversation.

"That's your church, Brandi!" Sarah exclaimed.

Brandi blushed and nodded.

"You're an Aussie," declared a young man in the group to Sarah.

"Yep!" she admitted, patting Honor on the neck.

"Where are you from?" asked another.

Sarah went quiet for a moment, "I came from inland Queensland, near Charleville."

They nodded, satisfied with this answer.

"Well, Sasha here, she's from Brisbane, originally, but we all came from a church in New South Wales."

Sarah nodded in acknowledgement.

"OK, folks," began Mark from up ahead. They had walked out some distance and were about to ride over a rise that would reveal the lowveldt where herds of wildebeest, zebras, impalas and the occasional giraffe or two would converge around the waterhole.

The Japanese couple behind Mark stopped their conversation and hushed each other to listen, pulling out their cameras. The rest of the group did likewise.

Mark began his usual spiel about where they were and what they were about to see.

Sarah slipped up next to Brandi and leaned over, "Hey, you didn't tell me that Aussies were coming over to your church."

Brandi looked apologetic, "I didn't think you'd be interested. We host mission groups all the time. It's fun having people visit from other countries. And other times, we send our own teams overseas to do outreaches and stuff."

Sarah looked confused, "Outreaches? So, you must have had

something to do with them coming on a trail ride, huh?"

Brandi blushed, "I might have."

Sarah grinned despite herself, "Well, I'm glad you did. I want to go see the orphanage they built."

"Do you?" Brandi's eyes went wide. "Well, ja! I can take you when we get a day off. It's very exciting! Up in Lebowa."

"OK."

Sarah stopped. Mark had pulled up his horse and was watching them. "Ladies," he called, "enough chatter."

A murmur of amusement rolled through the group of riders. He shook his head and, turning his horse Sniper, continued his talk.

The two-story orphanage was in Lebowa, a Sotho community outside of town. The northern Sotho tribes people who lived there were poor and in desperate need of aid.

Mark, Brandi, and Sarah took a trip to the orphanage Monday morning. People from the Sunny Bank Church were moving furniture into the orphanage building that had been donated and built by various people in the church. Mark let out a long whistle, impressed with how people were teaming together to help one another.

His whistling drew an unimpressed look from Sarah, but he didn't care. He'd never before thought to visit these places, but when he heard Brandi and Sarah were going, curiosity drew him, in more way than one. He was determined to start to take an interest, see what was going on in Sarah's world.

Sarah had shrugged it off when Mark had asked to come, saying that she didn't care what he did. Brandi had allowed it, knowing his ulterior motive.

Early in Mark's childhood, his Afrikaans grandfather and father had instilled biases in him about not mixing with native Africans. He'd been taught about segregation, disfranchisement and other laws of that era, but try as he might, Mark couldn't see the logic or compassion in this type of thinking, and he found himself caught between a rock and a hard place. He didn't agree, and it left him at odds with his family.

The country was now going through the birth pangs of major change, and apartheid ideals were not something that were going to be able to hang on in the new nation. Nor were they ideals that Mark believed in, nor wanted to uphold.

He didn't consider himself racist, but Mark had never had much to do with the native Zulu or Sotho people who lived in the area, except for working alongside Solomon, whom he found to be strong, hard-working and trustworthy. Part of the reason Mark had stayed away from the turmoil of places like Lebowa was circumstantial, but it was also to do with his feelings of guilt. He felt that because of his bloodline, he too was somehow responsible for the atrocities that apartheid had wreaked on the less fortunate.

Knowing that the girls were coming here, though, Mark decided that it was time to see what all the fuss was about, to make some kind of retribution in his heart against the feelings he'd struggled with most of his life. He was his own man now, not that of his father or grandfathers before him. He'd decided to make his own judgments, and to follow his own belief system.

Sarah looked up at Mark, curiosity crossing her eyes, as he surveyed Lebowa.

What did she think about him coming along? Did it anger her, too? Mark's thoughts were interrupted as Brandi grabbed Sarah by the arm.

"Come! There's Max and Kim!" Brandi exclaimed.

As they approached, Max and Kim were talking with a couple from the village. Kim laughed and picked up one of their small, dark children, hugging him close.

Max beamed as he saw the trio approaching. He shook Mark's hand first, and then greeted the girls. Max introduced them all to Koto, whose name meant "pillar", and his wife, Lerato, whose name meant "love", and their two gorgeous children, Moses and Kagiso.

This family lived and worked in Lebowa. Lerato worked as a farmhand, tending the crops of local farmers for a meager pay, and Koto worked on the neighboring private reserve as a tour guide and tracker. Koto wasn't working today because business had been slow.

Brandi and Sarah allowed the children to take them away from the others to play a new game they had invented, leaving Mark standing awkwardly with the other two couples.

Max was the first to break the silence, "Mark, Brandi was telling me about the elephant culling in the Kruger and how someone came out and yelled at Sarah about it."

Uncomfortable, Mark shifted his weight, looking at Koto and Lerato. He scratched his head, "Ja. Some guy came out and waved a tusk and a rifle at her and yelled at her. She didn't understand him. She thought he was a shaman or elder or someone. I don't know much more about it," he was quick to add, looking again at Koto. He didn't want to offend the man by saying something out of tune by accident.

Koto nodded, "Ngaka!"

Koto looked at Max, who explained the meaning to a confused-looking Mark, "'Ngaka' is Sotho for shaman."

"Uh ha," Mark nodded, waiting for more. He looked over to where Sarah and Brandi were playing with the kids in the distance and wished that he hadn't come along for the ride after all. He felt trapped by the strained conversation.

"Do you know a Ngaka?" Max asked.

"Yeah," nodded Koto, "Thabo Masekela! He live that way." Koto pointed into the distance. "Some say, he gone mad. He very angry at killing, saying he go find answers. We all know that. It no good." The tall, swarthy man shook his head.

Mark looked confused, "I thought that it helped your people, the culling, that is. Don't the elephants destroy crops on the farmlands?"

"Yes, it is true," admitted Koto, "But most men now need tourism—to be a tour guide or tracker—to support our families. Foreign peoples don't like killing. It turns them away. That means no work."

Mark let this sink in as he looked around, taking in all the sights of children, teenagers and adults. They led humble lives;

they wore humble clothes. Some of the women sat in groups, creating colorful beaded necklaces, handbags, artwork and other traditional items to sell to tourists at the markets. The half-naked kids ran and played in dirt, and were perpetually dusty-faced over their shiny black skin. Most were underfed, and their homes were comprised of very simplistic thatched huts, which were more traditional open-plan rondavels, containing little else than an odd chair or table. There was something about these people that filled Mark with compassion and guilt at the same time, guilt from hiding his face against this for so long.

"Mark, everything alright?" Max touched his arm as Mark refocused on the group.

"Sorry, I just didn't realize," Mark exhaled, "I've stayed in my own area for so long that I didn't realize how other people have to live. I didn't know about how important tourism is for these, I mean, *your* people." Mark indicated Koto and Lerato, and the couple inclined their heads, smiling humbly.

Sarah and Brandi returned with flushed faces from running around with the kids.

Kim laughed, "Who wants to check out the orphanage?"

They all headed over to admire the church's work in this humble village. Mark remained quiet and thoughtful for the rest of the visit.

CHAPTER
ELEVEN

Sarah's love of God grew a little more each day as she read her bible and met with Brandi and her new friends. She started attending Sunny Bank Christian Fellowship, where she met up again with Koto and his family on a regular basis. She felt like she had been embraced by a whole new family, yet her pain still lingered.

She hadn't forgiven her father yet, and this gnawed away at her heart daily.

One afternoon after work, Sarah rode out on Honor to be alone and to try to spend some time with God. The days were growing longer as the summer months began to swell up, bringing with it heat and humidity.

Sarah had stripped off her saddle after the last trail ride of the day, and had set out on Honor bareback. She didn't intend to go far; she would stay on the Brennan's private property and head for the waterhole to so that Honor could swim. The waterhole sat close to the boundary fence, so she could still enjoy spotting the odd bit of game while she swam.

The pair trotted down the track to the low-lying grasslands that sprawled between the electric fence; the grasses were now swollen with water from recent rains. The fence line had been built up with dirt and cement, ensuring that the seasonal waters wouldn't short out the power or electrify the inhabitants of the waterholes.

Rolling up her jodhpurs, Sarah surged Honor into the cool waters. Honor splashed her nose back and forth through the waters before settling into a long drink.

Sarah cocked her legs up onto Honor's withers and looked out

131

over the glorious lands beyond the safety of the fence line. *Lord God, help me! You have given me so much, and yet I still struggle to give up this one thing: forgiving my father.*

Sarah sighed and, swinging her legs back down, sprawled over Honor's back and neck on her stomach. Honor snorted and started to paw at the water.

"OK, enough water for you, before you drop on me," Sarah laughed and kept Honor walking through the waterlogged grassland until they emerged up onto a slight rise where the grass grew lush and dry.

She slid off Honor's back and flopped down into the soft, long grass. Honor walked a bit away from Sarah, turned in a circle and put her head down before dropping to the ground and proceeding into huge luxurious rolls. When she was done, she stumbled to her feet and shook off all the bits of dried grass that had stuck to her golden coat, which now appeared a light shade of brown. Sarah laughed and sat up to watch the sun as it started its downward crawl toward the horizon.

A low trumpet resounded off the nearby mopane trees, and Sarah stood with trepidation. *Elephants!* They shouldn't be this close to Brennan's!

She vaulted onto Honor and headed in the direction of the noise. Sarah rounded the track through the mopane, which grew thick in this section, and gasped with dismay. The fence was down.

Frowning, Sarah grabbed a stick and tested the electricity. The power was out too, as she had suspected. The elephants would have shorted it out when they took it down.

Wary now, Sarah rode over the rise, listening for sounds of wildlife. If she could hear elephants nearby, chances were, they had taken out the fence.

She wondered if she and the group might have left the electric power off by accident on their way back into Brennan's. If that was the case, it would have been easy for the elephants to attempt to tackle the fence.

Better judgment told her that she should go straight back and get Mark and Piet, but then she heard it again: the soft trumpet of an elephant.

Swallowing hard, she pushed Honor onward until she spotted a small herd of elephants playing in a deeper part of the water. She kept her distance up on the rise, just out of sight of the intelligent beasts. Slowly, she moved along the ridge to get a better view. That's when she almost rode Honor right over the top of Mark, who was lying on his stomach watching the elephants.

"What the hell? Hey!" he threw his arms over his head, ducking instinctively.

Startled, Sarah was quick to back Honor up and jump off.

"Sorry Mark! Are you alright?" she asked, her voice hoarse.

Squatting down next to him, she quickly scanned the elephant herd to make sure they hadn't been startled.

"I think so, just my nerves," replied Mark, clutching his chest dramatically.

"Shhh," insisted Sarah.

"I know, I know. So you're talking to me now, are you?" Mark narrowed his eyes with confusion as he ushered her to get down low beside him.

Ignoring the question, Sarah gazed around and saw Sniper tied to a nearby tree. She led Honor away, tying her beside Mark's gelding. The horses looked toward the commotion of elephants, the whites of their eyes showing with fear.

"The fence is down," Sarah whispered, lying on her stomach next to Mark.

"I know," he replied, looking at her from the corner of his eye. "I was coming back to deal with it, but then I heard these guys. Just wanted to observe them for a bit and work out what to do."

A little perturbed, Sarah noticed how close she'd positioned herself next to Mark. Attempting to be discreet, she shuffled herself over.

"Maybe they'll just move off." Sarah craned her neck, trying to get a better view, "This is dangerous."

Mark turned toward her, his expression incredulous, "You're one to talk."

Sarah went to object, but Mark suddenly sat up, moving close to her and covering her mouth with his hand, "Shhhh! Look!"

Removing his hand, he pointed as a large elephant moved over. A baby elephant emerged from behind its legs and splashed in the water with its trunk.

"Oh," gasped Sarah, "it's so cute!"

She felt her face burn at Mark's closeness, but thought it would seem rude to move away again. *Had he done it on purpose?*

The baby elephant stomped its front feet in the water, splashing up mud. Mark and Sarah both chuckled in silence at its antics. The calf then meandered away from their view.

Caught up in the elephant calf, Sarah forgot herself and leaned into Mark's space so she could peer through the trees for a better look. Just then, she heard his sharp intake of breath. She looked at him funny, and the moment was gone. Settling back, Mark plucked a long blade of tasseled grass and began chewing on the end of it. He was unusually quiet, and Sarah wondered what he was thinking.

"Is this the D-12 herd? The one due for culling?" Sarah looked at Mark in concern.

"Ja," he remained calm, almost wistful.

Sarah rubbed the dirt from her hands onto her jeans as she got onto her knees. "We should move away, Mark. We're a bit too close to the calves, the cows will get aggressive." She gazed at Mark's rifle sitting on the grass beside them as she started to stand.

"Hang on a minute!" Mark grasped her wrist, pulling her back down, as a massive cow turned her attention their way, her intelligent eyes scanning the area. The horses were well hidden, but their scent could give away their position if the wind changed direction. Mark and Sarah crouched lower, holding their breath.

The cow blinked and moved on, turning back toward the herd and moving her youngster away from the smell of danger. Mark and Sarah exhaled, sharing relieved smiles as they turned to each other. Sarah noticed how close his face was to hers. The smile faded on her lips, as they looked into each other's eyes. A long moment passed before Sarah cleared her throat and pulled back.

"This is the herd they want to cull next month," she repeated, turning away to watch them. "It's a shame."

Mark continued looking at her for a long moment. "I know..." he admitted, unusually quiet.

Sarah raised an eyebrow at his tone, "I thought you didn't care. I thought you said it was necessary."

Mark stared ahead, chewing his stalk of grass.

"Well, isn't a man allowed a change of heart? Besides, even if it's necessary, it doesn't make it a good thing. Look at them, they're..."

"Magnificent!" Sarah finished.

"Well...ja," he spat out a piece of grass, and then resumed chewing on the stalk quietly.

Sarah went quiet, and he looked at her, a strange gleam in his eye.

"I have to know...isn't it unlike you to come and talk to me? You have your new friends now and all," Mark scowled, throwing away the stalk.

"Well, I couldn't help nearly walking over you, now could I?" Sarah looked cut as she regarded the Afrikaans man. "Mark, they could be your friends too, you know. You chose to come along the other day, what are you complaining about?"

The herd was moving away now, and they both relaxed a little more. Sitting up, Sarah pulled her sweaty black hair from its band in agitation and combed her fingers through the thick locks. She rearranged it higher off her neck to eliminate some of the heat.

"Besides, I didn't come looking for you," Sarah smirked at him, satisfied that her hair felt somewhat normal. She resettled into the grass cross-legged and watched the elephants as they appeared to move away.

She felt Mark's gaze fall upon her, and her pulse began to race, "Why did you come to Lebowa the other day anyway?"

Sarah kept her focus trained on the mopane, where the elephants had disappeared. Without their presence, she felt even more awkward in Mark's.

Mark sighed and picked another piece of spindly grass. "It's personal," he sighed after a moment, drawing Sarah's curious gaze toward him.

"Personal?"

Mark sat up and rested his elbow on his propped up knee, as he stuck the new grass between his teeth and watched as the last visible elephant lumbered out of the water onto dry land and disappeared after its herd.

"Ja," he said.

Sarah shrugged and plucked at the grass also.

After a moment, Mark continued, not wanting Sarah to get any wrong impressions, "It's nothing, Sarah. I just...I come from a family that used to be really racist. You know? Apartheid?"

She gave him a blank stare.

"Sheeesh! I'm Afrikaans, Sarah! A white African! We didn't exactly treat blacks that well," he exclaimed, shaking his head. "Don't they teach history in Australia?"

"I know what the apartheid is, Mark," Sarah snapped.

"*Was.* It'll be finished soon, then we can all start to rebuild this nation as one. I'm not racist!" he quickly defended himself as she looked at him with an odd expression.

"I'm not racist! I've just never actually had much to do with...you know...apart from Solomon, Jacob and Martha. I just wanted to see for myself how they live, what they're like. I don't want to live by what I've been taught; I want to know for myself." He hung his head.

"You mean the Sotho village?" Sarah quizzed.

Mark nodded and looked at down at the grass. Sarah recognized the heavy expression on his face, for it seemed similar to what she herself carried.

Sarah looked at him and wondered. He was being genuine, not wearing some kind of arrogant or desperate mask. It was a side of him that had her intrigued. She didn't understand the guilt and turmoil that Mark felt, and she sat next to him, trying to figure out what to say or do.

"I'm sorry," Sarah offered, redoing her hair to avoid eye contact.

She finished fidgeting and looked up at him sheepishly. He tilted his mouth sideways and leaned toward her, his tender hand brushing back a lock of her black hair from her eyes and tucking it behind her ear.

"You missed a bit," he stated softly, staring into her eyes for a long moment.

The blush that came to Sarah was instant. Tearing her eyes from his, she leapt to her feet, "We should go tell Johnno about the fence."

She hurried over to Honor, trying to hide her face. An embarrassed silence ensued, and Sarah fumbled to gather her reins before mounting. Mark made no move to stop her; he'd expected her to react like that. He was going to try to give her the space she needed, but she needed to know one thing.

"Sarah..."

She turned around to face him.

"Please know this...I want to help these elephants just as much as you do...and I'm not racist," he added.

Sarah nodded, trembling, "I know."

With shaking hands and face still flushed, she gathered her reins and her nerve, leapt up onto Honor and trotted off.

Mark watched her leave. He had been thinking about what Brandi had said to him about supporting Sarah and her endeavors. Getting on her side about the elephants was not going to be enough without making an effort to do something about it, but exactly what, Mark was still unsure.

He looked out toward where the elephant herd had disappeared back into Letaba. Right now, he was angry with his family and felt an unwarranted guilt that should never have been placed upon him in the first place.

He stood and dusted himself off, heading back to Sniper. The horse grunted as he mounted, and they moved with speed back toward the compound where he would need to rally the troops in the bakkies, or pick-up trucks, as tourists liked to call them, to help fix the fence.

The next day, they were scheduled for an overnight campout, staying at one of the bush camps in the Kruger. Sarah was walking into the office to retrieve her rifle, radio and first aid kit, when she saw a note in her staff pigeon hole. She plucked it off and read it.

Sarah,

I've organized a meeting with the authorities about the elephant culling. 4pm, tomorrow afternoon, when we get back from the bush camp. Meet me here after work, and I'll drive us there.

Mark

She scrunched up the paper and tossed it into the bin. Whatever Mark was up to, at least he was doing something right for a change instead of fighting with her all the time.

She breezed down the hall and grabbed her two-way and rifle, as always, and headed out to the tack-up area. She had the extra packhorses saddled up with the gear for the five riders, and for herself and Mark. They also had extra horses organized that would be led by the packhorses in case any of the animals fell ill or acquired an injury.

Johnno had not allowed Brandi to come along on this trip, and that filled Sarah with both consternation as well as disappointment on Brandi's behalf. He'd said that it was too small of a group and that he'd only allow two experienced riders to go. Brandi had been disappointed.

Mark met Sarah out at the kraals. "You get my note?" he asked as he brushed down one of the horses.

"Uh huh," nodded Sarah, checking the girth on Shar, who was being trained as a packhorse.

"We should talk about it, Sarah. What we are going to say at the meeting."

"Mark, leave it till tonight. We've got enough to organize right here and now."

She walked off again to grab something from her rondavel that she had forgotten. The least she had to talk to Mark at the moment, the easier it would be to try and work out her reaction to him yesterday and sort out things in her head. When he'd been that close, looked at her that way, she felt something, and it scared her.

She grabbed her bible from the rondavel, locked up and, jogging back to the kraals, tucked it into her saddlebag on Honor. She then left and checked the other packhorse.

Satisfied that all their loads were secure, she returned to Honor and touched her neck, "Ready for a long one, girl?" She laughed as the mare pushed her head into Sarah's hand for a scratch.

Smiling, Sarah pushed her head away and leaned against the fence, waiting for Mark to return with the riders. Sarah enjoyed these overnight rides, even if she did get on edge venturing so deeply into the Kruger. They would ride all day through, stopping to set up camp at Jacob and Martha's bush camp, a campsite within Kruger National Park with electrified perimeter fencing to protect people overnight from predators in the wild.

Often, bush camps took on more of a luxury accommodation status than a campsite feel, and the one they were visiting was no exception, complete with a pool and modern rondavels.

Sarah looked forward to seeing the caretakers again. Jacob and Martha were originally from Mozambique, but they moved across the border to take up the job of guardianship of the bush camp. Since working for Brennan's and doing several trips out to the bush camp, Sarah had become fast friends with the couple.

Soon enough, they were headed out of Brennan's. Sarah had already worked her way through the small group, ensuring that they felt at home in the saddle. She'd had to readjust a set of stirrups and help one gentleman relax into the saddle and ease up on the reins.

This group was one of the rare groups that wasn't made up of foreigners, except for one. A South African family in Phalaborwa had relatives visiting from Cape Town who had brought over a young English exchange student and they wanted to show her the sights of Africa. They didn't often venture into the wilderness, and this was their chance. They were spending their time off enjoying the beauty in their own backyard, while showing it off to the young woman visiting from London. Mark seemed to be eager to relate to them about Cape Town, conversing with them enthusiastically in both Afrikaans and English.

Sarah hoped he would be consumed with talking to them all night. That would free her to catch up with Jacob and Martha without him, and it would keep her from having to deal with the feelings he aroused in her. Any excuse not to spend time alone with Mark was going to be the safest for Sarah at the moment.

She was cross and confused with herself that her heart had fluttered when he touched her the other afternoon. She was nervous that it could happen again. The more distance, the better.

Sarah looked ahead at a herd of buffalo. Mark was rattling off his tour in Afrikaans, but that didn't bother Sarah. She'd heard it all before and was content to be lost in her own world.

The Afrikaner woman in front interrupted her thoughts, "You're Australian?"

Sarah nodded, reluctant to talk.

"How long have you been in Africa?" the woman pressed politely, as if she felt her new mission was to include Sarah.

"Four years," Sarah replied.

"Do you love it?"

Sarah nodded, "How can you not love this?" and waved her hand out over the lowveldt. A lone rhino stood in the distance, away from the grazing buffalo. He raised his huge head to regard the group absently as they passed.

"Do you ever miss home?" the woman continued.

"Sometimes," Sarah admitted, looking down at Honor's head, "But don't we all get home sick from time to time? I wanted to come here."

The woman thought about this. "Well, that depends. Some people make home where they are. They strike up new homes, and then it becomes hard for them to leave the new place."

"I guess," Sarah replied, unsure.

"Look!" the woman pointed, "A gemsbok!"

"I see it," Sarah answered, grateful for a change in subject. This woman made her feel like she had to justify her being here, and it made her uncomfortable.

140

CHAPTER
TWELVE

"Jacques!" Sarah bent and scratched the cheetah on the top of his neck.

Jacob came out smiling, "Welcome friends!" He greeted them all with his deep voice and large, ebony-hued out-stretched arms. He shook all the riders' hands and gestured for them to follow him to get cleaned up.

Sarah stayed back as the riders walked past; she was weary but content, relieved that they had crossed the Kruger unscathed and with no lion sightings.

Mark stopped next to Sarah, grinning from a day well done. Sarah looked toward the horse kraals and rubbed her hands on her jeans.

"I'll go and start unpacking the horses and get them fed up," she indicated and walked back toward the kraals. "Can you make sure Jacques doesn't follow me? He makes the herd nervous."

Sarah had only just finished her sentence when a tall, heavy-set, dark-skinned Sotho man came out with a heavy chain and approached Jacques, who had flopped over on his side in the dirt next to Mark and Sarah, and was panting from the heat.

"S'cuse me, riders." He inclined his head to them, "I'll be putting Jacques to bed now anyway." He clipped the chain onto Jacques collar and led him back into the buildings.

Jacques had been found as a cub. Jacob and Martha had raised him here and tried on various occasions to release him back into the wild. Unfortunately, Jacques—aptly named after his Afrikaans equivalent, jagluiperd—wouldn't have anything to do with the release. He had it too good here at the bush camp.

He had now been there long enough that release was not an

option. The plus side, though, was that he was good for business. Foreigners, in particular, loved to come and have their photos taken next to him.

Sarah smirked as she watched the large cat padding away obediently. She was relieved that he was out of the way, but also perturbed that he wasn't going to keep Mark away.

Then she jutted her chin and suggested to Mark, "Why don't you go and settle our guests in?"

"You can't get rid of me that easily," he grinned. "Jacob has it under control. They'll all want to settle into their tents, and then go for a dip in the pool. I'm helping you with the horses." He rested his hand on her arm.

Sarah looked at his hand uneasily, and with reluctance, he pulled it away.

"Besides," he added, "they expect us to be unpacking and feeding horses."

Unreasonable fear gripped Sarah as she turned and walked back toward the horses. She wasn't handling this attention well. Mark's affection for her was getting so strong that she felt like a frightened bird trapped in a cage, her heart fit to burst from panic.

She didn't know how to escape. What scared her more was that her flesh didn't want her to escape.

"You're shaking," Mark observed, as they walked. "It's hot. Are you feeling OK?"

"I'll be OK. I'm just tired," Sarah quavered. "Let's just get this done, hey?"

Mark set his jaw in concern, "Are you thinking about tomorrow afternoon?"

Sarah looked up suddenly; she'd almost forgotten.

"I don't know what to do about that anymore," she sighed. "I don't know any other options we could present to them to address the elephant problem."

"What about your mustering idea?" Mark inquired.

"Bah!" Sarah waved that away. "That was just one of my silly dreams, remember?"

She looked at him, raising her eyebrow, wondering why

he would bring that up now. Was he taunting her again?

"How about you? You feeling better after the Lebowa orphanage visit?" she queried to change the subject.

"I think so," Mark replied.

There was silence between them as they walked the rest of the way. The sun had just gone down and the horizon glowed a soft orange and purple, underneath a blanket of dark navy, polka-dotted with stars. It was magnificent and romantic, and filled Sarah with dread. Alone with him again.

Several horses nickered a soft greeting as Mark and Sarah arrived at the holding kraals. Shar had decided to roll in the dirt with his pack on and had strewn bits and pieces all over the kraal. All the horses began their soft nickers, asking for food as they saw Mark head over to the feed shed.

Groaning at the mess, Sarah went and started cleaning up Shar's kraal. They had given the other riders all their personal gear to take with them, so all that was left was the tack itself, the picnic gear and Mark and Sarah's personal gear.

Mark got the feed ready as Sarah untacked the horses, throwing their sweaty gear over the sheltered saddle racks to dry for the night. The horses all needed a good night's rest tonight for their return trip tomorrow.

Mark checked the electrified fencing, knowing that lions were common in this section of Kruger. After they had finished, Mark and Sarah grabbed up their own gear and lugged it back to the tent area of the campsite. Rondavels were plentiful, but staff from Brennan's left them for the tourists and opted for the smaller, but no less opulent, luxury tents.

Sweet aromas filled the air as Jacob and Martha had dinner started on an open fire, where everyone would later gather for dinner and stories of their adventurous day. Mark and Sarah went their separate ways, desperate to be rid of their heavy gear.

Sarah stepped onto the wooden platform, slipped through the woven petition, under the mosquito net, and dumped her gear in her private tent. After making sure she'd resealed everything against the onslaught of mosquitos, Sarah raced back to see Martha.

Martha had her wiry black hair pulled up into a colorful scarf on her head. She stood before several huge campfires, spit-roast lamb on one fire pit and a large pot boiling on the other. She also had jacket potatoes wrapped in foil sitting in the coals at the edge of the fire.

"Sarah!" The plump older African woman opened her arms for a hug. Sarah fell into a jog and allowed herself to be enveloped by Martha's large but firm embrace.

"Need some help?" Sarah asked.

Martha grinned, her white teeth bright in the fading light, "Don't be silly girl! You're our guest. How've you been?"

"I've been better," sighed Sarah, looking over her shoulder toward Mark's tent.

Martha followed her gaze, "That young man better not be giving you trouble, child!" She slapped a large wooden spoon into the palm of her other hand dangerously.

Sarah laughed with guilt, "No, it's not like that..." She gave the woman a coy look, and Martha's eyes went wide as she grinned broadly.

"Ahhhhhhh," she winked at Sarah, "I see." She turned back to the fires, chuckling to herself.

"See what?" Sarah's face flushed bright red as she saw the knowing expression on Martha's face. How on earth had she guessed?

Sarah stuttered, "You don't understand," her voice rising, "I don't want it to be like that. I have enough to deal with."

Martha chuckled again, her stomach moving up and down in rhythm. She looked at Sarah for a long moment and shook her head again, chuckling.

"What?" Sarah was getting frustrated. "What's so funny?"

"You'll find out soon enough, I suppose. So tell me," Martha squatted down onto a log, "how's the new girl? What's her name?"

"Brandi?" Sarah asked.

"Yes, Brandi. How is she fitting in? Last time you came, you said you weren't too sure how she would go. You'll have to bring her one day so I can meet her."

Sarah sat next to Martha on the log and looked down at her

dusty riding boots, "Well, I was wrong about her, Martha. She's a lovely person to work with. She's helped me a lot," admitted Sarah.

"And how is that?" pressed Martha.

"She showed me what it means to truly be a friend to someone, even if that someone doesn't like you. She and her friends introduced me to God...well...Jesus."

Martha slapped Sarah on the back. "Jesus? Ha! Hallelujah! We've been praying for you to find our Lord," laughed Martha.

"You're...you're a Christian?" stammered Sarah, eyes going wide.

"Have been for years, girl."

Sarah pondered this. Jacob and Martha had always shown love and hospitality to anyone who came to the bush camp, but that was their job. Sarah had always felt, though, that there was something else, something bigger in their love. How had she not noticed this before?

Just at that moment, Mark strutted past wearing a pair of board shorts and no shirt, carrying a towel.

"Enjoy the pool," called out Martha, winking back at Sarah.

"Enjoy the mozzies," Sarah mumbled under her breath. Flicking a look toward him, she tried not to notice his strong, tanned physique. Turning away just as quick, she swatted a mosquito on her arm.

Mark saluted the women and continued on. After he passed, Martha continued, "So, what about Mark? Does he know Jesus?"

Sarah scoffed.

"I guess that answered my question." Martha shook her head, "We'll keep praying for you all."

Sarah stood up and wiped her hands on her jeans, "I better go get cleaned up before dinner."

Martha regarded her, "You do what you have to do."

As Sarah walked off, she could hear Martha chuckling to herself over the dinner, "Our Sarah, a Christian. Thank you, Lord!"

After most of the riders had showered or taken a swim, or both, the whole group gathered under the stars for a campfire dinner. The area was surrounded with large torches, burning with citronella oil to ward off insects. There was laughter, stories and heaps of food. Sarah sat next to Martha, listening to all the funny tales Jacob told the group of Jacques's antics and other stories about various wildlife and visitors to the bush camp.

"So," continued Jacob, his laugh hearty, "I walked up to the storeroom and, behold, there was Jacques, up on the cupboard chewing on all the biltong! Had to order in fresh loads before the Americans arrived."

"What's biltong?" The young exchange student from London asked meekly.

The corner of Jacob's eyes crinkled into a broad smile. "Beef jerky," he explained. "Dried beef." She nodded in understanding, chuckling as she appreciated more heartily what the cheetah had done.

Soft laughter rippled through the group, as Mark caught Sarah's eye. His warm eyes settled on her as he bit into the hunk of fresh bread in his hands. His face shone bronze in the light of the fire, and Sarah had to admit to herself that he was indeed quite stunning.

She blushed and looked away. Feeling Martha's gaze on her and looking up, Sarah found the older woman chuckling again, her finger tapping her nose.

Sarah pursed her lips and leaned over to speak to Martha quietly, "It's not what you think."

"Uh huh!" laughed Martha, standing up. "Who wants desert?"

Several people shot up their hands.

"At this rate, the horses won't be able to carry us home," teased Mark from across the fire.

Martha shot him a look, shaking her wooden spoon at him.

Mark laughed and addressed the group, "Martha is the best cook I know!"

146

Everyone agreed. Martha bowed dramatically and began to dish up her famous rice pudding.

After the hearty meal, people began to crawl off to their rondavels for a well-earned rest before sun-up. Jacob, Martha, Mark and Sarah lingered behind.

"Thank you again for a wonderful night," Mark said sincerely.

Jacob slapped him on the back, "Our pleasure! You and Sarah are like son and daughter to us."

Mark glanced at Sarah, a cryptic look in his eye, before Martha cut in with more serious tones, "You need to come and visit more often without groups. We miss you up here. And bring along young Brandi next time, too. I need to meet this girl." She wagged her finger at them both.

"What's ol' Johnno Brennan up to these days?" queried Jacob sitting down and poking the coals with a stick.

"Not much," admitted Mark.

"He just bought two new horses," Sarah offered.

"We brought Shar with us. The large bay packhorse, but the nicest one we had to leave behind—Zulo, a pure black quarter horse."

Jacob and Martha nodded, impressed, "Does he get out much though? Johnno, I mean?" Jacob asked, his tone anxious.

Mark and Sarah shook their heads. "He's not been himself lately," admitted Mark with a quiet voice.

"How so?"

Mark raked a hand through his still damp hair, "Just cranky, I suppose."

Jacob shot Martha a glance, and Martha gave a slight nod. Sarah saw the exchange and knew that they were planning to pray for Johnno a lot more.

Mark looked at Sarah and stood up, "It's getting late. We'd better hit the sack. Early start tomorrow."

"Yeah, I'll go to bed soon," Sarah nodded to Mark.

He paused as if he had something more to say, but hesitated and said his goodnights, heading off to his tent.

Jacob turned his gaze to Sarah. "Martha tells me you have some good news!" he chortled.

Sarah blushed and told the couple the whole story of how she came to give her heart to Jesus. They nodded with delight, tears of joy threatening to spill down, as Sarah told her tale. When she finished, Martha shook her head with amazement, smiling. Jacob sat back in deep thought.

"My only problem," finished Sarah, "is that I still can't forgive what my father did."

The couple nodded, sympathetically. They knew Sarah's story well. Without reason, she had blurted it out to them the first time she'd met them. They were the first people in Africa who knew the whole story, apart from Kim, who also knew now. Sarah realized that it must have been the spirit of God within Jacob and Martha that had allowed her to feel safe enough to share with them.

"That's understandable," Martha took Sarah's hand in hers. "That's a big thing for a little girl to live through. You should never have had to go through that. You did nothing wrong!"

Her words were too much to bear, and Sarah burst into tears. How had she harbored that for so long? She *did* used to think that it was somehow her fault.

Martha held Sarah close to her, and Sarah let the tears come.

"Let it all out, girl. Get it all out." Martha gathered Sarah closer. The Aussie's tears slowed into great heaving sobs, as if her heart was breaking.

Jacob nodded to Martha and took his leave, squeezing his wife's shoulder.

"Sarah, I want you to do something for me," Martha held Sarah out at arm's length and looked her in the eyes. "I want you to shut your eyes and picture what I describe. Can you do that?"

Sarah wiped her eyes, nodding. She'd done this before, but it hadn't worked.

"Forgiving your father is a choice, Sarah. You don't have to feel it; it's a decision. Often the feelings follow later. Do you understand?"

Sarah blinked.

"Shut your eyes, girl," Martha enveloped Sarah close against her chest. "Now, picture the cross. Jesus is at the cross, but not on it. Can you see Him?"

148

Sarah closed her eyes and took a moment to visualize the scene. At first, she found it hard to picture Jesus, but then the fog cleared and she saw Him crystal clear, just as she had in her dreams. She felt his loving gaze on her again. His compassion, his mercy. In previous dreams, she had felt so unworthy and dirty before Him. However, now she felt like she could stand before Him clean and redeemed. *Forgiven.*

"Sarah, you are holding onto your unforgiveness. It looks like your heart is in a cage. The unforgiveness is the cage, and it has a huge lock. Can you open it?"

Sarah tried the lock, but it was solid and hard. She shook her head and looked at Jesus. Sarah lay silent in Martha's arms for a long while, her eyes clamped closed as she imagined the scene.

"Wait...Jesus has a golden key!" Sarah then exclaimed, gasping.

"Hmmm," answered Martha, in a knowing tone.

"I'm holding out the cage, and Jesus...," Sarah broke into fresh waves of tears, "He is unlocking it, He's letting my heart out!"

Sarah couldn't talk for a long while. She wept and wept. The cage disappeared, and Jesus held her heart close to Him. It was torn open. She watched in awe as He stitched it back together. He then covered the stitches with His hand, and a warm glow emanated. When He took His hand away, the stitches were gone and the heart was brand new.

Sarah felt overwhelming joy. She broke into tears and laughter. Martha could tell what had occurred, and she laughed with Sarah, crying some herself.

After a long while of holding Sarah, the African woman spoke up, "How do you feel, child?"

Sarah regarded her weakly, "Light. Exhausted. I had no idea how much weight I was trying to carry. I feel like I'm floating."

Martha's smile grew, "Now, do you think, after everything Jesus has done, that you can say you've forgiven your father?"

Sarah looked up at Martha through tear-streaked eyes, "I believe I have. I do forgive my dad."

Martha laid a hand on Sarah's head and prayed for her,

thanking God for His goodness and sealing her in protection. "Now, you need your rest," she patted Sarah on the hand and got up, heading into her house.

Just like that, Sarah was astounded at how easy that had been. She felt extremely tired all of a sudden, and stumbled off to her tent.

Mark lay on his back in his tent, staring at the ceiling. He had heard bits of what had happened but decided that if he intruded again, it would not help matters. He tried to roll over and get to sleep after he heard Sarah go to bed, but sleep eluded him. He tossed and turned in agitation. What was all this Jesus stuff? Did it have any credibility?

"God, if you're there, please show Yourself to me. Blow me away with Your so-called power," he muttered with sarcasm under his breath.

Grabbing the corner of his sleeping bag, he rolled over. Unbeknownst to Mark, that was the very fleece that would set things in motion.

CHAPTER
THIRTEEN

Sarah rose early and listened to the first songs of the morning bird chorus as she lay snuggled in her sleeping bag. She thought about what took place the night before, wondering whether it really happened or not. *Did I really forgive my father?* She had an instant warm glow in her heart and knew that she had. It was the most liberating feeling she had ever felt.

She sat up, stretched, grabbed her bible and settled back into her sleeping bag on her stomach to read some more from the book of Matthew. The words sprang off the page like a delightful meal, which she inhaled with desperate ferocity.

So deep was she engrossed in the word of God that sometime later, she had lost track of time. Sarah looked up, startled as some boots shuffled past the entrance to her tent area. She could see a shadow on the woven screening.

"Sarah? You awake?" Mark scowled and tapped the bamboo.

"Yeah, I'm coming," Sarah quickly slipped on a fresh pair of jeans, slipped on her work uniform over her singlet and began to button up.

"Breakfast is ready," Mark stated in a drab tone and shuffled off again. Sarah rolled her eyes. *Apparently his stomach was calling.*

As they ate another lavishly prepared breakfast, Jacob took Sarah and Mark aside. Sarah had finished eating, but Mark was still munching on an apple as they walked away from the main group with Jacob and another man.

"This is Kgomotso," he explained as he thumped the thick-set African man across his broad shoulders. Sarah recognized him from the evening before as the man who had put Jacques away for the night. "He desires to go across the Kruger to visit his family in Lebowa. He asks if he could accompany your group."

Mark regarded the tall Sotho man and looked regretful. He glanced at Sarah, who was thinking about how to arrange it so they could manage the horses.

"We could always spread some of Shar's packs among the other horses," she suggested, not wanting to turn away a man in need when Jacob and Martha had done so much for them.

"Oh no," said Jacob, "he has a mount."

Mark nodded with satisfaction and shook Kgomotso's hand, "Welcome."

Kgomotso's face lit up broadly, and he kept bowing in thanks to Mark and Sarah. He then turned and ran as fast as he could to go prepare his horse for the trip.

"He's easily pleased," laughed Mark to Jacob.

"You don't understand. It's dangerous for him to travel alone, and he is very superstitious about the way. I wouldn't allow him to travel without company anyway, and none of us were driving into town for another week or so." Jacob's mouth formed a hard line as he waited for more questioning..

Mark shrugged and returned to his breakfast.

Sarah looked at Jacob apology in her smile, "Sorry about Mark."

"Hey!" Mark protested as he was walking away. Sarah watched him leave for a moment before turning quietly to Jacob.

"Why is Kgomotso superstitious about his own land?"

Jacob looked over his shoulder then leaned closer, "Well, he believes that he could be tormented by evil spirits for spending time with us."

Sarah glowered, "Because we're Christian?"

Jacob nodded with sadness, "He doesn't realize that we've been praying for him ever since he started to work for us. He is under God's holy protection, but he doesn't know it yet."

Sarah nodded, "Well, all the same, sorry about Mark's attitude this visit."

"There's no need, Sarah. He hasn't changed a bit. It's you that's changed."

Sarah's face flushed as she walked with Jacob back to the group that was finishing their breakfast. Mark jerked his head toward her as she arrived, indicating that they needed to go and get the horses ready.

She nodded and said her thanks to Martha for a great meal, before slipping off to gather her things from her tent. The other guests had packed their bags and placed them along the fence line. This made it easy for Mark and Sarah to grab and pack the gear onto Shar and Mac, who were the two designated packhorses.

Sarah beamed as she hefted another pack onto her other shoulder and headed for the stalls. Nothing was going to steal her joy today.

They began to head out by eight a.m., late by Mark's standards, but they still had to wait for their extra charge. All were settled back onto their mounts as they waited. Soon enough, newcomer Kgomotso arrived, riding a large dark brown gelding.

Everyone had said their heartfelt goodbyes to Jacob and Martha, and some even posed for photos with Jacques, who had been let loose again and was prowling around the campfire from last night, looking for leftovers.

Jacob and Martha stood inside their closed gate, waving goodbye to the trail group. Jacob noticed that Martha had a tear in her eye, smiling and shaking her head. She was so happy that Sarah had come to the Lord.

They rode on in silence for quite some time, enjoying the contentment of full stomachs and great memories. However, everyone was weary that morning after yesterday's long ride. Mark and Sarah were familiar with this. People would pay for the great adventure of an overnight ride, but often they didn't ride enough to have the stamina for day two.

153

Mark set a steady, easy pace for the group, letting them enjoy the panoramic views of the African wild. They saw herds of zebra grazing alongside wildebeest and antelope. The birds came in all sizes and colors along the trail. From storks to hornbills, and the robust and the bright-colored kingfishers.

It was a beautiful day of wide expanses of rich blue skies, broken up here and there with soft white clouds. Even Mark settled back in his saddle, trying to enjoy the morning. The only person on full alert was Kgomotso. He rode up front with Mark, so that his restless eyes could scan the area.

"Hey," Mark got his attention, "relax." He patted his rifle.

Kgomotso eyed the rifle for a moment, and then kept looking around in nervousness.

"What's the matter? I thought you'd be at home out here," Mark sat up and looked at the Sotho man with interest.

"This area. Bad spirits. This part of land, no good," Kgomotso looked behind himself as if speaking it out somehow confirmed his fears.

Mark nodded, understanding. He remembered what Jacob said about superstitions among tribal people. To Mark, though, it was all superstitious mumbo jumbo. It wasn't real.

Mark tipped his hat at Kgomotso, "We'll be fine. We came through this way just yesterday, and it was safe."

They rode on for a while longer before Mark started to get nervous with Kgomotso's glancing about. He followed the Sotho man's gaze behind them at the group stringing out behind.

Mark was up front leading Mac with the pack. Directly behind him were four of the riders who had paid for the ride. Then there was a large gap, followed by the fifth rider. Several horse-lengths after the middle-aged rider in fifth place, rode Sarah, who was leading Shar.

Mark hadn't noticed the gap before now, and he wondered why Sarah hadn't radioed him to slow down. He looked at Kgomotso, and then began to feel the hairs prick up on the back of his neck. Something was not right. Wary, he narrowed his eyes across the expanse of long grasses.

Mark picked up his radio, "Sarah. You on radio?"

"Yeah, why wouldn't I be? Over," answered Sarah a few moments later, cheerfulness in her voice.

"Can you guys at the rear pick up the pace? There's a gap. Over."

Mark half-halted Sniper to slow him down. The others started to catch up, bunching up, but the fifth rider was still off by himself and too slow in catching up.

"There's often small gaps on the way home. These guys are tired. Over," replied Sarah.

"That's what I'm worried about," muttered Mark, looking back over at Kgomotso, who was staring at the long grass to the side of them.

The African suddenly pointed a frantic finger toward the swaying grass, "*Sebatakgomo!* Lion!"

Mark swung his head around, trying to locate the beast. They needed to locate the animal, stay calm and walk away from it. No sudden movements and keep their voices loud and calm. Then he spotted her, a lioness was stalking through the grass, her eyes trained on the fifth rider in the middle of the group.

Mark pressed the radio to his lips, "Sarah! *Sarah!* A lioness! It's stalking toward the rider in front of you! Move away to the left. Get that rider ready to sit a gallop if need be!"

Mark spun his horse away from the group and out toward the lion, pulling his rifle out from its sheath.

Sarah saw the lioness, "Sir..." she said, ready to remind the rider of the safety brief and about what to do, but things started to happen way too fast as the man sitting on Snow, the white horse, suddenly spotted the cat and froze. The lioness leapt into a charge toward the horse, which stood oblivious.

Sarah dropped Shar's lead, letting her charge run loose as she yelled out to the man to get out of the way. He wasn't responding fast enough, and Sarah charged Honor straight at the lioness, which was pounding toward the stunned rider. Hoping the bold move would stun the cat into backing off, she intercepted just as the lioness leapt into the air to strike the horse.

Breaking out of a catatonic state, Snow shied sideways and then leapt into a canter, slowing only when she got to the front of the main herd. Honor and Sarah slammed into the flying cat, knocking Sarah from the saddle. She thumped on the hard ground, knocking the wind from her lungs. Honor trotted off after Snow, leaving Sarah sprawling and dazed in the hot grass next to the stunned lioness.

Horrified at her predicament, Sarah felt like she was in a bubble with just her and the lioness, as she lost awareness of the other riders gathering further away. Only Mark was trying to get closer with all caution, speaking in a loud, clear voice, trying to deter the lion.

Sarah didn't take her eyes from the great cat as it quickly got to its feet, blinked, spotted her and opened its mouth in a loud snarl. The cat then hunched into a pounce pose, ready to strike again, this time at Sarah. She was defenseless to do anything. She got to her feet and did the only thing she could think of.

"Jesus, help me!" she prayed in a loud voice.

The lioness blinked, hesitating before it circled, bearing its huge vice-like fangs at her and snarling again.

"Oh, Jesus!" Sarah turned as the lioness circled, not taking her eyes from the cat. Where was Mark?

Mark was almost close enough to make the shot, but he didn't want to risk hitting Sarah. He shut one eye, focused on the lioness through the sight on his rifle, and took aim.

Without any obvious cause, the lioness stopped and simply lost interest, stalking away, twitching its tail in agitation. Mark blinked and looked up as he lowered the rifle. Standing directly in front of Sarah was a huge man dressed in white, his arm outstretched toward the lioness. Sarah didn't seem to notice him. She sat bewildered, watching the lioness slinking away through the grass.

The man then turned and looked straight at Mark with power and authority in his fiery eyes. Mark gulped and then looked behind him at the group of riders, who were gathered on a clearing with Kgomotso. *Could they see the man?*

Kgomotso had taken charge of the group and kept them all together during the drama. He sat, appearing stoic on his horse now, staring back at Mark.

156

Mark turned back to Sarah, the color draining from his face. The man was gone. He shook his head, dazzled. Was he seeing things?

"Hey, you just going to sit there?" Sarah stumbled to her feet, grimacing, and wiped the dirt from her hands and clothes as she staggered over to Mark. She had several slight grazes along her neck and arms that were weeping, and she limped with pain as her back protested.

"You OK?" gasped Mark, breathing heavy. He was still looking wide-eyed toward the grass where he had seen the man.

"I'll be better when I get back on my horse."

Pulling her hand to the small of her back, she turned and stretched out her sore back, calling Honor with a soft whistle.

Honor lifted her head from the grass and gazed in Sarah's direction, all the while snorting with nerves. Sarah whistled again. Lowering her head, Honor trotted over to Sarah.

Wincing, Sarah climbed back into the saddle. Settling in, she looked at Mark, who was pale.

"What? I just fell off! I'm ready!. Let's get this group cracking! I don't want to stay out here any longer."

Mark shook his head, trying to clear his thoughts. He definitely saw a man there who had saved Sarah. There was no doubt. But now he was gone. Did Sarah see him?

"Who was that? Did you see him?" stammered Mark, pointing to where Sarah had been with the lioness.

"Don't you mean her? It was a lioness, Mark. I'm completely fine!"

"No...I mean the man!"

"What man?" Sarah cocked an eyebrow at Mark.

"Never mind. If you're right to ride, then let's get this lot home," he said as he slid the rifle away and trotted back anxiously to gather the group.

Kgomotso kept staring at Mark, his eyes emotionless.

Mark looked at the Sotho in surprise. "You saw him, didn't you?"

The Sotho man shook his head. "I told you this was bad place."

Mark ignored him and straightened out the group when Kgomotso continued, "That girl! Is she Ngaka?"

Mark grimaced, "Sarah? No way! why?"

"She has a power in her, power like I have never felt before. It protected her."

Mark tossed a curious look at Sarah, then turned back at Kgomotso, "Hmmm," he thought out loud. With a start, he recalled his words from the night before: *"Blow me away with your so-called power!"*

Sarah fetched the two packhorses that had wandered off, and bringing Mac to Mark, resumed her place at the tail with Shar. Sarah made sure that she and the other riders stayed close to the group from then on. Tired riders made attractive and easy meals.

The middle-aged South African man who was riding Snow was still quite shaken up at being the target for a lion's lunch, and he changed positions to ride close to the front of the group. Rather than being tired, he was now on full alert.

Mark kept them going at a steady pace until lunch. They stopped for a quick break and bite to eat, then remounted their horses to get home. Sarah looked over her shoulder as she pulled herself wearily into the saddle. Kgomotso was watching her. Curious, she held his gaze until he turned away.

The lion attack had left a bad taste in everyone's mouth, including Mark's. Sarah struggled on, riding at the back of the group. She was sore from the fall in her lower back and her arm, but she tried not to show it.

When they returned to Brennan's and said their goodbyes to an unusually quiet group, Kgomotso approached Sarah and Mark on his horse. He looked straight at Sarah for a moment, nodded his head with approval, before turning and trotting off.

Sarah raised an eyebrow and looked at Mark, "What was that about?"

He grimaced, not knowing how to tell her what the Sotho had said about her. They watched in silence as the man trotted out the gate toward Lebowa, dust forming a soft cloud about him.

CHAPTER FOURTEEN

Sarah showered after the ride and got ready for the meeting about the elephants. She noticed a large bruise on her side and one on her upper left arm, but the worst one was coming through on her lower back, plus various scratches and grazes. Her back was what hurt the most as she had landed on her tailbone.

She dressed in a long-sleeve shirt and a clean pair of jeans, grateful to be able to cover up all her scuffmarks. Sarah knew that by tomorrow, she'd be really sore, but it was nothing that wouldn't heal soon enough. She was grateful for no broken bones.

Not in the mood to go to this meeting with all that had taken place, Sarah was reluctant to agree when Mark asked her if she still wanted to go. She met Mark at the office, where he was talking to Johnno about what had happened and filling out the all-important incident report.

"Don't forget!" Johnno wagged his finger at Mark, who nodded as Sarah walked in.

"We're also taking you to the hospital to get checked," Mark explained.

Sarah shook her head, "I'm OK."

"Really?" asked Johnno, he squeezed her left arm, releasing a yelp of pain from Sarah.

She yanked her arm away, grimacing as she rubbing at it. "That was unfair!" she complained.

Mark looked on in concern, his mind made up. "We're going! Even if we have to wait all night."

Sarah groaned and adjusted her handbag on her good shoulder. "Can we just go?" she insisted.

Nodding, Mark signed off on the report and escorted her to his car.

As they drove, Mark glanced at Sarah, curiosity in his manner, "Sarah..." he said then his mouth dried up.

She looked at him in question.

"Out on the trail, when the lioness and you were on the ground, I...I saw a man," he stammered, rolling his tongue around his mouth.

Sarah stared at Mark, "You said that. What did you mean? What man?"

"Well, I don't know..." he shook his head, wondering whether he was losing his mind. "He was with you! He stood over you and sent the lioness away."

Gritting her teeth against the pain, Sarah sat herself up, her eyes going wide, "Really? What did he look like?"

"Well, that's the other thing...he came out of nowhere, then he just vanished. And he didn't look normal. He was tall—larger than life—and he was dressed in a white robe. He also had a glow about him. He looked at me, then he just disappeared. I think that Kgomotso saw it too, but he didn't directly say so." He shook his head with confusion, "Maybe I'm just seeing things. Maybe I need a vacation, or a CT scan." He laughed self-depreciatingly.

Sarah's sat back, staring ahead.

Mark focused on his driving, worrying about the pause.

"You think I'm crazy, and maybe I am," Mark sighed.

A loud exhale escaped Sarah's lips as she looked at Mark, smiling, "No, I don't think that at all." She started to laugh, feeling an extraordinary release in tension.

Mark looked at her quizzically, "So...what? You believe me?"

"Yeah, Mark. I do! I think you saw an angel! I cried out to Jesus to help me when that lioness was lining me up... God saved me!" She jumped in her seat with excitement.

"Wait a minute," Mark stopped her, "you think that because you prayed, God sent an angel to save you from that lioness...and that was an angel I saw?"

Sarah nodded, emphatically smiling to herself.

"Hmmm!" Mark rubbed his chin, turning up the air conditioner. He remembered lying in his tent the night before, challenging God to show Himself. Was that God answering? How could he be sure?

Mark drove for quite a while, lost in his thoughts. In silence, Sarah was thanking God for His goodness and praying that somehow, in some way, God was starting to reveal Himself to Mark, too. She pondered Mark's silence, which in itself was unusual.

They arrived in the center of town and Mark turned into a large driveway outside a government building.

"We're here. OK, we...uhh...never talked about what we're going to propose to these people," Mark said as he unclipped his seatbelt and looked at Sarah with expectation.

"Mark, stop." She touched his shoulder. "Just wait a minute...why are you even doing this?" Sarah confronted him. "You've never been this interested in stopping the culling. The only reason you rang that other time was because I was pushing you."

Mark shrugged, "I told you, I've been thinking about it. I went out to see the herd, you saw that for yourself."

He stepped out of the car and ducked around to open Sarah's door. Sarah sat for a moment in thought, before she got out of the car. She stumbled, and Mark caught her by the elbow.

"Sarah!" he exclaimed, his cool fingers adjusting their grip on her arm to support her. She groaned, trying to straighten, as the pain shot through her back. "You really are hurt! Blow off this meeting, you need help."

"It's just my back," Sarah admitted and slipped back into the car seat with relief.

"Can I see?" Mark asked, expecting to be rejected.

Sarah exhaled with exhaustion, nodding numbly as she leaned forward. She lifted her shirt with reserve, just enough to reveal an ugly purple mass sitting on her lower spine. Mark gasped, immediately leaning over her and pulling from the car his new cell phone. The new gadgets were becoming all the rage. It was his first chance to test it as he pulled a business card and dialed a number on the large black device.

"Hi, Ja, this is Mark van der Merwe from Brennan's Safari

Trails. I'm good, thanks. And you? I'm just ringing in regard to the meeting we had planned this afternoon..." Mark plonked himself back into the driver's seat, shut the door and clipped up his seat belt, "...I need to cancel. Uh huh, I'll call you back regarding another time. Thanks for that, ja, bye."

Sarah sat looking at him for a long moment, "You didn't have to do that," she said in a mousey voice, closing her door. "You could have gone in."

"Ha! Truth be told, I don't know what I would have said either. I was winging it. Besides, you need a doctor, and you need one now."

Sarah laughed, "You needed a scape-goat!" Sitting back, she offered him a weary smile, "Thanks, though."

He cocked his head at her, not sure how to take her response.

Sarah caught on to his confusion, "I mean, thanks for trying to line up a meeting, Mark. I mean it. I appreciate your effort, and thanks for caring."

"You're welcome."

Mark covered his sudden awkwardness by starting the ignition.

The triage nurse pulled up Sarah's shirt so the doctor could have a good look at her bruises. Mark sat waiting in the next room. He was worried about her. She was in more pain than she was making out—they could all see that.

She came out soon after, and Mark sat up waiting to hear the verdict. Sarah groaned with exhaustion and pain as she walked stiffly from the examination room.

"I'm alright, just some major bruising and tissue damage. They said I'll feel it tomorrow, though. I told them that I can feel it now."

"Good." Mark was relieved, and then looked in horror as he realized how his comment sounded.

Sarah rolled her eyes at him.

"I meant, 'good that you are OK,'" he corrected himself.

"Maybe Johnno will let you have the day off tomorrow to recoup. Let's get back and call it a day." He yawned. "Brandi said she was taking care of feed-up today."

"Nice," Sarah said then stopped and touched Mark's arm, "Mark?"

"Ja?"

"Thanks again."

"You already thanked me," he replied with amusement.

Sarah nodded in agreement before adding, "I know, I'm just glad that you insisted I get my back checked out, even though I figured I'd be alright."

Mark nodded, feeling a warm glow inside as they headed back to the car.

Soon after leaving the hospital, Mark noticed that Sarah had dozed off, her gentle form rising and falling in soft rhythm, as she rested against the doorjamb of the car.

Johnno Brennan reclined in his office chair and exhaled loudly as he was put on hold. He adjusted the phone to his other ear and took a swig from a bottle of soft drink.

"Tom here..." a voice said on the other end.

Johnno sat up and looked behind at the doorway. "It's me, Johnno," he spoke quietly, wondering whether he should have shut his office door.

"Johnno! I told you never to call me at work!"

"I know. I'll be quick. She's up to something; we need to do something to neutralize."

"Damn! Do you think she knows?"

"No, I don't think so. But if she puts a stop to it..."

"I know. Let me think..." the man on the other end of the phone relayed an idea he'd just formed to Johnno, who scratched his head, reluctant to agree.

Johnno hung up the phone and ran his hand over his polished wood-grain desk, sighing with depression. If this didn't work, he'd have to call it quits and sell the safari business. If anyone discovered anything, he'd have to leave town or he'd lose more than his business.

With the help of Solomon, Brandi finished feeding the horses their extra portions of food after their long trek across the Kruger. The job done, she nodded with satisfaction, saying goodnight to Solomon. With a bounce in her step, she headed toward the offices to put away the stable keys.

She didn't think it was odd at all when she heard Johnno in his office talking. She slipped inside and put the keys on their hook in the key cabinet. On her way back out, she heard Johnno lower his voice. Feeling an inexplicable discomfort, Brandi was quick to pad out from the office and rush home to her rondavel.

Something wasn't sitting right, and she spent the rest of the evening trying to pray through an unsettled feeling in the pit of her stomach. *What was wrong? And were Mark and Sarah alright? They'd been gone a while.*

After a long time, Brandi heard Mark's car pull into the drive and she ducked outside to see how things went. Mark shushed her as she raced out to greet him. Brandi stopped in her tracks, as Mark motioned toward Sarah, asleep in the passenger side.

"Is she alright?" Brandi asked in hushed tones. "I was worried; I thought something had gone wrong."

Mark shook his head, "She'll be fine. She'll just feel it in the morning."

"Hmmm." Brandi was thoughtful. She watched as Mark gave Sarah's shoulder a gentle nudge. Sarah moaned before blinking up at him with confusion.

"You fell asleep," he explained in his soft accent, disappointed that she'd awoken and he couldn't scoop her into his arms and carry her home.

With much effort, Sarah got out from the car and groggily allowed Mark to escort her to her rondavel. He helped her find her keys and unlock the door before heading off to his own place. Brandi followed suit.

Within minutes, everyone was in a deep and blissful sleep, except for Brandi, who lay awake wondering why she still didn't feel right. She prayed until, at last, she fell into a disturbed slumber.

SARAH'S GIFT

CHAPTER
FIFTEEN

Groaning, Sarah tried to roll over as pain shot up her back. She felt like she could barely move that following morning. Just as well, bookings were light that day and were able to be handled without Sarah.

Johnno conceded that, not being fit to ride, she could clean the gear from the overnight trek or do office work with Romy. Brandi stayed behind to help Sarah, while Mark took the first ride of the day with Solomon, some honeymooners on a romantic sunrise safari.

It was shaping up to be another hot day, so the women set up the gear on the large shaded deck surrounding the office and worked on cleaning and polishing leathers in the cool breeze, while overlooking the valley paddock.

"How are you feeling today?" asked Brandi as cheery as ever, though Sarah suspected she saw dark rings under the girl's eyes.

"Very sore," admitted Sarah as she scooped up some more oil from the tub with a rag and rubbed it into the saddle she was working on.

"Mark's been acting strange since yesterday. Well, strang-er! Not just upset because there was an accident, but spooked," Brandi stated, seeming to be curious as to Sarah's take on the matter.

Sarah stood watching in thought as Brandi put together a bridle she'd just finished oiling.

"Yeah," Sarah began and went on to tell Brandi what Mark had seen. "I believe it was an angel," she said.

Sarah's eyes glazed over with wonder as Brandi replied, "That's an amazing testimony, Sarah!"

167

"I know," Sarah agreed.

They settled into comfortable silence for a bit, both pondering what had occurred.

"So, anything interesting happen while we were gone?" Sarah inquired.

They both looked up as they heard Johnno pass by the doorway leading out onto the deck.

Brandi looked at Sarah worriedly, "Well, I don't know. Everything went along as normal, but..."

"But what?" asked Sarah, lowering her voice.

Brandi gave a half-hearted smile and shrugged it off, "It's nothing. I don't think so, anyway. I just feel really unsettled for some reason. I don't know what's wrong with me."

"Maybe you need a holiday," offered Sarah sympathetically, looking under the flap of the saddle. It was filthy. She grabbed a wet cloth from a bucket of soapy water and began to wipe it down. "Oh yeah, Martha and Jacob want to meet you," she added.

"Really?" Brandi looked up, surprised that they would even ask after her.

Nodding with enthusiasm, Sarah went on, "Maybe we could take a drive out there during the holidays and spend a couple of days or something."

"That would be great, provided we can get the same time off," agreed Brandi. All of a sudden, she felt distracted, like someone was watching them.

Sarah followed Brandi's gaze as they scanned the windows. Sarah got up and peeked in through the doorway. No one was there, but Sarah also started to feel awkward.

Fearing he'd just been caught, Johnno turned and scuttled into his office and took a seat at his desk. He put down his coffee and pulled out some paperwork that needed his attention. He had been in the kitchen, making a cup of coffee and trying to overhear what the girls were talking about. He had to try to find out what Sarah knew, if she anything at all. Or what she was up to with these elephants. All he overheard was something about wanting to visit the bush camp on their time off.

Johnno leaned back in his chair and sighed with relief. Nobody had noticed him. He took a sip from his coffee. Still too hot! He placed it down again and looked toward the door in agitation. How would he find out more from Sarah, without appearing suspicious?

Johnno fiddled with the pens in their holder, remembering what Tom had said. Maybe he should just sit and wait and let things play out. That way, he wouldn't feel so paranoid. He needed to stop stressing and relax about it all. He would find out soon enough.

The engine of Mark's car took a bit longer to turn over this morning. He tried it several more times before it sprung into a deep purr, smoke billowing out from the exhaust. Mark groaned; he toyed with the idea of trading it in and getting an upgrade, but then wondered whether he should just opt for the repairs the vehicle needed.

He left the engine running for a moment before turning off the choke and pulling out of the driveway. The gravel crackled under his tires. He picked up the piece of paper he'd placed in the crook near his gear stick and turned it over idly in his fingers. It contained the name and address of the family in Lebowa he'd met when Brandi and Sarah had taken him out to see the new orphanage. Koto and Lerato.

Mark had been impressed with the church's charity, and he'd also had his eyes opened to the way people lived outside his own circle. He felt compelled to visit again today and find out more, perhaps even talk with Koto about what else they could do to stop the elephant culling. He also thought that talking to Koto might allow him to sort out the feelings in his heart. Either way, he was nervous about the prospect of going out there on his own, but he felt something strange drawing him to do so.

Mark had asked Brandi for the address and name of the

family. Brandi had been quite curious about Mark's intentions. When he explained, she was more than accommodating and gave him the information. Brandi knew that after Koto, Lerato and their family had gotten to know Sarah more from church, they had heard all about Mark and would welcome him with open arms.

Moses, Kagiso and some other children from Lebowa were the first to see the car approaching, and they ran eagerly to see who was visiting. Through her window, Lerato looked up from the rice she was cooking and squinted in the bright light to see who it was. When Mark stepped out of the car, she rushed to find Koto.

Koto and Lerato both approached Mark, who was standing in the village and looking around, lost.

"Mark, is it?" Koto asked.

Mark tilted his lips, still somewhat reserved, and stuck out his hand, "Ja, that's me. I wasn't sure if you'd remember me. Koto? Lerato?"

The couple inclined their heads, pleased that he remembered their names. They invited him back to their home and, feeling awkward, Mark accepted the offer.

"How's Sarah doing?" asked Lerato as she went back to her cooking task.

"She's good, but she had an accident last week," Mark said as he sat down on the ledge next to Koto.

"Accident? What happened?" Koto sat up worried.

"Will she be at church tomorrow?"

Mark blinked. "Church?"

"She goes to church with Brandi. We all go to same church, when we can be picked up," he added as he looked at Lerato.

"Sunny Bank Christian Church. Sometimes a group of us go in the church bus," Koto explained with pride.

Mark rubbed the back of his neck, "Oh...I didn't realize that Sarah was going too. Brandi's usually gone by the time I get up, and Sarah usually goes for a horse ride."

Lerato looked up at Koto, who went on, "Well, she does, but...what accident did she have? Is she OK?" Lerato went back to stirring, but listened with concern.

"We had a lion attack on the trail. Sarah was knocked off her horse while trying to protect another rider. The lion ended up leaving," Mark paused, not knowing whether or not to elaborate, "and Sarah is sore from her fall from the horse."

Koto's eyes went wide, "So, it's true!"

"What?" Mark sat forward, wondering what Koto had heard and from whom. All of a sudden, he realized. "Have you met Kgomotso?" asked Mark, trying to fit the puzzle pieces together.

Koto considered the question, "Kgomotso is the cousin of Thabo Masekela. He came here last week on a horse, telling people about this girl who he claimed had great power to turn away lions. Even the spirits can be commanded by her. They are making praise songs about her. We didn't know it was you he travelled with." Koto sat forward, level with Mark, and looked at him with scrutiny, "Was he talking about Sarah?"

Mark nodded and added, "There was something else," then paused, gauging whether to reveal what he saw, "Sarah said she prayed to God, and God sent an angel. That's what she told me afterward, but at the time, I saw a huge man dressed in white. He turned the lion away. He glowed."

Koto gave a vigorous nod of his head, turning to Lerato, who was looking wide-eyed with excitement, "So, it was an angel. It was Sarah, not some other. Kgomotso is claiming that it was a white Ngaka. Her praise song is going around Lebowa!"

"Praise song?" Mark queried.

"Yes, yes! It is a song created to honor. Our praise songs are mostly about our ancestors or leaders."

"But Sarah's neither of those," creases appeared between Mark's brow.

Koto tilted his head, "I know you do not yet know our culture. Her praise song honors her courage and the power behind it. That is why they made one for her."

Mark's head was starting to spin. He nodded in thought, folding his hands together and changing to a safer subject, "So, how's work, Koto?"

The Sotho man shook his head slightly, curious as to the sudden steer of topic, "Not too bad. It is going slow though, since the cull. Tourists are no longer coming as much. I only get work when they have groups. But it will get better. God looks after us," he shared a loving look with his wife, and her eyes sparkled in response.

Mark looked at the ground in dismay. How did they keep so hopeful and joyful when they had an uncertain future?

"What do you think could be done to bring back the tourists and stop the culling?" Mark found himself asking.

"Hmmm, you're asking me? Only the government can do anything about that...and they won't." Koto threw his hands in the air.

Mark tilted his mouth in thought. He too was stumped with what they could do about it.

After spending a good part of that Monday with Koto and his family, Mark was determined to head home. He decided that he liked this family, and he wanted to get to know them more. The guilt in his heart remained, but he started to feel better with himself for making the effort. He was even planning to sneak into church the following week to see what all the fuss was about. After all, he wondered whether God had answered him by sending that angel, or vision, or whatever it was. And what better place to find God than at church?

Sarah and Brandi walked into church the next Sunday morning, and after finding Max, Kim and the others, they went over to find some seats. Sunny Bank Christian Fellowship was an unusually large church, boasting over seven hundred people. Most towns this size would have less than half of that if they were flourishing. But the move of God in this town over the past year had caused an influx in people coming to know Jesus. As a result, they had healthy numbers that far exceeded the expectations for such a place.

The worship team was practicing as the friends organized their bags under their seats and greeted one another. Eric stopped tuning his guitar from the stage and waved down at the girls who had just arrived.

Sarah and Brandi waved back as Sally came up to the group, "Hey everyone. I want you to meet someone. He's new to church, and he was just saying that he wanted to be part of a bible study group."

Everyone looked up smiling.

"Declan," Sally went on, "This is everyone! Everyone, Declan."

Declan waved, grinning. He caught Sarah's eye, and winked at her. Sarah regarded him with curiosity. He was tall and handsome, with dark red hair and a clean-shaven face. His eyes were a deep green color, and he had a strong jaw line and a smattering of freckles across his boyish face. When he spoke, Sarah noticed he had an Irish accent.

Sally took him under wing, showing him around, introducing him to people and insisting that he sit with her. Brandi looked sideways at Sally, then rolled her eyes Sarah's way, smiling as they settled into their seats.

"I hope this one is a Christian," she confided to Sarah.

Max and Kim sat on the other side of Sarah, and Max kept looking over at Sally with disapproval. She'd done this before and just gotten herself into trouble. The more Sarah hung around Brandi and her friends, the more she realized that Christians had the same weaknesses and problems as everyone else. The difference is that they possess the tools to make better decisions, although often they still struggle to choose the right ones.

The service started, and they all stood up to join in the worship songs. Sarah felt Declan's gaze keep falling her way, so she maintained her eyes forward, reading the lyrics from the big screen. He was making her feel uncomfortable.

Mark met Koto and his family outside Sunny Bank Christian Fellowship as they'd agreed the week before. Mark felt uncomfortable and dubious about going into a church. The last time he'd gone to church was for his sister's wedding.

As Koto's family stepped out from the church bus with other

Sotho families, the kids were chattering with excitement, looking forward to going to children's church. Lerato helped in children's church and, touching Koto on the arm affectionately, said her goodbye and took the children away to the large hall.

Koto stepped up to Mark and nodded, "Ready?"

"Don't know," admitted Mark.

Koto clapped him on the shoulders, "You will be fine!"

They both laughed, walking into the large auditorium, and headed toward the balcony seats that overlooked the vast rows of chairs.

Mark was amazed at how large and modern this church was. Koto greeted some other people, and then he and Mark each took a seat. Mark leaned over the rail, peering down at the seats below. He began to scan the dozens of rows, looking for Sarah and Brandi. He spotted Max standing near the back of the room beside a greeting area, handing out some flyers to people and chatting. If he kept an eye on where Max went, he knew he might catch a glimpse of where Brandi's other friends – and Sarah sat. His breath hitched slightly with nerves as he thought about her.

A woman approached the microphone on the stand in the middle of the stage and gave a welcome. Her words echoed through the elaborate sound system as the worship team started playing their first song. Mark located the lyrics being projected onto two large screens on either side of the auditorium.

He watched as Max made his way back toward the seating area. Lots of people who had been mingling at the back were filing their way back to their seats. Mark lost sight of Max as Koto leaned over and pointed out to him one of the backup singers on stage, "That's my sister," he boasted.

Mark nodded and tried to find Max again. He'd lost him. Mark resigned to stop stressing over spotting Sarah. After a while, he decided that he rather enjoyed the atmosphere. It was relaxed, it was modern and it was relevant, unlike many of the churches Mark had been to, which were old-fashioned and traditional. And while the other churches were very beautiful, Mark had been too scared to even breathe, lest he offend God.

At Sunny Bank, though, Mark was impressed about how real

the pastor was. He was practical, and Mark felt like what he taught was good advice for how to live a good life. He didn't understand a lot of the stuff about sin or repentance, though.

After the service, Mark and Koto made their way downstairs to find Sarah and the others, but Koto kept getting waylaid by people who wanted to visit. This was Koto's main day for getting out of the village, and he looked forward to catching up.

Sarah, Brandi and the others all made their way outside straight after the service. It was going to be a hot day, and they wanted to get out into the breeze, away from the crowds. They'd also decided that they would leave right after church to get good seats at Portico's for lunch.

They slipped into their cars and drove off before Mark had a chance to find them.

The group of friends settled into their favorite spot at Portico's and looked over the menus. They decided that since they were sitting in the soft couch area, and not at proper tables, they would order a large amount of finger-foods and just pool it together on the table.

Declan found an excuse to sit away from Sally so he could talk to the others, which Sally appeared to take in stride. Trish, who normally looked very business-like, shed off her high heels and tucked her legs under herself on the large couch next to the bookshelf. Max, Kim, Eric, and Brandi were still deliberating what to order, as Sarah sat back on the single couch next to Sally and Declan.

Declan spoke first, "So, Sarah is it? What do you do for a living?"

"Yeah, I work at a trail-riding place. I'm the stable manage," Sarah replied, her voice tight.

"Oh, wow. I'd love to ride. I haven't done it in years," Declan hinted, which Sarah ignored.

Eric came to the rescue, "What about you Declan? What do you do?"

Declan tipped his chin, "I work for the local council." He looked back at Sarah, who had gotten up to look over the books in the shelf.

Sarah found one about how to discover your God-given potential and follow your dreams. She turned it over. It was a second-hand book worth ten ZAR. She brought it to her chair and flicked through, while half listening to the conversation. Every now and then she would look up to show that she was still listening.

"What kind of music are you into?" continued Eric.

"Contemporary. But I don't mind some of the golden oldies either," Declan talked with Eric for a while.

Sarah sighed, grateful to be rescued. She felt awkward with the subtle flirting that Declan was aiming her way, particularly since the others didn't seem to approve of Sally's interest in him.

"So, tell me how about you getting attacked by a lion, Sarah? Brandi told us!" Sally started, breaking her from her thoughts.

"I wasn't attacked," corrected Sarah, amused at the term, "It nearly attacked someone else, though. I just knocked it away. I fell off Honor doing it."

Declan and Eric stopped talking and looked at Sarah, wide-eyed.

"What? Tell us!" Eric insisted. "I'm sorry; I didn't even notice you were hurt."

"That's OK. I'm fine now," declared Sarah, feeling like she was about to have to launch into her tale again.

Trish leaned over, "Brandi said something about an angel..."

Brandi, Max, and Kim looked at Sarah grinning. Sarah gave a patient smile.

"Tell them the story, Sarah," Brandi urged.

Sarah nodded, and began to retell the story to all their friends, who all exclaimed and chimed in on how amazing it was.

Trish looked day-dreamy, "You and Brandi lead such romantic, adventurous lives."

Sarah and Brandi shot each other amused glances before breaking into laughter.

"Well, it does include the odd picking up horse poo and other mundane jobs too, you know," teased Brandi.

"Bah!" groaned Trish, "You can keep that. I'll stick with my shoe shop."

They all laughed.

The food came out and everyone tucked in. Declan fitted into the group well enough, taking genuine interest in the lives of others. Sarah tucked the book next to her bag, deciding she would buy it on the way out and that, perhaps, she'd misjudged Declan.

He wasn't so bad; in fact, he was funny, charming, and charismatic, and he was easy on the eye—*very* easy on the eye. He was no Mark, but as the afternoon wore on, Sarah found herself feeling more and more comfortable with him around. As she sat nibbling her lunch, she enjoyed listening to the unusual sound of his Irish accent as he related funny tales from Ireland and Europe, much to the delight of the group, who were laughing until their sides hurt.

Declan had eased back from all the initial attention he had paid Sarah, and she began to feel at ease, thinking that she was no longer in his sights. He was just another Christian, new to this church, trying to find where he fit in. Harmless.

CHAPTER
SIXTEEN

Making up the feeds for the horses that evening, Mark pondered everything he had seen and heard at church that morning. Something spoken during the service kept tugging at his mind. They had said how God speaks to people in many different ways, but people had to be open to listening to him. If Mark spoke to God again, would He answer? Would God help him with these feelings in his heart?

He grimaced as he put several feeds under the tap and added just enough water to mix them. Brandi and Sarah arrived just in time to help Mark, laughing and talking as they leaned down to grab some buckets of feed Mark had finished mixing. They each took them to the individual horses, which were in their stalls for the night, ready for a new week. Mark finished up the last of the feeds, washed his hands and started to sweep out the feed room as the girls whisked the buckets off to their hungry equine charges.

He stopped and watched the women working for a moment, leaning on the broom. Sarah was becoming just as happy and contented as Brandi had ever been, and this made him wonder. Just the other week, she was a constant blubbering mess, dealing with stuff from her past that she refused to tell him about. Now, all of a sudden, she'd moved on.

Nobody changes that fast. He shook his head in wonder. *God, I don't understand what you've done to her.*

Sarah glanced his way, questioningly. Looking away quickly, Mark flicked the broom across the floor, sending the pile of feed dregs and dust out the doorway onto the driveway outside the stables. He stole a second glance Sarah's way as he worked, and saw that she had left. Mark stood up, looking around openly. They must have gone back into the tack room.

He finished his sweeping. A short time later, Brandi and Sarah finished their jobs, laughing and talking as they approached Mark.

"Sarah, could I talk to you for a moment?" Mark inquired as they walked past.

She stopped in her tracks, the same questioning look in her green eyes.

"Sure." She hesitated, and looked to Brandi who waved, indicating that she was going home.

"Night, Brandi." Sarah looked at Brandi, a plea in her face. Mark wondered if she was trying to avoid being alone with him.

"Goeie nag!" Mark waved.

"Night, guys," replied Brandi. "See you tomorrow." And then she was gone.

Mark noted that Sarah seemed very reserved around him. He wished she'd relax. He went and sat down on the bench, wiping his hands on his jeans.

"I went to your church today, Sarah."

Her eyes lit up as she went and joined him on the bench. "You did?"

Mark feigned hurt, "Don't look so shocked! Ja, I went with Koto." He nodded, took a deep breath, and went on, "We were looking for you and the others after church. Where were you sitting?"

Sarah shook her head, appearing amazed that he'd gone to church. What did she take him for? Mark started to wonder if she were really pleased or not. She did seem suddenly more relaxed around him. Mark tilted his head, not sure how to read her.

"That's great that you went with Koto! We left early, to go to lunch. When were you talking to Koto again? When did you organize to go to church? That's so great!" she answered.

Mark shrugged, cautiously moving on, "Last week, I went out to visit them. They invited me to church, and I thought I'd come and check it out."

"And?" pressed Sarah, her eyes sparkling, "What did you

think?"

Mark scratched his head, uncomfortably. "I don't understand a lot of it, but what I do know is that I saw that man out in the Kruger...and I think there's something to this God thing. I heard what happened to you at the bush camp that night." He looked down, suddenly embarrassed.

Sarah tilted her head, a vacant look in her eyes.

Mark elaborated, "I could hear from my tent...you know...when Martha and you were alone at the fire, and you cried."

He looked away, feeling guilty. When she said nothing, he glanced meekly up at her. Hot color had risen to her face. Mark took another deep breath and went on, noticing how Sarah's beauty was heightened by the blushing. Her olive skin seemed to glow with the added color, and her lowered green eyes seemed to be endless deep pools of emerald, under her long dark lashes.

"Annyway," he drawled out, getting himself refocused, "I challenged God. After I heard you, I wanted to know if it was real. I told Him to show Himself to me, in a powerful way. Then the next day, I saw that...angel."

Sarah regarded Mark silently for a long moment. Her eyes were intense in their focus on his, and he shuffled uncomfortably on the bench. Had he said too much? Was she angry at him? He still couldn't read her.

Then something amazing happened. Sarah's whole countenance shifted, and she looked upon him with understanding and compassion even. Before Mark could think on it further, Sarah launched into a full account of what Jesus had done for her. She elaborated on how Jesus had taken away that pain and burden and given her a new life and a new purpose.

"I know He has a special purpose for me. I just don't understand what it is yet. I haven't had any of those dreams for a while. He used to tell me that I have a gift. Everything seems to have slowed down at the moment, and I believe it's because God wants me to spend time getting to know Him before I move on."

Mark sat looking at his feet. With everything she'd just explained about God and Jesus, she still hadn't told him what he really wanted to know.

"You never told me what happened to you in the past. When you were upset last week, I wanted to help you. I was worried about you. You just kept pushing me away."

Throwing him an apologetic smile, Sarah seemed to brush that aside. "It doesn't matter now; it's over. I've moved on."

"But, what about when you got upset at me for mentioning your father? What did he do, Sarah?" Mark insisted.

Sarah sighed and looked out into the distance, as if remembering something.

Mark glanced at her and noticed a single tear roll down her cheek. Looking directly at her now, he noticed her eyes were brimming with tears, threatening to cascade at any second.

Sarah tried to control them, as Mark waited. His heart melted for her. He wanted to wrap her into his arms, but knew she would push him away. He wished that Sarah would allow herself to be comforted by him when she needed it.

She was still trying to be strong in front of him. Whatever her father did, it must have been pretty bad. Mark started to doubt that Sarah would talk about it to him, and he sat back sighing, thinking it was time to leave her be.

"My mum..." Sarah sucked in her breath all of a sudden. Mark held his own, sensing that she was about to open up to him. She shut her eyes tight for a moment, tears escaping onto her boots, before looking up at Mark with clear, watery eyes full of pained memories. "Dad...he..." She breathed in a sharp, shuddering breath.

He saw that it was still too painful for her to talk about. It was killing him, seeing her like this. Throwing caution to the wind, Mark moved closer, slipping his arm around her, and pulling her close. She didn't resist. Mark breathed an almost inconceivable breath of relief. Sarah open her mouth to speak, but Mark stopped her, putting his finger to her lips.

"Shhh..." He squeezed her to him. "You don't have to talk about it if you don't want to."

Warmth flooded his heart as he held her close. He wished he could take away the pain of whatever it was, but he was comforted with the fact that she was allowing him to be part of it.

After a while, Sarah looked at him with both sadness and wonder, and then tilted her head to rest upon his shoulder, allowing tears to fall. Mark was taken back at the unexpected move on her part, but he accepted it. After a moment, Sarah sniffed and wiped her eyes, shifting her weight from him.

Reluctant, he let go of her dainty form and sat back against the wall, savoring the afterglow of that soft interlude. God had somehow helped Sarah to get over the worst pain ever. A pain that still lingered, but not with that resentment and bitterness that she had held onto not that long ago. If Sarah's father had done something unspeakable to her mother then no wonder Sarah was always distant with Mark. He started to understand that she would have carried a deep mistrust of men for a long time.

But now, Sarah wasn't so distant. She was allowing Mark to try to comfort her. She was allowing him to come closer to her. Only God could have done something like that.

"Mark," Sarah said after a while, tearing him from his thoughts, "God can take away all your burdens too, you know."

Mark blinked back his surprise at the sudden revelation, and then looked into the distance, "I don't have any burdens. I'm pretty good. I don't need God's help. I know plenty of other people, though, who do." He thought of Koto and his family in Lebowa. "I don't want to waste God's time when He has more important things to do, like help you with your past." He turned to her seriously.

Sarah looked at Mark, sadness in her luminous eyes. That look broke his heart.

"You think God doesn't have time for you?" she asked, tilting her head to peer into his eyes.

Looking away with disdain, Mark quavered.

"I know He doesn't. I can look after myself. I always have." Mark set his jaw proudly, trying to mask the look of longing that passed his eyes. He wasn't weak. He had learned to be strong. He couldn't rely on other people, or on some God.

As if guided by some unseen force, Sarah continued on

relentless, "What about your family? What does your dad do for a living?"

A muscle jerked in Mark's jaw. "He's an ambulance officer. A paramedic," he replied, with an edge of bitterness. "He's always out saving other people's lives."

"How do you feel about that?" Sarah asked.

Mark gripped the bench he was sitting on, and stared out into the deepening colors of the evening. What did that have to do with anything? A deep weariness began to wash over him.

"Honestly," Sarah urged.

"Why do you want to know? What does this have to do with anything?"

"Trust me, it does!" urged Sarah, convincingly.

Mark squirmed with discomfort, not liking the turn the conversation had taken. It was nice, however, that it was Sarah there and not someone else, like Brandi...or his mum.

He wanted to change the subject, move to safer grounds, but he sensed that Sarah would keep pursuing it tonight for some reason. *Should he bail and go home?* Frowning with indecision, Mark started to peel the old paint from the bench they were sitting on. If he wanted to bail, he would have done so already. Truth was, he didn't want to leave. He was finally getting some answers out of Sarah, finally starting to understand, and finally, getting closer to her.

He took a deep breath. "Dad was always too busy for us," Mark began, struggling to open up. "My little brothers, my sister, and me had to look after ourselves. Mum was always making excuses for him, but it didn't help. Even on days off, he was too tired to spend time with us. I don't feel like he was there when I needed him, so...," Mark paused, exhaling loudly, "we learned to look out for ourselves."

"What about your mum? Surely, she looked after you?" Sarah looked saddened. Did she know what it felt like?

"Mum still looked after us. She's great. But it's not the same thing. We craved dad's attention. We needed a male mentor, not always Mum. Kids need dads! Especially boys!" Mark shook his head bitterly. "Boys need dads," he repeated, his voice fading as he looked away.

Sarah nodded. "There you go, Mark."

"There I go, what?" He looked at her.

"That's your burden. You are resentful that your dad wasn't around for you and your brothers and sister."

"Well, Ja! I have every right to be!"

A flame was ignited in Mark, and his eyes flashed with resentment.

"You know," Sarah murmured, "I never found peace with God until that night at the bush camp."

Mark shook his head. "I'm not like you Sarah. I can't even think about forgiving my dad the way you forgave yours. I don't have your strength."

Sarah at up straighter, raising her voice, "I'm no different from you, Mark. You think it was easy for me to forgive my dad?" She glared at him. "Yours didn't kill your own mother!"

Mark jerked his head up in shock, staring at her. Her eyes burned into his with an intensity he'd not seen in her before.

"I...I'm so sorry," he stammered.

The moment passed, and Sarah relaxed her firm expression.

"It's OK," she sighed. "God was the one to give me the strength to forgive him." She looked Mark in the eye again. "He can do it for you, too."

Mark led his eyes wander toward the wooden floorboards of the shed, resting his elbows on his knees, deep in thought.

"I suppose..."

"He could do it now, even," she pressured.

Mark looked her in the eye again.

"I don't really feel like talking about family anymore." He shifted on the bench, feeling queasy in his stomach after hearing about Sarah's father.

He watched as she clamped her lips together, somewhat dejectedly. He felt drained right now. He didn't mean to put her off; he just wasn't ready for this.

She put her hand on his shoulder and hefted herself to her feet, leaning on him. Mark grunted in jest as she pressed against him. At least she wasn't putting more distance between them.

Reaching out, he caught her by the elbow. She stopped and looked down at him. Her skin felt warm to the touch, and he thought he saw her shudder.

Mark stood and faced her, looking deep into her eyes. His hand lingered on her soft skin, sudden passion rising up. Sarah blinked, her green eyes staring at him defiantly under her thick eyelashes, almost daring him to take another step.

His gaze fell upon her soft features and perfectly shaped lips. He took a step closer to her, his breath brushing her face. Sarah blushed and Mark was once more swept away by her beauty. He was close enough to kiss her. All he had to do was...

His thoughts were cut off as she looked away, taking a step backward. The moment was suddenly gone.

"So, are you going to come back to church?" Sarah asked, sounding breathless.

Mark cocked his head to one side, disappointed at the emotional distance that Sarah had just put between them, but also aware of the effect he'd just had.

"I'm not sure. I'm still searching for answers."

Sarah nodded, then added, "Hey, thanks for the talk."

"Hmm?" Mark raised an eyebrow.

Sarah tipped her chin up, "I know how hard it is for men to talk about some things. I feel honored that you shared with me."

Feeling the warmth return to him again, Mark smiled. Her words were formal, but offered hope. She reached out and squeezed his arm.

"Well, we've got work in the morning. Goodnight," she said, her voice soft, as she turned to slip back to her rondavel.

Mark watched her leave, her dainty silhouette alluring as she stepped out into the moonlight, his breath caught in his throat.

Sarah rushed back to her rondavel and shut the door behind her. She tried to slow her heavy breathing. If they'd lingered any longer in the stable, Sarah was sure he would have tried to kiss her. She didn't know what she thought about that, but she knew that she still wasn't interested in any romantic relationships.

She touched her fingertips to her lips, feeling a gush rise in her chest. No, she couldn't think about it. She had to shove aside the strange feelings that he instilled in her. Getting involved with a colleague would not work; it would become too complicated. Sarah was still trying to get used to her new faith in God, and anything else at the moment would be an unwelcome distraction.

She went and fixed herself some leftovers for dinner and, plonking on her couch, flicked on the TV. She tried to focus on a natural horsemanship training video that was still in the player from an earlier viewing. Sarah sighed; the video wasn't sinking in. All she could think about was the way Mark had looked at her. The feeling of his arms around her. The electricity that seemed to buzz inside her from the moment he grabbed her elbow.

CHAPTER
SEVENTEEN

The beginning of the week rolled in as usual at Brennan's Safari Trails, with rides booked up for the whole week. Sarah was back in the saddle, riding the trails with Mark, Brandi, Piet and the other staff. They had large groups this week, and all hands were on deck.

Sarah now had Shar integrated into the group, and today Brandi was trying him out, lending out her horse, Jet, for the tourists. Mark was also trying out a new horse, as he strode ahead on the impressive-looking Zulo. Piet and several others rode the old reliable horses, in case a rider needed assistance. Mark was happy to let Piet take the lead for some of the rides so he could work the smooth new Zulo.

Sarah played things safe on Honor for the time being, her back still quite tender. They were on their last ride for the day, and in the heat of the afternoon, Sarah was contemplating swimming Honor in the Brennan's waterhole after work.

Mark loved Zulo so much that he kept joking that he might have found a new horse, and that Sniper would get put on the shelf, much to Sarah's disgust. She didn't like the way some people could so easily dismiss their equine partner for another. Sarah would never give up Honor for anything. However, riding off to the side, Sarah watched Mark and Zulo and conceded to herself that, indeed, he did look like he suited the horse very well. His long, strong legs and well-muscled body complemented the large black quarter horse.

Zulo made Mark look more heroic and masculine, as the horse strode out with new-found poise in the world. It had taken Sarah quite a while to help Zulo gain that confidence, but now he had it, the horse took on a proud and enthusiastic pace, which Mark said was the smoothest he's ever felt.

Sarah's eyes lingered on Mark and Zulo as her thoughts drifted back to the night before. She felt a tingle run up her spine and hot color burn her cheeks. She was blushing again. Annoyed at herself, she turned away.

Sarah glanced over at an experienced older man, who was mounted on Sniper, and felt a stab of sympathy toward the horse. Mark turned, gazing back over his shoulder at the group, his eyes flicking her way. He smirked and patted Zulo on the neck, launching into his talk about the elephant herd they were tracking. He was acting as he always used to, and this annoyed Sarah. What did he feel toward her?

She began to wonder too long about it, before she caught herself. Why did she even care? They were trying to find game.

Earlier, they had come across the herds of plains game and noticed that several had new offspring. With Sarah's new-found freedom in Jesus, she was having new beginnings, too. These newborns represented that for her.

On their way back to Brennan's, the group had stopped under the shade of some baobab trees to watch as a herd of elephants close to the campsite were wading and drinking from the Letaba waterhole.

Sarah tilted her mouth, hoping they hadn't taken out the fence again this time. D-12, this was the herd scheduled for culling by the parks board, thought Sarah with great sadness. The matriarch of the group was a large, old female with massive tusks. She stood in the center of the waterhole, swinging her great ears back and forth trying to keep cool, her trunk idly flicking the water's surface.

Behind the matriarch, the rest of the herd were drinking, squirting water in the air over their backs and each other, stirring up all the mud. Since Mark and Sarah had seen them, which was not that long ago, there had been another calf born. The two calves now circled each other, playing and splashing water and mud all over themselves, trumpeting with glee. The tourists 'ooed' and 'aaahed' and took lots of photos.

Brandi, Mark, Sarah, and Piet watched with pride, and pulling out their water bottles from their saddlebags, took long swigs. They were growing close to this herd and liked to think of them as *their* herd.

The herd would be at this waterhole most days, and was fast becoming the highlight of the safari rides. Sarah looked into the distance over the bushveldt. Far off on the horizon, dark clouds were gathering, and very distant rumbling could be heard.

More summer evening storms. Brennan's welcomed the summer storms, which brought green pastures with them—feed in the paddocks that would help them get through the winter months. Sarah noticed that Mark had seen the clouds too and was smiling to himself. A storm would cool everything down after another hot day. She continued to watch as he took his hat off and wiped the sweat from his forehead.

"Right! We ready then?" Mark suddenly looked directly at her, gathered up his reins and took his position again, toward the front of the group. The tourists had tucked their cameras and water bottles away and were ready to ride home.

"You're not going without us," Mark declared as Sarah tried to slip away, alone. She was riding bareback on a sweaty, unsaddled Honor, later that afternoon, after all the tourists had left Brennan's.

Sarah grinned and stopped to wait for them. Piet had shaken his head and headed home to Romy. Brandi and Mark ditched the new horses they had ridden that day, in favor of their own mounts, Jet and Sniper. They jumped onto their sweaty horses bareback, ripped off their boots, throwing them to the dust in the tack-up area, and rolled up their jeans and jodhpurs. They then rode bareback, back out toward the Brennan's waterhole that Sarah found was empty of dangers and just the perfect size for swimming horses.

They plunged their hot and weary, but eager, horses straight into the cool waters, feeling just like the herd of elephants that were playing further round the bend in their bigger, muddier waterhole on the other side of the fence.

The horses drank deeply. A moment later, Jet pawed and, before Brandi knew it, went down, rolling in the water, sending Brandi sliding into the cool water. Mark and Sarah laughed, and Brandi splashed out toward them.

Mark waded Sniper to the edge of the deepest part of the waterhole, and standing on his horse's back, jumped into the water. He re-emerged moments later, grinning from ear to ear.

Sarah lay along Honor's back, allowing herself to float as Honor swam into a deep area, where her hooves couldn't touch. She began to swim as Sarah took her weight off the horse's back, holding onto Honor's mane. Sarah was dragged along the surface of the water. As Honor found her footing again, Sarah settled back onto the mare's back, and they emerged from the water a dripping mess.

Sarah's work shirt clung to her singlet in a revealing way, and she felt herself blushing again as Mark looked her way. Mark and Brandi remounted their horses, Mark shaking out his thick brown hair like a shaggy dog.

Mark and Brandi donned their broad-brimmed hats, which were floating atop the water, and they all meandered out of the waters, refreshed and satisfied. Finding some soft, dry grass in the shade, they slid off their horses, finding trees to tie them under. Plonking back down onto the grass, they sat back, sighing with contentment.

"Just the ticket on a hot afternoon." Mark lay back on the grass, folding his arms up behind his head and shutting his eyes.

"Do you think we'll get in trouble for not finishing up the jobs yet?" Brandi inquired, starting to worry.

"Probably," laughed Mark, still relaxed and unmoved, "Unless Piet and Solomon beat us to it."

Brandi looked back toward the track leading to the stables as she wrung out her wet hair. "We need to sort out the other horses, though."

Mark didn't move, but responded, "They've got hay and water in their stalls, and they are untacked. They can stay there until we get back, then we'll turn them out into the paddocks."

Brandi nodded, reluctant still. All the talk droned into Sarah's peaceful thoughts. If only she'd managed to escape here on her own, like she usually did.

The chatter simmered down and Sarah began to relax, when she suddenly heard something. She sat up and looked through the trees to their right, pointing. The others followed her gaze.

The new baby elephant calf had pushed its way through the bushes and stood with a stick in its truck, waving it around like a musical conductor.

"Didn't you fix the fence?" Brandi sat up with alarm.

"Ja!" Mark narrowed his eyes. "Did you turn on the electric fence when we all got home?"

The look on Brandi's face gave her away, as Sarah and Mark sighed in union.

"The fence will be down again. They like the green over here," Mark spoke in a quiet tone, as he sat up. "We should clear out now. We have no protection if big mama comes through for her bub."

As one, they turned and looked at their bare horses, saddleless and unarmed.

They sat motionless, watching the calf for a moment. It flapped its huge ears nervously at them and then stomped forward, waving its trunk and giving a defiant trumpet.

Sarah got up and headed for Honor and the other horses. The palomino looked up at her, then back at the calf, her eyes growing wide. Curious, the calf lowered its trunk and came toward Sarah. Abandoning her horse, Sarah watched with intrigue. Mark and Brandi gasped.

"We need to go, *right now!*" Mark insisted. He snuck over and untied both Sniper and Jet from their trees. He led the horses, cautious of his proximity.

"Mount up, girls; we need to get out of here now!" Mark insisted.

He and Brandi mounted up, but Sarah crouched and held out her hand, transfixed by how close the calf was venturing toward her.

"Sarah! What are you doing?" Mark got urgent, backing Sniper into the trees. He could hear the rest of the herd of elephants approaching, and he was worried that they were about to get confronted by overprotective parents for being so close to the calf.

A loud trumpet resounded in the distance. The calf lifted its trunk and called out in reply, snapping Sarah out of her fascination. She was way too close to the herd now. She turned toward Honor, who was standing at the tree.

Sarah stood and turned back toward everyone with uncertainty. A huge crash resounded as the matriarch elephant burst through the mopane trees, right in front of the startled group. Terrified, Sarah fell to the ground covering her head in alarm, expecting to get trampled or gored to death.

"*SARAH!!!*" Mark and Brandi screamed in union.

Jet and Sniper reared and backed up in fright, jolting Mark and Brandi, who almost lost their grips and fell off. Honor reared and pulled, snapping the branch she was tied to. She spun and bolted away from the elephants. Well behind Jet and Sniper in the distance, she stopped and turned, watching on full alert.

The matriarch elephant flapped its ears with aggression at Sarah and raised its trunk, trumpeting, but it didn't charge. Sarah clamped her eyes shut, arms still over her head, as the matriarch let out a thundering angry trumpet again. *Is this the end, Lord? Am I about to die? Please let it be quick!*

She opened one tentative eye when nothing happened. The calf lumbered behind its mother. The matriarch lowered its head to regard the infant with tenderness.

Sarah took the moment as her chance for escape. Standing with extreme caution, she started to back up, step by step. Keeping her eyes on the great elephant, she stopped as the pachyderm turned its ancient eyes toward her, regarding her with a deep intensity. It flapped its ears, back against its head and stood watching Sarah.

Mark and Brandi got control of their horses and started walking them through the trees back to the waterhole, looking over their shoulders toward Sarah.

"Get ready, Sarah. You may need to run," Mark kept his voice low and clear. "Ready...*now!*"

Sarah looked back at Mark, then at the elephant and hesitated. The matriarch lowered her trunk and great head, letting out a long breath of air. Standing and watching, Sarah got a sudden impression that this elephant wasn't going to attack.

"What are you doing, Sarah? Now's your chance! Get out of there!" Mark's voice was shaking.

"Hang on," Sarah replied in a steady voice, stepping forward. She grabbed a branch of mopane shrub that elephants liked to eat and, breaking it off, offered it to the elephant. The great matriarch elephant regarded the offering for a moment.

"*Sarah!* What the hell are you doing? Get out of there now! That's an order!" Mark's voice became desperate.

Disregarding the warning, Sarah's outstretched arm didn't waver. Time slowed down as the impressive animal stretched out her trunk and gently took the branch, taking it to her mouth and crunching at the plant fibers. Sarah gasped with awe and looked back toward Mark and Brandi to see if they'd seen the exchange.

Only Mark was watching as Brandi was further out in the open with Honor and Jet. His eyes were burning with fury at her audacity. She knew she'd overstepped the boundaries this time.

Taking her time, Sarah edged backward with care, out of harm's way, and made her way back to Mark. Full of awe, she looked at him, expecting him to chide her.

Mark gaped, his face flushing red with both anger and fear. He looked from Sarah to the elephant with urgency.

"Let's go," he growled as she walked up beside Sniper.

They walked out from under the trees into the open, and Sarah called Honor over. The horse trotted over, perturbed. Dismounting with speed, Mark gave Sarah a leg-up before vaulting back upon Sniper. Brandi was down near the waterhole waiting for them as they rode over.

"*Look!*" She pointed behind them.

Mark and Sarah turned around at the same time and sucked in sharp breaths. The whole herd of elephants had emerged from the trees and was following them into Brennan's. They regarded

Sarah with mild curiosity, led by the matriarch.

"Just ignore them and keep riding," Mark directed, turning his gaze forward.

Sarah swallowed and urged Honor forward. The three of them continued along the fence line, hoping to deter the trailing elephants.

"They're still coming..." Brandi informed them, alarm in her voice.

"What do they want?" Sarah wondered, hearing the quaver in her own voice.

"It doesn't matter!" Mark snapped. "We can't have them at Brennan's. "Blast, I wish I had my rifle!" He abruptly stopped, turned, and cantered toward them, shouting.

"Stop! Gaan terug! Get back!" He waved his arms above his head, trying to send them away.

His balk didn't work. An adolescent male threw its ears forward and charged toward Mark, fury in its eyes. Sniper bolted into action, fighting against the bit. For a moment, Mark struggled to remain seated.

Regaining his balance, the horse leapt sideways and rushed into the shrubs, away from the pursuing elephant. Soon enough, the young elephant gave up the chase and Mark checked his horse, spinning Sniper to face up to the fray.

The elephants continued straight past him and kept moving. His eyes widened with alarm. They were heading toward Sarah!

Mark and Sniper jumped sideways again, as another older elephant broke away from the herd and took a swipe at them with its trunk.

To Mark's horror, Sarah turned Honor around to face the herd squarely.

"Forget it, Sarah! They won't listen!" he called anxiously.

She didn't make a move.

"*Sarah!* Get out of there, now!" Mark bellowed in a panic. He'd nearly just been killed for doing the same thing. "Sarah, *NO!*"

She could hear the worry in his voice, but ignoring him, she stared straight at the approaching matriarch. Dropping her reins across Honor's neck, she held up her hands with authority.

"SARAH!?"

Mark's anguished cry was only just distinguishable above the sound of her own heartbeat reverberating in her ears. Sarah jutted her hands forward. "STOP!" she yelled with authority. Without warning, the nearest elephants, led by the matriarch, stopped abruptly, directly in front of Sarah. Mark and Brandi both gaped in disbelief. Sarah had done what Mark could not. The matriarch's great ears flapped forward with annoyance, as she lifted her trunk, trumpeting a warning and shaking her great head.

"Whoahh!" Sarah stayed calm and kept her arms raised. She could sense Mark and Brandi both looking upon her with fear in their eyes. She didn't dare look their way, but kept the matriarch held in her steady gaze, her hands raised.

The elephant let out a long sigh, lowered her gaze, and turned away. The herd copied her lead, and as one big family unit, they all headed back from where they had come.

Sarah sighed with relief, feeling light-headed all of a sudden, and looked at Mark and Brandi, who had appeared silently at her side. Nobody knew what to say, but Mark kept looking at Sarah like he had seen a ghost.

In silence, they began to ride home. It was Sarah who finally broke the silence.

"I'm sorry," she apologized to Mark, as they got safely back into the stable area and were heading for the paddocks to offload their horses.

He was still speechless.

Brandi seemed to pick up on an unspoken cue and was suddenly all business.

"We need to get that hole fixed in the fence and the electrics back up and running. At least the inner fence is turned on and not broken," Brandi piped in as they dismounted.

Mark merely grunted his approval of her words, as he continued to stare at Sarah with trepidation.

"I said I'm sorry!" Sarah repeated insistent. Mark's unwavering appraisal of her was making her feel slightly unnerved. "I did what I had to do. I thought I was going to die!

What more can I say? Mark?" Her eyes began brimming with tears, like the roiling emotions that were accosting her heart.

His eyes only grew bigger.

"Mark?" Sarah was just as shaken as Mark was, and she seemed determined to justify her actions. All of a sudden, Sarah felt as though they were in their own private world, where she was trying to gain his approval. Nothing else seemed to matter. Her emotions began to conflict with themselves. *Why did she want his approval anyway? Why was she doing this to herself?*

Mark shook his head, as if trying to shake a dream. He stared at her, gaping. Sarah saw him move his lips, attempting to speak.

"Who are you?" he managed to gasp after a moment. He ran his tongue over his lips.

"Really? I mean, first the lion...then...that! What was that?!" His voice shook with fear, as he indicated toward the closed inner fence gate. "This God business! It's real, isn't it?" He breathed heavily, wide eyes not straying from hers. "You could have been killed!"

The intense emotion in his eyes tore at her heartstrings. Sarah felt her knees buckling. She gasped as she started to drop, but Mark was instantly there, catching her before she collapsed with emotion. Sarah closed her eyes and buried her face into his shoulder, trembling.

Brandi approached the paddock gate, shooting Mark an approving smile. She led Jet to the paddock, and taking off his bridle, she released him. Sarah hadn't seen the exchange, in fact wouldn't have wanted Brandi to see her how she was now. In his arms.

Flickering open her eyes, Sarah heard Brandi and quickly pulled away from Mark, looking at him with a strange intensity. Trying to salvage some dignity, she lifted her chin.

"I'm a normal person, just like you. I've just found freedom in Jesus, and I am just trying to discover my God-given purposes." She moved back to her horse and released Honor in the paddock, walking away.

Mark did the same with Sniper as he quirked an eyebrow in confusion at Sarah, "Purposes? What purposes?"

Back out near the waterhole and broken fence, the elephants settled back to eating the mopane. It grew lush on the Brennan's side of the fence, due to not being kept in check by the elephants.

An old Sotho tribesman sat with his cousin, under the trees. Behind them, an old brown horse was tied to a lone tree. They spoke in hushed voices to each other of the scene that had just taken place before their eyes. Kgomotso had seen something similar happen not that long ago, it had involved the same woman.

His cousin rubbed at the white whiskers jutting from his chin. Whoever she was, she had a greater power in her than even he. Whatever it was that he felt within the girl, he feared it. She was going to be the one.

CHAPTER EIGHTEEN

Sarah and Brandi met with Max and Kim again the next afternoon.

"What if the dream—*the gift*—is an affinity with animals, just like Adam had before the fall of man?" Kim wondered out loud.

"Well, that would make sense," admitted Max, nodding. "After we receive Jesus as our personal Lord and Savior, we are supposed to be able to break the curses that originated with Adam and Eve. Before the fall, their job was to look after the animals. They had a way with them, the animals respected and listened to them."

"But for what purpose would God restore that kind of gift to Sarah now?" Brandi queried.

"To save the elephants from this next cull," Sarah explained. "Maybe I am to be leading them over the border to Mozambique. They are endangered there; they'd be welcomed. I just need to convince the Parks Board to let me try it." Sarah bubbled with excitement, and Brandi looked at her in alarm.

"What? Like cattle?" Brandi asked.

Sarah's face was ecstatic with the prospect. "Yeah, I'll lead, and others can drive from the back, keep them together. You'd come along wouldn't you, Brandi?"

The younger girl looked at Max and Kim, curious about their opinion.

Max shook his head, "That sounds dangerous! You need to be absolutely sure that God has told you to do something like that, Sarah. Don't just go ahead with it. You need confirmation."

Kim looked at Max, worry lining her face.

Sarah reassured them, in all confidence, "Oh no, I wouldn't

just do it. I would just like to have a look into the possibilities, maybe try to make contact with the elephants again." She tried putting them at ease. "It's OK."

Kim looked at Brandi, and Brandi cut in, "I don't think Mark will let you do that again anytime soon. Neither will I, for that matter! You really scared us back there with those elephants, Sarah. Mark and I thought you were going to get killed. It was way too close for comfort." She looked at Max and Kim to back her up, and they nodded their agreement.

Sarah scoffed in disbelief, "What if this is what God wants me to do? I feel like it's my destiny or something."

The others watched her with uncertainty.

"Maybe it is," admitted Kim, her voice trailing with uncertainty, "but we just want you to be sure that God is in it. We don't want you to get hurt."

"To never risk is to never live." Sarah looked straight into their eyes, daring them to challenge her. "I'm not going to do anything stupid. These things take lots of planning, too. But I've made up my mind, that this is something I want to do."

"But if it's not God's will for you, Sarah, you'll probably die trying." Brandi's eyes went wide with alarm at the thought. "And I would have allowed it."

Sarah considered this for a moment before her mouth slanted sideways. "It's all good, Brandi. Just forget I even mentioned it. If I die, I die. At least I died doing something I believed in."

The younger girl looked at her, dubious.

"Are you going to tell Mark?" Brandi asked on the quiet.

Sarah blew some hair from her eyes. "You really think he'll be in on it? No, he'll hear about it once I've established a relationship with D-12 and we're ready to roll..." she scanned the group, trusting them to keep her secret, "...and when he's ready to hear it."

"Wait!" exclaimed Brandi with stress in her tone, "Did we...ah...you, just decide something? I thought you were just going to look into it first? Not try anything dangerous?"

"Make sure you seek God first. You *must* wait for a clear cut, green flag from Him first!" Max cut in, narrowing his eyes at the aloof expression on Sarah's face.

Sarah picked up her orange juice and sipped it with finality. The conversation was closed.

Brandi looked away with growing consternation. Could she just sit by and let her friend get killed when she could have done something to stop it?

Dust billowed out from under the tires as Mark's car pulled up next to Koto and Lerato's home in the Lebowa village that night. The soft orange glow of various fires flickered off the walls of different thatch huts, as Sotho families cooked their evening meals. Children ran around in the twilight, playing and squealing with delight, as they chased a ball or each other, and every now and then, Mark could hear women calling their children to dinner.

He walked with confidence to the door and was greeted by an anxious Koto and his family, who were eating. Koto came to the door and ushered Mark in, indicating that he should sit on Koto's own seat, while Koto dragged over an old wooden box from the corner.

Mark put his hand up, declining. "I'm fine. I don't feel like sitting," he said, feeling awkward at their hospitality.

Koto shrugged and resumed his seat.

"Did Sarah come with you?" asked Lerato, eyes wide.

"Uh, no. Why? Should she have?" asked Mark, raising an eyebrow.

"Because, she is the talk of the village," Koto continued for his wife. "They are calling her *Phlôfôlô Thapa*, Wild Animal Tamer. They speak of her like she is great Ngaka. We tell them she is not Ngaka. She is God's servant, but..."

Mark kneaded his temple, shutting his eyes, "Whoah. Whoah. What are you talking about? The lion?"

"Yes, yes! First the lion, now the elephants," Lerato explained as she tidied up the empty dishes from Kagiso and Moses, and moved over to a bench to start cleaning up.

203

"The elephants? Don't talk to me about elephants right now." Mark pinched the bridge of his nose, closing his eyes against the oncoming headache he could feel creeping its way up the back of his skull.

Koto touched his shoulder.

"The elephants that broke the fence and spoke with Sarah," Koto clarified.

Mark looked up sharply. "Broke the fence? You mean yesterday? How do you know about that?" Mark sat down on the box, suddenly feeling very weak.

Koto nodded, helping the white man down, as young Kagiso ran through the room crying out, "Elifence! Elifence!" and making Moses laugh. Lerato chided her children in love, leading them away to their sleeping mats. The two children skipped away, laughing.

Mark turned his serious attention back to Koto.

"How do you know about that? Who told you about it? Brandi and Sarah?" Mark tried to work it out.

"No, no. It is going around the village. If Brandi, Sarah or anyone from church told us that, we would never have spread it around. People get the wrong idea. It was the Ngaka, Thabo, and Kgomotso. They say they saw it happen. Sarah had a herd following her and then she stopped them and sent them away with a single command."

Koto dragged his chair closer to Mark and regarded him with curiosity. "Were you there? Did that truly happen?" he asked in a quiet voice to a silent and somber Mark.

Mark nodded, "It did. I can't explain why or what happened...but after the lion business, I don't know what's going on anymore." He dropped his head into his hands, running his fingers through his hair stressfully.

Mark then looked up at Koto, a furrow in his brows, "You say Sarah is God's servant. Does she *really* have some kind of power?"

"Not Sarah. Sarah has no power herself, but as God's servant, she has access to His power. God's power!"

"Ja, she keeps saying that she is no different than anyone

else."

Koto smiled and continued aloud, "Oh, but she is. She has a special gift from God! I wonder what He wants her to do with it."

Mark massaged the pressure points on either side of his temple again, as the headache assailed him with full strength. He sat silent for a moment, wrestling with the thoughts running through his numbed mind. *It must be real! God...must be real after all,* he thought. First God answered him when he challenged Him to show Himself in a powerful way, and Mark saw the angel at the lion incident. He later went to church and got even more confused. But then the elephants...Sarah had something supernatural going on that helped her to do that. No one could do that normally. It didn't make logical sense—she should have been dead!

The only logical explanation was that God was real. *God is real!* Mark let that sink in.

He gradually got his head around that one. *And if God is real, then the stuff that Sarah was saying about Him was also real.* But surely God wouldn't have time to be bothered by him.

"Are you OK?" Koto jolted Mark from his thoughts.

"Ja. I just think...I know...that there is definitely a God out there," he began.

Koto focused on some distant memory and looked out the open door at the brightening stars. "Yes, discovering that is half the battle won for you, Mark."

"But that means...He answered my prayer. He's trying to get my attention." Mark rested his elbows on his knees, looking out the window toward the stars.

"Hmm," Koto confirmed, his voice low.

"But why? What does the God of the Universe want with me?" Mark continued, looking confused.

Koto put a hand on his shoulder, his eyes warm, "Because He loves you, Mark, and He has a purpose for you."

Mark squirmed under Koto's hand, renewed guilt flooding his heart. Guilt over how he'd lived his life. Not giving his parents honor and respect. He felt guilt over his family having a part in the racial segregation that had flooded the nation. Guilt then mingled with pain over his father not being there for him and his siblings. The thought of God loving Mark filled him with discomfort.

"But why would He love...this?" he indicated himself. "Who am I, that God would even notice me?" Mark dropped his head in despair.

Koto grinned, "Because you are his child, too. He is calling you to Himself. All you have to do is accept His gift and ask forgiveness for your sins."

"His gift? Sin?" Mark was not familiar with what Jesus offered when He died on the cross. Mark felt like he was free from sin.

"I don't sin, though. I haven't killed anyone; I'm not *that* bad a person."

"Sin is not just the *really* bad stuff. Have you ever lied? Have you ever felt selfish? What about pride, pride in yourself? Anger?"

"Pride? Pride isn't a bad thing," Mark protested. "How is that sin?"

Koto tilted his mouth, his demeanor patient, "Pride is what made the devil fall from heaven. When we are full of pride, then we cannot accept God's gift to us. We are, in a way, saying that we are better than Him and that we don't need His gifts."

Mark let that sink in. He didn't mean to insinuate to God that he thought he was better than Him, that he knew better than Him.

"I have pride," Mark admitted, dropping his gaze. "So again, what would God want with me if I have sin?"

"He wants to take it away. That's the gift part."

Koto went on to explain to Mark about sin in more depth and how there is nothing we can do to get rid of it. He explained God's gift of salvation through His son Jesus.

Mark hung his head in silence and amazement. Why had he not realized before? Koto and Mark talked long into the night about the things of God, until Mark admitted his need for a Savior and prayed the prayer after Koto, to ask forgiveness, and for Jesus to come into his life. Mark then also spoke with Koto regarding his family. His relationship with his father in particular.

"So, let me get this straight. You're telling me that how I view my father is how I view God?" clarified Mark.

Koto nodded before carrying on, "Yes. You have been calling people 'God-Botherers' because you think God doesn't have time for people...that's because you've found that that was true of your own father. Mark, God is *never* too busy for you."

Mark was amazed at how misinformed he'd been. This also made him angrier at his natural father.

Mark decided that in light of what he'd just discovered, he was not going to let unforgiveness rob him again. He knew that if Sarah could find forgiveness in her heart toward her father with what he had done to her mum, then he should be able to find that same forgiveness toward his family.

He forgave his father out loud in his second formal prayer ever, and also prayed to forgive his grandfather.

"Your grandfather? You did not tell me about him," Koto said.

Mark fumbled his words with embarrassment, "Well," he began, his mouth drying up, "I'm an Afrikaaner...and a white man. We have not treated your people that well. For that, on behalf of my family, I ask your forgiveness."

Koto dropped his gaze, nodding in understanding. He knew those times well. He also knew that people still had prejudices today.

"You have my forgiveness," he replied with no hint of malice. There was a long pause.

Koto lifted his head, looking Mark in the eye, "My family and I are privileged that you count us as friends, Mark." He held out his hand.

Mark's shoulders dropped with relief. "And that, you definitely are," he assured Koto, grasping his hand firmly.

"You still feel guilt, don't you?" Koto asked.

Mark was slow to nod, his brows burrowed.

Koto went on to explain about generational sins. He prayed with Mark to break those curses and to ask forgiveness on behalf of his family.

Later that night, Mark left Lebowa, feeling both as light as a feather and also exhausted from going through so much in such a short time. He still couldn't believe how he had just discussed all his deepest, darkest fears and problems with people he hardly knew, and yet totally trusted.

CHAPTER NINETEEN

"Sarah!" Mark found her and Brandi in the office that morning ready to ride. He slapped the startled women on their shoulders as he gathered up some radios.

"Guess what, you won't be getting troubled by tribesmen anymore!" he said.

Sarah raised an eyebrow at Mark and opened her mouth to speak, but Mark continued, "You are the talk of Lebowa! That Ngaka, a shaman or whoever he is, thinks you're a holy person...another Ngaka more powerful than he. They are very respectful and reverent of you and the wildlife now. "And," he paused, "They know for sure that you are not culling elephants."

"Hmmm," Sarah tilted her head to the side in thought. "Well that's good...I think." She shot him a sarcastic look. "How'd you know all that anyway?"

He tapped the side of his nose like Martha would, and then added, "Also, I've arranged another meeting with the Parks Board on Thursday. Piet's covering the trail with the girls, so we're going early. Oh," he looked at Brandi, "You want to come along, too?"

"No thanks," replied Brandi, "If Johnno doesn't have me riding, I'll pick up those new saddles that he ordered from Phalaborwa on Thursday. Can you believe it? Me spanking new saddles! We must be doing well. Thanks for the offer though, Mark. You guys go ahead."

She then looked at Sarah, "Will you tell them about your idea?"

Sarah was reluctant as she looked at Mark.

He sighed deeply, retrieving the keys to the gun safe from the key cabinet, "I know what you want to do, Sarah..." He stopped, an anguished expression crossing his tanned features, before being replaced with an uncommon calm. "I don't know if I can let you get that close again, though."

Sarah and Brandi blinked with surprise at the lack of angry passion they thought they'd see on display.

"Sarah's been having dreams, Mark. Dreams from God."

Brandi took two of the radios from him, handing Sarah one.

He looked at them one at a time, under his lowered brows and asked, "A God dream?"

"Ja...where she keeps being told she has a gift." Brandi looked at Sarah as if seeking consent to continue.

Pressing her lips together, Sarah stepped toward Mark. "In the dreams, I was leading and subduing wild animals ..." She waited for him to process the information.

"And how long have you been having these, ah, dreams?" He rubbed his chin.

"Almost a month." Sarah lowered her gaze. "I truly believe I'm to muster D-12 across to Mozambique," she murmured.

Mark regarded her a long moment, "Like you told me once before, and I thought you were crazy?"

She nodded in reply. Both girls waited for the imminent attack on the dangerous idea.

Mark tilted his head to one side, handing Sarah her Winchester from the gun safe. "If God told you to do it, I suppose you'd better."

Sarah shook her head insolently, believing he was mocking her and God again.

"Just try and stop me," she challenged, leveling her eyes at him.

Mark stared straight back, neither contempt nor bitterness in his expression. "You be safe!" he warned, turning his gaze away.

Sarah exchanged surprised glances with Brandi before taking a deep breath and lightning up.

"Let's do some work! Who are you riding, Brandi? Jet or Shar?"

"I've got Jet ready. Mark thinks we should try Shar with an experienced tourist today."

Sarah nodded and looked at Mark with approval.

"Sounds good," he said and he gave a tight smile, moving outside.

Mark didn't let on to Brandi and Sarah about his new-found faith in Jesus; he had hoped that they would notice themselves. His reservation against Sarah's dreams and mustering idea didn't go down too well, though, and he felt like he was blowing it. The truth was, God or no God, elephants could still kill, and he couldn't bear the thought of losing Sarah. He had serious doubts about her going near any elephants again.

Rifles, radios, and first aid in hand, the trio left the main building and headed for the horse kraals. Johnno, coffee in hand, watched them from his office window. The corner of his mouth twitched as he thought about Mark organizing the meeting with the Parks Board. He had overheard snippets from their conversation, and it filled him with dread. He needed to talk to Tom again about his oh-so-brilliant plan. So far, it didn't seem to be making a difference, but rather spurring on the girl. They'd have to come up with something else if she couldn't be deterred.

"Oh yeah, I forgot to tell you. Guess who's coming for a trail ride today?" Brandi teased, pushing Sarah's arm as they arrived at the tack-up area.

"Whoah! Watch the rifle! Who's coming?" Sarah laughed, guessing that it was Max, Kim and their other friends, but played the game to humor Brandi.

Brandi laughed at Sarah's pre-empting, "Everyone! And they're bringing Declan."

Sarah nodded, "Nice!"

The thought of Declan with his charming Irish accent and suave ways intruded her mind. She remembered how he'd hinted that he wanted to ride again; she'd ignored it at the time, and now she was thinking it might be fun to teach Declan how to ride.

"What are you smiling about?" Mark asked as he walked past, the last saddle hanging over his arm.

"Oh nothing," Sarah replied, waving it off. "I'll go collect the group from the office this morning. Is that OK?" she asked.

"Sure, no problem," Mark said as he looked at Brandi questioningly.

Brandi shrugged and then chortled, before going over to start girthing up horses, as Sarah jogged up the track toward the offices. Mark shook his head at Brandi and watched Sarah head off.

Sarah returned soon after, laughing and talking with their friends from church. Mark touched his hand to the brim of his hat politely as he saw them approach, the reason for the fuss revealed. It was their church friends coming to ride.

Max came straight over and shook Mark's hand.

"How are you?" he beamed, pleased to see Mark.

Kim appeared at Max's side, looking ready to ride in jodhpurs, chapettes and riding boots. Max was more casual in soft jeans and a soft shirt, looking nervous.

"Good. thanks. How are you both?" Mark said, remembering the last time they'd met.

"Good! Good! Koto tells us that you've been out to visit them more," Max added.

"Ja, I enjoy going out there. I even went to church with them one week."

"So he told me," Kim acknowledged.

Mark shared a laugh with them before Max introduced the Afrikaans man to their other friends Sally, Trish, Eric, and Declan. Brandi and Sarah stood behind the group, ready to ride, as Mark greeted them all and then went through his standard initial safety spiel. He organized who was riding which horse, and Brandi and Sarah began to mount them up after they had fitted their helmets.

Sarah helped Sally onto Shar as she was horse savvy and, thus, the most experienced. Sally looked back over her shoulder at Declan across the shelter, eyes sparkling, as Sarah adjusted her stirrup length. Sarah smirked at her.

"Still chasing after him, huh?" she lowered her voice, a hint of laughter tinkling though.

Sally sighed and looked at Sarah, "Is it that obvious?"

"Just a bit," admitted Sarah, fixing the other stirrup. "Try standing up in those and we'll see how even they are."

Sally complied, "Ja, that's great. I could have done that myself, you know."

"I know. All part of the service," replied Sarah.

"Thanks." Sally leaned over and checked her girth.

Sarah put her hands on her hips, tilting her chin with mock hurt, "And I certainly wouldn't let you go out without checking that!"

"I think I've given up on Declan." Sally ignored Sarah's ruse about the girth and went on.

Sarah looked at her in question, and Sally explained, "He's not interested in me...in fact..."

"Hmm?" Sarah looked up, stopping what she was doing. There was a long pause and Sarah glowered a little at the way Sally looked at her. "What?"

"Oh, it's just that...we all went out for lunch yesterday, you know, the one you couldn't make it to because you and Brandi were working?"

Sarah nodded.

"Well, all Declan did the whole time was ask about you."

"What? Me?" Sarah shot a glance over the kraals toward Declan, who was busy getting mounted on Buster, the tall brown gelding. Mark got him settled and adjusted his stirrups the way they did for every rider.

"Yeah." Sally followed Sarah's gaze and frowned. "Plus, well...that's kind of why we came today. They all decided that we'd come out for a ride for the fun of it and because Declan was asking so much about this place, and about you and Brandi. He wanted to visit."

"Oh." Sarah was both relieved and disappointed at the same time. "So it was more about Brennan's and how Brandi and I work here, huh?"

"Sort of. He *was* asking about you...a lot," Sally said pointedly.

Sarah shrugged and looked over toward Declan again, who

swiveled in his saddle, flashing them a smirk and a thumbs up, as Mark moved on to mounting up Eric. Hot color rose in Sarah's cheeks at his attention.

Sally looked at her with meaning, and Sarah set her face with determination.

"I'm not interested in any relationships," she stated matter-of-factly. "Enjoy the ride today, Sally. I'm glad you all came out. I love spending time with you all," Sarah said with sincerity as she moved over to help Kim, but she felt a discomfort regarding Declan.

They set off on the ride as normal, except that they already knew each other, which made it the more enjoyable. Mark, who only knew Max and Kim, kept more to himself. He treated the ride as normal, going through all his safari guide talks. Sarah and Brandi, on the other hand, were chatting away with everyone in bliss.

They passed through the open gateways leading into Letaba, waving at the other staff members and tradesmen who were working on repairing the broken fence for the second time. With the extra voltage and reinforced steel mesh, Mark doubted the herd would try to bust through a third time. They were smart animals, though. Piet had mentioned that, upon closer inspection, it appeared that they knew to take out the electric fence convertor first.

Leaving the safety of Brennan's behind, Mark led them around the trails of Letaba, searching for the now-elusive herd of elephants, who seemed to avoid them when they were carrying firearms. The day was fine, choruses of birds completing the background noise, and they wound along the bush track.

Brandi noticed that Sarah spent a lot of time riding flank near the center of the group where Declan was riding. On a regular ride, she would flow back and forth along the line, helping people equally. Granted, Sally didn't need any help on Shar; she glided along, perfectly natural on the silky horse. While Kim looked the part, she hadn't really ridden much and needed a bit of attention, which Sarah gave. Eric and Trish were also intermediate riders, needing touching up on their riding.

It was Declan, however, who confused Brandi. When Sarah wasn't looking, he appeared to handle Buster quite well, but then when Sarah appeared, he asked lots of unnecessary questions and appeared helpless. Brandi pondered this as she looked away. He kept feigning ignorance to get Sarah's attention, and Sarah seemed too naive and happy to give it. Brandi narrowed her eyes at the man's audacity. Why would he lie just to get closer to her? Why not be direct?

Mark stopped the ride to point out a white rhinoceros that was resting in the shrubbery. The white rhino was an endangered species and often quite elusive, he explained to the group in hushed tones as his eyes flicked over to Sarah, who was still talking to Declan. He cleared his throat, loud enough to be heard by all, causing Sarah to pause and look up at him sharply. Nodding in irritated gratitude, he then continued his monologue about the rhino, feeling more than put out by her apparent interest in the Irishman.

Sarah blushed and moved Honor up the line toward Max, Kim, and Mark. She touched her hat and gestured toward them, sidling her palomino next to Sniper. Tipping her chin at Mark with apology, she rode beside him, listening as he continued his observations of the rhino.

Despite Declan's charm and good humor, Sarah wanted to be free to catch up with the others, too. When Mark didn't speak to her, she gave him an apologetic look again, and turned and trotted up the line to Brandi. They filed past the rhino to continue down alongside Letaba River.

Sarah spoke to Brandi, "Do you need a break from being the tail rider? I'll sit at the rear for a bit if you want a break. You don't have to teach anyone; they know what they're doing now. Declan might need a bit of coaching, but he'll be alright."

Brandi smirked, "He doesn't need coaching, Sarah..."

They rode side by side for a moment, observing Declan. He did look fine, but then he fumbled again with his reins, flicking a glance over his shoulder at the two girls.

Sarah gave Brandi a sideways glance. "Like I said, he'll get there. Have fun."

Brandi rolled her eyes and rode ahead.

Sarah chatted with Trish and Eric at the back of the trail about God and church and how her journey was coming along. She told them about the book she bought after church at Portico's that week. The book about discovering your God-given potential and following your dreams.

"Could I borrow it after you read it?" asked Trish.

"Sure."

"So, what about Declan?" asked Eric, his voice coy.

"Oh, don't you start too." Sarah's dry reply cut him off. Eric looked hurt.

Sally was three horses up ahead and turned, glancing at Sarah.

"I'm not looking for anything like that..." Sarah repeated, eyeing off Declan, who was sitting tall on the brown gelding.

They stopped soon after for morning tea. Sitting on a grassy rise overlooking the beauty of the lowveldt, the horses tied under the trees, the group sat enjoying each other's company and their pastries and fruit that Sarah and Brandi had packed in insulated lunch bags.

Mark found that he enjoyed Sarah and Brandi's friends. He was itching to share his decision he'd made at Lebowa, but every time he thought of mentioning it, he thought he would sound silly and grew embarrassed.

Along with his nervousness, the Irishman didn't sit well with him. He was flirting with Sarah again, and whether she realized or not, she was responding in a way that made Mark uncomfortable. And just when he felt he was getting somewhere with her. Mark plucked a blade of grass and studied it as the conversations whirled about him.

Max leaned over and nudged Mark on the shoulder, "By the way, welcome to the family, bro."

Mark looked at him, taking a while to register his meaning.

"Thanks," he responded after a while, bewildered that the news of making a choice for Jesus would spread so rapidly.

Sarah and Brandi shot each other looks, and then looked at Mark with amazement.

"You didn't tell us that!" Brandi accused, stealing Sarah's words away.

Sarah stopped gaping and remained quiet and sulky. She'd thought Mark was close enough to her to tell her something like that. She was hurt that he would pursue her, yet neglect to tell her something so important. *Why didn't he tell her ages ago if he cared so much for her?*

Sarah started to wonder whether he really did care. While Sarah still held firm to her decision that she didn't want a romantic relationship, something inside her twanged with pain when Mark failed to tell her this one thing, especially since she'd been aware of his interest in her for so long.

She grimaced and bit into her apple, turning away to listen to another conversation going on next to her. Why was she so upset about it? She contemplated her own feelings toward the man.

Mark caught Sarah's disapproving look and wondered why she made such a face. He thought she'd be happy for him.

She paid him little heed for the rest of the morning tea, turning her attention to the others and their idle talk of music and fashion. Declan sat off the side, listening, but not joining in. When he noticed Sarah starting to observe him, he went quiet and moved away from the group a bit more, turning and looking out over the wilderness in thought, hoping to draw her closer. He heard a rustle of someone approaching from behind and knew she'd taken the bait.

"You're not into fashion?" queried Sarah, a hint of sarcasm touching her tone.

She moved to sit down next to him. She'd just fetched some drinks for everyone and passed the Irishman a can of soda. She glanced back at Mark, hoping to catch his eye and looking for a sign of interest.

She saw a scowl cross his face as she moved over to Declan. *Was he upset with her now? Perhaps he'd moved on, lost interest in her because she took too long. Was he really that shallow?* Sarah felt an aching emptiness in the pit of her stomach as she turned her attention back toward the Irishman.

"Fashion?" he scoffed, "Not really."

"What are you passionate about then?" she probed, tearing her attention further away from Mark.

Declan's eyes turned full onto hers, shining. He looked out on the lowveldt with longing.

"This," he gestured outward with a sweeping motion, "...well, actually, conservation in general." He gushed, ducking his head as he turned red, "Did you know that zebras are getting poached left, right and center in the Kruger, and in other reserves in other countries, too? Zimbabwe is getting hit like something chronic. All for their coats! Rhinos and elephants are not holding out either in those smaller countries. Ivory...white gold. Poaching is still such a huge issue everywhere." He sighed and took a deep breath through his nostrils, drinking in the scent of the land. "It's just such a crime! We can't keep enjoying all this tomorrow if we don't do something about protecting it today."

Sarah looked at him in wonder, her eyes glazing over. *He was speaking her language. Did he know it?*

She followed his gaze over the majesty of the lowveldt and its wildlife. A small herd of impalas wandered through the long grasses, grazing. Sarah pointed as a majestic gemsbok raised its black and white head from grazing. His sharp, straight horns in contrast to the elegant twisted horns of the neighboring impalas, pointed up to the heavens with pride as he began to strut about, dipping his head now and again to graze.

Off to their right, zebras drank from the waterhole, while their peripheral mates stood guard around them, waiting their turns. In the distance, they could see giraffes drinking on the other bank, their front legs spread apart, heads craned down. Under the trees in the distance, Sarah knew that lions would be lazing around, soaking in the warmth from the morning sun.

"I wonder if this is what Eden was like before Adam and Eve were banished," Sarah posed.

"Hmmm," Declan replied deep in thought.

It was a scene of beauty and peace, and one that Sarah also felt a strong urge to protect.

Declan hung his head, smiling. Sarah watched him with a new admiration. She thought about telling him about the elephants, but didn't think it was the time, nor the place.

"You *really* wanted to come out here today, didn't you." Sarah pressed, her voice quiet.

He nodded. "It wasn't just for the wildlife," he paused, seeming unsure whether to go on, "I wanted to see you and Brandi again...well...just you, actually."

Sarah felt herself blush, and looked away.

"I...," he looked behind them at the others, then spoke quietly as he closed the distance between himself and Sarah, leaning in and speaking for only her ears, "was wondering if you wanted to get dinner sometime?"

Embarrassed, Sarah's head shot up, gazing back at the others, wondering if they'd heard. She caught Mark's eye, and he glowered at her, clearing not approving how close the pair were. *He hadn't approved of anything she ever did. What hope did she ever have with Mark?*

Turning away from everything she knew, she crossed the boundary into unfamiliar territory, gazing steadily into Declan's eyes.

"Sure," she answered. "What about Saturday night?"

Declan appeared shocked that she'd agreed, then he broke into a broad smile.

"Great, I'll pick you up at, say, six?"

"Deal," agreed Sarah, looking back at Mark darkly.

She resolved in her heart that she still wasn't planning on getting involved romantically, but she was interested in talking more about her and Declan's shared passion in stopping poaching and culling. Perhaps he could offer some help in her venture, being on the council and all.

Sarah kept gazing back at Mark, hoping for a reason not to go out with Declan. She noticed that Declan was still watching her, his face clouding.

"I'm not cutting anyone's grass here am I?" Declan asked.

Sarah cleared her throat, growing angry that Mark was still ignoring her.

"Not at all. I'm not with anyone. And this is only a dinner, to talk. Nothing else. OK?"

"Sure," Declan conceded, his tone mild.

Despite justifying it to herself, in her heart Sarah felt that it was more than just dinner to Declan and that she was giving the wrong message. A dull ache toward Mark grew in her heart, and she struggled to shut it out. She had to forget him, accept he just didn't want her and move on.

CHAPTER
TWENTY

Mark and Sarah were driving into Phalaborwa for their meeting with the Parks Board. Both feeling heated about things other than elephants, they attempted to discuss and agree on Sarah's ideas for leading the elephants over the border, but to no avail.

"I know you disagree, but I'll have to get out there with the herd and get to know them better before we get set up to do this," Sarah insisted.

Mark didn't like it, but he eventually called a reluctant truce.

"You'll wait until Piet and I are there with rifles to back you up?"

Sarah waved it off, "Of course."

Mark grunted and turned down a small street. He was too distracted to really think about this elephant business, let alone enjoy the fact that he had time alone with Sarah. *What was the point anyway? She made her position quite clear yesterday.*

He was troubled that his new faith seemed to have something to do with Sarah's sudden rejection of him. Just when he thought he'd had a breakthrough with her, she was angry and closed off, refusing to share her feelings, or even talk about God or anything on a personal level. She was keeping everything surface. She wouldn't tell him if he'd done something to upset her. But worst of all was her new interest in the Irishman.

He thought something had changed between him and Sarah. Perhaps he'd been wrong. One thing was sure, though, what he'd discovered in Jesus was important to him, and he was not going to let anyone take that away. Every time he thought about bringing up the subject of his new faith, Sarah would cut him off and continue with her plans for the elephant rescue. At least she was positive about his steps toward helping her with the elephants now, but were his efforts for nothing?

Mark sighed and kept driving, "You'll have to get a formal proposal plan set out for them. But first things first. We'll explain the contact that you've made and what you think could be done."

He pulled into the car park and killed the engine.

Sarah nodded, and looked at Mark. He refused to return her gaze as he stepped out from the car. He didn't open her door for her, but began stalking away toward the stately building.

Setting his face toward the concrete steps, Mark heard her falling into step beside him. Without a word, they walked through the doors of the council building. Mark was feeling somewhat confident and ready to make their proposal to stop the cull.

The lady at the reception ushered them into the boardroom. Sarah paused at the closed doorway, drawing Mark's gaze. She began to play with her hair, hesitating to even open the large wooden door.

"You'll be fine," he said as he leaned toward her, his voice stiff.

Giving a slight nod, Sarah kept tugging at her plait. Mark narrowed his eyes, she was acting strange, and he knew it wasn't just because of the meeting.

He pulled open the door, and they entered. The room was large, featuring a long board table in the center of the space, surrounded by elegant chairs. They both stood looking around for a moment.

A door at the side opened, and a group of officials entered the room. Mark and Sarah's eyes simultaneously widened with differing reactions when they saw none other than Declan O'Doherty among the group of people, ready to meet them.

They greeted everyone, shaking hands with them all. Mark sat, feeling despondent as he noted Sarah's reaction to Declan's presence.

"You work for the Parks Board?" she breathed lightly.

Mark's heart sank at the way they regarded each other, and he looked down at the table as he heard the shuffling of other people sit.

Declan gave a smug chuckle, "I told you all I worked for the council."

Mark lifted his eyes toward Sarah and jerked his head, indicating that she should sit. Sarah went and took her seat next to Mark, as Declan took his on the other side of the table with the other board directors. Mark eyed the Irishman with consternation.

A man who looked to be in charge asked about her proposal. Sarah took a deep breath and launched into her story about the elephants, and how she had found that she could not only contact, but also influence, an entire herd through the matriarch.

The group of officials said nothing throughout her explanation and proposal, except for a few questions to clarify here and there. Their expressions gave away nothing as to what they thought of her ideas, all except Declan, who wore a broad grin and a sparkle in his eye as he nodded at various points. Mark found him to be very plastic and fake in his enthusiasm for the project, but Sarah didn't seem to notice.

Finally, Sarah was finished. She sat back with relief. Now it was time to await their verdict.

The main officer lowered his eyes, the furrow in his brow very pronounced beneath his shining, balding forehead. He rubbed at his eyes and looked over at the men next to him. One slight man shrugged at his gaze. He looked back at Mark and Sarah and coughed, clearing his throat.

"You'll need more research into this. How do you know that the elephants won't turn away from you halfway to Mozambique? How do you know they won't turn on you? How many people would you require to aid this venture? It could become quite costly..." the man said.

"I would take it all on myself," Sarah explained. "I would find my own men, and supply my own provisions. All I am asking is a delay in the cull. I just want to buy time," she pleaded.

"It would ease up the strain that culling is putting on the tourism industry, and Banhine National Park needs more elephants," Declan suddenly spoke up.

The shiny-headed man turned to look at Declan, nodding in thought.

"Hmmm...If we spared this herd, would twelve months be long enough for you to pull off your project? After twelve months, we would need to cull again." His shrewd eyes penetrated into Sarah and Mark's.

Sarah gave a quick nod. A look of immense excitement lit up her face. She looked at Mark, eyes bright. He wished she'd look at him like that when she was thinking of him.

The officer interrupted Mark's thoughts.

"We'll spare the D-12 herd for now. You have twelve months to see what you can do about it," the man said, looking to the others, who nodded their agreement.

Mark saw Sarah catch Declan's eye, and the Irishman winked at her, smiling broadly. A muscle jerked in Mark's jaw as he tried to control his rising emotions.

They all stood and shook hands again before exiting the room.

"That was intense, huh?" breathed Mark, as they walked outside into the fresh air.

He was trying to draw conversation from his companion, gauge what she was thinking. Was she still going to let him be part of this?

She sighed with relief, looking back at him for a long moment.

"Twelve months." Sarah sounded worried.

To Mark, her features instantly transformed, looking drawn and tired, not like she had moments earlier when she was talking to Declan. He mustered a light-hearted attitude.

"It's fine! You can do it! We'll all help you!" Mark reassured her, hoping she would still let him.

Mark's strained disposition darkened further when Declan jogged out to the car park to meet them. Mark thrust his hands into his jeans pockets, trying not to let his face reflect his mood.

"Thanks for your input in there." Mark pressed his lips into a tight smile.

Declan nodded, appearing to size up Mark.

"That really helped," added Sarah, the tiredness falling away again.

Mark watched her transformation, an emptiness filling the pit of his stomach.

"Well, I'd heard about it, but I didn't know that *you* were the one wanting to liberate the elephants," said Declan to Sarah. "I'm honored to finally meet such a hero." He bowed low to her, and she giggled.

Mark raised an eyebrow, feelings of jealousy and hurt rearing up inside to replace the emptiness. He suddenly felt like a third wheel in the conversation, a spectator to something he wasn't invited to, and he struggled to suppress the feelings it invoked.

Pushing his hands deeper into his jeans, he turned away, watching the traffic passing by.

"So, I'll see you Saturday night at six?" confirmed Declan to Sarah.

Mark spun a look over his shoulder at the other man, and Declan flicked him a smirk.

Without waiting for her answer, Declan waved goodbye and jogged back into the building. Sarah turned toward Mark, guilt in her eyes, but it was too late. Mark had already slipped into the driver's seat, his brows heavily furrowed. Sarah grimaced at his expression, ducking into the passenger seat of the car.

Mark felt like he'd just taken a blow to the stomach. Keeping his eyes set forward, he waited until she was in the vehicle and buckled up. He then pulled out of the driveway, brooding.

They sat in uncomfortable silence for a while as Mark drove out of town toward Brennan's. Mark was lost in his thoughts, and so was Sarah.

"So, he asked you out, I see," Mark ventured.

Sarah offered no more than a quiet nod.

Silence ensued for a long while, before Sarah exhaled loudly, "Mark, I'm not dating him. We share a similar passion; he's into animal conservation and so am I. Knowing now that he is on the Parks Board, well, it could work in our favor."

Mark's jaw tightened as he looked ahead, "Maybe. Or maybe it could work in *his* favor!"

"Are you upset with me?" Sarah looked at him with concern.

The corner of Mark's mouth twisted with the anguish he was

225

trying to hide.

She frowned, "Declan?"

Mark didn't answer, but the blood vessel at his temple pulsed, and she saw his hands grip the steering wheel tighter as he fought against anger.

"Declan hasn't done anything wrong, Mark," Sarah defended. "I agreed to go out to dinner with him. It's not like you...," she stopped herself, touching her fingertips to her lips.

"What? Not like I what?" He looked at her, his defenses rising with his voice.

His intensity seemed to catch her off guard, and she clammed up again.

"Nothing. Forget it." Sarah sighed, and they sat in heated silence again.

"I respect you, Sarah," Mark began, glancing over at her, "And I don't want you to get hurt, by animal or person."

She didn't answer, but tightened her lips. Mark scratched the back of his head with frustration. This was going nowhere. If he kept it up, she'd never speak to him again. Mark decided he was going to drop the conversation.

Sarah interjected into his thoughts again, "I can look after myself, Mark. I am just going to dinner to talk about elephants."

Sarah looked out her window. The conversation was finished, and that was fine with him.

"Evening," Declan flashed his perfect teeth handsomely, as Sarah opened her rondavel door. He took in a sharp intake of breath. "You look lovely."

Sarah blushed and replied, "Thank you!"

She was wearing her soft denim jeans, a flowing, dusky-pink cami top and dress boots. Her black hair, smelling of shampoo and conditioner, fell in soft, blow-dried waves down her shoulders and her makeup was applied with modesty.

Declan's gaze fell in open admiration over Sarah's delicate curves as they walked down the steps. He opened the passenger door to his shining black off-road vehicle, gesturing for her to take a seat within the plush interior. He jogged around to the driver's side and, getting in, inhaled deeply, breathing in Sarah's stunning perfume.

They chatted on the way to Phalaborwa, where Declan had booked a reservation at an expensive restaurant. Sarah found herself loving the sound of his Irish accent, and drank in the attention of his charm and attention, something she wished had come from Mark.

Regretful, Sarah thought about when Mark had offered this sort of attention in the past. All she had done was pushed him aside. She wasn't accustomed to being treated like a princess, and that was how Declan treated her—like she was precious.

She knew that, in the past, Mark would have done likewise. In light of his present mood toward her and his neglect to share important things such as his new faith, she figured she'd missed the boat. Mark wasn't interested in her anymore and maybe never would be.

Sarah resolved not to think of Mark for the rest of the night. If he was so quick to drop her then perhaps he hadn't ever been worth it.

Declan and Sarah arrived and exited the luxurious vehicle, and Declan offered his arm as they moved lightly up the steps into the restaurant. Sarah felt color flush into her face as she shook her head, feeling underdressed for such extravagance.

"I just want to be clear. We're here to discuss animal conservation. This is not a date," she said.

Declan blinked, "As you wish. And so we shall...but in style."

Sarah cocked her head to one side, reluctant, "OK."

She took his arm as they walked through the door.

They ate splendidly that night, talking about almost everything. The initial reservation about overdoing the night fell away as Sarah relaxed. She felt comfortable around Declan, and began to tell him all about her past, her hopes, and her dreams.

In particular, they began to discuss in detail what strategies to use to move the elephants.

Sarah felt relief when they focused on this subject, feeling sure that she would get confronted and quizzed on the night by Brandi and, more to the point, Mark.

Declan offered to come aboard and help with the translocation. He said he had friends that could already ride horses well. Declan just needed more lessons himself from Sarah, and they would all be ready for action.

Sarah wondered about what Brandi had claimed to observe on the trail about him already being a good rider. She dismissed her concerns. She would find out for herself sooner or later.

By the time they got back to Brennan's, Sarah was feeling confident that it was all coming together well. She and Declan made plans for him to ride with her after church on Sunday afternoon. She would start teaching him personally, to get him up to scratch for the translocation.

They sat in the car for a moment, enjoying the silence.

"Thanks, for tonight." Sarah regarded Declan for a moment. "I really appreciated that you were not racing into a relationship or something. It was nice, dinner with a friend," she said.

A feigned look of pain shot across Declan's face, but he quickly covered it up and smiled.

"Well, I'm glad you enjoyed it. But honestly, though, I kind of hoped that perhaps one day we might become more than friends."

Sarah gave him one of those motherly, apologetic looks that you give a child whom you've just said no to. He played along, hanging his head. She lifted his chin with her finger.

"You never know," Sarah surprised him by saying.

Declan's eyes lit up, and he leaned over, giving her a peck on the cheek. Sarah blushed as she stepped out of the vehicle.

"Good night," Declan called after her, before pulling out of Brennan's. She could hear the stylish truck's engine purr, long after it disappeared from view.

Sarah noticed the lights on at both Mark and Brandi's rondavels as she slipped into her own. She didn't want to talk to them at the moment; they would just rip through her for going to dinner with Declan. The last thing she felt like doing was explaining the whole night to the others.

Stopping on her doorstep, she gazed at Brandi's rondavel and saw two silhouettes move across the window in the kitchen. So, Mark was at Brandi's.

Maybe Mark had given up on Sarah for Brandi, Sarah thought despondently as she closed her door. The thought made her feel both regret and betrayal.

Brandi arrived home Saturday night after going to bible study with Max and Kim, and she noticed that Sarah wasn't home yet. She knew that Declan was taking Sarah out for dinner, and she didn't feel comfortable with it at all. Despite Sarah's reassurance that it was going to be related to elephant rescue due to Declan's position on the council with the Parks Board, something did not sit right with Brandi.

Something about Declan didn't quite add up. Brandi was sure that he was lying about his riding ability. But why he was lying, she didn't know. What she worried about more, though, was that he was trying to get closer to Sarah.

Brandi sat in her car for a moment in deep thought. Sighing, she grabbed her knapsack and stepped into the cool night air, locking the car for the night.

The click of a door opening jolted Brandi from her thoughts as she was heading for her rondavel. Mark stepped out from his place and regarded her as he leaned against the wall.

"Not back yet, huh?" Brandi tilted her head toward Sarah's rondavel with the porch light on and dark inside.

Mark shook his head as he thrust his hands into his jeans pockets.

"I'm worried about her, Brandi. I don't trust him. And I don't know why."

Brandi gave him a strange look, "It's not just you, is it?"

"Me?" questioned Mark.

"As in, being over protective...or jealous?" Brandi wondered, her voice sheepish.

She strode over to his rondavel.

"I don't know," he admitted, looking lost.

"She can look after herself, you know."

Mark looked at Brandi sideways, "You're not too convinced about his good intentions either, are you?"

Brandi relented, "She's still a new Christian...like you. She could get easily misled. Something about it all just doesn't feel right."

"You're not making me feel any better here, Brandi," groaned Mark. "But I'm sure she'll be fine," he said, trying to convince himself.

He pulled his hands from his jeans and folded them across this chest, resting one of his feet up on the rail of the balcony.

"Let's just keep an eye on it," Brandi cautioned Mark. "Sarah would trust anyone calling themselves a Christian at the moment. Speaking of which, what happened with you? Are you going to tell the tale?"

Mark hesitated.

"Koppie koffie?" Brandi offered to sweeten the deal.

Mark thought about it a moment.

"Sure, why not," he replied vacantly, looking back over his shoulder toward the driveway.

"You're easily convinced," Brandi chuckled as they walked into Brandi's rondavel for coffee.

Mark shrugged, anything to take his mind off his anxiety.

CHAPTER
TWENTY-ONE

Both a brown horse and a palomino horse cantered across the open lowveldt of the Letaba Reserve, alongside startled giraffes and zebras, as Sarah and Declan whipped through the long grass. Sarah tried a few more tricky maneuvers to test Declan. He handled each turn with ease and agility, and Sarah frowned to herself. He *HAD* lied to her.

They slowed to a trot, and Sarah allowed Declan to catch up and move up beside her and Honor.

"Why did you lie to me about your riding ability?" Sarah accused, her tone hurt.

Declan wiped some moisture from his brow and shrugged as they stopped under the shade of a baobab tree.

He still breathed heavily as he stammered, "I...well..."

Sarah faced him, waiting for his lame excuse.

"The truth...the truth is...that I wanted an excuse to spend more time with you." He blushed and looked away. The color made him look more boyish.

"And Thursday?" Sarah took her feet from the stirrups and stretched her legs.

Declan offered a meek nod, "Uh huh. Same reason. I hoped you would come and ride with me to help me, so I could...see you."

Sarah rolled her eyes and snorted, "You're as bad as Mark, you know?"

She took off her hat and wiped her forehead, fanning her face. As bad as Mark *was* in the past. The thought caused pain, and she pushed it aside.

"Mark? He's interested in you, too?" Declan asked.

Sarah shrugged. She didn't want to talk about Mark with Declan. Putting her hat back on and gathering her reins, she began to trot down to the waterhole, leaving Declan full of questions.

He followed after her, allowing Buster to pick his footing through the water. Buster snorted and pawed at the water as if he wanted to roll. Declan lifted his horse's head, giving him a sharp kick to move on, and up the rise, out of the crossing.

"You're doing well," commended Sarah with sarcasm, dismounting Honor on the grassy bank. Tying Honor to a branch of mopane, she pulled her rifle free and stepped over to the thicker scrub, peering through. "You're a little hard on his mouth, though," she continued, distracted.

Declan shook his head and dismounted Buster, tying him to the same shrub as Honor and throwing himself down on the grass for a rest. He stretched out his legs.

"So...how *do* you feel about Mark?"

"Shhh!" Sarah frowned at his words as she moved deeper into the mopane.

The two horses exhaled and cocked their back hooves up on the tips in a relaxed pose. Declan sighed with relief, taking his cues from the horses, and sat watching Sarah.

"If you won't talk about Mark, at least tell me what you're doing right now," he chided in jest.

In an instant, she had disappeared from his sight and he sat up, somewhat bemused. Sarah pushed aside a branch and emerged into a clearing that had been ravaged by a certain herd: D-12. They were all there, foraging and eating among the mopane trees and scrubs. At least they hadn't broken into Brennan's this time. *The new fence must be working well.*

The elephant calves were growing bigger each day, and getting more and more adventurous. Sarah walked with confidence toward the herd, making plenty of noise and staying out in the open, so they knew she was there.

She had been visiting the herd daily since her initial encounter. True to his word, Mark had allowed her the contact, as long as she was accompanied. Piet, Mark, and Brandi had accompanied her most times, carrying weapons as back-up.

Other times, she'd been allowed to move away from a riding group and they would watch as she approached the herd, re-establishing her new bond with them. The matriarch in particular had taken to Sarah. Having befriended the boss of the clan, the rest followed her lead.

"Hi, babies," Sarah cooed, as she walked with boldness among them, touching a young male on the shoulders.

They all stopped their foraging and looked at her with recognition and quiet acceptance. Even the presence of the rifle no longer alarmed the animals.

"Maggie," Sarah called, her voice gentle.

The matriarch elephant pushed through the herd and stood in front of Sarah. Maggie, as Sarah had named her, had become her favorite in the herd and the one elephant that she had the best communication with. The elephant lowered its majestic head, and Sarah embraced the rough hairy trunk that was etched with years of experience. The elephants' warmth comforted Sarah and, closing her eyes, she savored the moment.

Feeling the great animal shift her weight, Sarah's eyes fluttered open as she heard a bit of commotion off to their right. The herd, who had long since returned to their foraging, stopped as one and looked toward the mopane scrubs. Sarah leaned around Maggie to see the intruder, Declan, trying to claw his way through the bushes into the clearing. He stopped short with wide eyes when he saw Sarah embracing the elephant's trunk.

"Whooah!" he gasped, staying right where he was. He took in the scene with shock and amazement.

Sarah's eyes lit up as she left the matriarch with caution and walked back to Declan.

"I've been spending a lot of time with them," she explained.

"Still, this is so dangerous! What if one of them trampled you by accident? What, what if they turned on you?"

He had never been this close to wild elephants that were alive before, and he kept staring at them in awe.

"They are so aware of where I am that I trust that wouldn't happen. Though, I do keep on my toes."

233

"Apparently...you just had your eyes shut girl!" Declan shook his head and started to back out from the clearing.

Sarah followed him, looking over her shoulder at her elephants.

"So, you *really* are going to be able to do this translocation thing?" Declan looked amazed.

"What? Did you ever doubt it?" Sarah put her hands on her hips.

"Well," admitted Declan rubbing the back of his head, "it did sound a bit far-fetched, but now I've seen this...I don't doubt it." He nodded his approval.

Sarah looked him up and down, not knowing how to take him. He looked awkward before he gave her his most charming smile. Confusion crossed Sarah's face, and she thought of how to fix the problem with his nerves.

"Here, come over here," she beckoned him to follow her back through to the herd.

Taking his hand, she pulled him over to one of the nearby elephants. He pulled his hand away, fear in his eyes. Sarah stopped at the elephant to establish contact. Sarah's face lit up with joy as the elephant lowered its head, fumbling the tip of its trunk over her hand. Sarah broke off some mopane foliage from nearby and held it to the trunk, beckoning the Irishman.

Declan hesitated.

"It's OK. He won't hurt you." Sarah reached out her hand to him as her other hand rested easily on the elephant's face.

The young elephant, content with the branch offering from Sarah, stood chomping away, his eyes half closed, body swaying.

Declan stepped with caution over the tree roots and made his way to the great beast. Movements slow, he reached out. The male inhaled as it finished eating. Declan jumped and recoiled his hand. Sarah urged him on with her eyes as the elephant settled back into a lulling sway, enjoying the sun that baked the mud onto its back. Declan was ginger as he reached out again and connected his hand to the ivory the animal carried. He sighed and ran his fingers down the modest length of the cool tusk. Breathing a sigh of relief and intrigue, Declan looked into Sarah's

234

eyes.

"See?" she whispered. "He won't hurt you."

They spent a moment there in silence before Sarah decided it was time to leave the elephant be. Just like that, she left the Irishman standing helpless.

Glancing back at the male elephant and the rest of the herd, Declan hurried after Sarah, back through the mopane tunnel. Sarah could feel his eyes on her as he followed, and she felt a wave of concern. What kind of desire would rise within him at them being so alone out here in the wilderness? Was she safe with Declan?

Sighing with contentment over the elephants, but also quivering with nervousness, Sarah walked over to Honor. Untangling the reins from the branch, she prepared to mount her horse when she saw that Declan was right there. In a flash, he grasped her by the hand, and pulled her away from Honor and toward himself.

He looked deep into her startled eyes a moment before pulling her closer and pressing his lips against hers. Palms pushing against his chest, she struggled against the rough force for a moment before finally giving in and melting into the most wonderful sensation she'd ever felt. A tingle ran down her spine, as Sarah returned the kiss.

He pulled back and looked into her eyes again, running the back of his finger down her soft cheek. Caught off guard, Sarah blushed and looked down. She'd never been with a man before, and it all felt so strange, yet wonderful at the same time. The intimacy of the moment felt askew, however, in light of the fact that she barely knew the man.

"You really think that much of me?" she breathed quietly, fumbling for the right words.

Declan took hold of her hands, "Ever since I laid eyes on you at church." His Irish accent melted her heart once more, and Sarah found herself sighing and melting into his embrace once again.

She laid her head against his shoulder. It felt so good, but something didn't sit right in her spirit.

Her heart was thumping hard against her chest. *Oh, Lord, this is not what I wanted. Why does it feel good and so wrong at the same time?*

She let go of him and stumbled backward.

"We should get back," she said as she moved back to her horse and touched Honor on the neck, preparing to mount up again.

Declan smiled and went over to get Buster.

Mark strode with purpose toward Sarah, as she watched Declan's black off-road truck drive off, down the road from Brennan's. She looked at Mark with consternation, heat flushing up her neck with the remembered interlude with Declan, moments before.

"This is an intervention," he stated, his voice flat as he tried to hide his agitation.

"What?" Sarah furrowed her brow. She didn't want him to grill her about Declan, not now. Not after what had just occurred. "Can this wait, Mark? I've got stuff to do. Don't you have anything better to do on your day off?"

Mark shook his head, "No. Brandi and I are worried, and I need to talk to you about it now."

Sarah flinched, thinking of the kiss again. Would they see it in her face?

Irritated, she followed him down to the horse tack-up area, where he ushered her to sit at the lunch tables, under the trees. After they both settled, she waited, expecting the onslaught. Mark hesitated under her daring scrutiny.

"Wait! Let me guess? Declan?" she started the conversation for him, folding her arms across her chest. Swiftly, her guilt was being replaced by anger.

"Firstly, you can stop being so angry at me. I just need to voice our concern," Mark said, not understanding her sudden hostility.

"'*Our*'? What, so now you and Brandi are conspiring against me? What else don't I know about, Mark?"

"Sarah! What's gotten into you? Why are you so defensive?" Mark was exasperated.

Sarah erected her emotional walls. Nothing he could say or do was going to penetrate them.

A fearful expression crossed Mark's features.

"Did something just happen to you?" he changed tactics, growing more and more worried about what Sarah's behavior meant.

She didn't answer.

"Did Declan do something to you?" strained Mark, his voice rising.

Sarah shook her head and left the lunch table, wounded, as she stepped out onto the lush lawn. Mark slipped from his seat and chased her down, stopping in front of her and grasping her by the shoulders. He tried to look into her averted eyes. Sarah could feel her face flush red. She wouldn't look him in the eye.

"What did he do?" Mark demanded.

Sarah thought she heard a note of panic in his voice.

Sarah reached up, shoving his hands off her shoulders in frustration, "I know what you're going to say: 'Watch out for Declan! Don't trust him! He lied about his riding.'" She continued on, "Declan lied about his riding because he wanted to get to know me better and couldn't think of a better way. He's shy. He's also caring, considerate, and wonderful. Declan is going to help me with the elephant translocation! He believes in me! He doesn't get angry at me..."

She stopped at the wretched look on Mark's face, which tore through her heart.

When he did managed to speak, he was hoarse with emotion, "You think I wasn't going to help you? That I didn't believe in you? You'd rather some guy who you just met, a guy who doesn't even know you like I do..."

Mark stuttered, not able to finish his sentence, his heart was shattered. He drew back from her and looked away.

"Mark, I didn't mean..." Sarah began, guilt welling up in her along with bitter tears.

She reached out to touch him, but he stopped her.

"No. Just don't," Mark said and held his hand up, silencing her, the grief constricting his heart almost unbearably. "If you'd rather do the translocation with Declan and his cronies, then fine. Do it. I'll hold down the fort back here."

Mark couldn't look at her. In his heart, he knew now for sure that she didn't want him, she never had. He would just have to face the facts and move on.

He stood up, looking tired and withdrawn across his strong tanned features.

"Mark..." Sarah implored him, the desperation clear in her eyes.

He put his hand up again, closing his eyes to her, "Just leave me alone."

He turned his back, shoulders sagging, and walked home.

Brandi knocked on Sarah's door earlier than usual Tuesday morning.

"Come on Sarah! I'm coming on your dawn ride before work. We'll make sure D-12 isn't near the fence."

The door was ajar, and Sarah emerged with reluctance, as if she was carrying a heavy weight.

"Are you?" Sarah smirked, half-heartedly as she stepped onto her porch, zipping up her chapettes.

In silence, the two women walked down to the stables to get their horses, the light just starting to break through on the horizon of the still-quiet and dark pre-dawn hours.

Cool dew was still falling, and Sarah found that she was damp by the time she stomped onto the loud wooden floorboards just inside the stable complex. Brandi flicked on the halogen lights, which took a few moments to glow into action. Brandi gave Sarah some distance, sensing that something was wrong.

"Did Mark talk to you last night?" Brandi pried bravely, as she opened the tack room.

Sarah sighed dramatically and looked at her, "I half expected this, you know." She glanced sideways at the younger blonde woman.

"What's that?" Brandi quizzed, pulling down her saddle and pad.

"That you and Mark would come at me about Declan. About how he is all wrong and such. Well, I got my point across to Mark," she added with regret.

Brandi went to speak again, but Sarah snapped, "I don't want to talk about it, Brandi! I'm tired. I just don't want to go there."

She sighed emotionally, tears threatening to flood her eyes again.

Brandi came up and put her hand on Sarah's arm with sympathy, "I know Declan is easy on the eye," she began in a soft voice.

"No, please, Brandi," Sarah said as sat on the bench and put her face in her hands.

Brandi left her a moment, getting their bridles out. She soon rejoined Sarah on the bench, determined to say her piece.

"Please just hear me out, Sarah."

Sarah raised her eyes to meet Brandi's, her face red.

"There is something that Mark and I see, that we don't think you've noticed."

"There it is again," groaned Sarah.

"What?"

"You and Mark! What's going on between you two anyway?" Sarah shot her a hurt look.

Brandi regarded the slightly older woman with shock, "You think there is something going on between Mark and me? What's going on is that we're worried about you. We noticed something in Declan. Haven't you?"

"What have you noticed?" Sarah raised an eyebrow, reluctant to hear it.

Brandi grimaced, and Sarah shook her head and said, "You don't know, do you?"

"I'm not sure. Something just doesn't sit right. We don't trust him," Brandi replied.

"He's from the Parks Board, what's not to trust?" asked

Sarah, pushing aside her own feelings of doubt.

"It's not that. It's something else. Like he's shifty under his charisma," Brandi said as she rubbed her hands together and got up, grabbing her grooming bag.

Sarah shook her head again, incredulous and just laughed it off, "You're just jealous!"

"Not at all," Brandi tilted her lips, a hurt expression filling her face. "Just promise me you'll be careful!"

Sarah wanted to believe that Brandi was sincere in her concern. But Sarah still wondered about Brandi and Mark, and it filled her with discomfort.

"That's fine," Sarah said, trying to lighten up. "You'll be coming on the translocation too, anyway. I'll work it out with Johnno that you can get the time off. We'll pass the bush camp and you can meet Jacob and Martha. And if you're right about your fears, you'll be there to point them out to me, keep me out of trouble."

"I will?" Brandi shrank back, with apprehension, "Wouldn't it be better for Mark to go?"

"He doesn't want to go, he made that perfectly clear to me. He needs to run the trails here anyway."

Sarah thought about the look on Mark's face yesterday afternoon and tried to shake the vision away. She really did care about him, but he had upset her, and he was wrong about Declan.

CHAPTER TWENTY-TWO

Sarah could feel her pulse race as she clutched the receiver to her ear. The park ranger from Mozambique was quite an amiable man who was just as excited as Sarah about the upcoming translocation proposal.

"That's great, Sarah! Well, you let us know when you set out and we'll be on radio, channel 10, once you cross the border. We'll have some people there to meet you, too."

"No worries. I'll give you the dates once I've set up my supplies and men," proposed Sarah as she began to pace the office floor as far as the phone cord would allow.

"Sounds good. Are you sure it'll work?"

"Absolutely. Tried and tested." Her face flushed with nerves as she said farewell to the man from Mozambique on the other end of the phone, then hung up the receiver. She looked at Declan and Johnno, who were drinking coffee in the office with her. Her eyes sparkled brilliant green, and it made Declan stare in open admiration.

"They are good to go in Mozambique. We just have to call with the dates, and they'll be ready at the other end. They're very excited; their elephant populations have been dropping rapidly due to poaching."

"Good for you!" Johnno gave her a jovial slap on the back, as he and Declan shared a look.

"It's just a pity that Mark doesn't want to help," Sarah said and looked toward the window, guilt welling in her heart.

Declan looked at her with mock concern, "Ahh, it's all good, Sarah."

He put his arm around her, tipping her chin upward with his

thumb, to look him in the eye.

"If he doesn't want to be part of it, he doesn't want to be part of it. Didn't you say that at one stage he was against it anyway?"

"No, I said that he didn't think anything could be done, so he didn't believe in trying." A slight scowl crossed Sarah's lips.

Johnno glanced at her.

"Sarah, he'll come around. In the meantime, I will need him here. So it may be for the best," Johnno said and looked at Declan with meaning.

Sarah missed the exchange and glanced out the window again, wishing that Mark would change his mind. *Perhaps Mark didn't think that the rescue was worth it after all. Maybe he thought she wasn't worth it either.*

Declan jolted her from her thoughts, "The Parks Board wouldn't give me any men to work with for this. They were pretty upset that I'd asked for time off to help, in fact. I think they believe they'll be culling as usual in twelve months' time. I'll have to take holidays for the translocation. I've lined up lots of help, though. My friends are horse riders, and they have their own mounts."

He turned to Johnno, "Are we able to use your place as a base to get prepared?"

Johnno nodded.

"Great. I'll organize them all to bring their gear and horses here. How many of your horses can you spare, Mr. Brennan?"

Johnno shot him a strange look, "Call me Johnno. You can have six, plus Sarah and Brandi's horses. Take the pack-trained horses, Sarah." He jerked his head at her.

Sarah sat feeling numb, like Declan was taking over the running of this operation. *Whose rescue was this?* She sighed. *It wasn't for her; it was for the elephants. It was God's rescue, not hers.*

She threw a tight smile toward Declan, who was still relaying his ideas to them both. His words fell on deaf ears as Sarah turned away to gaze out the window.

Johnno watched her and stroked his moustache in thought.

The door opened in the office, causing Johnno and Declan to

look up suddenly. Sarah followed their gaze, seeing Mark standing politely at the doorway. Her eyes lit up, until she heard his still, formal tone.

"Ahh...just wondering if I'm right to steal Sarah back for work? The group is here and ready to go," Mark's eyes flicked onto Sarah and he gave her an urgent look, beckoning her to come.

"Sure. We're finished here now, aren't we?" Johnno said as he looked at Declan and Sarah.

She gave a quick nod, turning to Declan, "I have to work."

"I'll see you later on, babe!" Declan winked at her, before casting Mark a dark look.

Feeling somewhat violated, Sarah walked out the door past them both. *Men! Why did she bother?*

Sarah didn't look at Mark as they walked back to the tack-up area. She heard him sigh beside her, but he didn't offer any other words. Sarah felt sick to the stomach over the change in him.

"Honor's ready for you," he said finally, his tone formal.

"Could you get the riders?" he asked and turned away.

"Thanks, and sure," she murmured turning in the opposite direction to get the tourists. She couldn't bear to look back and see if he was watching her.

The big day was fast approaching, and Sarah had met the people Declan was bringing on the ride and had tested their riding abilities on Brennan horses. She did it according to protocol, knowing that it was her operation. They were bringing their own mounts, so it didn't matter. Whatever they did was at their own risk. Still, she was pleased to know within herself that they wouldn't be useless to have on the rescue. Her main misgiving involved how scruffy a bunch of people were that Declan had rustled up.

As things were getting organized, Brandi felt both dread and excitement rising within her. *What if it didn't work? What if something went wrong? Those men...*

She sighed deeply, looking towards the sky as she drank in a shuddering breath. *Trust in God! Trust in God. At least I'm going to finally meet Jacob and Martha! And Sarah was doing it! She was saving the elephants like she'd dreamed.*

Mark became more and more moody as the day got closer. More than anything, he wanted to apologize and offer to help, but his old friend, pride, had raised its ugly head again, and he struggled to even speak to Sarah regarding the rescue. She wouldn't want him along anyway; now she had Declan helping run the show. Mark kept his conversations with Sarah professional and shallow. Sarah struggled with Mark's distance and moodiness as they worked together.

She was growing weary of Declan's constant presence and interference with the rescue plans. It was her operation, not his. He said he loved her, but Sarah started to feel uncomfortable with his affection, his clinginess. It was too forced upon her. She couldn't honestly say that she loved him back. She'd just liked the affection and attention. Now, she found that it wasn't what she wanted at all, and she made every excuse to be too busy to get alone with Declan.

With Mark giving her the silent treatment, Sarah found herself relying upon Brandi to help her to get last-minute preparations ready.

"Are you going to tell Declan?" Brandi blurted out one day.

"Tell him what?" Sarah frowned at Brandi's cryptic question.

"That you don't like him like that," insisted Brandi, looking over her shoulder to make sure Declan wasn't around.

"How'd you know that I had a change of heart?" Sarah smirked at her perception.

"I can tell by your expressions, your body language, how you talk to him and about him. He's taking it too far. You said that you told him where you stood right at the beginning, and he's walked all over that."

Sarah sighed, "I need him. I need him to help with this rescue. I'm afraid he'll bail out and take his friends with him. But you're right. I let him kiss me once, and now he acts like he owns me, and my dreams."

"So, you're going to use him? Lead him on?" Brandi queried, her tone carrying an element of disbelief. One look at Sarah's dull expression, told Brandi everything she suspected.

"Sarah!"

Frowning defensively, Sarah shook her head at Brandi.

"Don't start lecturing me. Of course I don't want to do that. I just don't know what to do." Sarah sighed and went to sit on a nearby tree stump.

Brandi walked over and put her arm around Sarah's shoulders, "Who cares if he bails on you? You have twelve months. And you have friends of your own. Aren't we all your friends? I mean, you haven't been to church for a while, but you have a lot of friends and support there."

Sarah looked up, giving Brandi a warm smile, "I'm sorry...you're right. I should just tell him the truth and deal with the consequences."

She stood up with purpose and marched off to the stables to find Declan.

Brandi bowed her head. *Please, God, help her to know what to do and say.*

Sarah found Declan sitting with a map of Kruger National Park sprawled over his lap, working out the safest routes for a large herd. Sarah rolled her eyes, because they'd had it all worked out before. They were using pre-existing routes. *Mark wouldn't have needed to sit and work it out like this.* Sarah rubbed her sweaty palms together.

"Declan?" she approached quietly.

"Hmmm?" he asked, concentrating on the map.

"Can I talk to you for a minute?" she said as she swallowed, but the lump in her throat refused to budge.

Declan looked up from his map with concern, "You OK, Sar?"

He patted the seat next to him, and she sat, annoyed at everything he did that insinuated that she belonged to him—like calling her pet names. Declan slipped his arm around her waist and pulled her close.

"Nervous, huh? It'll be fine!" He kissed her on the forehead.

She shut her eyes and tried to work out what to say, let alone to find the courage to say it. Being squashed into his shoulder, Sarah spoke in a quavering voice, "I'm ready. I'm excited about the translocation...and I am so grateful to you and your friends. But I need to talk to you about something else..."

"Huh?" Declan blinked.

"I needed to talk about...us." She sat up, looking for his reaction.

"Us?" Declan hesitated, tearing his attention from the map and searching Sarah's face. "Have I done something wrong?"

"Well," she hesitated, and then opened her mouth to speak again.

Before she formed any words, Declan had moved in and covered her mouth with his own warm lips. She felt powerless against his tight grasp. He tilted his head, kissing her deeply. Sarah started to lose herself again in his amazing kiss. *What am I doing?* Shaking herself out of it, she struggled and finally managed to pull away.

"Stop!" she cried.

A wave of frustration flashed across Declan's eyes, before he stopped and studied her face, his face crinkling with hurt.

"I love you, Sarah!" he whispered softly.

It was more than she could handle, and she started to cry, tears slipping down her cheeks and falling in wet patches onto her jeans, unhindered.

"Declan! How can you say that? You don't even know me!"

"Oh, Sarah!" he said as he slipped his hand around the back of her neck, pushing his fingers into the back of her hair and pulling her face into his chest, holding her tight. He set his eyes toward the window.

Sarah heard her heart pounding in her ears. *Why is he so desperate and forceful with me? With this relationship? He's scaring me.*

She tried to pull away again, and he let her.

Sarah swiped at her teary eyes, trying to gather her strength,

"Declan...you're great, but remember our dinner? I told you it was just business. I didn't want a relationship. But now it's just happened, and I don't...I don't think this is going to work."

"Why?" He wiped a fresh tear from her face with the back of his finger, and then took both her hands in his.

She took a deep breath, "I think this is becoming too serious, too soon...and the truth is, I hardly know you." She swallowed hard. "I don't feel the same for you as you feel for me."

"You don't love me?" he queried, pain etching into his handsome face.

Giving a meek nod, Sarah's gaze dropped down to her lap gingerly.

He let go of her hands and looked away.

"I see," he uttered, barely above a whisper.

Sarah felt queasy in her stomach as she continued, "And I understand if you want to pull out of the rescue because of this."

She looked at him, waiting to see what he would do. Would he get angry? Would he storm off?

Declan sat quietly for a long moment.

"Sarah," he began, turning to face her again, "I won't lie and say that I'm not heartbroken, because I am. But as for the elephants, I am not going to stop helping you with this venture. Rescuing these elephants is bigger than you and me. It's for the greater good of conservation and the environment. I always finish what I start. Sarah, I am sticking with you until the end."

She looked at him with amazement, relief filling her heart.

"You'd do that?" she gasped, eyes glistening from fresh tears of joy. It seemed too good to be true. And maybe it was.

"Aiy!" he chuckled.

Sarah's smile was tight, "Thank you, Declan!"

She got up and left the stables with rapid steps. Declan sat watching her go, exhaling slowly as he hung his head in mild sadness. He hadn't really loved the black-haired beauty from Australia. He'd liked her, though. He would miss the feel of her body pressing up against his, the scent of her hair as he kissed it. The taste of her sweet lips.

He sighed and rolled his head, easing the tension in his neck.

She was right about one thing...it was just business. And it was time to refocus his attention on the job at hand. Moving some elephants.

Now that he didn't need to pretend, maybe he'd still get his way with her later, the easy way.

CHAPTER TWENTY-THREE

———◆———

The sun rose that morning, bright and full of promise as Sarah sat on her rise with Honor, praying for safety for the trek. Declan's men had arrived the night before, and they all camped out. Now, they were getting their gear prepared.

Sarah had noticed them polishing their suspicious-looking weapons, boots, and saddles, ready for action. They seemed normal enough, but not the sort of people Sarah would have counted as friends of Declan. He seemed so high flying and sophisticated, and they seemed so...gritty and tough.

She had walked past the group, shaking her head and shrugging. *Oh well, friends come in all shapes and sizes.*

She stopped, flinching at one of the men sitting with legs outstretched in the dirt, his rifle cradled in his arms as he worked on polishing it. She narrowed her eyes as she flicked her fingers toward the box of ammunition next to one of the men.

"You don't need that caliber for this job," she commented, clearly upset.

The man squinted at her, then turned his gaze upon the point seven hundred magnum nitros bullets in the box.

"Wha? These?"

Sarah looked down her nose at the Holland & Holland double-barrel elephant gun cradled between his feet and gave a snort of derision.

"Nice, isn't she? Bought her last year," the man beamed.

A broad Cheshire cat grin spread across his face as he ran his hand down the length of the weapon. He focused on Sarah, revealing a staggered row of unkempt teeth, some black, some missing.

Sarah cocked her head to one side and folded her arms across her chest. The man's name was Mick; he was supposed to be one of Declan's finest choices for the trek because of his wildlife savvy and extraordinary riding skills. To Sarah, he looked like a pirate belonging on a page in history with his oily black hair pulled back in a ponytail with a rubber band and his odorous, rumpled clothes.

Mick continued to grin at Sarah, and she squirmed with discomfort. Huffing at him, she snapped her focus away, scanning the motley crowd of men and their weapons. Among them, she saw that Mick wasn't the only one packing the heavy gear. Several more elephant guns were spotted and some A.K. forty-sevens.

"Why are you all carrying elephant guns? You only need regular hunting rifles!" she demanded with vexation.

Mick patted his shotgun tenderly. "Insurance!" he said and spat on the ground.

"Well, I don't think we'll..." Sarah stopped midsentence when Declan appeared out of nowhere.

He wrapped an arm about her waist, and whisked her away from Mick, looking over his shoulder at the older man.

"Declan! Let me go." Sarah struggled against him with confusion and anger.

He pushed her roughly around the corner of a building, out of earshot of the men.

"They've got elephant guns, Declan! I said that I didn't want..."

The Irishman pushed her back against the wall and covered her mouth with his hand, causing her to knock her head against the wood. He didn't seem to notice or care. A mixture of fury and fear rose in Sarah's eyes. He lingered, pressed up against her, longer than appropriate, and Sarah squirmed, fearful of his strength.

"Shhh, Sarah." He looked back at the dangerous-looking crew, "I know they look, rather...odd." His light-hearted voice only served to enrage the imprisoned girl more.

Reaching up, she reefed his hand from her face, retorting

sharply, "You can say that again! Let me go!" Tears came to her eyes, and her breath came short and rapid, "They look like criminals, Declan. Like poachers! Please, Declan, you're hurting me!"

Declan covered her mouth with his hand again, and Sarah stiffened, her eyes growing wide. *Where is Mark, Piet, Brandi...anyone?*

Declan spoke to her in a slow, deliberate tone like she was a child, "They look like poachers, because they used to be! They work for the Parks Board now. For me!"

Sarah's eyes widened even more, as she pushed his hand away again.

"You said they wouldn't give you any men!" her hushed tone bordered on panic, and he pushed close to her again, but didn't cover her mouth. She could feel his body, rigid like steel, pressing her into the building.

"They're contractors, Sarah." He spoke with beguiling venom. "What better way to catch poachers than by using ex-poachers? They are very good in the saddle, and they are great protection from any unwanted attention."

Sarah stared into his eyes, looking for a sign of trust. Could she trust him? Did she have a choice anymore? She shuddered.

Declan stepped back from her, releasing his grip. Sarah remained stiffened against the wall a moment, afraid he'd pounce on her again. Terrified of what he could possibly be capable of, were they completely alone again.

"Oh," Sarah straightened, unsteadily on her feet and smoothed out her rumpled clothing as Declan stepped further back from her.

He continued to stare at her, a look of frustration and lust, burning in his eyes. Sarah felt sick to her stomach as she moved to the corner of the building and peered back at the group.

"I'm not comfortable with them carrying those weapons, or that weight of ammunition, Declan. They're packed to go on an elephant-hunting spree. Johnno would gladly lend out more of our Winchesters or the R-ones."

She glanced sideways at him, afraid he would attack her

again. He didn't.

Instead, Declan scoffed, "R-ones? NATOs?"

Sarah's face creased seriously, and the Irishman tensed. "You can't be serious!? I already asked Johnno. He said there was no way he would issue out his good rifles...and there's no way I'd carry a NATO!"

Sarah raised an eyebrow, "What about the Parks Board? Wouldn't they lend some weapons?"

Her cocky attitude pushed Declan back to the edge, and ignoring her words, he grasped her shoulders and forcibly turned her to examine the crew. Letting out a slight yelp of shock, she could feel him pressed up against her back, and the feeling left her cold.

"I know they look rough, Sarah, but you can trust them."

She bit her lip, *But can I trust you?* she wondered. She looked over at Mick and the others. A.K. forty-sevens, nitros, elephant guns? Sarah felt a wave of nausea sweep over her.

She felt Declan's hands slowly run up the length of her arms, coming to a rest on her shoulders. Her skin crawled at his touch.

He gently turned her to face him, a strange look in his eyes.

"OK?" he asked, his words soft and deceptively charming again.

"Sure," she was reluctant to agree, struggling to regain control of the situation, "But you are responsible for them. One slip up, and you deal with it."

Declan grinned, and crossed his hand over his heart. "You have my word."

Then, with a patronizing pat on her shoulder, he walked away.

Once out of sight, Sarah's shoulder drooped with relief. She needed this to work. She couldn't tell anyone about what Declan was doing to her. They'd force her to call the whole thing off. One thing was sure though, she had to make sure he couldn't get her alone again.

252

Sarah had dinner with Brandi in her rondavel that night. Sticking with light topics for the evening, they poured over their plans, making sure that they were equipped with enough gear for a long trip.

Declan had popped in at one stage, heard the plans, then opted to leave and spend the time briefing his friends.

Brandi looked odd at Sarah after Declan left the room, "What's wrong, Sarah?"

"Nothing," she answered, a warm smile covering her face.

"How did Declan take the news?" Brandi pressed.

"I don't really want to talk about it," snapped Sarah. Then feeling guilty, continued with, "Sorry, Brandi. It seemed to go well enough." Sarah looked down at her meal to avoid eye contact.

"Are you going to talk to Mark before we head out?" Brandi urged, hopeful.

"Why would I do that?" Sarah looked up.

A small smile played on Brandi's lips, and Sarah felt her face burn.

"Brandi! I've just been with Declan. It was all wrong!" she gasped. "Why are you looking at me like that?"

Brandi chuckled, "Because it's been obvious for a while who you *really* want to impress."

Scowling, Sarah squirmed in her seat, reaching for the bottle of apple juice on the table. She filled her glass and screwed the lid back on the bottle.

"Yeah, well, I've blown my chances now, haven't I? He was the one who turned down dinner tonight. He's giving me the cold shoulder about this, still. Why should I go chasing after him? If he is going to treat me like this, then... He just needs to grow up."

Sarah sloshed her drink down onto the table. Brandi's eyebrows raised in surprise.

"Is he still angry about Declan?" she asked, chewing on some garlic bread.

Sarah twirled some spaghetti on her fork, "I don't know what he's angry about. I think he's just given up on me. I don't know what to do."

"Do you love him?" Brandi tried to avoid eye contact, as she asked the unsuspecting question she'd longed to ask for ages. Her eyes flicked up to see Sarah's reaction.

Sarah sat in silence, twirling her food. She finally looked up at Brandi, tears in her eyes.

Brandi smiled, leaning across the table to grasp Sarah's hand. Sarah didn't need to answer the question, and Brandi let her off the hook.

Sarah wiped her sleeve across her eyes, sniffing as Brandi passed over the tray of garlic bread, "More?" she asked.

Sarah accepted the bread and ripped into a chunk none too delicately as she wiped again at her red-rimmed eyes.

"I can't afford to get emotional now. We need to concentrate on this translocation. I need my wits about me."

Brandi nodded at her friend, "We need to be praying for absolute protection in this, protection for everyone involved."

Sarah nodded her full agreement. Brandi didn't know how right she was.

Sighing, Brandi tipped her chin toward the window, "I still feel unnerved in the pit of my stomach. I don't know what it is, I'm just praying that the Holy Spirit guides us, and helps us through this. I...I don't like the people coming with us very much."

Sarah smiled, trying to hide her own tension.

"I think we can trust Declan," her voice quivered. "He works for the Parks Board. His friends might look rough, but they're not criminals...anymore, that is."

She gathered their plates.

"Desert? I need some chocolate! And coffee! Coffee and chocolate, lots of chocolate," Sarah said.

Brandi didn't know whether to laugh at Sarah's nerves or be worried. She nodded with uncertainty, watching Sarah pass into the kitchen.

"Sure," she replied quietly.

Sarah sat upon her palomino mare, back in her special spot up on the rise. She looked out over the magic colors of the morning in the African lowveldt below and thought about the night before. She was apprehensive. She still wanted to ask Johnno about lending out some Winchesters and leaving the heavy double-barrel shotguns at Brennan's.

The day had arrived, and Declan's friends were saddling up and getting ready back down at Brennan's. Johnno had ventured out to meet everyone and talk about the translocation. There was a general atmosphere of excitement back at camp, which was why Sarah chose to escape to the solitude of her spot, to think and pray.

Up here, alone, Sarah felt sadness that Mark was still upset with her, that he still refused to come along and help on this venture. Surely Johnno could have shut up shop for the week and let him come along with the other staff. Or, at the very least, let Piet and the others run the show. Mark didn't push it, though.

Sarah poured out her heart to God about how she felt about Mark. She repented that she'd not gone about things the right way. She prayed that they would all be safe on the great elephant muster.

Bending Honor's neck to face back down the track, Sarah squeezed the mare to step out toward Brennan's and back to the buzz of the camp.

The sounds of leather snapping into buckles and hooves moving restlessly in the dirt greeted Sarah and Honor as they moved into the tack-up area at Brennan's. The tranquil atmosphere of the kraals was transformed into something akin to chaos. It was full of the bustle of strangers and their horses, preparing for a long ride. The occasional squeal resounded, as one of the other horses met with a Brennan horse that it didn't like.

Brandi was among the crowd, getting the packhorses ready to go. Sarah had organized the inventory for the packs with Brandi earlier that week. Food and water, supplies, spare clothing, first aid equipment, extra rounds of ammunition, radios, and other bits and bobs.

Sarah approached Brandi and the horses to double check that all was secure. Brandi finished tightening a girth and straightened up, looking around the group of gathering men. Sarah sidled up to Brandi, and leaned close.

"Did Mark come out?" she asked on the quiet.

The young woman shook her head, regretfully, "He's in the office."

Sarah glowered. A new feeling was growing against Mark. This time, for not feeling the need to protect the two women from this hungry hoard of ex-criminals. More than that, she was vexed that he was continuing, even at this late hour, to shut her out.

Sarah located Johnno, who was speaking with Declan as he stood stroking Zulo. Declan and Johnno had hit it off quite well, and Johnno had decided to let Declan ride his favorite new horse.

Sarah scowled. He was supposed to be riding Buster. Declan wasn't ready for Zulo. Why was Johnno overriding her decision?

She put on a tight smile and got straight to the point, as she approached the two men.

"Johnno, have we got some spare rifles for these men?" She waved her arm, indicating Declan's motley crew.

Johnno looked at Declan and shook his head, leaning closer to Sarah so Declan's men wouldn't hear.

"Now, Sarah, why on earth would I entrust our expensive firearms to these...?" Johnno replied.

"But they've got..." Sarah began, her stern expression melting into grave concern.

"I know," he shushed her, putting up an uncompromising hand. "But, they won't need to use them. I'm putting my foot down on this one, Sarah. You're already using a lot of my equipment, supplies and money on this little greenie crusade of yours."

Sarah's mouth dropped open, "Is that what you think of this?"

Johnno laughed, slapping her on the back and looking at Declan, who tilted his mouth, seemingly amused.

"See? She takes me too seriously, this one!" Johnno said as he slapped her again, jolting Sarah's mouth shut.

She tensed at him with hurt, and Johnno stopped jibing abruptly, "I was joking Sarah!" He glared back at her seriously, the joviality suddenly cut off, "But, no...you are *NOT* going to take any more Winchesters or NATOs. You and Brandi have yours; that's enough."

She flicked Declan a glance, imploring him to back her up. He merely shrugged at her and turned away.

Johnno jerked his head over at the group, "You two better get going anyway, before that sun gets too high."

Sarah nodded her head and stalked over to the group, who were trying to calm their excited horses.

"Right!" Sarah slapped her hands together officially, trying to shake away her disillusions. She needed focus. She went and stood on a stump, so that everyone could see her, and inhaling a deep breath, she stuck two fingers in her mouth, whistling shrilly. It got their attention.

Taking another breath, she projected her strong Aussie accent toward the men, "First of all, thank you all for coming along to help with the translocation of the D-12 herd. You can count yourselves as part of something big. You will have had the opportunity to help save one of the herds of elephants that are being culled every year in the Kruger. Now, I've been up on the trail this morning and have located the elephants down in the Letaba waterhole again. I know they are protected in Letaba, but they are originally from the Kruger. The Letaba waterhole is their current favorite hangout. We'll head out really quiet, so please try and settle your horses."

She looked over at the men before continuing, they were perched nonchalantly on their jig-joggy, nervous mounts before continuing, "I want most of you to hang back, so that they don't feel trapped. Culling teams will often make a circle, and then close in. We're not going to look like a culling team. Whatever happens, keep your shotguns in their sheaths." She glared at Declan with meaning and he saluted her.

Disconcerted, she went on, "So, Brandi and I will go ahead and get the herd moving by leading them out into the open. Once we have established a good pace, the rest of you can ride along the flanks and rear of the herd—from a distance, please. I don't want them feeling hemmed in."

She looked around the group to let the instructions sink in. Mick was murmuring away to someone next to him, the other man's horse sidestepping with nerves.

"Do you understand?" she questioned, looking hard at Mick, who looked up at her mockingly.

Sarah groaned and continued, "This will be like droving cattle, nice and calm, cool and quiet. No heroics. We'll make camp at the bush camp that Brennan's often uses in our two-day rides. The herd should stay around if I camp out with them. But to be doubly sure they don't wander home, we've organized electric tape as well. Then, on day two, we'll make for the Mozambique border, where there are crews waiting to aid us with the final crossover into their national park. Questions?"

People looked at one another, shrugging, and then shook their heads at Sarah.

She nodded, "OK, if anyone does have questions, Declan, Brandi or I will be here. If you haven't already, let's mount up."

She stepped down from her stump and strode over to Brandi and their horses.

"Ready?" She winked at Brandi, trying to lift their spirits.

Sarah grabbed up Honor's reins and led her away to a clear area, preparing to mount.

"*SARAH!*" some yelled.

Hearing her name, Sarah paused, looking over her shoulder. Her breath caught in her throat as Mark jogged to meet her, breathless. She let Honor's reins fall and turned to face him, heart beating.

He stopped in front of her, glancing over at Declan and then looked into her eyes.

"Please...please be careful! I'm praying," he breathed quietly, letting his eyes scan over Declan's friends.

His eyes settled on Mick the longest, and he frowned deeply, as if trying to recall something.

Sarah followed his gaze and moaned, "I know! Creepy!"

He looked at her and said, "These people! This is all wrong!

Something feels very wrong here. You can still pull out now, you have time."

"What?" demanded Sarah, blinded with emotion. "I knew it! You don't want this to succeed!"

She glanced over her shoulder, as Brandi appeared with them, leading Jet.

"That's not what I mean!" Mark breathed through gritted teeth.

He kept his voice low, and Sarah noted how Declan and Mick had noticed the conversation and were suddenly taking interest.

Sarah shook her head at Mark in disbelief.

"You could still come if you want," blurted out Brandi, causing Sarah to fume even more as she glared at the younger woman.

Johnno and Declan appeared, interrupting their conversation, "Mark, the tourists will be here at eight a.m. That gives these people time to clear out so you can start work."

Johnno put his hand on Mark's shoulder and squeezed it, his grip rough, "You'll be alright for two days. I've only booked small groups. You, Piet and Solomon can handle it." He gave Mark a severe look.

Declan moved up next to Sarah, draping his arm over her shoulders, as he smirked at Mark. Sarah caught the flash in Mark's eyes and tried to shrug off Declan's arm. Johnno cleared his throat and stalked off.

Ignoring Declan's presence, Mark looked from Sarah to Brandi with apology, then back at Sarah, "I didn't think you would want me cramping your style anyway." He shrugged, trying not to look at Declan as he looked into Sarah's eyes.

Her face burned as she looked from Mark to Declan, feeling awkward and uncomfortable.

Giving Mark a final cocky wink, Declan removed his arm and shuffled off to mount Zulo. They all watched the Irishman leave, and Mark's face twisted with pain. Sarah struggled to control her rising emotions. Struggled against begging him to come, if only to protect her from Declan.

No, it wouldn't work. They'd call the translocation off. She had to be brave and see this through. She couldn't let Mark sense her fear of Declan.

Setting her jaw, she kept her emotions in check.

"You know that's not true, Mark. We'd be happy to have you help," Sarah stated, and turned back to mount Honor.

Mark shook his head at her, incredulous.

"Happy? Really? As happy as you and Declan?" he murmured numbly.

His words cut through Sarah's heart, and she shook her head with vigor, tears pricking her eyes. Mark's jaw went slack, and he looked extremely tired. What could she tell him?

"I know you don't understand me, Sarah. I'm not trying to thwart this thing. Just PLEASE be careful." Mark cleared his throat, trying to quell the rising emotions.

Looking to Brandi he added, "Mooi bly! Asseblief sal jy uit kyk vir haar, veral met daai man!"

Brandi looked at Sarah, then over toward Declan.

Sarah was very flustered. With very little understanding of their language, hot color rose in Sarah's face, not appreciating them speaking about her in Afrikaans.

"Brandi?" Mark demanded urgently, requiring an answer.

Sarah caught the tight emotion in his tone.

Brandi was quick to nod, "Natuurlik."

Looking one last time at Sarah, Mark turned and walked away.

Sarah gazed after him in confusion and pain, before turning on Brandi.

"What was that?" she demanded, her voice quivering.

"He's still upset about Declan. He doesn't trust him with you. You didn't tell him, did you?" Brandi asked, incredulous.

"About what?" Sarah stammered, wondering what the pair knew.

"Breaking it off with Declan."

"How could I, with Declan pulling a stunt like that? Besides, when did I get a chance? He's off being Mr. Grumpy all the time," growled Sarah, mounting Honor.

Battling with feelings of regret, Sarah tried to shove her

emotions aside.

"I'm sorry, Brandi. We've got a bigger priority here."

Brandi shook her head at her friend and mounted up Jet. They took to the front of the group and headed off at a steady pace toward the electrified fences that would mark their passing into Letaba Reserve. Once they located the herd, they would be heading onward into the Kruger and beyond.

Johnno waved from the kraals, grinning at Declan, who took up the rear on the magnificent Zulo.

Sarah shook her head and looked at Brandi, "I know he lied about his riding ability, but I'm not sure he can handle Zulo if that horse spooked."

Brandi shrugged, "His choice. They did it behind your back; he can live with the consequences. You're not responsible for his bad choices."

"I know that, Brandi, but I don't want anything slowing us down. I want to keep this herd moving. It's going to be a longer than normal ride. Elephants will slow us all down."

Sarah squinted into the sun; she was getting a headache.

"Hey, it's OK. It'll all be fine," Brandi said, trying to be cheery for Sarah's sake before looking back at the crew behind them.

Sarah saw the spark in Brandi's eyes fade slightly.

"You just keep trying to convince us both, huh?"

They both laughed and settled into their saddles, looking ahead toward the track.

After a while, Brandi ventured a coy glance over at Sarah, "I still can't believe you didn't tell him. It would have changed everything. Still think he's given up on you now?"

Sarah tightened her lips in thought.

"He was really worried about you, Sarah. It was so sweet. You should have told him."

"I know," Sarah snapped.

Brandi looked hurt, the way she had in the past. Sarah scolded herself for reverting to her old ways of thinking. She didn't need to take it out on Brandi. It was her fault.

"I'm sorry, Brandi. I just..."

"It's fine. I just would have felt safer with Mark around too,"

Brandi admitted, looking back toward their companions.

Sarah couldn't agree more. Nodding, she rode, eyes fixed on the upcoming gate.

"I have to keep my mind on the job right now. I believe this is what God gave me—I mean, *us*—to do now. It was in my dreams. Mark or no Mark, the show must go on," Sarah explained.

Smiling bravely, but with an ill feeling in her stomach, Brandi set her eyes ahead on the goal.

"Of course," Brandi murmured. "I'll sort out the gate."

The group slowed down and waited as Brandi unclipped the electricity and opened the large reinforced gates. Then the group all trotted their heated-up horses through into Letaba.

Moving with caution through Letaba, it wasn't long before Brandi and Sarah rounded the track and came upon the great matriarch and her herd of elephants at the waterhole. The great elephant lifted her head, seeing the pair of riders and trumpeted in greeting.

She left the main herd and approached Sarah and Honor without fear. Warmth filled Sarah's eyes and she held her hand out toward the old elephant with the great tusks. Maggie extended her trunk out, undaunted by Honor and Sarah. Honor, who had grown used to this unconventional treatment, lowered her head and flicked her ears back and forth, wondering what Sarah required of her.

Brandi sat upon Jet a few horse-lengths back. It still amazed her to see how Sarah had developed her relationship with this majestic herd.

Maggie and the other elephants stepped back, recoiling in sudden nervousness. Sarah looked over her shoulder and heard the chatter of Declan and his men approaching. They were too close.

Looking back at the withdrawing matriarch and her herd with concern, Sarah picked up her radio, "Declan? You copy?"

"Sure, Sarah. What's up?"

"You and the men are getting too close. The herd is getting nervous because the group is too big. They are moving away. Do you think you guys could move way back at this stage? Over."

Sarah watched the elephants, butterflies in her stomach. *What if this didn't work?* The elephants had stopped and were warily watching from a distance. *What if she couldn't get them to follow her?*

"We'll go back to the gates and wait until you start them moving. Yeah?"

"Sounds good. Wait for me to radio before you move on. Over and out."

Sarah glanced at Brandi, then back at Maggie. She flicked her head, directing them to make a wide birth around the herd. The two girls then rode in silence, flanking the herd at a slow pace until they were on the opposite side, facing toward the track that would take them into the Kruger.

Maggie and her herd turned around to follow Sarah and Brandi.

Sarah stopped and looked back over her shoulder as the Matriarch hesitated.

"Com'on Maggie," she cooed in a soft voice.

The proud matriarch raised its head, and then sauntered after the two girls and their horses. It was working.

The other elephants followed suit, and the herd was now following Sarah's lead. Sarah nodded at Brandi, breathing a huge sigh of relief.

"Let's hope they stay hooked on now." Sarah's voice quivered with nerves.

SARAH'S GIFT

CHAPTER
TWENTY-FOUR

"So, it's all in place then?" Tom's tone was wary over the phone.

Johnno shifted the handset to his other ear and sat back in his leather desk chair, his eyes narrowing.

"Ja. They got away well enough. I don't like it, though. I think she suspects something. She cracked about the guns."

"What makes you think that she suspects something?" Tom grated, an edge to his voice.

"Well, Declan told me that she broke it off with him. So we can't count on that as back up. They're supposed to still be friends, but she was asking lots of questions about the men. Why did you use them? They don't look the part."

Johnno wiped the sweat from his forehead with a soggy handkerchief.

"Just keep it cool, Johnno! You must make certain that the other guy doesn't get wind of it."

"Who? Mark?" Johnno leaned backward and gazed out his window toward the meet-and-greet kraals, where Mark, Piet and Solomon were busy putting people on their horses.

"He'll be too busy. I made sure of it."

"Yes, well, just don't get too overly confident. We must ensure that all possibilities are checked. They are expecting the white stock in a week. So, make sure you're on radio for when they pull the switch. I can send in trucks for clean-up and get it done quickly and cleanly."

Johnno's brows rose.

"What about the Parks Board?" he said.

"What they don't know won't hurt them. Remember, Declan is

the Parks Board. He can tell them anything, and they'll believe him. Hasn't he done that for years for us, so far? He'll just say that the elephants turned savage or something, and it was self-defense."

"It's much cleaner getting the stock from the storehouse than off the field, though," Johnno sighed, reaching across his desk and fiddled with an elephant carving.

Tom was quiet on the other end of the phone for a moment then said, "This is bigger than just the stock off the field, man. We can't have that woman succeed in this translocation. It'll shut us down for good. Not just this herd, but others to come. This is an unwanted doorway she is trying to open!" Tom's voice hit an almost hysterical note.

"Just as long as they don't hurt the girls. I need them for work." Johnno looked out the window again and saw Mark and Solomon leading the trail of eight horses and riders from the property, followed by Piet at the tail.

There was a long silence. Johnno sat up, his tension growing.

"Tom! Don't harm them!"

"I know! I know! I understand what you're saying. There's just no guarantees, though. You can always hire more people. This is more important. I've got to go."

Tom hung up abruptly, leaving Johnno sitting in a cold sweat, grinding his teeth. He'd never agreed to that. He should have gotten out while he still had the chance, but with a flailing business, he'd needed the money to keep afloat. The recent boost of cash advancements had seen Johnno out of some tight spots, but now he wondered if they were just a way of buying his cooperation. Tom depended on him as a powerful ally in keeping an eye out on the reserves for potential threats to their operation and, in return, Johnno received commission in white gold and cash.

Using Declan as a diversion seemed like a great idea at the time, but he was supposed to lure Sarah away from the rescue, not lure her into danger. What had Tom told Declan to do with her? Despite their differences, Johnno was fond of his Aussie employee and his onsite saddler, and he was not willing to simply throw them away.

He put his head in his hands and tugged his hair. What was he going to do? Should he send out Mark after all?

No, he shook his head. He'd have to wait it out and hope for the best. If he got involved against Tom, he'd lose more than just his business.

The sun shone high overhead as the unusual grey mass of elephants crawled across the bushveldt, kicking up an impressive dust cloud. They had long since crossed into the Kruger and were headed in the direction of Olifants River so that they would have plenty of water stops for the horses and the elephants on the way.

Declan wiped the beading sweat away from his upper lip. He looked over at Mick and the others, who were meandering along on their now-calmed horses with boredom, some slugging water down their throats from their flasks. The horses had long since lost their fizz and had settled into the long hot walk. The humidity clung in the air like a wet blanket, and they were all certain that a summer storm would be eminent and almost welcome in the afternoon.

Declan squinted toward the sun with apprehension. The heat was not going to be pleasant. Lowering his gaze, he watched the grey herd ahead move as one slow unit, trudging through the bush. He planned to make the switch before they got to the bush camp for the night. Out in the open, away from civilization, would be the safest move. He'd studied the maps and had decided on the perfect spot.

Most of the Kruger was flat, dry country, covered with dense mopane tree and scrub. According to the map, there was an open section of grassland surrounded by heavy foliage. It was secluded, but open; perfect for an ambush. Once they got over the next few miles, they would cross into the open grasslands, and he could put his plan into action.

Declan thought about the largest beast in the herd with greed. The matriarch. She carried by far the richest load of ivory in the herd, and she was old. She and the herd wouldn't put up too much of a fight after such a long, hot walk, he figured.

Declan smirked over at Mick, and the man nodded, his grin wicked. This heat was starting to take its toll on all of them, but Declan knew it would get worse before it got better, and it would work to their advantage.

His mind kept wandering back to Sarah. He'd ordered his men to keep her alive, if they could, but the bigger priority was the white gold. Declan reasoned that, if she survived the switch, at least he could have a little bit of pleasure with her before the end. The main goal was to stop her venture, and to stop her, and he planned to do it.

Sarah and Brandi took the lonely position at the lead of the herd, but they were grateful and making the most of it. They enjoyed not having the company of Declan and his gritty crew surrounding them and eyeballing them with a flirtatious hunger. They were able to pray together, sing songs that Sarah had learned recently in church and, best of all, talk about what how exciting it was that Brandi would get to meet Jacob and Martha when they reached the bush camp. They also looked forward to the return trip, when they wouldn't have the responsibility of the herd to worry about any more.

Once Sarah had coaxed Maggie, the whole herd had followed her without hesitation. It was a great feat just to get them moving in such a way, and Sarah praised God for such an amazing gift and exciting adventure. She didn't take the responsibility lightly, making sure that the D-12 herd's welfare came at the forefront.

They stopped often in the heat of the day by Olifants River to water the herds and allow the elephants to pick at the foliage. The men often had to hang right back and wait their turn, or go upstream to water their horses. It was a slow and tiresome process, but nobody complained about having cool water to wet down their hot skin. The danger of Nile crocodiles and hippopotami was ever present, and as the lead trackers, Sarah and Brandi needed to keep on their toes, selecting appropriate water stops.

It was getting to be midafternoon when Sarah gave the call that they were to leave Olifants and head off again for their final leg of the day. Next stop: the bush camp.

After relaying the information to Declan and his crew, Sarah put the radio back on her hip and sighed wearily. Gazing toward the sun, which streamed through the trees above in golden dappling on the ground, Sarah released her reins.

Unbuttoning her long-sleeved shirt, she shrugged out of the light pink fabric, revealing her white singlet top. She tied the outer shirt about her waist, before picking up her reins again. Nodding to her friend that they were right to go, she and Brandi headed off again, calling the elephants to follow.

The heat was starting to drag the herd down too, and they hesitated, preferring the cool shady banks of the river to the heat and dust of the trail.

"Maggie!" Sarah cooed in a gentle voice.

The great matriarch regarded her with interest as her trunk stripped a branch of its leaves, folding them into her gaping mouth. Other members of the clan were also browsing the thick mopane, reluctant to leave the small oasis.

"Com'on Maggie!" Sarah repeated, spinning Honor to face the lowveldt beyond.

"Maybe we'll need to wait a bit longer," Brandi suggested.

Sarah sighed, urging Honor away from the herd and out through the thick foliage to face toward the bush camp. Brandi followed her, praying, as she sidled up next to the stricken form of her friend.

"What if we've made a big mistake?" Sarah asked, worried. Her face tightened as she spoke the words out loud, "What if I can't get them to follow any further? If we camp out here tonight, we'll all be in danger and they'll just wander back home."

Unsure of what to say, Brandi offered no advice but pressed her lips together in thought. She prayed.

Unbuttoning her own shirt, Brandi peeled it off and tied it around her waist as Sarah had done earlier. Sarah glanced over at her, a small smile playing at the corner of her mouth as she saw the kitten decal printed on Brandi's black singlet.

After a moment, Brandi spoke in a hush, "What do you believe God asked you to do?"

The smile faded from Sarah's eyes as she stared into the distant bushveldt.

"To move these elephants," she replied without hesitation.

A rustling of branches nearby drew both their heads back toward the herd. Nothing. They weren't coming.

Sarah's countenance fell.

"Well," began Brandi, running her tongue over her dry lips, "if God gave you this task then He will supply all the tools. He will make it happen."

"How?" Sarah shrugged.

Brandi considered the question as she slipped her flask from her hip. Tipping her head back, she upended the remaining contents into her parched throat. She swilled it in her mouth a moment, relishing the feeling of the liquid soaking into her dusty throat. She then swallowed hard, looking into Sarah's eyes.

"It's just a matter of a little faith, I guess," Brandi said and turned to look out at the hot horizon, not looking forward to their next leg either. "We're halfway there, Sarah. Don't give up."

Brandi smiled warily. She slipped the empty flask back into her saddle pack, her expression showing regret.

A crease marred Sarah's soft features, as she looked upon Brandi with despair, "It's easy for you to say when you don't have to be the one getting them to follow..."

A loud crash resounded behind them, like a branch snapping. Startled, Sarah and Brandi spun in their saddles as they heard a rustling sound now, which then turned into more snapping of what they could tell were rather large branches.

Gasping with relief, they saw Maggie bust suddenly through the foliage, followed by several others. They were following! Hope wasn't lost!

Sarah turned to Brandi, apology in her face, "A little faith?"

"A little faith!" Brandi mirrored, laughing with delight.

Declan relayed Sarah's message to the men. Time to move on. In unison they groaned, reluctant as they urged their horses out of the water.

"It's too hot, boss!" one of the men said.

Declan was quick to reprimanded them.

"Shut it!" he snapped. Remember why you're here, men! Keep on your toes. We are about to cross into the lowveldt I mentioned. Once we are in, I will give the signal. You all know what to do."

The men looked at each other, knowing what to do.

Mick spat and put his hand on the hilt of his rifle as he trotted his mount out of the water. His horse paused on the bank, dropping his head and shaking droplets of water everywhere.

Soon enough, the herd that had been weaving through the mopane spilled through the thick bordering shrubs and found themselves surrounded by a pleasant lowveldt of grassland. It beat the prickliness of the thorny scrubland they had just left.

Mick and Declan couldn't contain their nerves as they prepared for the switch. On Declan's nod, Mick started to direct his chosen men to go ahead and flank the herd of elephants from a distance, and overtake Sarah and Brandi, closing around them to stop their retreat. Declan ordered his three men to do the same on the opposite side.

The six set off at an eager canter, clearing a large distance around the herd in no time. Mick and Declan looked at each other, cruel pleasure in their eyes, as the men were lost from sight, hidden among the clouds of dust that the meandering elephants were throwing into the heavy air. Now all they had to do was wait.

It wasn't long before the men returned, breathless, at a trot. Declan face flushed red.

"What's going on? We're going to miss our window!" he

271

shouted.

"Sorry, boss. They sent out a party," one of the men explained.

Declan scowled at Mick, who shook his head.

"It's the bush camp, boss. They sent out people to welcome us in. They say they've even set up an electric fence kraal for the herd. They have dinner cooking, and a pool!"

Declan slapped his reins on Zulo's neck, startling the black quarter horse.

"Damnit, man! Forget the food and pool! Do you think we're doing this for our health?! Keep your mind on the job! You'll miss out on more than food and a pool if we don't get this job done!"

The messenger shrank back at the Irishman's furious explosion.

Mick trotted up next to Zulo and Declan.

"It's not lost. We can wait until tomorrow. There's another spot," he said without a hint of distain.

"We'll bloody well have to wait now, won't we?" growled Declan, loosening his reins again on the black gelding, who was snorting and prancing. The whites of Zulo's eyes flashed in response to Declan's rise in temper.

"Relax, Declan!" Mick said as he caught Declan's eye, his expression turning cold and serious. It was an order. "We can't afford anyone to lose their head, alright!?"

Something in the seasoned man's voice called Declan to reason, and Declan's shoulders relaxed with deliberate control.

"Right," Declan agreed.

The staff from the bush camp drove out in the old bakkies and Land Cruisers to greet the translocation party half way. Escorting the weary travelers, they ushered them through the gates with great ceremony.

Jacob had prepared for their arrival and had set up extensive electric fencing kraals for the elephants, to prevent them from wandering off through the night. This saved the girls from having

272

to set up their flimsy attempts that they had carried on the packhorses. Jacob also informed the girls that his staff had volunteered to stand watch that night, to save Sarah and Brandi from sleeping outside with the elephants.

"You need your strength for this. You can sleep in real beds tonight," Jacob said.

Grateful, the girls dismounted their dusty horses and went to help settle the elephants in the kraals. They made sure that they were settled, and had access to the self-filling water trough. Remounting their horses, the girls then headed for the horse kraals.

Jacob had even thought ahead enough to provide foliage for the elephants to eat, as well as hay for the horses. Sarah was relieved to be able to leave the elephants and horses in good care and to make her way to the bush camp sanctuary and Martha's food.

Brandi rode beside her, dirt and sweat smeared across her beaming face. Sarah noticed her scuffed-up, bare upper arms. The blemishes of dirt were hiding some light scratches from the thorny shrubs they'd passed through.

Sarah glanced down at her own bare arms. Though tanned and glistening with sweat, they also carried the battle marks of the scrubby bushveldt. Sarah's white singlet was stained and carried a fine layer of dust, which turned it a light ochre color. Never mind, she could wash it at Martha's and it would be dried by morning in this heat.

"You wait!" Sarah laughed, enjoying Brandi's look of pleasure at their surroundings. "You think Jacob is great, well Martha's just as lovely. They'll feed us up and we could even go jump in the pool," Sarah explained. She was thrilled that Brandi had gotten to take a trip out here to meet her friends.

Declan, Mick and the men trotted up behind the girls, heading also for the horse kraals. Even from a few meters away, the smell of sweat, dirt, and body odor that extruded from the raucous men was enough to make the girls screw up their noses.

Brandi sighed with delight, "A pool? That should be the first stop."

Sarah nodded her agreement.

Her expression dropped as they slowed at the kraals. Declan's men were dismounting their horses and laughing raucously with each other.

"Of course, the pool may be filled with others tonight," Sarah said.

Following Sarah's line of sight, Brandi shuddered, "Perhaps we shouldn't swim this time, then."

"Unless you want to try and beat them to it. They don't know where it is yet!" Sarah replied.

They shared a laugh.

Sarah slid off Honor and sauntered toward the water trough, her back stiff. She leaned against the fence post, rubbing her tired eyes, as Honor drank deeply. A staff member approached Sarah, offering to attend to her horse. Shaking her head no, Sarah watched as several staff members walked off to attend to other people's horses. She watched with dissatisfaction at how most of Declan's men passed their horses over, slipping their weapons loose and strutting back to the camp common area. Preferring to attend to Honor herself, Sarah shook her head against the sight and went about fussing and settling her horse in for the night.

Brandi did the same with Jet, feeling nervous in a new place and preferring to stick close to Sarah. Sarah approved of her actions. The two women met up again after attending their mounts, and walked tired but happy into the common area to dump their loads and rest their feet.

"Sarah!" Martha rushed over and took both of Sarah's dusty hands in hers. "I'm so proud of you for taking on such a noble task. And this must be Brandi!" she exclaimed and took a blushing Brandi's hands in hers. "Welcome! Welcome! Come and rest yourself. We've heard so much about you." Martha chuckled, as she walked them back to the common area, "But Sarah, you have a rather...erm...unusual team working with you. Where's Mark?"

The joy in Sarah's eyes faded, "Long story." She grimaced. "And one that I'd rather not discuss in front of...these others."

Sighing, she jerked her head toward Declan's men, who were raucous as they headed for the pool.

Brandi pulled a face at the sight of their hairy, unwashed upper bodies as they sauntered past with no shirts on, trying to catch the women's eyes.

"Ugh!" Sarah grimaced.

I hope your pool filter works well, Jacob. She thought better than to voice her thoughts, knowing full well that Martha would scold her for her lack of hospitable thinking.

"Come," Martha picked up on the cues that something was not right and whisked the girls away to her own house, where they could shower, rest and talk in private.

Brandi and Sarah spent the remainder of the evening there. Martha and Jacob had to step out from time to time in order to cater to their other guests, but most of the entertaining of Declan and his men was left up to the bush camp staff. Not that they complained or even seemed to care, but rather, soaked in the luxuries that Jacob and Martha's hospitality offered them.

Sarah, Brandi, Jacob, and Martha talked long into the evening, discussing how the translocation had developed and how Sarah had landed such a rough-looking team.

"I saw the weapons they were packing out there," Jacob said as he narrowed his eyes with concern and walked back into the house at one stage. "Looks like an elephant hunt, not a translocation."

"Don't remind me," Sarah groaned. "That's another thing that set me off yesterday."

Jacob and Martha were concerned about the types of people that were working with Sarah, and although they were a little disappointed in Sarah for her lapse in judgment with Declan, they felt that a God-ordained mission was not going to get thwarted, despite the devil's tricks, and they committed to keep praying during the rescue, even more so than before.

During the night, the group enjoyed each other's company, between Jacob's interim comings and goings to check on the others.

He walked back in at one stage, looking more than worried.

"Sarah..." he said.

"Hmm?" she looked up, seeing his concern.

Jacob cleared his throat, "Declan wants to see you. He's been asking after you all evening. I've been putting him off, but now he is getting more urgent. He wants you to check the elephants with him."

Jacob looked at Martha with worry.

"We'll send someone with you," he added.

"Yes, please," Sarah tried to keep the quaver from her voice as she jumped up from the couch.

In all her catching up with Jacob and Martha, she'd forgotten to go back and check on Maggie and the others. She pulled her riding boots on and hurried out of her hosts' home with Jacob in tow.

Martha shook her head at Brandi, "I wish Mark had come with you both. I don't like these people. I'll send some staff to go with you both for the rest of the way."

Brandi tilted her face, "It's alright. I think it will be fine. The Lord is on our side. If He is for us, who can be against us, right?"

Martha's mouth grew wide with appreciation; she liked this young girl.

Declan was quiet as he sat around with the others, watching the fire. His eyes were smoldering with anger. He didn't expect that Sarah would come out, not after being rejected all the other times tonight. He'd asked the owner of the bush camp more than once to bring her out. *What was she up to in there?*

He was getting more and more infuriated with her lack of respect. What he wouldn't give to get his hands on her! He was just pondering going up to the private house and breaking down the door when he saw her, her fine figure glowing in the firelight as she stalked over to him.

She was pulling her hair back into a ponytail as she walked, and he could see immediately that she was put out. He didn't care for her feelings; he was put out, too.

Declan stood up and left the group.

"Where have you been all night?" he demanded.

"I told you. These people are old friends of mine. I was

276

catching up. Is that a crime?" Sarah retorted, defense flashing in her eyes, "Are you my keeper?"

"Well, I have to be involved in any discussions that you have regarding this rescue," scowled Declan, not bothering to conceal his anger.

Sarah stopped and stared. "Who made you the boss of this translocation? You don't need to know everything, Declan! I was not visiting on business; I was visiting people who are like family to me!"

She momentarily stammered with embarrassment, as they were approached by extra company. The tall, swarthy, Zulu staff member that Jacob had sent to accompany Sarah stood quietly to the side, appearing to look elsewhere.

The muscles in Declan's neck tightened. *A bodyguard?* His face flushed with anger.

Jutting out her chin with indignance, Sarah continued on her verbal rampage, "Just because you work for the Parks Board doesn't mean that this is your project. You are doing this on your time off, and you are doing it under *my* direction!"

She spun and stormed off toward the elephants, wrapping her pink long-sleeved outer shirt tight around her. The Zulu man was quick on her heels, his long legs matching her furious strides as he stayed close.

Declan jogged after her, trying to regain control of his emotions. He was furious at her for pulling rank. *If it wasn't for that Zulu....* No, he needed to stay calm. He needed to bide his time. *Tomorrow. Just wait till tomorrow. Then she'd pay for her insolence.*

Declan narrowed his eyes into the darkness. The Zulu man walked off by himself, a little to her right, but still in sight.

"Sarah, wait!" Declan caught up in no time. "I'm sorry. I know this is your thing. But I'm up the back of the herd and in charge of the men. I can't see what you want to do—what you want me and the men to do. I need to know what plans you have."

She tossed her head, glancing at him with curiosity, "I'll radio you, if something changes...you know that. Nothing has changed."

She shook her head with irritation, wanting nothing more than to be alone, "I can check these elephants on my own now if you like. I have help," she said and tossed a smile toward the Zulu man.

"You know..." he struggled to speak as he tried to keep up with her grueling pace, "...you're cute when you're angry."

He shot her his famous charming face, and then winked. She scowled at him.

Sarah slowed once they reached the elephants, which were still munching away at the copious amounts of greenery that Jacob had organized for them. They were beautiful under the moonlight. Seeming much more relaxed with the Zulu man in tow, Sarah sighed, leaning against a nearby post, smiling at the elephants. She appeared to completely ignore the Irishman's presence.

"S'cuse me, miss?" the Zulu man approached them, inclining his head with respect as he addressed Sarah.

"Yes?"

"Would you like me to fill the water again?" He pointed toward the water troughs that had been laid out for the elephants.

Sarah nodded, "That would be lovely, thank you!"

Bowing his head again, the Zulu stepped away to fetch a bucket and began hauling water. Declan watched him leave, then positioned himself closer to Sarah. He searched her silhouette.

"So, there are no other changes I need to know about for tomorrow? No extra people coming along or anything?" he pried in a singsong voice, glancing back at the Zulu in the distance.

"No," she snapped.

There was an awkward silence between them. She still refused to look at him, even though he was openly staring at her. Finally, her eyes met his and her impudence was suddenly replaced with a look of fear. He savored that look. Her wide emerald eyes seemed overly large in her delicate face. Her soft olive skin appeared to shudder under his scrutiny. This look. It gave him a feeling of power. How he wanted to reach out and use that power. But he couldn't. Not yet.

She stepped back with alarm, and he quickly looked away

toward the Zulu. Returning his focus to her, he saw that her gaze had fallen in the same direction—toward the Zulu. All she had to do was scream. Declan knew that his strength, as good as it was, was no match for the tall, heavily muscled Zulu man.

Trying to calm her down, Declan decided to act bored. He shifted his weight and kicked at a clump of dirt.

"Right. Then I'm going back to the fire."

With that, he left her there with the elephants. Walking back into the shadows, Declan tried to control his rising desires.

Sarah started breathing again with relief. *Finally!* Her brows pulled together in deep thought as he left. He didn't seem too upset about their break-up. She had figured he wanted to get her alone to try to talk her into salvaging the relationship he thought they had, but it was not so. He didn't seem interested in the elephants either. All he appeared to want was to make sure he was in the loop. It was what he didn't say that scared her the most. If it weren't for Jacob sending someone to be with her, Sarah couldn't tell what might have happened.

Shaking slightly, she found another bucket and helped the Zulu finish topping off the water troughs. They then pulled out some more foliage for the elephants, spreading it out within the makeshift kraal. Saying goodnight to the man, and assuring him that she would be OK now, Sarah then slipped over to the horse kraals to check the horses.

The night air was quiet as she approached. Shivering, she wrapped her arms around herself, watching the horses that stood sleeping in the darkness. The night air was not cold, but she felt chilled to the bone.

Spotting a fallen log, she went and sat, watching the kraals for a moment. Gazing up at the three-quarter moon, which glowed comfortably back down on her, Sarah sighed. The last time she'd been at these horse kraals at the end of the day, she'd been with Mark. She remembered how much she had thought she wanted him to leave her alone, like she'd just done with Declan, except when she was with Mark she hadn't really wanted him to leave.

Troubled, Sarah tried to separate the feelings in her heart.

Fear of danger, regret about Declan, a deep longing to make things right with Mark.

Frustrated, she stood and paced. It was getting late. Tomorrow would be a big day. She had to stop worrying. Passing the wooden horse kraals, she slapped her hand against a post, sending stinging pain up her wrist.

Pushing all thoughts of Mark aside, she headed back to Jacob and Martha's for the night.

They set off early the next morning, leaving right before sunrise. Jacob and Martha waved goodbye from the gate, as they had custom of doing, and Sarah felt a twinge of sadness that Brandi hadn't had more time here to get to know them. Perhaps on the way home, they would stay longer, if Johnno would let them.

Sarah nodded to Brandi, her expression solemn, before looking over her shoulder at the herd of elephants that were trudging after them eagerly. A good night's rest and plenty of food had transformed the elephants, and they stepped out, impatient to move on. It was a good sign. It was going to be a glorious day to get these elephants to their new home, and to have that feeling of accomplishing something great—having saved them from certain death.

Sarah got on her radio, "Declan, you copy?"

"Declan here. I copy you, Sarah."

"How are you and your crew feeling today? You all set back there?"

Sarah turned in her saddle, trying to make them out. During yesterday's ride, they were able to begin to skirt closer around the herd, as the herd grew used to them.

"We're all set. Over and out."

Sarah turned with relief to Brandi, "The final leg. Mozambique or bust."

"Don't say bust!" laughed Brandi with a mock grimace. "This is a God-given mission. It will happen!"

Sarah laughed, despite the feelings in her heart.

"That it is! Onward to Mozambique!" she said as she held out her arm, pointing dramatically.

CHAPTER
TWENTY-FIVE

The afternoon was waning outside at Brennan's. Solomon would soon be saddling up the four horses for a honeymoon couple that he and Mark would be taking on a sunset ride. Piet and Romy had knocked off work and headed home to their rondavel. Mark and Johnno still lurked about the administration building. Mark worked as he ate a late lunch, and Johnno filed paperwork in his office.

Mark took a sip from his coffee, setting it down among the newspaper clippings, before he began to sift through the various folders of articles he had collected over the years on the Kruger. He was certain that he knew some of the faces of the men in the group that Declan had hired. He doubted that they were from the Parks Board. In particular, the man Mick worried Mark. He had seen him somewhere recently, but couldn't place where.

Flicking his thumb over his tongue to moisten it, he sifted through the saved news article pages on the Kruger. Articles that spoke of natural disasters, political impacts and, most of all, the numerous poachings that had occurred; articles that listed statistics, arrests made, horrid discoveries found and the other trappings that went hand in hand with poaching reports.

Turning the pages of his folder, he paused on a particular article. Mark reached across the broad table for his plate of food, and grabbing up a piece of steaming toasted sandwich, he took a bite. Melted cheese dripped from the bread onto the clear plastic protecting the article. Sighing, he wiped it away with a paper napkin as he continued to read. Nothing. Maybe he was wrong about those men.

Placing the half-eaten slice back on the plate, he grabbed up the coffee again and rocked back on his chair, taking conservative sips, as he thumbed through the pages of yet another folder. Then something caught his eye, and he paused. He scanned over the title a second time: *Michael Conway. Convicted of Black Market Ivory Trade and Poaching.*

Mark pushed the chair up, hunching over the page as he located the photo of the so-called Michael Conway. Squinting closer, Mark recognized him as Mick from the group. His eyes went wide with trepidation.

"Poacher?" Mark said to himself.

He read the article again. All the men mentioned were ex-poachers. So why did this one stand out? Reading on, Mark noted with dark foreboding that Mick's main atrocities and crimes concerning the black market were with the grueling dealings of poaching. Right where the action was; not just a suit that stood in his office behind it all. Mick was one to get his hands dirty on the field. He'd also been convicted for assault and two accounts of murder.

The last bit caught Mark's attention. There was a warrant out for the man's arrest. He was wanted. He was no *ex*-poacher.

The blood drained from Mark's face as the words blurred together in a tangle of emotions. *Brandi and Sarah!*

He leapt away from the table, sending the chair careening backward onto the floorboards with a loud crash. Moving to the key cabinet in the other room and removing the appropriate keys, Mark rushed into the storage area, cranked open the gun safe and grabbed a rifle and ammunition. Fumbling as he relocked the safe, he also grabbed a charged radio, first aid kit and keys for the work bakkie.

Hearing the frenzied commotion, Johnno stepped out into the foyer in alarm, "Mark? What's going on?"

"Can't talk!" Mark glanced at Johnno, his voice sharp. "I have to go. I'll be back in a while."

"What about the trail this afternoon?" Johnno's face grew red and flustered.

"Blow the trail! Piet can do it!"

Johnno positioned himself in the doorway, bracing his hands

on the wooden frame.

Mark's eyes flashed with fury.

"Get out of my way! Sarah and Brandi are in danger!" Mark snarled and went to push past Johnno, but was met with resistance.

He looked at his boss with growing rage and confusion. Why was Johnno stopping him for something this important?

Johnno stood up straighter, a look of satisfaction in his eyes at Mark's hesitation.

"Leave it, Mark," he growled.

Mark's face warped in anger as he pushed past the older man with force, storming out the door.

"You go, and you're finished here!" Johnno threatened, wagging his finger.

Mark's eyes widened as he stared at Johnno in disbelief, "Then consider this my notice!"

With that, he bounded down the stairs, two at a time, rifle and other gear bundled in his arms. Breath shaking, he jumped into the work bakkie, stowing the rifle and other items beside him. Anxiety growing, he turned the key in the ignition and, after the second try at getting the engine started, roared away, kicking up a cloud of dust.

Johnno watched him skidding out of the driveway and down the road toward the gate. He knew that Mark had figured it out.

Urgency in his step, Johnno ducked back into the office where Mark had been going through his folders on the big table. He scanned the article that was sitting on top in the open folder. Trying to suppress his rising panic, Johnno picked up the phone and dialed.

"Hello? Police? Ja, I'd like to report a stolen vehicle."

Hanging up from the police moments later, Johnno cursed himself for his premature call and then dialed Tom.

"We've got a problem!"

Out in the Kruger, Sarah and her translocation crew had all

just finished watering their horses and elephants at Olifants and were headed back out into bushveldt country. It felt like déjà vu to Declan, as he sent out the flank riders to overtake Sarah and Brandi and circle the herd again, putting his plan into action.

The riders slowed as they faced up to Sarah and Brandi, their faces blank. The women looked up in confusion.

"Hey! What's up?" called out Sarah, seething that Declan hadn't radioed.

The men stared at them, their eyes cold. Sarah and Brandi halted with consternation. The six men then pulled out their shotguns and leveled them toward the women. In alarm, Brandi shot her hands into the air. Sarah shrank into her saddle, but held her ground, eyes wide.

"What...?" Sarah's voice faltered as she tried to think what to do.

One of the men changed his aim toward the herd and lined up the matriarch. The old elephant had grown accustomed to the sight of the weapons and trusted the people that were riding with Sarah. She continued to meander onward toward Sarah.

The man holding the Nitro elephant gun snapped his gaze back at the other men, awaiting suggestion. He knew that elephants could not be taken down that easy, and he would need careful aim, before all hell broke loose. Head shots needed to be aimed with precision to hit the brain outright. An injured elephant was a dangerous elephant.

Maggie felt the tension in the air and changed course to examine the man with the gun. An expletive word issued from his lips as he took a haphazard shot toward the elephant, grazing the bullet across the top of her ear. The round echoed across the bushveldt.

Recognizing the threat as pain was shooting through her ear, Maggie charged forward, eyes red with fury. Wheeling his horse out of harm's way, the shooter cantered around the other side of the fray, lining up with more care.

"Hey!" Sarah screamed with panic. "Stop!"

She went to grab for the radio on her hip, but another rider suddenly appeared, ramming his horse up next to Honor. Their stirrups locked as the horses skittered to a stop in confusion. The bearded man roughly grabbed Sarah's arm, twisting it as she growled in pain. She spat in his face and he lunged forward, pulling his fist back, ready to knock her from the saddle. Their horses teetered a moment, before his grey mount reared in fright as an elephant came careening their way. Sarah dropped the radio and, grabbing her reins, cantered away just in time.

The second loud gunshot pierced through the air, cutting down not the matriarch but the male behind her. A direct hit to the side of the skull felled the beast in a heaving crash of dust and chaos. The herd went into panic and turned tail, running back toward Olifants River. The men all broke after the herd, shooting as they let out a triumphant bloodthirsty cry, leaving Sarah and Brandi in a startled panic.

Sarah sprang into action, galloping after the herd. Brandi and Jet followed.

Crying out in rage, Sarah realized that Declan would have been the one issuing the orders. Gripping her reins, she galloped into the frenzied cloud of dust, hot tears streaming down her face. Righteous anger drove her into action, and catching up to the fray in no time, and pulling loose her faithful Winchester, Sarah knocked one of Declan's men off his horse with the butt of the gun. The man was being dragged by one stirrup, and Sarah looked to her left and saw Brandi and Jet racing up next to her.

The elephants skidded to a stop and looked around in confusion. If cornered, elephants were known to attack with great force. Declan and the other men must have stopped the herd up ahead, using Olifants River to block the path to their escape. They were cornered against where the eroding of the land gave way into a deep muddy part of the Olifants River, a section frequented with many Nile crocodiles.

Sarah heard more gunshots, and then heard Declan through the cloud of dust, barking out orders. Cantering around the side of the mass and coming into view, he looked straight at Sarah with cold and hungry eyes.

Masses of grey bodies and dust thundered perilously across the land as the elephants fought back. Sarah called out to

Maggie, and several elephants turned to her voice, charging away from the fray.

"Damn it!" Declan lunged Zulo away from an oncoming male, moving with the horse as they leapt sideways to avoid being taken out by another swinging head.

Pulling Zulo into a clearing, Declan swiveled his gun toward Sarah's horse. Seeing his intention, Sarah didn't have time to think. She gripped her reins, leaping into a gallop, back into the roiling dust clouds.

In that instant, Declan let fire, missing Sarah and Honor by a fraction as she ducked. Honor reared and whinnied as she bailed into another horse and rider. Gasping with surprise, Sarah turned and spotted Brandi to her right, pulling Jet up with urgency. Something was wrong with them.

Time appeared to stand still. Jet backed up with impatient agitation as Brandi clutched at her stomach, surprised as blood seeped through her fingers.

Gasping with horror, Sarah spun back toward Declan, who was cursing and trying to line up Honor again, the range of his rifle up to his eye.

Elephants were rushing in every direction in earth-shuddering confusion, kicking up billowing dust and blocking Sarah from Declan's view. Sarah heard him order his men to get behind him, firing his rifle into the air in frenzied fury, sending the elephants trampling away from him in a sudden wave toward the women.

Sarah looked up in terror, the rush of elephants hurtling toward them, "*Brandi!*"

She didn't have time to act as she saw Jet and Brandi disappear under a cloud of dust and grey bodies, before a sudden gut-wrenching jolt knocked her from her saddle. Gasping for breath, Sarah tried to pull herself up, but strength failing, she collapsed into comforting blackness.

Only four elephants and three men were lost in the chaos at Olifants, but Declan rationalized that he could still move the rest of the herd to a more accessible place so that Tom's trucks could move in and efficiently cull and clean up before anyone else came.

He spat in the dirt as he cantered after the herd, pushing them onward with the blast of rifle fire into the air. He wanted this over with! He wanted Sarah!

The elephants were still in a terrified frenzy but were starting to tire, being ever pushed on by Declan's cruel men.

Declan called for all gunfire to cease so he could survey the remaining herd. Minutes passed with no gunshots, but after a time, the exhausted herd began to slow down. Declan examined the weary beasts, reasoning that the cull should be easy with them all so worked down.

Mick rode up next to Declan, pleasure showing through his rotten, jagged row of black and yellow teeth.

Declan scowled at him and spat, "We need to go back, finish the job and clean up that mess. Collect survivors."

Knowing that Declan meant the girls, Mick sat back in the saddle.

"You mean prisoners! Take it easy, boss. It's too late for that now. Let nature take its course...and this heat," he added, looking woeful at the hot midmorning sun. "This heat will finish the job."

Declan grimaced in frustration and went on with business.

"We need to get to that secluded grassland in an hour. Tom's waiting for us there with a clean-up crew. I want to go back and finish."

"Whoah!" Mick laughed, "It's too late! There'll be other women! Leave it be. Better off not putting more evidence out there. It looks like an accident, leave it be."

"I hit one," retorted Declan, his pent-up aggression being replaced with fear. "I need to..."

Mick stopped him, "Oi! The vultures will mess it up soon enough. Or the cats and dogs. Relax! You never look back!"

Declan wasn't convinced, and he shook his head with anger. No amount of carrion, hyenas, or jackals was going to remove a bullet. He ruefully thought about how much worse it would have looked if he'd blown a massive hole in someone with an elephant gun, instead of the dainty Winchester Sarah insisted he use.

"Leave it be!" growled Mick. "Leave it be! I should know. You're still a greenhorn at this business; you should've let me take care of it, my way! If you go back now, you create more evidence against you. The elephants will have covered it."

"Probably..." Declan tightened his lips, thinking again of Sarah.

Mick was right, he should have done it. Mick had the record. Declan didn't.

Tom leaned against the truck, looking casual as he regarded the pleasant vista view of the lowveldt. His team had their trucks open and their knives, rifles, ropes and other gear all laid out ready for the job.

It was a dirty business, but necessary to protect future investment. They could not allow this Sarah White to succeed in her translocation efforts or it would become the normal way of handling elephants in the future.

He squinted into the distance where he knew Declan and his men would appear from. Where were they? They should have arrived by now. He wasn't concerned by Johnno's phone call; they could deal with that one man if he showed. What worried Tom more was the fact that he'd had to leave his clean office to come out on the field. If he was spotted out here, it would be over.

Declan wiped the sweat from his brow and cursed. The very young and very old elephants began to drag behind the others, slowing down the whole herd, which was being driven by ruthless whips and gunshots.

They were taking too long out here. The longer it took, the more chance they had of being discovered, or worse, the girls being discovered.

This was not the regular way things were done, Declan reminisced. *In the good old days, you found the herd, you killed what you could of the herd and got the bloody hell out of the way of the rest, running for your life. Then you took what you could, and made off with it.*

Declan spat the dirt from his mouth. *Blast that Tom and his grandiose idea of using Sarah's method to bring the chaos to him.*

Declan booted Zulo with cruelty in the flank, ramming the black horse at a canter into a baby elephant.

"*MOVE IT!*" he screamed at the calf with impatience.

The young one trumpeted in panic and tried to leap into a run, but stumbled, falling on its face. Exhaustion was setting in, and the calf struggled back to its feet and meandered onward.

"Blast it!" he yelled.

Temper rippling, Declan ripped out his rifle and shot the baby elephant square in the side of the head. A clean brain shot. Its front legs buckled under it, as it skidded on its face into the hard ground, dead.

Declan snorted with irritation, but then looked up with surprise. Another kill had set off the elephants with renewed vigor, and the matriarch elephant charged through the herd, trumpeting with anger, and slammed into Zulo and Declan. Declan was sent airborne as the injured Zulo limped for cover in the dense mopane.

Hitting the ground with force, Declan somersaulted onto the dirt and leapt back to his feet in fear. He scanned the ground in desperation for his gun, calling to his men.

"Hey! Back up!"

Turning with a mixed look of confusion and fury, he stood helpless as the matriarch bared down on him at a furious pace, swinging her great tusks from side to side, ears flapping forward. The look of fury turned to anguish as Maggie closed the distance, reefing him into the air with a sweep of her great tusks and trunk. He landed in the dirt, limp and groaning, the great female thundering after him. Grasping her trunk about his leg, she caught him up into the air again. He was not so lucky on his descent as she swung her head, catching and impaling him on one of her slender long tusks.

A strange, fuzzy thought flashed through his mind. It was the same tusk he had rested his hand on and marveled over when he first saw the elephant with Sarah. With a quavered breath, Declan exhaled his last time, his head going limp.

Head off balance from the weight, Maggie shook him loose from her tusk, sending the rumpled heap sprawling into the dirt. Eyes livid with rage, she continued to bear down upon him and trampled him into a bloody mess. When she stepped her scarlet feet away from him, he was abnormally flat.

The other men stood watching in horror as she raised her scarlet-stained trunk into the air and trumpeted. She then turned to stare with empty eyes at Mick and the rest of the men. She meandered over to the limp body of her calf, running her trunk over the limp form.

Mick saw the opportunity and, crying out in rage, charged his horse at the matriarch, lining her up in his shotgun. Intolerant of their presence now, Maggie turned on him in an instant, sending him from his horse and careening into other elephants before he'd even fired a shot.

The other elephants moved out of the way, anxious as Maggie chased Mick down and trampled him into the dirt, meters away from Declan's body. Two more men yelled at her with fury and raced toward her on their horses. The speed at which she closed the gap was alarming as she swept her great trunk across their startled faces, flinging them from their horses and leaving them moaning on the ground in agony. They would be as good as dead in a moment.

The rest of the men, blood draining from their faces, turned their horses and galloped away, leaving the mess as fast as they could.

Sarah opened her eyes with pain and spat the dirt and blood out of her mouth. Every part of her body screamed with pain. With effort, she lifted her head and looked up, straining to see. Exhausted from just doing that, she rested her head once again upon the hard ground, allowing her eyes to try to focus on the sideways view.

Memories started to flood back of what had occurred, giving Sarah a sudden sick feeling in her stomach. *Brandi!*

She gathered her strength and lifted her head right up, looking around. Her vision blurred, and the scene appeared to spin. Clenching her eyes closed, she groaned, trying to lift herself to her knees. Dizziness accosted her.

Sarah gritted her teeth and forced herself shakily into a sitting position. Pain shot through her head, and she felt a wave of nausea hit her. Rolling onto her knees and doubling over, she retched.

While throwing up, Sarah tried to steady herself, as the bitter bile burned her dust-filled throat. *Help me, Jesus. Help.*

She put her hand to her dizzy head. Withdrawing it from her hairline, she saw from her crimson hand that she was bleeding from her head. Her jeans were ripped and streaked with blood and dirt, but as the pins and needles eased in her legs, they seemed to look and feel alright, although scuffed up.

Hesitant, she took a deeper breath, trying to gauge if she had any broken ribs. The throbbing in her side sent a shiver of nausea back through her.

"Brandi," she murmured, looking around urgently, trying to push through the dizziness that kept trying to overwhelm her.

She needed water. She spat some more blood and bile, her mouth getting drier. Then she saw her.

"*BRANDI!*" Sarah choked, staggered to her feet, and scuffled over to the limp form in the dirt. "Brandi?"

She collapsed down next to her, placing her trembling hand on Brandi's burning cheek. She was alive! Tears poured down Sarah's dirt-streaked face, creating salty rivulets in the muddied skin.

Brandi's eyes were slow to open, and she turned her head stiffly to focus on Sarah.

"Wha...?" she said as a spasm of coughing racked her frame, and she shut her eyes in agony against it.

Sarah looked down and saw the gunshot wound in the side of Brandi's stomach, leeching blood at a steady rate. Gasping, Sarah struggled out from her pink outer long-sleeved shirt and tried to staunch the flow.

"It...it's going to be OK, Brandi. You're going to be fine. I'm going to get us help."
Sarah looked over her shoulder helpless. *Please, God! Please, God, help us!*

Brandi brought a weak hand up, resting it over Sarah's, who was firm in pressing the shirt over her wound. Brandi gave a feeble smile. Sarah looked at her in consternation. She had lost a fair bit of blood, and Sarah thought she looked pale.

"Sarah?" Brandi tried to lift her head.

"No, no. You're OK. Lay back and rest. I need you to stay still."

Sarah put Brandi's hand over the bunched-up shirt that was now stained crimson.

"Can you try and hold this for me?"

Brandi moaned in reply and clutched at the moist clump.

"My back's not broken..." she gasped as Sarah started to move away.

"What?" Sarah trembled, returning to her.

Even like this, Brandi's mind was at work on first aid.

"My back. I can feel all my limbs," Brandi repeated. "Oh boy, can I feel them!" she groaned.

Sarah touched her shoulder, "You're not allowed to move, Brandi. I'll find a way to move you somewhere safe. But for now, please, be still." Standing on shaking feet, Sarah shielded her eyes from the sun as she surveyed the landscape. They were out in the open lowveldt, unprotected. Surely there would be something. Sarah brought her hand to her head as if that would stop the new onslaught of dizziness. Then she saw it. A line of trees in the near distance. *Shade! The river!* Those tree would offer protection if she could just get them there.

Sarah was frantic as she looked around for something she could use to move Brandi into the shelter. She needed to get her away from the sun that was now high and scorching above. It must have been close to noon. She looked with longing toward the line of shady mopane and baobab trees that she knew nestled close to the Olifants River.

Her legs still felt like jello, but Sarah felt strength begin to return to her body. Still trembling under the heat, the need to shelter now diminished, Sarah's focus fell on the area before her for the first time since the attack.

The scene struck her with a horror that was inexplicable. Her mouth began to dry up as she shuddered involuntarily. Three dead elephants lay strewn in the dirt, along with several trampled bodies of Declan's men. How could she have been so stupid to let all this happen?

Hot tears flooded her eyes, blurring her vision. No! Brandi was her top priority now. The sound of her friend coughing suddenly spurred Sarah to action. She searched among the debris and bodies to find something she could use to move Brandi. Sarah gazed back over her shoulder toward Brandi with apprehension. She wouldn't last in this heat. And what if they were discovered by big cats? Or even scavengers? Sarah would be too weak to fight them off. How were they going to survive out here?

Blinded with worry, Sarah lurched over to the first fallen horse, where she pulled furiously to loosen a rolled-up riding jacket from behind the saddle of the dead beast. She shook it loose, realizing with horror that it was her own. Taking a double take at the horse, realization hit her like a kick in the stomach. She touched the ruffled and scuffed golden coat of her best friend with trepidation. The fur was cool under her fingers, despite the heat of the overhead sun, as rigor mortis had already set in.

Sarah crumpled onto her knees in agonizing grief over the lifeless animal, tears streaming down her dirt-streaked cheeks. Coughing startled Sarah from behind, and she turned anxiously to see Brandi heaving under the pain of her wounds. She spun to her feet and rushed the riding coat over to Brandi.

With extreme care and effort, Sarah shuffled Brandi onto the outspread coat and dragged her with much exertion over to a line of shady trees, closer to the Olifants River, but far enough up the steep bank not to attract Nile crocs. Once certain that Brandi was as comfortable as she could be under the circumstances, Sarah rushed back to the carnage to collect whatever provisions she could find from other saddles and gear that had been strewn around.

Brandi watched, numb from shock, as Sarah carted over her gear from her saddle, then various bits of other gear, such as a water bottle, a small blanket and another bag with some food.

Dismay sunk in as Sarah's used her survival instincts. She thought about the flimsy electric fencing that lay attached to one of the deserted packhorses. She could use that now as extra protection.

At last, Sarah returned carrying her saddle, rug and Honor's bridle. Brandi blinked in confusion at the last acquisitions as realization set in.

Sarah caught her watching and smiled with encouragement, "You'll be fine, OK? There's some water in two of these bottles, but the rest are empty."

Knowing that the water from Olifants wouldn't be safe enough to drink, Sarah restrained from the temptation of even filling the empty bottles to use the river water to clean Brandi's wounds, knowing that it could infect her. Cracking open one of the precious bottles of water, Sarah helped Brandi take some of the life-giving liquid, which ran down her dried and dusty throat. She took a small sip herself, savoring the feeling of the liquid as it connected with her parched throat.

Careful not to drink too much, she replaced the lid. As much as she needed water, Brandi needed it more. She offered the bottle again, and Brandi nodded with gratitude. Sarah watched with grave concern as the color refused to return to Brandi's face after she drank sip after sip with slow precision.

The effort of sitting upright created a fresh stream of blood that soaked through the already crimson cloth. Sarah grimaced, wondering what else she could do. She fashioned a fresh bandage in the form of another recovered shirt that had been folded into a saddlebag. Bunching that up, she put the new bandage in place.

Running back down to the river and cleaning out the old bandage, she started to rip up her now-stained pink shirt so she could at least tie it around Brandi's body to secure the fresh bandage. Diluted blood ran down the river, causing Sarah to cringe about attracting crocodiles, as she raced back to Brandi.

After her novice attempt to secure the new bandage with the old ripped one, Sarah slumped with resignation next to Brandi, as her friend closed her eyes for much-needed rest. She wasn't as good as Brandi with first aid or survival skills, and Brandi, fading in and out of consciousness, was of no help in directing her.

Picking up a trampled radio, she turned it over in her hands, trying to see if she could get it to work. It would do no good; the side was busted in, the batteries were missing and some blue and red wire was sticking up out of it, along with a spring. Dropping it beside her, Sarah gazed out toward the glaring wilderness, where the sickening events of the day had taken place.

She couldn't bring herself to go back out there in search of more supplies. She didn't want to see Honor again in such a dismal state. How did it come to this? She wondered why God would call her and give her such a strong purpose, then just to let it all fall apart.

Her face fell into her hands, as Sarah sobbed, "God...why did you do this to me? I've failed! I've lost everything that was most important to me!"

A soft hand brushed against her, resting upon her shoulder. Sarah looked over, seeing Brandi watching her with wide eyes, full of sympathy and love.

"No," her voice was hoarse, "No, you haven't failed. Neither has God." She swallowed hard, forming words a stilted effort, "Sarah, don't give up."

"Don't give up?" Sarah let her hands flop into her lap. "It's all over. How can I start again? I don't even know how we'll get out of this mess we're in now. I don't even know if you will...," he stopped short, Brandi watching her with a strange calm.

Brandi was silent for a long while, her eyes glinting, then said, "Sarah, look at you..."

Sarah raised her brows.

"You're fine," Brandi went on, her words only making Sarah feel worse.

Looking down, Sarah reflected on what had occurred out in the lowveldt. She was lucky to be alive. It would have been so easy for her to have been killed, or even maimed, but here she was, unscathed except for a few bruises and scratches.

Sarah sighed and looked at Brandi and her injuries, "But you're not!"

Brandi stopped her, "Sarah, you *still* don't see how God is protecting you? You have a great purpose...and it could be for the here and now. Who knows?"

Brandi started to cough, pain wrenching across her features. Sarah thought she saw flecks of blood appear on her lips.

Pressing her hand down upon Brandi's bandage, she attempted to staunch the potential flow of fresh pulsing blood, caused by the coughing fit.

"Shhh, Brandi. Don't talk," a shadow crossed Sarah's face.

Brandi settled and waved her hand away, "Who knows? You could have been born for such a time as this," she quoted from the book of Esther.

Sarah sat back, looking out into the wilderness.

"He's kept you alive, Sarah. You are still needed."

Sarah looked back down at Brandi, her jaw set with determination, "As are you, Brandi! I refuse to lose you too! I'm not going to let you die."

"Sarah," Brandi sighed, "You can't change the way things are. I don't know what my future holds, but I know who holds it. It's not up to me or you."

Satisfied, Brandi settled back and shut her eyes, sleepiness overcoming her. Anxious, Sarah watched her, and then, getting up, wandered over to the edge of the tree line and gazed out into the huge sky, forcing her eyes to deny what lay upon the horizon.

"Lord," she murmured, "what do I do now? How do I get us back?"

No answer.

Sarah dropped her gaze and stood looking at her hands.

"Please, God...I need to know you are with us."

A cool breeze licked up from the dusty lowveldt and kissed Sarah's heat-stressed body. She closed her eyes against the dust and exhaled deeply, a calm settling over her. She needed to think about survival.

It was drawing closer to dusk, and she hadn't thought of how to keep scavengers away from them, scavengers that would be attracted to what lay upon the blood-stained grasslands. Vultures had since discovered the feast, and littered both the ground and the skies above like black beacons that would soon be attracting much bigger clean-up crews.

Tom looked at his watch in frustration. Something was wrong. The sun was getting low and there was still no sign of Declan and his crew. He'd sat here all day, waiting.

He tried the radio again. Nothing. Looking at the bored crew with concern, Tom made the decision to call it off. Declan wasn't on radio, so he must have run into trouble. They would have to regroup and find out what happened.

CHAPTER
TWENTY-SIX

Sarah placed some bigger branches upon the fire that blazed in the clearing where she and Brandi were settled. She had collected as much dead wood as she could find from around the area, and had stacked it nearby.

Fire could be used to scare off curious wildlife. With no usable rifles or other weapons at their disposal, Sarah was going back to use one of God's oldest resources.

As well as the protection that could be offered by waving a large, burning torch toward would-be attackers, the fire would bring comfort and warmth. Sarah had found several packs containing dried biscuits from the bush camp and a few pieces of squashed and damaged fruit. It would still buy them survival until they could get more help. Brandi had already turned down food, and was fast asleep by the flickering warm glow of the flames, her breathing was labored.

Sarah sat, her hair messy, face and arms scratched and dirt streaked, nibbling a dry biscuit by the fire with her eyes watchful, ears keen and mind in prayer. She could hear the frightful laughing of hyenas not too far away as they entered the feeding frenzy on the field. She closed off her ears to the noise, not bearing the thought of her beloved horse's fate.

The sun had just taken its leave, and a soft orange glow lingered on the horizon as a heavy, navy blanket began to push away the day, stars blinked their way into their heavenly domain. Sarah prayed hard. She prayed that she would stay awake, that she would not have to face any animals given her current state of fatigue. She prayed that Brandi would make it through the night, and she prayed that Declan and his men wouldn't return, lured over by the distinctive plume of smoke that was weaving its way into the night sky.

Jacob opened the gates with joy as Mark drove the bakkie through into the bush camp.

"Mark! It's a pleasure to..."

Jumping from the vehicle, Mark, looking stricken, stopped Jacob mid-sentence. The dark-skinned man frowned.

"What's wrong, my friend?"

"Sarah! Did she, I mean, they, when did they leave?" Mark spluttered as he looked around with urgency.

Martha walked out from their home, tea towel in hand, worry in her eyes.

"They left this morning," Martha replied as she looked at Mark with worry, waiting for an explanation to the fear she heard in his voice from her kitchen window. Now standing next to Jacob, she went on, "Why?"

"Do you have any idea which way they were going?" Mark strained. "I...I think they're in trouble. Big trouble."

Jacob looked confused.

"The girls!" Mark blurted, impatient.

Martha and Jacob's eyes went wide. They hadn't liked the look of the men that stayed with them last night and, in an instant, they understood.

"Here! Come!" Jacob led Mark over a large map on the wall of the building and pointed along several tracks and Olifants.

"Thank you! Thank you!" Mark squeezed Jacob by the shoulders, before rushing away to the bakkie again.

"What are you going to do?" Jacob looked nervous.

"I'm going after them! I need to make sure Sarah and Brandi are safe."

Martha stepped forward, "The sun will be setting in a few hours, shouldn't you wait till morning?"

Mark shook his head, "Can you do me a favor? Ring Mozambique. See if they got there. Those men are poachers!"

Jacob and Martha looked at each other, fear in their eyes.

Mark looked at them for a moment as they agreed, and then setting his face, turned back toward the bakkie.

"I have to go!"

He slipped into his seat, his shaking hands sweaty on the steering wheel.

"What else can we do?" Jacob asked urgently after him.

Mark leaned out from the window of the bakkie, "I've already called the police. I'm hoping they are coming, too. If you see them come past, can you direct them the same way as me? I'm on channel fifty on radio. Can you tune in?"

Jacob was solemn as Mark backed out from their drive.

"And pray!" he called out from the utility vehicle, as he slammed into first gear and drove out.

Martha was anxious as she looked to Jacob, who put his arm around her with comfort. They watched Mark drive down the track.

"Did he just say what I think he said?" she asked. Turning a sharp eye toward her husband, "Did he just ask us to pray? Do you think...?"

Jacob squeezed her shoulder solemnly.

"The Lord works in mysterious ways," he conceded.

Johnno rushed out onto the deck of the administration building as he saw Tom pull up in his Land Cruiser. Tom emerged and slammed the door shut, stalking over to Johnno and throwing his hat in the dirt!

"They didn't show! Something's up!" he exploded. "You were meant to make sure it all happened from this end!"

Johnno stepped back, flabbergasted, "I warned you that Mark was coming out. What more can I do? Declan and those rogues know how to take care of themselves. Can you get hold of Declan?"

"No!" Tom wiped his brow, trying to think.

"Maybe they couldn't do it. They could be over the border by now. There were rangers meeting them there. They may have called it off." Johnno scratched his neck, clearly nervous.

Tom shook his head in agitation, "He would have called my cell phone by now. I think something's happened.

"He hasn't called yet? Well, did you send some of your crew to find out?" Johnno's eyes widened in alarm.

"Of course not! That's your job!" Tom snapped, further infuriated by Johnno's benign suggestions.

"Well, we'd better do something! If there is...you know...a mess out there, it could get traced back to us. The police could..." Johnno paused mid-sentence at the glare on Tom's face.

Holding his finger up to stop Tom from replying, Johnno turned and strode back toward the office, returning soon after with two rifles.

"What are you doing?" asked Tom with disgust, taking the rifle offered to him.

Adjusting a rifle strap on his shoulder, Johnno looked toward another work bakkie, "You mean, what are *we* doing. We have to see what happened before someone else does."

"Oh no, I can't get involved!" Tom pushed the rifle back into Johnno's arms. "I work for the government, Johnno, remember? I can't afford jail time. I organize, I traffic, I don't get in the messy stuff. I shouldn't have been out there today! If I get busted, the whole gig's gone! For everyone...that means you, too!"

Johnno narrowed his eyes, opened the driver's side door of the bakkie, then took a seat, defiance set in his jaw.

The whole gig will be up if it's not dealt with," he assured Tom and started the engine.

The tall man watched with consternation as Johnno drove out the gates. Straightening his suit, he strode back to his own vehicle, agitated. At least if something went wrong, Johnno didn't know Tom's *real* full name. Nobody would believe his story, and Tom could disappear into the shadows again while Johnno took the wrap.

Mark drove into the night, the spotlights of the bakkie illuminating the African wilderness with a strong yellow beam that pierced through the grasslands with limited range. He would stop every now and then, listening for signs of elephants, sounds of voices—anything. He was upset at himself for letting such petty things come between himself and Sarah.

So far, all he could find was more of the same; expanses of eerie dark bushveldt that seemed so far removed from the beauty reflected in the daylight. The rumble of the engine his only companion, Mark started to feel the weight of fatigue take over. Then he saw it. Bloodstained grass in his headlights.

He stomped on the brake, halting the vehicle. Soft dust floated forward from behind his still tires, shifting into the beam of light, partially concealing Mark's discovery in the mysterious ochre clouds. He stepped out from the bakkie and into the headlights, straining to see beyond, into the darkness ahead.

Up ahead, he saw the dark shadow of what appeared to be a large rock, then more grass. *You don't get boulders like that out here,* he thought to himself. Smaller, sleek shadows began to slink back and forth into Mark's view, and he got back into the bakkie to drive on.

A kill. But what did the blood come from? The boulder had to be a carcass.

Cautious, Mark pulled the bakkie forward. A hyena scurried past his headlights. Then another stopped and looked at the vehicle nervously, blood staining its muzzle. Their faces confirmed his theory: there was a kill up ahead.

Squinting, Mark turned the bakkie, bringing one of the large shadows into view under the glare of his headlights. The boulder-shaped kill was an elephant calf. The calf was surrounded by hyenas feeding with greed, as they leered and laughed at each other, fighting for the best parts. As Mark's bakkie approached, several of them hurried away from the vehicle again, hiding in the grass until he passed.

Mark frowned. A lion kill? They often took down the young and the old. He looked for signs of a lion attack, but there were no gaping wounds around the throat, save where the hyenas had started to have a go. The main area where the hyenas had struck was the soft underbelly, which was the easiest to access through the tough hide.

Tilting his head as the vehicle passed the fallen infant, Mark pressed his foot on the brake again. A hyena was licking the calf's forehead. The hyena stopped and regarded the bakkie before scuttling away. Once out of the way, Mark saw a small, neat bloodstained gunshot wound on the side of the calf's head. A brain shot. Seasoned hunters and poachers were the main people with the knowledge and know-how to kill in one shot like that.

Mark pulled on the hand brake, staring at the calf for a long moment in thought. One of the hyenas returned to eat, drawing Mark's attention to a squabble that was breaking out to his left, between two other hyenas, which were fighting over a hunk of intestine. Others moved on ahead to something bigger and better. *Is this from Sarah's group, or is it something unrelated?*

His eyes were drawn after the hyenas, who were whooping with noise as they took off further ahead. *Was there another kill?* He rolled the bakkie past the elephant calf. All tiredness had left Mark and he started to get a nauseous feeling in his stomach as the bloodied grass continued on.

Stopping the bakkie and reefing the hand brake back on, Mark grabbed the powerful flashlight from the back seat. Opening his door, he leapt outside and swung himself onto the back of the bakkie, scanning the area with the light. He could hear hyenas everywhere in the darkness. He could also hear the presence of jackals somewhere out there.

Every direction he looked, he saw more bloodied grass. This was more than just an elephant calf. The hairs on his neck began to stand up on end as his flashlight caught the glint of metal. Staring for a moment, he recognized the double barrels of an elephant gun.

Vaulting off the tailgate and swinging back into the safety of the bakkie, Mark drove the vehicle over to the thing. More blood. Leaning out of his window with the flashlight, he saw a clear trail of blood leading up a dirt track. Perhaps someone was still alive, but injured, somewhere out here.

"SARAH! BRANDI!" He risked calling into the night.

He was answered with the sudden silence of the hyenas as they regarded the unfamiliar noise in their territory. Driving on slowly, he followed the trail until it stopped at the line of heavy foliage and trees. The trunk of an acacia boasted smears of blood as Mark approached.

Holding the flashlight out his window again, he strained his neck as he trained the beam further up the tree. Blood was smeared on a lower branch. Mark stretched his head further out from his window, shining his light high up into the tree.

"Hello?" he called, hoping to find a wounded soul hiding in the safety of the tree.

Knowing the signs of a leopard kill involved it being taken into a tree, but feeling anxious as to what it was, Mark gagged as he smelt offal from above. Definite signs of leopard. His light caught sight of the kill. There it was. Mark squinted in confusion, not recognizing what he was seeing of the shadowy form. The sight of jeans and a boot stopped him in his tracks.

Dropping his flashlight into the dirt and jerking open the bakkie door, Mark vomited violently onto the ground. Sense of danger was lost as the overwhelming urge of basic natural reaction took over.

After his now-empty stomach stopped heaving, Mark forced himself to look up into the tree again, hands shaking as he groped through the dirt for the flashlight. Swallowing back the taste of bile, Mark shone the light back into the tree. The leopard had long since left, leaving the unwanted remains hanging.

Ripped jeans and other clothing, stained with blood, hung limp on either side of the branch. Mark forced himself to study it, trying to see whose it was. It wasn't Sarah or Brandi's, he realized with relief; it was male, judging from the once-hairy arms. Then Mark recognized Declan's watch sitting snug upon his pale wrist.

Eyes wide with horror, Mark swung the flashlight around the lowveldt. His fears confirmed that this carnage had occurred to Sarah's team. Mark gasped against the rising panic in his chest. *Sarah! Brandi!*

He took his rifle and flashlight and leapt from the bakkie,

racing along the grass, looking for more blood.

"SARAH? BRANDI?"

He was answered by nothing, except for the sounds of startled hyenas and yapping jackals that called out to each other in response.

He spotted another mound of huddled scavengers. Tears exploded from Mark's eyes as he tore toward the group of hyenas around their meal.

"MOVE! ARRGHHH!" He waved his arms around, furious with no thought to his own safety.

Scattering the beasts in anguish, he found another man, his lifeless eyes staring dismally into the darkness. Looking toward another group of hyenas, Mark hurried on, finding more bloodshed, but no sign of the girls. "BRANDI? SARAH?"

Mark felt his knees buckling, as he left the remains of Mick and another man. Feeling sick again in the stomach, he stumbled back to the safety of the bakkie that was still running, high beams glaring, a welcome sight in the midst of such a terrible scene in the darkness.

Collapsing into his seat and slamming the door against the horrors outside, Mark squeezed his eyes closed. *Please, God! Where are they? Let them be ok!*

Shaking again, he took up his radio, "Jacob!" He cleared his throat. "You online? Jacob, please!!! It's Mark..."

"I'm online, Mark. What have you found? Over."

Mark's mouth went dry and he couldn't speak.

"Jacob here. Mark, do you read me? Over."

"I read you, Jacob. Please call the police. Tell them to come to Olifants River, near Thompson's bend. It's carnage, Jacob." Mark exhaled a quavering breath, "I won't be here. I have to find Sarah and Brandi. Tell them I've found four dead. Over."

Mark dropped the radio into his lap. There was no reply for some time.

Finally, Jacob responded, "Copy that, Mark. I'll get right on it. Please be careful. We're praying. Over and out."

Mark gritted his teeth and sped off along the river, calling out his window for the women.

CHAPTER
TWENTY-SEVEN

A twig snapped, jolting Sarah awake from where she leaned against a tree. Cursing that she'd fallen asleep, she sat up, grimacing against the pain in her neck. She was still holding the thick branch, clasped in both hands. It had been her choice of weapon that she'd hand-picked to use if the occasion arose. The branch had attacked her first, leaving a crick in her neck as she'd drifted to sleep against it.

Sitting up, Sarah felt the blood rush back into her arm as she rubbed at it to eliminate the pins and needles sensation. She hadn't meant to doze off, and the thought filled her with dread. How long had she been asleep? What time was it? She gazed over at Brandi with fear and sighed with relief when she saw the younger woman was still sleeping, her chest moving up and down steadily, hand resting over her bandage.

Sarah stood, feeling stiff and sore, and put more wood on the decaying campfire. Tilting her nose into the air, she felt the coolness of dew rest upon her face.

Gazing upward at the stars, she sensed that it was into the early hours of morning. The fresh scent of the oncoming dawn caused her to recalculate her assumption. Perhaps it was closer to sun-up than she first supposed.

The fresh scent seemed in thick contrast to the pungent smell of death that also invaded her senses. She could still hear hyenas out on the lowveldt, though not quite as many as earlier, and their squawking, fighting, disfigured noises had quieted into grunts and barks as many of the overfed beasts meandered their way back into the African wilderness to sleep out the oncoming day.

Sarah gagged at the thought and felt a strong wave of grief wash over her again for Honor. If only she'd been able to keep them away from her, but how would she have done that without attracting more unwanted attention? She grimaced, trying to shake the vision of exposed white rib bones that invaded her mind. Her mission was now to protect Brandi and get them back to civilization. But how? She still didn't know.

Another feeling had fallen upon her, and it gnawed away at her stomach like a hyena on a dried bone. Hunger.

Sarah heard Brandi moan in her sleep, and she turned to regard her friend, grief twisting her gut. The younger woman's sleep didn't deprive her of the pain she was suffering as Sarah watched her rolling her head around in pain. Sarah grimaced. Brandi wouldn't last much longer. It was a miracle she'd lasted this long.

Feeling hopeless, Sarah looked out into the darkness as she tossed more wood into the flames, stirring the blaze again. Graceful embers eddied into the sky, along with new plumes of smoke as Sarah stoked the fire brighter. She thought she could see the pale light of dawn upon the horizon, but her exhaustion made it hard to tell.

Plonking herself next to Brandi again, Sarah found herself lulling back into an unwanted doze.

"Mark? Do you copy? Over."

The static noise blared over the rumble of the bakkie engine.

Mark squinted through his headlights, his eyes growing weary with fatigue. He fumbled next to him for the radio and pressed it to his lips.

"Mark here," he replied, his voice shaking. "Jacob?"

"The police are here, Mark. They came back here after they found it. They have to interview you, but an officer is here and wants to speak with you now."

Mark blinked. "OK," he answered, guarded.

"Mark van der Merwe?" another man's voice appeared over the

radio.

Mark adjusted the radio and pulled up the bakkie, "Ja?"

"We need you to return to the bush camp right now. We can take it from here. This is now a crime scene; we need you away from it. Where are you? Over."

"Officer, I haven't and won't touch any evidence. I'm not even near it now. Trust me. I need to find the girls. Over," he replied, tossing the radio onto the passenger seat and putting the vehicle back into gear.

The radio crackled to life again, "I understand how you are feeling, sir, but I repeat, you need to return to the bush camp. We have experts on the ground searching as we speak. Over."

Grabbing up the radio again, Mark gritted his teeth and spoke with anger, "And I told you, *sir*, that I am not stopping until I find the girls! They're still out here. Can you organize paramedics in case we need them? That would be useful! Over and out!"

Mark zoomed ahead as the radio bounced onto the passenger seat. It continued to crackle as the policeman on the other end tried to turn Mark back toward the bush camp.

Mark leaned over and turned the volume off. With eyes scanning the dark and eerie lowveldt grasslands with just the use of his headlights and flashlight, Mark continued on, hoping against all hope that Sarah and Brandi were still alive out there.

Hope. It was all he had. But was it enough?

"God! Where are they?" he shouted, slamming his hands down on the steering wheel in sudden rage.

Blinking back tired tears, Mark stopped the bakkie and got out, collapsing to his knees in despair. The dust from his sudden stop clung to the air about him, curling around, coaxing him to give in to his emotions. To face the inevitable. To give up.

Inhaling deeply, he looked up to the sky and bellowed despairingly, "WHY?"

Hanging his head and crumpling into himself, Mark wept, "Why did you let this happen?"

I've failed. I should have gone with them.

Crickets chirped away nonchalantly in the long grass, as Mark gazed toward the horizon. Just as he noticed the dull, deep orange appearing across the expanse, he heard the first cheerful songs of birds starting their early hunt for insects. He could feel the cool, wet dew seeping through the knees of his jeans, and it snapped him back to reality. It was then that Mark spotted a faint grey line twisting elegantly into the sky against the sunrise in the distance.

Smoke? Mark stood and squinted toward the ethereal wispy thread, without recognition.

All of a sudden, it dawned on him, throwing him from his sleep-deprived stupor. *A campfire!*

Hope restored, Mark jumped to his feet, threw himself back into the bakkie, then stopped. The smoke could have belonged to anyone, including Declan's men or tribesmen. If it was Declan's men, they'd get what was coming to them.

Determined, he turned the ignition on. Mark tried to calculate what dangers could be under the camp smoke; he needed to keep his cool. Despite this, hope welled in his chest, threatening to burst. Leaving a cloud of fresh dust, he sped down the dirt track toward the wispy beacon.

The colors of the radiant dawn began to spread themselves across the horizon. He felt the familiar stone feeling in the pit of his stomach as he approached several more elephant carcasses. Another crime scene? They had been stripped bare overnight by various scavengers, their clean, white bones sticking up like sentries, the sightless eyes in their intact heads agape.

Driving onward, he passed one of the fallen behemoths, and then came across the first fallen horse. That answered his first question. This looked to be part of the same ordeal that had occurred further back near the bush camp on Thompson's bend. Mark rubbed his chin in thought. *Why were there two sites of attack like this?*

He stopped the vehicle and stepped out. Gazing into the lightning sky, the smoke had gotten thicker, as if someone were trying to stifle it. Over in the distance, a line of mopane shrubs and trees hid the source of fire from view. Mark knew that whoever was there had now been alerted to his presence.

Breath heavy, Mark walked past the horse and then hid

behind the scarce corpse of another elephant. From this vantage point, he crouched and scanned the ominous line of trees, waiting for some sign of life. Nothing.

Glancing over his shoulder, Mark spotted the remains of another horse. Its body was hollowed out, ribs jutting into the air in a final act of defiance. All that remained intact was the head. Gasping, Mark scuttled over to the animal. Tracing his trembling fingers down the golden mare's pretty, bridle-less face, he turned yet again to the line of trees.

Jaw set with resolve, Mark stood, looking toward the smoke. Whoever had done this was going to pay!

Teeth grinding with both fury and despair, Mark stormed toward the tree line. He left Honor to stare unseeing into the morning skies, which were filling with black circling scavengers, eager for their second turn at the kill.

Grabbing her weapon of choice and inadequate sleeping companion, Sarah steadied herself behind the trunk of a baobab. She stared toward the open, where she had heard the vehicle.

Sarah stole a quick glance behind, toward Brandi. The younger woman was awake, clasping her stomach, as she peered out from under the protective shrub that Sarah had just moved her to. She was only partially hidden, but it would have to do. Brandi's breathe was way too loud, rasping and uneven as she gasped shallowly for oxygen.

Sarah mustered her courage. She turned her attention back toward the gap in the mopane. Someone was coming. Spacing out and planting her feet, she rocked nervously from side to side, branch held at the ready, preparing to strike like a cobra. How many were there? Did she even have a chance?

A stick snapped, followed by the approaching foot falls of someone near their camp area. Sarah swallowed hard, not daring to even breathe, lest the sound give them away.

She risked another quick look anxiously at Brandi, hoping that her lack of breath might somehow compensate for the loud panting noise issuing from her friend. It may not have been that bad, but it echoed loudly as Sarah's heart beat in her own ears.

A man's deep, authoritative voice rang out across the bushveldt, "COME OUT!"

Sarah heard the strain of emotion catching in the man's throat.

"I KNOW YOU'RE IN THERE! COME OUT AND FACE ME!" he shouted again.

Sarah gasped, recognizing the voice. Excitement rising in her throat, she threw down the branch with a squeak and staggered out from behind the tree.

Mark's eyes went wide with relief and he raced to embrace her. Sarah ran to meet him, jumping and wrapping her arms about his neck, her legs about his waist. He spun her around, holding her tightly, moaning with emotion.

"Ohhh, I thought I'd lost you!" he murmured, holding her tight at the waist.

He buried his face into her loose hair and began mumbling with emotional in Afrikaans. Forgetting herself, Sarah rested her face into the crook of his neck, weeping with relief. She didn't want him to let her go...ever!

Mark pulled back after a moment, putting her slight weight down onto the ground and holding her at arm's length. He looked hard into her eyes with concern.

"Brandi?" he asked.

Wiping her suddenly clear eyes, Sarah nodded. Pulling on his sleeve, she guided him back to the shrub, where Brandi lay gasping in pain.

"We need to get her to the hospital now. Do you have a radio on you?"

Mark stared in alarm at Brandi, the bandage against her abdomen stained with old blood, her face pale.

"In the bakkie," he said as he tore his gaze from the girl and wasted no time.

He ran back through the mopane, adrenaline pumping anew. Brandi tried to cough, but her failing strength prevented her. Sarah was quick to her side. Wiping fresh blood from Brandi's lips, she propped up her head and offered her the last of the water. When the girl gave a weak nod, Sarah tipped the bottle and let a trickle fall into her mouth.

Brandi swallowed with pain, then trying to sit up more, managed a weak cough. Small flecks of new blood spotted the side of her mouth and Sarah wiped it away, gazing back over her shoulder, praying that Mark would get back soon.

Mark returned, flushed in the face from running.

"They're coming now," he informed them, standing over Brandi to survey the damage again. "Jacob is calling an ambulance. They'll send air crew. The police will be here soon also."

Sarah sighed; she'd forgotten about the carnage out on the lowveldt.

"Well, they'd better get here quickly," Sarah stared into Mark's eyes with meaning.

He followed her gaze back to Brandi's wound.

"Jacob said he'll radio back when the ambulance is online. They'll want to stay on radio with us until they get here. May I?" he indicated the wound wanting to assess how bad it was.

"I'd rather you didn't." Sarah stopped him, clasping his hand away from the makeshift bandage. "She's lost way too much blood."

Choking up, Sarah turned away, not able to bring herself to look into Brandi's glazing eyes.

Mark touched Brandi's forehead with concern. Sweaty mats of blonde hair clung to her shuddering, pallid, and heated skin. Her temperature was rising.

"They'll be here soon. You'll be fine," he said to the injured girl.

Sarah hovered near, focusing on only the wound.

The radio crackled to life in Mark's hand. He was quick to bring it to his ear.

"Jacob here, Mark. Do you copy? The helicopter is coming. They'll want to talk to you. They know what channel."

"Copy that, Jacob."

It didn't take long for the radio to spring to life again. Static sounded, and then a man's voice came over the radio. Mark explained the situation to the paramedic and tried to describe where they were. The best coordinates he could give involved a lone vehicle and several dead elephants and horses near the Olifants River. The main thing was, help was on the way.

"Sarah! Crank that fire up again. The smoke will signal them," he instructed.

Mark watched as she leapt into action. He remained next to Brandi while on the radio, receiving instruction and answering questions about her condition.

When it came to specific information about the nature of the wound, Mark passed the radio to Sarah to fill them in. She stayed online with them from then on, as the primary person who had started first aid, she held most of the information.

Mark continued to stoke the fire as time seemed to hold still, like it was holding its breath for what seemed like an eternity. Then, the increasing thump-thump-thump sound of an approaching helicopter ensued, answering all their prayers. The welcoming sound was soon followed by the sound of police vehicles.

Sarah's world became a blur of motion as paramedics arrived, assessed, and whisked Brandi away to be airlifted to the nearest hospital. Sarah didn't know if she protested about wanting to go with Brandi out loud, or in a dream, but her last weary memory was of the world spinning. She felt like she was being carried to a bakkie and laid on the back seat.

The relief of being rescued decompressed the adrenaline. As it left her body, exhaustion overtook. Lying curled up on a soft, clean backseat of a vehicle, she felt safe at last. Even the sharp angle of a seatbelt clip digging into her hip didn't deter her as she drifted into slumber. The soft hum of the motor, settled her further into one of the deepest sleeps she'd ever known.

CHAPTER
TWENTY-EIGHT

Sarah's eyes fluttered opened in confusion. She stared up at a thatch roof with disorientation. Her tongue felt thick and dry and was stuck to the roof of her mouth.

She turned her head, trying to shake the dizziness and establish where she was. Every muscle ached as if she had lain in the one position for days.

Mark appeared in her fuzzy line of vision, smiling warmly, though his eyes looked anxious.

"Hey," he leaned over, exclaiming in a soft tone. He touched his hand to her forehead. "You've slept for almost two days!"

Sarah reached out a shaking hand, and he clasped it in his own. His hand was warm as he rubbed his fingers gently over her skin.

"Two days? What happened?" Sarah murmured, a look of disorientation in her dulled green eyes.

"The doctor said that you were dehydrated, had heatstroke and exhaustion." He took a weary breath before going on, "It caused the fever. I thought you'd caught something from the river. I thought..."

He choked up and dropped his gaze.

A frown crossed Sarah's face as she squeezed his hand, "I didn't drink from Olifants. I'm OK, Mark."

She looked up, locking her gaze onto his dark blue eyes. She'd never noticed how vivid their color was, like the deep, clear blue of the ocean.

He nodded, "When they assured me that you would be fine, they said you'd be alright to stay here, at the bush camp instead of the hospital. I think they wanted you to be somewhere where you feel safe."

Sarah offered a weak smile. She didn't like hospitals anyway. The hospital. The paramedics. Memory hit her like a freight train and she sat up with alarm.

"Brandi?"

The swift motion sent her world spinning. She put her hand to her head, the dizziness hitting her hard and fast.

"Whoah, girl! Not so fast!" Mark was quick to his feet, steadying her with his strong grasp around her back as he sat on the edge of the bed.

Picking up a glass from the bedside table, Mark held the water to her. Unsteady, Sarah took it, sipping it with care. Pulling the glass from her lips, a frown crossed her face as she saw the drip attached to her arm.

"The nurse put it in. You needed liquids," Mark confirmed. "Now you're awake, she'll be able to take it out."

"Brandi?" Sarah murmured, forgetting the IV.

Mark took her glass and put it back on the table.

"She's stable," Mark reported. "She's in intensive care in Phalaborwa. They're confident that she will be fine. Sarah...she's lucky to be alive, and she has you to thank for that."

Guilt ridden, Sarah couldn't look into Mark's eyes, "It's my fault she got shot. It's my fault that Honor's dead, and we don't even know where Jet is. So many lives were lost because of me!"

Hot tears of regret began to well in Sarah's still weary eyes, and she fought to hold them back.

Mark opened his mouth to protest, but Sarah stopped him, "I should have listened to her. I should have listened to you!"

She searched his face for confirmation, but what she found was something else. His face showed compassion. Compassion and something else akin to anguish.

She shook her head, not being able to read his thoughts. Tears began to escape and run down her flushed cheeks.

"I should have listened."

Breaking into heaving sobs, Sarah slumped forward, her hands making shaking fists in her lap. She couldn't look at him.

Feeling warm hands covering her own fists, she stopped

shaking and closed her eyes as she heard him speak.

"Don't think on it now! You need your strength back," he said.

Flicking open her eyes, Sarah felt numb as she stared at his hands over hers, allowing the tears to slip unheeded down her cheeks.

"I want to go to her," she said as she turned glassy eyes to Mark.

He squeezed her hands gently.

"We will," he promised.

Looking back over his shoulder, his tone changed to a more lighthearted note, "When the boss says it's OK."

Sarah saw him grin by his profile, as Martha came bustling into the room with authority.

"Who's using my name in vane?" she gaped in jest at Mark, as she placed a tray of food down on the table next to the bed. "I heard that you were awake, child, and I went to bring you some food. You must be starving!"

A white nurse slipped in behind Martha, fussing about the food tray. Her stocky frame shook with frustration, as she locked eyes with Martha.

"She can't go rushing back into full meals yet," the elderly nurse insisted. "Why didn't someone tell me she had woken?"

The nurse locked eyes now with Mark.

Martha laughed. "What, and have you prevent me from fussing over her?"

Giving up, the nurse tilted her mouth and went to check the IV drip and Sarah's blood pressure.

Sarah wiped her eyes and sat up straighter, a slight smirk curling the sides of her mouth.

"How did any of you hear I was awake?" she said, looking at Mark, who shrugged, and then back to Martha, who tapped the side of her nose, grinning like a Cheshire cat.

"Come! You must eat," Martha insisted, shooing Mark off the side of the bed and plonking herself down, plate of toast in hand.

"Not till I finish the blood pressure," the nurse insisted, fussing over Sarah's arm.

"Martha, you are always feeding us." Mark laughed as he

moved to the end of the bed.

"And I'm not about to stop now," she wagged a finger at him jovially. "Go and make yourself useful, boy. You've been here watching over this girl for hours. Jacob needs some help chopping wood."

Mark stretched, looking sideways at Sarah with a coy expression. Sarah suspected she saw color sweep into his cheeks. Looking somewhat embarrassed, Mark left the room.

"He's been watching over me?" Sarah asked of Martha when Mark was gone.

She shifted herself into a better position, nodding her thanks as the nurse left and took the toast from Martha.

"Sarah..." Martha began, holding out some toast, "...he's barely left your side for the last two days. He was so worried. Through everything, that man has never stopped caring for you. You should know that."

Sarah felt her eyes moisten anew at the revelation. She nibbled at her toast in silence, avoiding eye contact with Martha, who sat watching her, full of love and grace.

"It'll be OK, child, you'll see. You've just been through a big thing."

Sarah sighed, still trying to collect her thoughts.

"Two days? I've been passed out for two days?"

"Nearly two days. You passed out once they took Brandi away. It was like your body decided that it had done its duty and it was time to knock off. You ran a fever, too. You were knocked about by the whole ordeal, but you've never had a chance to recover. When we asked for you to stay, the doctor insisted on leaving a nurse here as well. We've been battling each other, fussing over you."

Sarah's face flushed with amusement. Martha patted her arm and handed over another piece of toast.

"I thought you'd find that amusing somehow. You need to stay here to recoup before you go anywhere," Martha said as Sarah took it all in. Then she continued, "We've had police, ambulance, the nurse—everyone has been crawling all over this side of Kruger. You have no idea! Some paramedics checked you when you got here. You've had major concussion. Plus they said you had sunstroke or something, plus all the bumps and bruises from falling off your horse. Once they left, I called our doctor to come out and do a more thorough check. He insisted that a nurse come out, got cross at me for not letting you go to hospital. But, most importantly, the doctor said that you need rest and that I was to see to that...and so I shall!"

Sarah stared into the distance after Martha finished, trying to process everything.

"Did they find Declan? The elephants? I think he meant to kill them. I can't believe that I was so stupid to believe him when he said his men were harmless. They were..."

Martha quieted Sarah by placing her hand on Sarah's shoulder.

"I know...poachers," she replied. "They found many dead." Martha shut her eyes, grimacing at the thought.

"I think there were three, plus the elephants and horses," Sarah remembered, her voice barely a whisper.

Martha looked at her, eyes wide, shaking her head, "No...you don't know the rest."

"What rest?" Sarah demanded, her dizziness returning.

"No, no, you will find out everything when you are better. Here," she handed a glass of fresh fruit juice to Sarah. "Drink. You must get better before you worry about anything else."

"That's not fair, Martha! You have to tell me what else happened. Martha?" insisted Sarah, handing back to juice.

Martha looked at her in sadness and appeared exhausted herself from the intense grief of it all, "They found Declan, Sarah."

"He's been arrested?"

"He's dead. Along with more of his men," Martha said as she watched Sarah's eyes grew wide.

"How?" Sarah whispered.

"The police aren't talking about it. I think they'll want to question you and Brandi later. I have a theory, though. How did the people die where you were attacked?" Martha asked, wording the question with care.

Sarah sat a moment, thinking back, "Well, when we were set

upon by Declan's men, they were aiming at me, but I moved. And Brandi..." Fresh waves of grief took hold of Sarah as the scene played again in her head. "Brandi took the shot meant for me. The elephants were going crazy. People fell and got trampled. It all became a blur. I don't know what happened next, but when I woke up, it was a mess. It was only Brandi and me who were alive. Everyone else was gone. Brandi—I thought she was dead, Martha—she took the shot that was meant for me!"

Fresh tears cascaded down Sarah's pale face. Martha shifted her generous hips to the edge of the bed and gathered Sarah into her arms. Sarah's frame was wracked with sobs as Martha held her.

"I know. Shhh." Martha held her close for a long time. "Sarah, listen to me."

Sarah stayed wrapped in the old African woman's arms, being rocked back and forth.

"You did what you thought was best. Nobody could have foreseen any of this happening."

Sarah stiffened in her arms and replied, "Brandi did. So did Mark. They were worried, and I didn't listen to them. Even you and Jacob were worried. I was the only person blinded by this whole thing. I didn't listen. It's my fault that Brandi is in hospital now, fighting for her life."

Martha held her at arm's length, "Now Sarah! Listen to me! This is not the time to dwell in depression and self-pity." Her directness caused Sarah to flinch.

"Jacob and I have always been praying for you. I believe you were played, Sarah. This didn't happen by chance; you are not to blame."

Sarah shook her head and Martha released her, tipping her chin.

"No, Sarah! Listen to me! You still have a mission to accomplish. One that you believe you heard from God. What's stopping you?"

"What?! You too? I tried, I failed," Sarah moaned, slumping back into her bed.

Martha went to say something else but stopped herself. The

322

creases in her brow smoothed away into concern for Sarah.

"Listen, we will talk about this more when you are better. But know this...we believe in you. Jesus is where you get your strength, not yourself. We are all praying." Martha stood and straightened out her bright-colored dress. "We all love you, Sarah. And when I say 'all,' I'm not just talking about Jacob and myself. We don't want to see you get eaten away from the inside. We don't blame you for anything. If you need forgiveness, you have it from God, and from us, but who you really need it from now is yourself."

With that, Martha breezed from the room and gently closed the door behind her, leaving Sarah deep in thought. *Do you forgive me, Lord? I am responsible for all those deaths, for Brandi nearly getting killed*

Sarah felt a warm glow spread through her from the inside. Of course God forgave her. But how could others? How could she forgive herself? It would be easier to not try and complete the mission. But then, the elephants would die and everything would have been for nothing.

Sarah slid back down onto her pillow and gazed at the thatch ceiling in turmoil. She wouldn't even be allowed to try this venture again. The D-12 herd would hate her now, and the Parks Board would definitely have something to say about it all.

Later that afternoon, as the sun was nearing its departure, Sarah awoke and found her arm free of the IV drip. Sitting up, she swung her legs over the side of the bed. She was wearing a light nightshirt that Martha must have found for her. At least it wasn't a hospital gown.

Blinking, she looked around the room for her clothing. Her riding boots were by the foot of the bed, and across the room on the dresser were some folded-up clothes. Slipping from the bed, she snuck across the floorboards and examined the clothing. It was her jeans, freshly washed and neatly folded. Her clean socks and underclothes were hidden in the folds of a new shirt and singlet. Her other clothing must have been damaged beyond repair.

She held up the jeans, remembering the rips that were caused by the accident. A smile played upon the corners of her lips. Not only were they clean, but also mended. The rip across the knee and thigh was hand-stitched with care. Martha! Sarah knew she was loved.

Closing the door, she dressed and slipped into her riding boots. The soft leather, a familiar comfort, was warmed from sitting in a patch of sun on the floor. Combing her fingers through her loose hair in an attempt to attack the knots, Sarah wandered out into the main living area of Jacob and Martha's house. Having been released from the bonds of the IV drip earlier that day, she now felt freedom to wander at her own leisure.

There was no sign of life in the expansive house, so she ventured with caution outside. Blinking into the brilliant oranges and pinks of the lowering sun, Sarah noticed that there were still several police vehicles parked inside the bush camp compound. Off to the left, Sarah could hear and smell the activities of a campfire going and concluded that Jacob and Martha were hosting emergency service crews, who were still cleaning up her big blunder.

She snuck down the steps and, avoiding detection, headed in the opposite direction toward the horse kraals. The last thing she wanted right now was to face all those people and the inevitable questioning that she knew she'd be required to face.

Approaching the silent stillness of the horse area, Sarah leaned against the familiar wooden kraals. She folded her arms upon the top rail, rested her chin on her arms, and gazed into the eerie emptiness. These kraals would usually be bustling with dust kicked up, snorts and flicking of tails, as flies annoyed the equine habitants. Sarah had never recalled being at the bush camp without horses, and she found the stillness of the kraals quite disturbing.

Gazing into the kraal that used to house Honor, Sarah heaved in a shuddering sigh, grief-stricken.

"Quiet, isn't it?"

Mark's soft voice startled Sarah, and her head snapped up with alarm.

She spotted him sitting on the log nearby. The same log she sat on just a few nights ago, as she thought about him. Jacques was sprawled out in the dirt at his feet, watching the sunset with boredom, his yellow eyes narrowed into the warm glow.

"Sorry, I didn't mean to scare you," Mark apologized, getting up to join her.

"No, don't get up. I'll come and sit."

Sarah went and joined him, her heart still pounding in her chest.

"You should sit. Are you even allowed out of bed yet?" he scowled, though his demeanor was gentle.

"I don't know." She shrugged in reply, "The drip was gone, and no one was around. Sorry."

"Don't be. It's great to see you getting back to normal," he looked at her, amusement touching his eyes.

"It's so quiet...," Sarah's face reflected deep sorrow as she looked over the kraals, "here, anyway," she added, glancing over toward the sounds coming from the campfires.

She leaned down and scruffed the sleepy cheetah around the neck. Jacques yawned in response, rolling his head around and closing his eyes.

Mark looked toward the communal area in the distance, "Ja, well, they have a big job to do here," he admitted, causing Sarah to worry her lip and stare into the sunset again.

Sarah thought she saw him grimace, following her gaze.

"I didn't mean...," he began, but Sarah cut him off.

"What am I going to do?" she asked.

Looking at her profile a moment, Mark closed the gap between them with care. They sat, shoulders just touching.

"Hopefully, set out to finish what you began," he replied, his voice light.

They sat in silence, watching the sun slip under the horizon, the brilliant oranges and reds fading into a splendid pink and purple, then navy.

Feeling Mark's strong, comforting confidence in her, an

unseen tear slid down Sarah's cheek.

"You, Martha and Brandi," she began slowly, "you all *still* believe in me to do this thing, even after... "

Sarah stopped, unable to go on.

Mark slipped his arm around her, squeezing her close.

"I can't speak for everyone, but I never stopped believing in you," he spoke fiercely under the dim light.

She looked at him for a long moment, denying his words.

"OK," Mark admitted moving away slightly little, "I was confused and torn why you turned to.... It's just that I couldn't understand why...Declan."

Sarah blinked back her tears. She'd forgotten that she hadn't talked to Mark about any of this. In fact, she had still been angry with Mark when she left Brennan's. Angry over a silly little thing, like him not sharing about coming to know Jesus.

She turned her face away, angry with herself anew. She had treated Mark so wrong, and didn't deserve him to treat her with this much forgiveness.

Mark searched her face and flinched, "Did you love him?"

Sarah bit her lip, more tears spilling down and shook her head.

"I didn't even know him, Mark," she declared with frustration. "He was throwing himself at me, and I was fooled. Before we set out on the rescue, I told him that it wasn't going to work, that I hardly knew him. He made me feel...awkward." She shuddered.

Mark stared at her.

Sarah continued, "I expected him to pull out from the rescue, but he was adamant. Then he got nasty once we set out. Always demanding to know what was being planned. I just, I...feel like such a fool."

Sarah looked at Mark with deep sorrow.

"I wanted you to come with us, but I was afraid to ask, and I was stressed about the trip. I didn't treat you right, Mark. Through everything, all you ever did was..."

"Love you," he finished, his voice almost a whisper.

Sarah looked up at him with bewilderment, her eyes wide, full of question.

"Ja," Mark nodded in confirmation. "And I still do."

"What?" Sarah breathed, touching her hand to her neck. "I thought you didn't care. When you didn't share about finding Jesus, I thought that you had given up on me. And it served me right." She hung her head, ashamed.

"Sarah." Mark took her hands in his, drawing her eyes to his own. "When you went with Declan, I felt no hope for us, but I never stopped caring and praying that you would be safe. And although I surrendered my heart for you to God, I never stopped loving you. I couldn't."

Sarah sat forward staring into the oncoming darkness, the crickets beginning their nightly chorus. Had circumstances been different, the evening would have been a marvel to enjoy, but Sarah's heart was heavy with the burdens of how she'd treated those whom she cared for the most.

"I don't understand why," Sarah spoke into the night.

Someone in the distance called out, and Jacques, recognizing his name, jumped up, trotting off toward the sound.

Mark continued to watch Sarah with such intensity that she squirmed. *How could he still love me? After everything I've done?* She didn't deserve his love.

When Mark continued, Sarah's heart twisted in a knot as she tried to erect the barriers around herself again, not to protect herself this time, but to protect him from her.

"I love you, because I...just simply do," Mark replied, his voice husky.

Taking her chin in his hand, he turned her to face him, and before Sarah could protest further, his lips enveloped hers in a soft, warm embrace. It was quick and unassuming, and it was over before she could pull herself together enough to stop it. He pulled back and looked into her tear-filled eyes.

"I don't deserve you, Mark," she whispered, her tone hoarse.

She kept shaking her head. Rising to her feet, Sarah hurried back toward the house.

Mark sat bewildered.

"Sarah!" he called after her, but was only answered by the sound of Jacob and Martha's home door closing amidst the chortling of crickets.

I'm a fool. Mark got up, dejected, and walked off.

CHAPTER
TWENTY-NINE

A rap at the door drew Martha bustling from her kitchen, where she was washing dishes after their midday meal. Sarah tossed her tea towel on the bench and took over the dishes, relieved to have a break from drying. She looked over her shoulder into the living room, where Mark and Jacob talked in quiet tones. Mark's eyes rose to meet hers, and Sarah turned back to the dishes.

"Sarah." Martha appeared at the kitchen bench along with an apologetic-looking police officer, holding his hat under his arm, "Sarah, this is Lieutenant Tim Naicker."

"Ma'am," he nodded to Sarah quietly.

Sarah dried her hands, returning the tea towel to the bench and faced the officer.

"I know you've been recovering," he began politely, "But we need to interview you regarding this case."

"I'm ready," Sarah lifted her chin, heading into the living room with the officer.

Jacob and Mark stood to vacate as they entered.

"Do you want me to stay?" Mark touched Sarah's arm as she breezed past.

"It's alright. I can manage." She nodded at him, wishing that he wouldn't be so accommodating, almost wishing that Mark would shun her and punish her like she deserved. She wasn't accustomed to this returning her sin with loving kindness business.

"With all due respect, ma'am, while I would prefer Mark to stay away for the statement, I will be requiring him to join us later on. What I have to tell you concerns Mark, too."

The officer faced Mark, who regarded him with confusion.

"Me? Well, I might as well stay for the interview then, if it's OK?" He looked at Sarah, who shrugged her reluctant agreement.

The officer nodded, and they all settled into the living room. Sarah relayed the whole story to the officer, who raised many questions about Declan. Where they met, how they met, even about the kiss and all the way to Sarah's detailed explanation of the attack near Olifants River. This was the first time that Mark had heard the entire story and he sat, stunned, shaking his head with regret at how much Declan had manipulated Sarah. When Mark met her eyes, Sarah turned away again, embarrassed.

"Here we go." The officer slapped his hands together to update them on the situation at hand, "you have all been very patient during this investigation, showing us hospitality as we set up base here at the bush camp. I just wanted to personally thank you for that, off the record."

"Thank Jacob and Martha, it's their place," Sarah informed.

"Of course," the Lieutenant agreed, but then hesitated, "But there's more, and I regret to say and it might shock you. It will involve your continued support regarding the business and premises of Brennan's Safari Trails." He looked at Sarah, then Mark in turn, as their faces creased with confusion and anxiety. "Among all the mess we've had to sort through, we also found who we believe to be one of the main suspects for this case. He was on his way to Olifants. Only, when he got there, he spotted our patrol vehicles and tried to make a run for it. We have made an arrest."

"Good!" Mark nodded with relief, glancing at Sarah to gauge her reaction.

"The trouble is...," the officer hesitated, looking from one to the other, "The man arrested was Johnno Brennan."

"What?" Mark stood in alarm. "Are you sure?"

Sarah sat in stunned silence.

"That makes sense," she rationalized, causing both men to look at her. "Before we left, Johnno was chummy with Declan, acting like he'd known him for years. It was strange. And..."

Mark finished her sentence as his eyes flashed with

remembered fury, "...he was trying to keep me busy so I wouldn't get in the way. When I thought there was trouble and I wanted to come and find you, he tried to stop me!" he said and looked at Sarah, "And I got fired."

"And that's why he didn't want to issue Declan and his men our rifles. He wanted them to have elephant guns," Sarah's voice squeaked with alarm.

Lieutenant Naicker scrawled notes in his notebook, then cleared his throat, "The reason I needed to inform both of you of this matter is that Johnno Brennan is your employer."

He eyed them both waiting for confirmation. They both nodded, waiting for the officer to go on.

"You also reside at the safari horse park?"

"As do others," Mark confirmed. "What happens with that now? For some of us, it's our home."

The policeman scribbled some more notes.

"Well, I need to inform you both that there will be a thorough investigation taking place on those premises. We will have a warrant out to search everything." He gave them a stiff look.

"By all means, officer." Mark squirmed in his seat, wondering if the officer somehow thought that they too were involved in this great crime.

"We believe there is someone higher than Brennan, though, in this particular black market ring. Did he ever mention any names?" The pair shook their head no.

"Hmm. So, am I to understand that Johnno Brennan terminated your employment just recently?"

"Yes, two days ago. When I came out here to search for the girls. I told you, he was trying to stop me. It was a threat," Mark answered with hesitation.

"Nobody else is aware of this?"

"Only the two of you," Mark replied. "What has this got to do with anything?"

"You acted out of duty to a fellow employee, while Johnno Brennan was incapable of making rash decisions. You were terminated with no due cause. It was not in writing. There were no written warnings prior. Therefore, it is not binding."

"OK..."

"What I am getting at, sir, is that we would appreciate you and Sarah staying at the safari park and helping us with further inquiries."

The officer stood and folded his notebook closed.

"In fact, we require it," he added.

Mark looked at Sarah, and then nodded, "I'll continue as acting manager, then?" Mark asked.

"Yes. But that establishment cannot be open for business at the moment. We don't want anything disturbed. There should be men out there to cordon it off." Lieutenant Naicker softened as he reviewed the worried looks on their faces, "I will be heading up this investigation and will be available to answer any further questions you may have as they arise." He handed Mark a business card, "Please, you must understand that if there are others out there higher than Brennan, then you may both still be in danger. If you are concerned, or you have any other things that you remember, you must not hesitate to call."

Mark turned the card over in his hand.

"And the other staff at Brennan's?" Mark regarded the lieutenant from under his drawn brows.

"They are also under protection. They need to be available for interviews in this case anyway, so we require them to stay available."

"Right." Mark looked dubious.

Lieutenant Naicker cleared his throat, "Anyway, thank you for your time. You are free to leave the bush camp now when you are up to it. I hope you feel better soon, miss."

The officer inclined his head and then left the house. Mark stared after him, feeling as though they hadn't seen the last of him.

"Free to leave?" Mark queried, "Since when were we not free to leave?"

Sarah didn't reply, but sat in dismayed shock for some time before she spoke.

"Why? Why would Johnno do that?" she asked.

"I don't know."

Mark sat next to her, trying to answer the same questions that were whirling around in his head.

"What do we do now?" Sarah looked to Mark with concern, trying to process the enormity of it.

She had left everything she knew in Australia to start this new life here. Brennan Safari Trails was a place she had grown to love. The thought that she may have to leave when this was all sorted out filled her with despair.

"I'm not sure," Mark admitted. "But I do know that tomorrow we need to go and see how Brandi is doing."

He stood and held out his hand for Sarah to join him. She stood, not accepting his hand, her mind still filled with turmoil.

"Sarah, listen. It'll work out," Mark insisted, stopped her and gazing into her eyes. "For starters, when Johnno is away, I'm the appointed manager anyway."

"But you got fired, Mark." Sarah pointed out, troubled.

"That I did," Mark conceded. "But, he's been arrested, ja? The police are the law, and that officer told me that I still have a job. Johnno dismissed me with no due cause."

"Hmm," Sarah wasn't so sure.

She followed him into Martha's kitchen, where he placed the copper kettle full of water onto the wood stove.

"Here." He motioned for her to sit at the table.

Sarah obliged and watched as he fixed her a cup of sweet tea at the bench. She wondered at the change that was coming over Mark. She'd seen a vast difference since he came to accept Jesus in his life. *He was more patient, less moody, and he attempted to hold back his biting comments,* she admitted to herself.

The most obvious change, however, was how deep and mature his affection had grown for her. He never gave up on his pursuit, and he was willing to change himself to do so.

Sarah wondered in her heart if it was all just a phase and that if he got his way with her, would he go back to his old self? Watching now as he poured the boiling water and stirred in the milk and sugar attentively, she hoped and prayed that she was wrong and that he was indeed genuine in his change.

The biggest fight on her hands now was her own feelings of

guilt and unforgiveness toward herself. How could she expect anything out of these people now? These people loved and cared for her, and her only thanks had been to put their lives in danger in her own pursuits?

Sarah tossed and turned that night, her mind a jumble of emotions and worries. Was Brandi still alright? What would happen with Johnno and Brennan Safari Trails? What would happen to her? To Mark, Brandi, Solomon, Piet and his wife, and all the other staff? People would be out of work now, and it was all her fault.

No, Johnno made his own choices, I just exposed it.

Lying awake and staring at the thatch ceiling, Sarah frowned. Mark was taking her home tomorrow. Their first stop would be Phalaborwa to see Brandi.

She sat up and blinked, gazing out her window into the clear starry night. Crickets chortled under her window in undulating harmony with some nearby frogs, blissful and oblivious to the wretched chaos that had torn across their lands in the past few days. Far away in the distance, Sarah heard the low roar of a lion calling its pride. All else was silent. She settled back into her soft covers and, after more tossing and turning, she fell into a restless sleep.

It had been months since she had last had the dreams that led her to Jesus and His plan for her, but tonight, He returned to Sarah unexpectedly in her slumber.

"Sarah?" he whispered, *"Sarah?"*

She rolled over in her sleep, agitated.

"Sarah," the whispered voice persisted, carried by the soft breeze, *"have you forgotten me?"*

Sarah woke with a start. "Have you forgotten me" echoed in her head.

"Of course not," she whispered into the night air coming through her window.

Staring into the inky blackness and vibrant stars, Sarah

uttered her fears, hopes, and despair to the only person in the universe who could help.

The nurse leaned down toward Sarah, startling her from her thoughts, as she and Mark waited in the Phalaborwa hospital waiting room.

Mark touched her shoulder and they stood and followed the nurse into Brandi's room.

"She is still very weak, don't stress her," the nurse warned them in a low tone, and then walked over to Brandi's drip to change it.

Brandi's eyes lit up with delight as they joined her at the side of her bed.

"Hoe gaan dit, Brandi?" Mark greeted.

"Goed...sorta." Brandi winced as she tried to shift her position.

Sarah sat shaking.

"Sarah?" Brandi asked.

Sarah's mouth went dry at the sight of Brandi.

"I," she hung her head in despair and began to sob anew, "I am so sorry, Brandi!"

Brandi tried to sit up, watching Sarah with concern.

"This is *not* your fault! Don't you dare ever think it was. We were manipulated by criminals," she said as she slumped back onto her pillow, wincing at the pain in her abdomen.

Sarah watched Brandi in anguish.

"I never should have put you through this. It's my fault."

Mark put his hand on Sarah's shoulder, giving her a look that indicated he didn't want them to stress Brandi.

"Sarah," Brandi whispered, looking into the distance, "do you remember why you started this cause?"

Sarah nodded, blinking back tears in a sudden wave of emotion.

"Do you remember who gave you the gift, and therefore, whose plan it was to do the translocation?"

"Of course," wept Sarah.

"Do you doubt that you heard from God?"

"Never!"

There was a long pause before Brandi added, "He doesn't change His mind, you know."

Sarah wiped her eyes before staring at Brandi, "You still think I should try again?"

Mark tilted his head, "We all do."

"What about the Parks Board? They would never allow it."

Brandi looked at them, through tiring eyes, "If it's God's plan, He always straightens the path."

Sarah stiffened. Martha had uttered something similar a few nights back.

Brandi snuggled back into her blankets as the nurse came to check on her. Looking with apology at Mark and Sarah, she motioned for them to take their leave.

"Thanks, Brandi. You get better now. We'll see you soon." Mark waved at the younger woman.

Sarah said her awkward goodbyes, and Mark guided her out of the room.

Sarah stood outside the hospital and looked into the sky, weary. *How was it even possible?*

Mark stepped up beside her, trying to work out what she was looking at in the sky, then shrugging, he jogged down the steps in front of her.

"She's going to be fine, Sarah! You need some food, let's go!"

Reluctant, Sarah plodded down the steps after him and toward the car.

CHAPTER
THIRTY

Investigators had cleared the main offices, securing their evidence in plastic zip-lock bags and giving the "all clear" for Mark and Sarah to re-enter the room to balance the books and work on liquidation of the business.

Mark put the phone earpiece face down on the desk, giddy with possibilities. Where was Sarah?

He got up from Johnno's office chair and jogged down the hall to where she was working through paperwork in the main foyer.

"Sarah! The Parks Board is on the phone! It's for you." His eyes sparkled with excitement.

Sarah groaned, "I wondered when they were going to grill me about my failed muster."

"No! It's not that, Sarah! Just go take the call."

Sarah hesitated, but got up, curious now. She followed him back into Johnno's office and sat in the big leather chair.

"Hello, this is Sarah speaking," she began.

Mark watched with delight as her skeptical expression melted away into wonder and amazement. She hung up the receiver, hand trembling.

"Well?" Mark coaxed.

She looked at him, still shocked at the news.

"They said they heard reports of how far we took the elephants and how smooth it all went before, well, you know, and they were very impressed. They've been talking to the other national parks across the border, and they want us to try it again."

She stood up, gasping as Mark reefed her into a huge hug.

"I know! Isn't it wonderful! Brandi was so right! God works out the paths," Mark said.

Sarah stepped back, wary of his closeness.

"But, the horses...? The people to help man it? We have nothing anymore. A handful of horses are all that's left here, plus the ones that somehow made it home."

Mark nodded in thought and said, "Well, I guess we'll just have to see what God does there, huh?"

Sarah smirked, "But we can't make any plans if we don't know."

Mark looked at her and shrugged, "It's alright. It's not our plan anyway; it's God's. It always was."

She was still wary in working out her heart toward Mark. While she had erected walls again, she often thought back to that dawn in the Kruger. The fear in his eyes, the relief when he'd found her, like she was the love of his life. How he'd sat for two sleepless nights by her bed, until she awoke. The way he'd touched her. The way he looked at her now.

Was it too much to hope for that they could still have a future together? How could she overcome her own feelings of guilt? Of despair that it was a failed cause? If God made a way for it to happen, then Sarah knew in her heart that she could forgive herself, move on. Perhaps, there would even still be hope for her and Mark.

Several weeks passed with Mark and Sarah trying to balance the budget at Brennan's with no money coming in. They kept their dealings professional; Mark giving Sarah the space she needed to sort herself out. They had looked into the possibility of saving the business, but with much of Johnno's current investments being found taboo, many things were repossessed or confiscated. The best they could do was liquidate and put the property on the market.

They weren't going down without a fight, though, and Mark was determined to hold on until they could have another shot at the translocation. They had met with the Parks Board again and mentioned that they needed time to work things through before another attempt could be made.

Sarah and Mark just didn't have the resources this time, something that would have thwarted the Parks Board's permission the first time around, but this time they were understanding. They had heard about what happened out on the Kruger, and they blamed none of it on Sarah's efforts In fact, it was quite the opposite; they ended up offering some men and horses to help, people who had been checked out as having no criminal record. It still wasn't enough, though.

Mark watched, however, as Sarah appeared to slip into a deep depression, despite how bright things looked. He couldn't work it out. He still didn't know how she felt about him after his declaration, but he wasn't worried anymore. He loved her anyway and would be there to support her as she needed it.

Brandi had recovered enough to leave the hospital, but she wasn't up to coming on board at Brennan's at this stage, and so went back to stay with her parents for a while. With the lack of work there anyway, there wasn't much else she or any other staff could do.

Piet and his wife, Solomon and many of the casual staff were forced to leave and find other employment, saying that they couldn't offer to help, as they needed to think about their families. Mark understood. They never heard from many of them again.

Brandi, however, was different. She managed to keep in the loop, and she organized for Mark and Sarah to meet with their church friends about the new project. Surely, they would find some more volunteers.

They were successful in their pleas, and everyone who could ride was on board to help, and others would flank in vehicles with supplies. It started to shape up into something that might just be achievable. Sarah's main dilemma was lack of horses and lack of even making contact with the depleted and wounded herd of D-12 elephants. What if she didn't have it in her anymore? What if they were now aggressive?

Sarah sighed as she brushed down Buster, ready to go for a

morning ride. She hadn't been back on a horse in weeks...not since the accident. Sarah stopped brushing and leaned against the brown horse, a tear slipping down her cheek. She gazed into the light rising on the horizon and thought about her morning rides on Honor, her blonde mane flying out behind her, the feeling of absolute freedom and the bond that she had with that one horse.

Mark had suggested at one stage that she try and ride Bunny. But the sight of the smaller palomino only made it hurt more. Sighing, Sarah moved away from the dull brown gelding, slipped through the rails, and sat on the bench seat, staring into the distance. *How could I even contemplate taking on the translocation again? How can I even ride again?*

Shaking her head with determination, Sarah got up, slipped back into the kraal, and finished saddling up, then swung onto the mount. She was going to do this!

Tightening the girth as she walked the horse down the pathway toward the park gates, Sarah wondered where she would look first in order to find elephants. Did Mark know that she'd snuck off this morning? If so, why had he not bothered to stop her, or go with her? Had he given up?

In autopilot, she went through the motions of turning off the electric fencing, moving through, shutting gates, switching the power back on, swinging back into the saddle and trotting down the track into Letaba. She knew she shouldn't be alone in the reserve, knew that Mark would have wanted to accompany her with a firearm if she was looking for elephants, but she couldn't care less anymore. *If I perish, I perish,* she thought, gazing at her empty rifle sheath.

She wasn't far into the reserve and trotted down that fateful stretch of track where she'd first encountered the Sotho Ngaka holy man. She remembered the day in vivid detail. She didn't want to remember it again.

All of a sudden, she was accosted by déjà-vu. Thabo Masekela himself stepped out from the mopane scrub and onto the track again, causing Buster to shy as they halted. Breathing heavily, Sarah stared at him, her heart beating wild in her chest. He

340

stepped forward, staring at her with an intensity that unnerved her.

"It wasn't me!" she called out to him, frustrated hot tears welling up in her eyes. "I made a mistake! I didn't kill the elephants, I was *trying* to save them," she insisted. Her whole frame crumpled onto the front of Buster's saddle as she wept bitter tears.

The holy Sotho man looked confused and spoke into a mopane shrub. Sarah looked up at him through puffy tear-streaked eyes. *Was he talking to a bush?* She then understood, as Kgomotso emerged, nervous to make eye contact with Sarah.

She wondered why she hadn't seen him around at the bush camp. Perhaps, he'd stayed back at the Lebowa village instead. Sarah glared at Kgomotso. He would know the truth.

"Tell him, Kgomotso! It was just a huge..." she stopped, her heart not bearing to go on, "...it was just a dream."

Kgomotso stepped forward.

"You no understand. Kgomotso said, "Thabo is not here to punish you."

The Holy Sotho man with the limp shifted his weight onto his good leg with some effort.

Sarah regarded him, assuming he was Thabo. She noticed that he was now wearing regular clothing and not that of a traditional witch doctor. She frowned with confusion, wondering what they wanted with her. How did they know she would come today?

Thabo looked at Sarah with deep sympathy. Kgomotso spoke to him in Sotho, translating what Sarah had said.

After a brief dialogue, Kgomotso spoke again to Sarah, "Please, I know you are sad, but if you will listen a minute..."

Annoyed, Sarah wiped at her eyes, dismounting Buster.

Thabo spoke in his mother tongue, and Kgomotso translated again, "He asks that you won't refer to him as an Ngaka, or even Thabo anymore. He asks that you now call him Israel. He has changed name."

Sarah rocked on her feet, her mind reeling with confusion. *Why would he do that? Why are you even telling me?*

Israel continued to speak in Sotho, and Kgomotso followed, translating stiffly, "Israel, saw the power you had over the beasts of Africa and saw the power that protected you...and he sought after this himself...after your God. He is now reborn."

Kgomotso beamed at both Sarah and Israel, clearly proud of his translation efforts before adding,

"We both are. We know Jesus now, and we no longer fear."

Sarah edged forward, skeptical, "How?"

"We spoke with Koto," he explained.

Sarah allowed the information to sink in, happy for them both and relieved at the same time.

"I...," she started to say.

"Wait...Israel and I are not finished." Kgomotso cut her off in his stunted English.

With much ceremony, Israel shuffled himself forward, passed Kgomotso his walking stick and stood up straight in front of Sarah, looking deep into her stunned eyes.

"If I may," Israel spoke out in a smooth, eloquent English.

Sarah gaped with surprise as he went on in perfect accentuated English, "I have a message for you, Sarah White, from the One whom you follow."

Sarah gasped again. The man who knew no English. Had he known all along?

Sarah's doubts of trickery were put to rest. He spoke with eloquence and didn't stammer like someone new to the language. The only explanation was it was an act of God.

Sarah's jaw dropped open.

"I'm sorry...what?" Sarah shuddered with renewed fear overtaking her.

"He has come to you in dreams. He asks if you have forgotten Him."

Eyes widening in disbelief at his words, Sarah stumbled backward, gripping the stirrup leather on her saddle to steady herself.

"Jesus! What do you want?" she breathed hard, tearing her eyes away from Israel's and looking at the brilliant sapphire sky above her.

She then lowered her gaze back into Israel's piercing eyes.

"Sarah, He says, 'I need you to finish what you began.'"

Nodding, Sarah looked at Kgomotso, who was watching the ordeal with wide eyes. Fresh tears welled in her eyes and dropping her reins, Sarah slid to the dirt on her knees, crying.

"I don't know how!" she moaned.

Buster stood beside her, his head dropped near the top of her weeping form. He breathed out and began to munch away at some grass beside Sarah.

Israel approached Sarah and looked down upon her. She gazed up at him, her face red and puffy with emotion.

"You are not alone, Sarah," the old man revealed.

Kgomotso spoke up for the first time with excitement, "No, no! This is true! Horses...horses came from white people in the South, tribesman in the North. Good, strong native horses. Given to tribesmen and also to this," he gestured toward Sarah.

"This?" she stood, wiping her eyes again.

"Yes, yes! The trans-location....mu-ster? Your mu-ster! Our men, we are strong! We are strong riders, too! We ride with you! You must lead us!" His voice rose with excitement.

Sarah chuckled, nervous at his enthusiasm and overwhelmed by his words.

"I need to find the elephants first," she admitted, looking behind them toward the lowveldt.

Israel frowned with confusion. All of a sudden, he could not understand Sarah's words, and he questioned Kgomotso in Sotho.

Kgomotso laughed. "The miracle of the tongue is now over," he reported with gaiety.

His excitement was not the least bit diminished, however, as he set to explaining to Israel the conversation that had just occurred. Israel smiled and praised God in his mother tongue, looking heavenward in awe. Kgomotso motioned for Sarah to remount her horse, which she did eagerly as he pointed down the track.

"Come. Follow us!" he said.

They took their time walking, as Israel's leg still ailed him, but when they came to the crest of the hilly track, Sarah gasped as she beheld a brilliant vista below of elephants in the watering hole. She recognized some from the previous herd, as well as some new ones that had joined the herd since their last trip. Was that the D-13 herd, joined with the remaining D-12?

The two Sotho men stepped aside the track, allowing Sarah to trot down to get a closer look. Sarah knew that family groups stayed together in the one herd, only meeting with other family groups occasionally to propagate and sometimes swap some herd members. Most of the time, though, clans were loyal to each other for life. What they were beholding here was a strange phenomenon where two family herds were meeting and blending to bring up the numbers.

Sarah felt both a pang of guilt as well as admiration as she observed several of the beasts surrounding another that was wounded, looking after it and tending it as they browsed the mopane for fresh foliage. They were intelligent and magnificent animals.

She didn't know most of these new animals from D-13, as she had only seen them on occasion from a distance. She was also wary of the reaction of the original D-12 herd. If Maggie no longer accepted her, then none of them would.

Sarah approached the group of behemoth creatures with caution, her heart racing. She almost cried out for joy when she recognized Maggie among the lumbering herd. At least she was alive!

Hesitation prevented her from racing up to the great matriarch. Would Maggie blame her for what happened? Would she allow her near, or even attack her? Sarah stayed in the saddle just in case a speedy exit was needed and edged Buster closer. The horse snorted and balked, not happy with the proximity.

Sarah urged him forward a few more steps, then stopped. The horse tossed his head, snorting again. Maggie's head shot up from the mopane, and she stared in their direction for a long moment before edging forward. Buster stood motionless, the whites of his eyes growing large as the matriarch elephant approached. As Maggie moved through the foliage separating them, she stopped, recognizing Sarah. The pause seemed like an eternity to Sarah, who held her breath, her muscles tensed, ready to allow Buster a quick escape if needed.

The elephant's ancient eyes looked as solemn as they'd ever looked, but they held no animosity or grudge. Settling Buster somewhat, Sarah watched as Maggie approached and extended out her trunk. Still jittery, Buster sidestepped. Sarah corrected him, speaking to him with soft words. He then relaxed, licking and chewing to show his acceptance of the situation.

Sarah reached out her hand toward the trunk, and they connected for a moment, as the ancient matriarch gripped Sarah's outstretched hand with gentleness. Elation flooded Sarah's heart as all her reservations crumbled away. *This could be done! It was still do-able!*

Maggie released Sarah's hand and returned to browsing the shrub close to Sarah. Feeling lightheaded, Sarah left the elephants and cantered up the track to find the Sotho men. She was filled with an excitement that had laid dormant for many weeks.

The men were gone. Sarah stopped at that rise on the track for a moment and gave thanks to God. This was bigger than her. It wasn't her thing at all. It was God's thing. She was but a tool in the hands of God, a tool that was being used for a greater purpose—greater than herself.

Sarah cantered back to Brennan's and dropped Buster off back in the kraals, throwing her saddle onto the fence. She raced to the offices to find Mark. *Mark!*

She stopped. He told her at the bush camp that he loved her. She thought hard, trying to recall how she'd responded to him since. Her heart skipped a beat as she realized that she felt the same way about him. She loved him. She'd been so caught up in herself that she now realized with horror that, despite her giving him the cold shoulder, he'd continued to love her.

"MARK!" she called through the foyer as she jogged through.

Nothing. Stillness echoed back down the empty halls.

She raced to his rondavel and rapped on his door. No answer. She jogged back up toward the stable kraals, near the entrance to the park, and then stopped in her tracks. A dozen horse floats and vehicles and several horse trucks were parked out the front of Brennan's, and people were bustling to unload horses of all size and description.

She stood a moment in a daze of confusion. Mark saw her and came sprinting over with jubilation. He grabbed her hand, tugging her toward the bustle of activity.

"Check it out! They came out of nowhere, some as far as Cape Town and Johannesburg. Can you believe it? Cape Town!" he slapped her on the shoulder.

"What?" Sarah stopped and stared with bewilderment.

Mark looked at her and, positioning himself in front of her, gripped her by the shoulders. He looked into her green eyes, trying to get her hear him.

"Sarah! Somehow...they heard about what you were doing...and...about what happened..."

Sarah murmured, "Was it on the news, perhaps?"

Mark shrugged. "I guess. We've been too busy to watch, I suppose," he admitted. "But anyway, look!"

He moved to her side, wrapping an arm about her shoulder and pointing, "They are donating horses. They are coming to help ride. Volunteers everywhere! Christians and horse people from around the country. They want to rebuild the herd here at Brennan's for us. They want you to try again! The translocation, Sarah!" He motioned to the fray with a sweep of his hand.

Sarah stood motionless in wonder. It was all happening so fast.

"I had something I needed to tell you too," she murmured, continuing to stare into the crowd of horse people dropping their loads into the kraals.

Her news! Her story about Israel, Kgomotso and the elephants.

Mark snapped her out of it, "What? What do you have to tell me?"

His eyes danced as he turned his full attention to her, turning her back to himself, hands resting easily on her arms.

She gazed into his deep blue eyes for a moment. Her hands trembled as they ran up the front of his khaki shirt, before she gripped the fabric. She pulled his face down to hers, kissing him deeply. Mark's eyes lit up with shock, before closing. Tilting his head, he kissed her back, his arms slipping around her, pulling her close. She didn't have to say a thing.

Nothing would fail now; it was God's plan. God had made the path and provided everything they needed. They just had to be obedient to His will and their greatest desires were going to be realized.

Finally, as Sarah settled into Mark's arms, she felt a strong peace that she had found her hope, meaning and purpose, not only Africa, but in life.

The End

ABOUT THE SERIES

Sarah's Gift is the first book of Skye Elizabeth's *Dare to Follow* trilogy about a group of friends who find God and themselves in the midst of adventure, danger, and beautiful vistas.

Sarah's Gift (Book One)
Mark's Strength (Book Two)
Kwan's Choice (Book Three)
of the

TRILOGY

Mark's Strength

Mark and Sarah van der Merwe think they may have escaped the attention of the ivory smugglers they faced in the past while saving the elephants in Kruger National Park. However, now fighting depression and isolation, the backslidden couple venture back to the place that caused their greatest grief in order to find closure for their current pain. Little do they know that evil raises its head once more and uses a lost little Zulu boy as bait. Will they show him the way to God, or will they end up in more trouble than they can possibly handle on their own?

ABOUT THE AUTHOR

 **SKYE ELIZABETH WIELAND** lives in Queensland, Australia with her two children, Daniel and Rachel. She is an artist and secondary high school teacher who has a love for horses. Skye is passionate about helping people discover their dreams in life and to strive for them.

ACKNOWLEDGEMENTS

I wish to personally thank the following people for their contribution to my inspiration and knowledge in the creation of this story.

- First and foremost, to God – my Lord and Savior - whom without I have no inspiration to create stories.
- To my husband, David, and my kids, Daniel and Rachel, who have been patient and supportive during this process.
- To Sophie Neville of London, who has lived and worked on horse safaris in South Africa for many years and has been a tremendous support and help in bringing an authentic Africa to this story.
- To Ant and Tessa Baber
  Ant's Nest Safari trails, The Waterberg, South Africa.
  www.waterberg.net / www.ridingsouthafrica.com
- To SANParks for all their hard work, dedication, and generally fantastic work that they are doing daily in the National Parks of South Africa.
- To the Sotho people of the Limpopo region and beyond in South Africa who work hard to provide for

their families.

- To New Hope Church, Crows Nest, who are consistently modeling a loving Christian community.
- And finally, to the following people in South Africa whom I've sought for various bits and pieces of information, and who have helped me with the various steps of producing this work: Romy Sommer, Kathy Bosman, Kirsty Redman, and Portia Ndlovu.

LETTER FROM SKYE

Dear Readers,

Thank you so much for reading my debut novel, *Sarah's Gift*. As I've been on the journey of creating and distributing this story, I've discovered that many questions have cropped up from the themes within the pages, and readers would like to know more about:

- Does God really take away our burdens? Does He wipe clean the slate to start a new life?

- How do I find forgiveness towards something unforgiveable? And why should I?

- Can God really speak to me through supernatural encounters and dreams? And how do I encourage/ask Him to do so?

- How do I come to know God and find a loving Christian community?

I was compelled to set up a blog site, where I endeavor to answer as many of these questions as I can, and to steer people in the right direction for any other questions they have.

If you have just read *Sarah's Gift* and have decided that you want what she found in Jesus and you've realized that sometimes the burdens in life are just too much for you, then the next step for you is to say "Yes" to Jesus. All you need to do is read the following prayer aloud, and the confession of your mouth will do the work in your heart.

Dear Jesus,
I acknowledge that I can't do everything on my own. I confess that I have sinned in both my own ways and also by putting myself above others and You. I ask now that you will forgive me Lord, and I invite You into my heart, to be my Lord and Savior. Thank you for the work that you did on the cross for me. Amen

I encourage you to visit my blog site to follow up on your decision and to start the journey of finding out more about this marvelous God we serve. As an author, I also love hearing from my readers. If you would like to leave any comments or you find that you cannot find an answer to a question, feel free to email me on the link provided. Thank you again for your support and I look forward to hearing from you.

Blessings,
Skye Elizabeth
Blog: http://skyeelizabeth-author.blogspot.com.au
Email: skyeelizabethauthor@gmail.com

ANT'S NEST SAFARI TRAILS
THE WATERBERG, SOUTH AFRICA

We specialize in riding safaris and have recently also been awarded Best Riding operator in Africa. Both Ant's Nest and Ant's Hill offer the opportunity for some of the greatest game viewing in the African bush – from horseback. We cater for riders of all riding abilities and have fit, reliable and responsive horses, providing a choice for both the professional rider and the absolute beginner

Ant's Nest & Ant's Hill are private bush homes in the magnificent malaria-free Waterberg. Specializing in a home-from-home experience, they can be booked exclusively or not. Enjoy fabulous horse riding safaris, guided bush walks or game drives on their privately owned reserve and enjoy al fresco wining and dining with a view. Flexibility is what they pride themselves in, tailor making guests stay with them. Suitable for families, riders, honeymooners or just good friends traveling together.

www.waterberg.net
Tel: +27 81 5722 624 or +27 83 287 2885
Email: reservations@waterberg.net

Lightning Source UK Ltd.
Milton Keynes UK
UKOW04f1338121113

220885UK00004B/8/P